BEAST
BEHAVING
BADLY

BEAST
BEHAVING
BADLY

SHELLY
LAURENSTON

KENSINGTON PUBLISHING CORP.

www.kensingtonbooks.com

BRAVA BOOKS are published by

Kensington Publishing Corp.
119 West 40th Street
New York, NY 10018

All Kensington titles, imprints, and distributed lines are available at special quantity discounts for bulk purchases for sales promotions, premiums, fund-raising, educational, or institutional use. Special book excerpts or customized printings can also be created to fit specific needs. For details, write or phone the office of the Kensington special sales manager: Kensington Publishing Corp., 119 West 40th Street, New York, NY 10018, attn: Special Sales Department; phone 1-800-221-2647.

BRAVA and the B logo are Reg. U.S. Pat. & TM Off.

ISBN-13: 978-0-7582-3168-0
ISBN-10: 0-7582-3168-7

First Kensington Trade Paperback Printing: June 2010

10 9 8 7 6 5 4 3 2 1

Printed in the United States of America

Chapter I

The face slammed into the protective glass, blood spurting out as cartilage was demolished, bone shattered.

The crowd around her either roared and howled in approval or hissed and barked in disapproval, depending on which team they supported. But Blayne Thorpe could do neither. Instead, she only gaped at the behemoth hybrid continuing to force that poor, battered feline face into the glass by using nothing more than his hockey stick and overwhelming size.

She had heard he'd gotten bigger since she'd last seen him nearly ten years ago, but she thought they were talking about the man's career. Not his size.

Career wise, the minor shifter league's onetime left defenseman from nowhere Maine had gone on to become one of the greatest hockey players the pro shifter league had ever known. Bo "The Marauder" Novikov was one of the first—and at one time, one of the *only*—hybrids to ever play on a professional team in any league. Of course, his saving grace had been that he wasn't one of the more feared—and, to be quite honest, more unstable—canine hybrids like Blayne, but a rare by-product of species crossbreeding. Specifically a polar bear–lion. Or, as Blayne always secretly thought of him, a mighty bear-cat. A much cuter name in Blayne's estimation than polar bear–lion. But bears breeding with felines was such a rare thing—and damn near nonexistent more than twenty-five years ago—that they didn't have any cute nicknames like coydogs for coyote-dogs or ligers and tigons for lion and tiger mixes.

Yet that didn't mean Blayne saw Novikov as one of the top representatives of the hybrid nation. How could she? He represented *everything* she loathed in sports. Where was the sportsmanship? Where was the team spirit? Where was the loyalty?

Nowhere.

In ten years the Marauder had become one of the most hated and feared players in any shifter league in the States, Asia, and most of Europe. Although in Russia and Sweden, he was merely considered "tough—for an American." Adored and loathed by fans in equal amounts, Novikov was equally detested by both his opponents and his own teammates. Bo Novikov had made a name for himself by being what Blayne could only describe as pure asshole on skates. If you were in his way, Novikov would either make you move or plow right through you. If you had his puck—and it was *always* his puck—he'd find a way to get it away from you, even if it meant permanent damage and learning to walk again for the opposition. From what Blayne had heard, he never had a friendly word for anyone, even the cubs and pups who worshipped at his feet.

None of this surprised Blayne. How could it? She'd met the man when he was a much shorter, nineteen-year-old minor league player. Tracey, a tigress that Blayne liked about as much as her best friend Gwen detested her, had seen Novikov playing and had begged Blayne to somehow get Gwen to invite her to one of her uncle's practices. At the time, the O'Neill males ran the Philly Furors minor hockey team. Two of Gwen's uncles were the managers and six of her cousins were either coaches or players. Although Blayne was invited anywhere that the O'Neills were, Tracey couldn't risk just showing up whenever she felt like it. Not unless she wanted to get her ass kicked by Gwen and her female cousins. It took some pleading, begging, and whining on Blayne's part, but eventually Gwen agreed that Tracey could come to one of the practices.

The idea had been that Tracey, wearing their Catholic school uniform—appropriately adjusted for after-school boy hunts—would show up and transfix the hybrid with her tigress beauty. It seemed like a solid plan as far as Blayne was concerned. And Tracey, not being real shy about that sort of thing, had made her move during one of the team's breaks. Blayne had barely noticed, too busy sitting in the stands and wolfing down a cheesesteak from the bear-owned restaurant across the street. She was halfway done with her sandwich when she felt like she was being watched. She had been, too. She'd looked up to find piercing blue eyes staring at her through the protective glass between the stands and the rink.

He didn't say anything, either. He just . . . stared. And he kept staring while glaring. He glared at her like she'd stolen his wallet or cut him with a razor. The bite of cheesesteak in her mouth went down her throat hard, and she tried to figure out if she could make it to the exit before he reached her. He looked like he wanted to eat her alive, and coming from a predator that was *not* a good thing. Especially a predator who, it was rumored, had descended from Genghis Khan on his mother's side and the Cossacks on his father's.

Putting down the remainder of her sandwich, Blayne had slowly stood. As she did, those blue eyes studied her every move. He watched her pick up her backpack and, in her saddle shoes, slowly make her way down the aisle. He'd skated along with her, oblivious to the fact that the O'Neills had noticed his interest. Blayne had reached the end of the bleachers and took the steps down to the massive hallway that the players entered through. Slowly, not wanting to startle him, she'd eased the straps of her bag over her shoulders. With the bag on, she'd looked over her shoulder one more time, expecting to see Bo Novikov still on the ice. He wasn't. He was right behind her. Blue eyes fierce as they glowered down at her.

And Blayne, as always, handled it with her usual skill and subtlety. She screamed like someone was stabbing her to death and took off running. Gwen called her name and ran after her, but

Blayne didn't stop until she'd run out of the building, across the street, and all the way home. She burst into her father's house, slamming the door behind her, locking it, pushing her father's favorite chair in front of it and then the side table. She was working on getting the piano over there, when her father had walked in from the backyard. "What are you doing?" he'd asked, and Blayne had been forced to calm down because there was little her father "tolerated" from his daughter. And her "irrational bullshit" was at the top of his "No Tolerance" list.

After taking a breath Blayne had replied, "Nothin'. Why?"

Her father didn't seem to believe her much, but he let it go. Tracey, however, did not let it go. She blamed Blayne for blowing the tigress's chance at being the future—and very wealthy—mate of a hockey star. Tracey never spoke to her again, which Gwen was very happy about, while Novikov lasted another month with the minor league team before landing his first major league deal. She hadn't seen him since that day and didn't bother to go to many hockey games, so she hadn't seen him play. But she'd heard about him. It was impossible to be around sports lovers and not hear about Novikov.

To quote her father, who loved sports so much he even watched the full-humans on TV, "That boy would take down his grandmother if she had his puck." And as usual, her father was right. If she had any doubts about the accuracy of his statement, all she had to do was continue to sit in this stadium with five thousand other shifters and watch that vicious barbarian batter the much smaller leopard into the ice. And why was he doing that? Because the smaller leopard had taken his puck.

The opposing team, the Charleston Butchers, tried to stop Novikov, but he tossed them off his back like they were puppies. The buzzer sounded and Novikov immediately stopped what he was doing, which somehow made Novikov seem even more cold-blooded.

The New York Carnivores newest center and enforcer stood. He was no longer the six-one, two-hundred-fifty-pound serial killer looking sub-adult she'd met all those years ago. Nope. He was now a seven-one, three-hundred-seventy-eight-pound serial killer looking adult.

Thankfully, though, she couldn't see his face or those frightening eyes because of all the blood he'd splattered over the protective glass between Blayne's and Gwen's primo seats and the rink. But Novikov didn't move away. She could see he was just standing there, facing in her direction.

"He can't remember me," she thought desperately. "There's no way he can remember me." She kept chanting that in her head while a gloved hand reached up and wiped at the glass. The blood smeared, but it was clear enough for Novikov to look through it and directly at her.

He was chewing gum. So was she. Cold blue eyes that had not changed to gold like most lion and lion hybrids gazed coldly at her. Blayne gazed back. She wouldn't run this time. She'd done her research and had a better grasp of serial killers. Not that she had proof Novikov was one, but a girl could never be too careful. And what she'd learned was to not show fear. Serial killers preyed on those they considered weak. She may not be all wolf but she had enough of her father in her to give her a backbone. So . . . so there!

If someone asked Blayne later if she had any idea how long they were staring at each other, she knew she'd have to honestly say she had no clue. It felt like hours, but basic logic told her it was more like thirty seconds or so. Long enough for one of Novikov's teammates to push his shoulder to get him to move off the ice. Probably not a good idea. Novikov caught the pushy wolf's right arm and launched him the entire length of the rink and right into the other team's unprotected goal. He didn't score anything by doing that, but the crowd loved it.

Her mouth open, Blayne gaped at him. That was his *own* teammate. Not the opposition. *Where's the loyalty?* she wanted to know.

She wouldn't know there was any fan love, though, from the way Novikov looked back at her, ignoring all his cheering, screaming fans. That impossibly angry—*okay, fine! And gorgeous!*—face glaring at her through all that blood.

The man may have been a sub-adult bear-cat when she'd first met him all those years ago, but he was a full adult predator now. Not only had he hit his bear shifter growth spurt, but his gold-brown lion's mane had grown in under the white hair that poured from the crown of his head, the two hair colors mixing into a silky mass that tumbled to just above his wide shoulders, giving him a kind of "rock-and-roll meets punk" look that worked for him. And although his eyes may be blue, the shape of his eyelids combined with sharp cheekbones, full bottom lip, and blunt-ended nose that faintly resembled a cat muzzle revealed his Mongolian descent.

Blayne would never say it out loud, but there had to be a cool factor to saying that his birth-Pride had descended directly from a lion shifter bloodline dating from the time of Genghis Khan. Novikov's ancestors ran before Khan's armies, destroying—and eating—whatever was in their way, helping the barbarian leader expand his territories until the cats grew bored and wandered off. Of course, Novikov's family on his father's side wasn't exactly filled with peace lovers, either. Nope. The Novikovs were descended from mighty Siberian Cossack polars dating back to the early 1600s, and they still ran some tough towns near the Arctic Circle.

Finally, after their endless staring, Novikov glided back from her, gave her one last hard look, and skated back to his team.

Once gone, Blayne crumpled into her seat.

"You're panting, hon."

"I am *not* panting," she told Gwen. "I'm trying to not breathe in fear. I thought he was going to rip my face off."

Gwen held out a bag of popcorn. "I don't know why you find him so scary."

Now Blayne gawked at her best friend. "Gee, I don't know. Maybe it's because it looks like he wants to cut my throat and watch the life slowly drain from my body so he can fuck my corpse without all that screaming-and-putting-up-a-fight distraction!"

Blayne cringed and, ignoring Gwen's shoulders shaking as she silently but hysterically laughed, turned and smiled at the family of six behind her. The youngest about five. "Sorry," she croaked out. "Sorry about that."

The father, a jackal, gave her a disapproving bark.

Blayne turned back around. Once again, she'd have to keep reminding herself that only the derby league had a twenty-one and older rule for their bouts. All the other sports, no matter the level of bloodletting, were family friendly. *Because your five-year-old pup should always know how to eviscerate a cheetah that had the misfortune of holding your ball or taking your puck.*

"Popcorn?" Gwen asked.

Not looking at her friend, Blayne dug into the bag and took a handful. "I hate you," she reminded Gwen.

"I know, sweetie. I know."

Bo sat down on the bench, the second string hitting the ice. He tugged off a glove and reached under his helmet to scratch his sweat-soaked hair. After he finished, he pulled his glove back on and studied the ongoing game.

She was here. In this stadium. Sitting in ridiculously expensive seats with that same girl she'd been friends with in high school. She hadn't changed much since the first time he'd seen her—running away from him. Screaming. Her reaction had been a bit of a blow to his extremely sensitive ego, but he didn't let it get to him because he'd been too busy studying those powerful legs under that Catholic school girl uniform as they'd bolted off. *Purr.*

Yet even now she looked at him the same way, didn't she? Like she'd stumbled between a grizzly sow and her cubs. Funny, most females didn't look at him like that. Then again most predator females were direct and rarely scared off from what they wanted. He always knew that some of them had more interest in his money or the hope they could breed the next big hockey star. Some hoped he was as charming and witty as the rumor mill—shifter sports didn't have any media covering their every move—had made him out to be over the years. Uh . . . he wasn't. Charming and witty that is. He was definitely direct, curt, and as one ex-girlfriend told him, "I used to think you were shy, which is cute. But you're not shy. You're just an introvert who doesn't really like other human beings!" And his answer hadn't made her any less unhappy. "Yeah, but I told you that up front." He had, too. Bo was all about being direct. He liked direct. Direct cut to the heart of the matter in seconds rather than hours of asking, "Are you all right?" Only to get back the answer, "I'm fine." More than one female had left his ass because he'd taken their "I'm fine" exactly for what it was, only to find out later that it was code for, "I'm unhappy and it's all your fault but you should know that without me telling you!"

So, after several years of that constant bullshit, he'd been on his own. He liked it that way and had had every intention of keeping that his status quo until the day he died. Then he'd done that thing he did every couple of years when he got an itch that could only be scratched in one way. He'd called his agent, Bernie Lawman, of the Lawman Clan—say what you will about hyenas eating their young, they made *phenomenal* agents—and said what he always said to the man during these calls over the years, "I'm bored." In less than three days, Bernie came back to Bo with offers from nearly every major hockey team in the American league, Russian league, and Asian league. The only team that pointedly refused to make an offer was the Alaskan Bears and that was because they didn't have to offer anyone anything. The entire team was made up of bears with two foxes as their centers. Just surviving a game against them was considered a win. But for Bo that was a little too easy. An entire team of bears was not exactly a challenge unless he was playing against them. And Bo needed challenges because when he got bored, he moved on.

Every offer involved a several-million-dollar signing bonus and perks that full-human sports stars could only dream of. His own seal farm was still his favorite, and he'd debated long and hard on that one. The deals were all fabulous, and he'd narrowed it down to the Hawaiian team—complete with his own untouched territory in the Antarctic during his off season, so he wouldn't have to sit around melting in the Hawaiian weather—and the Utah team—seal farm! While he debated, his agent had called.

"Didn't you say you wanted to go to New York to stop at that used bookstore?"

"Yeah. Figured I'd go next week sometime. Why?"

"Wanna go for free?"

Sure. Why not? Plus Bernie got to go and see his New York family on someone else's dime. That someone else turning out to be Ulrich Van Holtz. Round-trip flights on a private jet—although nothing beat the entertainment value of watching the horror of a full-human flight staff when they saw Bo heading their way with a suitcase—and one dinner meeting with Van Holtz at one of his family-owned and -managed restaurants.

Bo had played against the Carnivores before. They were . . . okay. They definitely weren't the worst, but they weren't exactly taking anyone by storm. Van Holtz, who had a financial stake in the team, was also the goalie. And the offer was, again, okay, but when Van Holtz excused himself to check on the meal, Bernie had crossed his eyes and ordered more bread from a passing waitress. The fact he wasn't even discussing what they'd already heard with Bo meant Bernie wasn't taking the offer even a little seriously. To be honest, neither was Bo. But the surf and turf—moose and walrus blubber in a delightful peppercorn sauce—was killer and Ulrich Van Holtz more interesting than Bo would have thought.

As the dinner wound down, Bo excused himself for the bathroom and cut through the restaurant. The place was big and extremely busy. When he found a waiting line at one bathroom, he went off in search of another. He found it, used it, and was heading back up the stairs when he heard someone singing . . . badly.

Curious—he was half bear after all—Bo peeked around a corner. That's when he saw her and recognized her as the wolfdog who'd run away. She was sitting at a table covered with papers, notepads, and a laptop. She wore little white earplugs attached to a cheap MP3 player, and she was still singing. Still badly. He remembered her hitting a note that made his eyes water a little, but he liked how she sang with such abandon. Such honest enjoyment. He found himself attracted to the same thing he'd been attracted to all those years ago—besides those ridiculously long legs. Her energy. There was just something about it that pulled him in. He couldn't explain it and didn't feel the need to. Instead, he'd gone back to the dining room, sat down at the table, and said to Van Holtz, "We have a deal." It was, other than the obligatory "Hello. Nice to meet you," all that Bo had said for the entire meal. Of course Bernie's wails of despair were a little disturbing, but Bo knew the hyena would get over it.

Besides, he'd only signed with the Carnivores for a year. A year to find "Legs"—his nickname for her since none of the Philly Furors would tell him what the wolfdog's real name was or where to find her—and then . . . well, he really didn't know. Sex, of course, was a definite "must have." Again it was those legs. He had to see what those legs looked like on his shoulders. Whether anything else happened from there, he didn't know. But life was always full of surprises. It was a surprise just seeing her in the VIP seats, looking decidedly un-VIP-like in stained cargo pants, work boots, and an abused sweatshirt that said B&G PLUMBING.

Bo scratched the back of his neck again, not bothering to take his glove off this time. His mane was irritating him. He'd stopped trying to cut more of it off because it kept growing back in less than twenty-four hours. Yet it was so thick and heavy that it made him want to shave his head. He had no idea how lion males lived like this.

Readjusting his helmet, Bo finally realized he had the attention of the team's goalie and captain, Van Holtz.

"What?" Bo asked, when the wolf kept staring at him.

"Do you know Blayne?"

"Who?"

"The female you were just staring at?"

Oh. Her name was Blayne. That was a nice name. It fit her. "I know lots of people," Bo told the nosey prick.

"That did not answer my question." Van Holtz sure did like

those complete, grammatically correct sentences. It was like talking to Bo's tenth-grade English teacher Miss Marsh.

"That's true. It didn't answer your question."

A shoulder slam from his right side had Bo sparing a glance at the grizzly next to him. Van Holtz's best buddy Lachlan MacRyrie wasn't a half-bad defenseman and usually kept out of Bo's way. He appreciated that in a player. But MacRyrie was big on protecting the runt, even if it meant going up against Bo.

"Answer the man," the grizzly told him.

"I don't feel like it."

The two males stared at each other, MacRyrie trying his grizzly intimidation move on Bo. It probably worked on most bears, but the grizzly forgot the mane. The Mongolian Lion's mane pretty much ensured that no matter how logical it may be for Bo Novikov to walk away from any fight he wasn't positive he could win, like most rational predators, Bo wouldn't walk away. Not now, not ever.

So when the two "dropped gloves"—hockey code for fistfight—and hit the ice in the middle of the game, fists flying and claws imbedding into important facial tissue . . . Bo, as always, blamed the mane.

Blayne cringed, wondering what had happened that had Lock MacRyrie—the nicest of all bears—to get into a fistfight with his own teammate.

"Lock's fighting," Blayne told Gwen.

"Yeah, yeah," Gwen said, waving off the fight that had the entire Carnivore team off the bench trying to stop it. "Whatever. Let's get back to this. Why do you think he's here?"

"I don't know." Blayne pointed at the ice. "Lock might get hurt, ya know."

"He can take care of himself. He could be back because of you, sweetie."

"What are you? High?"

"Did you see the way he looked at you?"

"I did. I'll have nightmares about that look until I'm old and gray . . . if he lets me live that long or decides to add me to the body count under his basement floor."

"There's no evidence he's ever critically injured anyone—outside the rink."

"I find so little comfort from that."

"I think you should go for it," Gwen pushed.

"And I think you should own up to the fact that you still hate Tracey. And the only reason you're pushing that psychopath over to me is because of her."

"What's the big deal if you go out with him just to *spite* her? You know, if it makes me happy."

Blayne's eyes crossed. The cats, they really never forgot a grudge, did they? "Surprisingly, Gwendolyn, I have more important things to do with my time, like put bamboo shoots under my nails or drill holes in all my teeth. *And how can you ignore this?*"

Snarling a little, Gwen faced forward and briefly watched the melee in front of her. "Yeah, yeah. Fascinating." She turned in her seat again and demanded, "But seriously, you should totally go out with him."

Chapter 2

Not in the mood to stand in line to use the bathroom and needing a few minutes on her own before she headed into that locker room, Blayne made her way down a few floors to one of the main training levels and the wonderful and rarely used bathroom near the locker rooms that the derby team used. Blayne was happy because the Carnivores had won against another top-tier team. They were finally hitting their stride and making their way to the playoffs for the first time in years, and Blayne was ecstatic for all the guys.

She was even ecstatic for Bo Novikov. A man who didn't look happy at all about the win or anything else. Did he even know how to smile? Was he physically capable? He'd been the one to make the winning goal, yet he had the same expression on his face after the win as he'd had on his face when the second string Carnivore goalie let the puck get by him. And man, had she felt bad for that kid. He looked ready to pee his pants when Novikov skated up to him, glaring down at the poor jackal like he was moments from eating the kid's face off before devouring his young.

And, as she'd heard about his on-ice attitude, Novikov had let the kid have it with a verbal assault that even Marine drill sergeants would think was harsh. *No wonder every team he's been on hates him.*

She'd feel bad for Novikov if she wasn't convinced he was a

serial killer. Or, at the very least, extremely rude. Blayne hated rude. It was her one major pet peeve. Her father didn't call her Miss Black Etiquette of the East Coast for nothing.

Washing her hands in the sink, Blayne wondered what was it about her that attracted the sociopaths. The charming ne'er-do-wells who eventually proved they'd kill their mothers for their life insurance or their best friends if they thought it would make them laugh. It had gotten to the point where she'd stopped bringing men home for her father to meet because he'd start the conversation off with, "And what personality disorder do you have and that I'll eventually have to kill you for?" That often led into one of their father-daughter fights, the two of them going at it until Blayne realized the guy had left, never to be heard from again.

Of course, all those guys were . . . what was the right word besides charming? Sweet? Loving? Yes. They were all those things. Superficially so. Once she got past that initial layer, she usually didn't find much of anything else. Novikov, however, seemed to be nothing more than a hulking mass of murdering hybrid from the first time she'd met him. Except for that mane of his and his clear need to win at all costs, he didn't have any of the natural male lion charm that Gwen's brothers Mitch O'Neill Shaw and Brendon Shaw possessed. Nor did he have the sweet disposition and adorable bear geekness that Lock MacRyrie and his dad, Brody MacRyrie, had.

Like all hybrids, Novikov's DNA had borrowed from both parents and created something entirely different.

Well, whatever. It was not her problem, nor her business. Novikov meant nothing to her, and now she was going up to the team's locker room and congratulate all her friends and ignore the glaring hybrid across the room. He'd probably have his own swarm of females anyway, so Blayne would not allow herself to feel guilty for not being nice.

She dried her hands with paper towels and headed to the door. Pulling it open, she walked out in the hallway, saw Bo Novikov and his perpetual scowl leaning against the wall across from the bathroom, turned right around, and went back inside, closing and locking the door behind her.

There was a lengthy pause from the other side and then, "You have to come out of there eventually."

Good God, he said that matter-of-factly! She could imagine him using the same inflection with, "You know I'll have to cut out your liver eventually."

"No, I don't," she told him through the door. "I've done the research. A person could survive on just water for a good sixty days. Plus I have a toilet. In theory, I have what I need."

"Blayne—"

Blayne gasped, cutting him off. "How do you know my name? How long have you been hunting me? Well, you can take your cellar of death where you keep all the bodies of the women you've slaughtered over the years and go to hell. Because this target, which you probably refer to as 'it' in your head to keep me as merely an object, is *not* going down without a fight!"

Proud of her speech, Blayne waited for Novikov to walk away. Instead she heard a brief sigh, then silence, but no footsteps. Where were the damn walking-away footsteps?

Blayne waited a bit longer, and having absolutely no patience to speak of, slowly crept closer to the door. She was only a few inches away when the door was ripped off its hinges and placed aside by the brute who'd done it.

Blayne squealed and stumbled back as Novikov stepped into the bathroom. Glaring down at her, he said, "Now we can talk."

She was staring at him that way again. The way she'd stared at him when he first met her and when he'd looked at her through the bloody glass. Her brown eyes wide, her mouth open a little. One good growl, and he was pretty sure she'd either make a desperate run around him or go for his jugular. Of course, if she thought he had a "cellar of death" he wasn't really surprised by the way she stared at him.

Blayne finally did speak, though, but it wasn't exactly what he expected to hear. "I am *so* not paying for that door."

"I wasn't planning on charging you."

She wanted out of the bathroom. He could tell by the way her gaze kept searching for a way past him, but he made sure that he stood right in the doorway so she couldn't get past him.

After another minute, she screamed, "You'll never take me alive! I'll never let you get me to a secondary location!"

Bo shrugged. "Okay."

With a horrified gasp, she stepped back. "You're gonna kill me here?"

Should he be entertained by this? Why was he entertained? "I actually wasn't planning on killing you at all."

Her eyes narrowed. "You're not going to kill me, skin me, and wear my head as a hat?"

Yep. He was entertained. And, no. It wasn't normal. Instead of answering her question, he asked his own. "Do you want me to?"

"Not really."

"Then why are you asking?"

"Because according to my father, many teachers, and quite a few anger-management counselors, I seem to lack that little internal device that stops things that are best left unsaid from being said."

"I see."

"So?"

"So what?"

She took a step forward. "Are you or are you not a serial killer?"

"Not."

"You've never murdered anyone?"

"On or off the ice?" Her eyes grew wide again and he argued, "It's a valid question." When she continued to gawk up at him, her mouth open, he admitted that "I've never murdered or killed anyone, on or off the ice, male or female, shifter or full-human." She went up on her toes, staring up at him. After a moment, she said, "Closer." He leaned in and she gazed into his eyes. He held her stare for a full minute before she said, "You're not lying."

"I know."

"Cool."

"Seals and walruses don't count, though, right?"

She shook her head. "I will not judge," she muttered to herself. "I will not judge." Then, "For this particular situation none-thumb-possessing prey does not count."

"Then we're fine."

"Cool," she said again.

He probably should be insulted she thought he was some kind of deranged serial killer, but that sounded like work he wasn't in the mood to indulge in.

"So," she went on, "since we've come to the conclusion that you're not looking for a new hat or to add me to a collection in your dungeon of pain and suffering—"

"Thought it was a cellar."

"—why do you have me trapped in a bathroom?"

"Thought maybe you'd want to go out for coffee or something."

She blinked. "You want to go—" Her eyes narrowed. "Gwen put you up to this, right?"

"Who?"

"What is her obsession with that girl? I mean, seriously—get over it already! Trying to set me up with you just to get even with Tracey Lembowski is so extreme. Don't ya think?"

"Well—"

For the first time, her face softened and she no longer looked terrified out of her mind. It was a lovely change. "But it was really sweet of you to play along. I heard you weren't sweet at all."

"I'm sweet. I'm very sweet."

"Hey, Novikov," a hyena cut in from behind him, "think I can get an auto—"

Bo bellowed in to the sniveling male's face, *"I am talking here!"* He hated when these idiots cut into his conversations without acknowledging the fact it was impolite. *"Can you not see that?"*

Giggling in panic, the hyena ran off, meeting up with his clan at the end of the hall, which led to more hyena giggling. Annoying.

"So where were we?" he asked, turning back to the suddenly wide-eyed wolfdog.

"Uh . . ." She gave a little laugh and muttered under her breath, "I will not judge." Then asked, "Do you have the time?"

Bo checked. "Eleven thirty-two and fourteen seconds."

"That was very precise."

"I like precise." He motioned to her left arm. "You have a watch."

"Yeah I do." She smiled at it. "Of course, it says it's three o'clock. Maybe it's on Bangkok time or something."

"Do you need a good jeweler to fix it? I know a bear who can—"

She waved away his offer. "Nah. It hasn't worked in weeks. Besides, it's a piece of junk, so there's no use fixing it. I got it for forty bucks in the Village."

Appalled, Bo asked, "If it doesn't work, why are you wearing it?"

"It's pretty!" She stepped in closer and lifted her arm so he could see it better. "It's a Pra-Dah." She laughed. "Not a Prada watch. A Pra-*Dah* watch. Classy, huh?"

True, Bo could see the humor in that but still . . . "But it doesn't work. Shouldn't you have a watch that works?"

"There's always someone around with a watch on. Like you. Or Ric. Or Gwen. And it's New York. Depending on where you are at any given time, you can usually find a clock somewhere on one of the buildings or on a billboard."

How could anyone live like that? It was so . . . all over the place! To be honest, Bo considered it a form of hell.

"That's not a very good way to tell time."

"Why sweat the little things?"

"Time is not a little thing."

"No, but it's close enough." A little tinkling sound went off, and Blayne turned in a circle, trying to find where the sound came from.

"Your pants," Bo told her.

"Oh!" She dug into one of the many pockets of her cargo pants and pulled out a small cell phone. "See?" she said, pointing at the front of it. "This has a clock, too." She gaped at the phone for a moment and then shook her head. "I'm such an idiot. I had this on me the whole time, and I could have totally called the cops if you'd turned out to be a serial killer. Except that I forgot I had the damn thing. In theory, I could totally be dead right now."

"Are you going to answer that call or keep making really, *really* disturbing proclamations?"

"Oh, right."

She answered the phone and said, "Uh-huh," and disconnected. "Gotta go. Gwen, Ric, and Lock are waiting for me outside."

She walked toward him and he automatically backed up. He couldn't explain it, but he felt like if he didn't move, she'd find a way to walk right through him.

"Well, see ya," she said, heading down the hallway.

"Wait," he finally called out to her when he'd finally recovered from her complete disregard for the importance of accurate timekeeping.

She faced him but kept walking backward.

"What about getting some coffee?"

She snorted. "God, no." With that, she turned back around and headed off.

God, no? Did she just say "God, no" to me? Normally he'd assume the worst with a statement like that, but with her he really couldn't be sure.

But it wasn't until the wolfdog suddenly stopped in the middle of the hallway and spun around to face him one more time that Bo realized he could never assume that the words coming out of Blayne's mouth and what she actually meant were one and the same when she suddenly admitted, "Because I hate coffee!" She laughed. "I realized I hadn't actually finished my thought. I do that sometimes. Sorry. Anyway, hate the taste of coffee and caffeine is so not this wolfdog's friend." She gave him a smile so bright that it nearly seared his eyes in his sockets, winked, and headed off.

Leaving Bo completely confused, kind of insulted, kind of not, and weirdly turned on because she looked shockingly cute in those oversized cargo pants.

But he blamed the mane for the turned-on thing. He totally blamed the mane!

Chapter 3

"So let me see if I understand this," Sami said, her small fingers steepled under her chin. "All you know at this point is that her name is Blayne and that she thought—"

"Not thought. She was convinced."

"Convinced. She was *convinced* you were a serial killer?"

"Yes."

Sander sat down at the table, his plate piled with bacon, ham, and eggs. Bo had no idea where the pair had found all the food. He knew they didn't cook it, and when he went to bed last night, they weren't even in the state. But he woke up this morning in his furnished Central Park Avenue apartment provided by his Carnivore contract, complete with its own Olympic-size swimming pool, and a full breakfast waiting for him. He probably should find out where the food came from, in case the cops showed up again. That was always so awkward.

Sander pointed a fork at him. "Are you saying you gave up that seal farm for a wolfdog who thinks you're a serial killer?"

"I didn't know she had that perception at the time."

Sami sighed. "This is what you get for not talking to us first before making these big decisions."

"Talking to you about what?"

"About which offer to take. *We*"—she motioned between herself and Sander—"are the most important things in your life."

"You are?" Because that was a kind of depressing thought.

"Yes. And do you know why?"

"How would I know why when I didn't know you were?"

"Because we're *your* foxes. All three of us are linked. Forever."

"But you're never really around."

"Because we're young," she reminded him. "We're traveling the world, trying to find ourselves. But when we're older, ready to have a couple of kits, we'll be back. And you'll need to be able to take care of us. That's your job."

"Which would be greatly helped by the seal farm," Sander said around a mouthful of ham and egg.

"You do both remember I'm only *half* polar bear, don't you? The lion part would have no problems slapping you both around and biting your little heads off."

Sami reached across the table and patted Bo's hand. "But it's the polar half we both love."

Blayne took back her bacon and followed that up with a punch to Mitch Shaw's shoulder. This was her monthly brunch with *her* wild dog Pack and the lion male had forced his way in, as was the way of male lions, and was now stealing her food! Rude!

"Ow!" the big cat whined.

"Stop taking my food or I'm going to start biting things off."

"Stingy."

"Greedy."

"Here, cat." Sabina of the Kuznetsov Pack dropped a platter of bacon in front of him. "I kill whole pig just so you can feed fat head."

"I know somewhere in there's an insult, but it still sounds so sexy with that Russian accent that I'm going to overlook it." Mitch switched his breakfast plate for the entire platter.

Blayne shook her head. "How can you eat like that? People starving and you stuff your fat face."

"Boo-hoo. My heart bleeds. Poor starving people."

Blayne knew Mitch only said that sort of thing to upset her, but what appalled her was that she fell for it every time. She slapped at his head, ignoring his laughter.

"Not that we don't love having you here for our Sunday brunch, Mitch," Jess Ward-Smith said from her place at the head of the long Kuznetsov Pack dining table filled with adults, all the pups outside in the backyard playing or up in their rooms, "but I am curious as to *why* you're here?"

"Important wolf Pack business has brought me here with my lady love and her Dee-licious cousin."

"Dee's here?" Blayne said with real excitement, and she jumped up, only to be yanked back down by Mitch.

"No," he told her.

"But I just want to say hi!" She jumped up again, and Mitch yanked her back down again.

"No."

"Come on. Pleaseeeeee let me say hi to Dee-Ann!"

At this point, Mitch was practically curled into his chair, he was laughing so hard while he still kept a firm grip on her arm. "No!" he finally got out. "And whatever you're doing with Dee-Ann—stop it. Because at this point, I'm thinking there's a shallow grave with your name on it."

"No fun," Blayne pouted. Then she snapped her fingers, her focus moving to something else entirely.

She reached into the backpack she had resting against the legs of her chair. "Look at this book I found—" She stopped abruptly when the entire table groaned. "What?"

"Blayne," Jess said, "You can't keep buying me books on pregnancy."

"It's not for you. It's for me."

Mitch leaned in and sniffed her neck. "You're not pregnant."

She glared at him. "Yes. I'm well aware of that."

"The ol' Blayne lower-land territory a little unused lately?" Blayne slammed the book in Mitch's big lion head. "I was just asking!"

Blayne flipped through the book. "This book is about what to do to help a friend going through pregnancy. There's a whole section on what to do in the delivery room."

Mitch took the book out of her hand, his fingers covered in bacon grease. "What do you need that information for?"

Blayne reached for the book, but Mitch held her off by turning away from her and using his forearm.

"Hopefully I'll be able to help out in the delivery room when the time comes, and I want to be prepped for that."

"Is this in case the future Ward-Smith wolfdog is crazy like all the others and comes out of the womb trying to chew through the umbilical cord? I know! Maybe you can distract her with a squeaky toy!"

Blayne balled up her fist, ready to punch Mitch O'Neill Shaw in the nuts when the book was snatched from Mitch's hand.

"Hey—oh." Mitch faced forward. "Hi, Smitty."

Smitty slapped his hand down on Mitch's shoulder and squeezed, Blayne cringing from the pain she saw on the lion male's face. Well, the pain and the blow to his sizable ego. "What was that you said about wolfdogs and my soon-to-be-here baby girl, Mitchell? Don't reckon I heard you right."

"Nothing," Mitch spit out between gritted teeth.

"That's what I thought." Smitty pulled his hand away and kindly handed the book to Blayne before kissing her forehead. "Hello, darlin'."

"Hello, Smitty. And thank you." Blayne sneered at Mitch and Mitch sneered back.

Smitty's sister, Sissy Mae, grabbed up the platter still half filled with bacon and dropped into a chair next to Mitch. She put her feet up on the table, worn cowboy boots right next to Mitch's arm.

"That's my bacon," Mitch told her.

"You need to learn to share, Mitchell Shaw." Sissy smiled at Blayne. "Mornin', darlin'."

"Hi, Sissy." Blayne looked around. "Where's Dee-Ann? I thought she was with you."

"Oh, well—Blayne, no!"

But Blayne was already up and running to the front door. She snatched it open and quickly scanned the downtown street until she saw the She-wolf halfway up the block. Grinning, Blayne screamed out, "Dee! Hey, Dee! Where are you going? Don't go!" The She-wolf stopped, her shoulders tensing. Blayne held her breath, but it was for nothing. Dee moved on. "Dee! Wait! Dee! Ann! Dee-*Annnnnnnnnnnnnn*! Come back!"

Dee-Ann didn't come back, and Blayne closed the front door and went back to the dining room and the remainder of her breakfast. Once she sat down, everyone at the table staring at her, she picked up her glass of freshly squeezed orange juice and took a sip. "I guess she didn't hear me."

Mitch shook his head. "It's like watching someone drive straight toward a concrete wall and yet there's nothing you can do to make them stop."

"Don't know what you mean."

"Forget all that," Sissy said, leaning in a bit and grinning. "We saw Lock and Gwenie last night for dinner," she said to Blayne.

"It's like having a mountain at the table with you," Mitch complained about Gwen's grizzly. "And he moves nearly as fast."

"And," Sissy went on, ignoring her mate, "what is this I hear about you and the almighty gorgeous Bo 'The Marauder' Novikov?"

It was bad enough that Blayne spit out her own orange juice in surprise, but when half the wild dogs, wolf, and lion did it, too, she didn't know what to think.

Bo finished up his hundredth lap, resting for a moment with his arms on the edge of his pool. It was Sunday, so this was his day off as per his schedule. Four hours working out in the pool was like a walk in the park compared with his standard ten-to-fifteen-hour daily workout the rest of the week.

Relaxing in a recliner and wearing a minuscule white bikini with her shoulder-length white hair up in a ponytail, Sami flipped through Japanese *Vogue*. Sander slept stomach down on another recliner. No snoring, but there was drool. It was not pretty.

"How long you two staying this time?"

Sami dropped the magazine onto the floor. She'd only been back in the States for a few days, but Bo could tell she was already bored, ready to travel again. Foxes bored easy, and Bo had gotten used to his friends appearing and disappearing randomly. If he were really desperate, he could always track them down through their parents. But to be honest, he was never that desperate. He enjoyed his friends while they were around, but didn't think much about them when they were gone.

"I don't know," she said. "We haven't made up our minds. Taiwan might be fun." She reached for another magazine. "You know, we stopped home before heading here. Lots of people asked about you."

"Lots of people asked about me? Or lots of people asked about Speck?" A nickname he completely loathed.

"Does that matter?"

"You kind of just answered my question."

Sami turned on her side, facing him. "What about your uncle?"

"I can't speak for him, but he's never suggested he's in dire need to see me."

"You always talk like a lawyer when I mention your family."

As usual Sami made it sound like Bo had this big family back in Ursus County, Maine, rather than one uncle willing to take him in when his parents died. No one else had wanted him. His mother's Pride had no use for a male hybrid, and his father's other brother had no use for Bo. So, Bo's Uncle Grigori left the Marine Corp and took Bo back to Maine where he was mostly ignored by the locals. They ignored him, that is until they figured out he was good at hockey. Hockey was all in Ursus County.

It wasn't easy, though, in the beginning. Bo was considered "small" for a bear, and playing hockey against all-bear teams—even the junior and minor league ones—was not for the weak of heart or body. Yet Bo learned a lot in those years, playing against bigger, full-bred bears who found him small and useless. And what he learned was to be mean.

He knew his reputation as a hockey player and, as far as he was concerned, he'd earned every bit of that rep. There were two constants when he was on the ice. The puck belonged to him and if you tried to take his puck, Bo Novikov would do whatever necessary to get it back. The intensity of his attack would depend on how much of a threat Bo considered a player. The more the threat, the worse the damage. When he was barely six-one and playing against bears at least a foot taller, this made sense and the damage was mitigated by his lack of size. When Bo hit his growth spurt, however, he didn't change the way he played. The only difference now was that he had the size and power to amplify the damage twenty-fold.

Even worse . . . Bo didn't care.

Winning was his goal. Always had been, always would be. The money, the contracts, the women, all of it, were the outcome of winning, but it was the winning that got Bo to the rink every day. It was winning that made him do whatever he had to do to get the puck from the other guy. Funny, he wasn't this predatory when he was hunting down dinner, or this territorial about anything else in his life.

"You need travel money?" he asked Sami, not wanting to discuss his uncle or the town he'd left behind a long time ago.

"Nah. We have some cash left from our last job."

Sami's last "job" most likely being her and Sander's last con. They were foxes after all, and foxes liked to steal. Sami was an Arctic fox from a very old Eskimo line. Sander was an Alaskan fox, his people from Kodiak. Bo had been unable to shake them since he'd moved to Ursus County, the pair latching on to him his first day of grade school. No matter where his career landed him, at some point Bo would look up in the stands and see Sami and Sander watching him, or he'd come home after practice to find them lounging on his furniture and eating his food.

It was simply just something he learned to accept, and as long as they cleaned up after themselves and controlled their clutter tendencies, he enjoyed having them around.

"Well, let me know if you need any."

"You're such a good polar," Sami teased. "I'm so glad we made you ours."

"Like I had a choice."

"You so didn't!" she laughed.

"See this?" Mitch demanded, lifting up his mane so Blayne was forced to look at the back of his thick linebacker-size neck.

"What am I looking at?"

"I was trying to get Novikov's autograph at a game he had in Philly, and I must have startled him because I was hiding behind a door until he passed—"

"Why were you hiding behind a—"

"—and he slammed me into the wall so hard, I was bleeding and couldn't stand for like an hour. I still have the scar!"

"Dude, dude, that's nothing." Phil, Sabina's husband, pulled the neck of his long-sleeve thermal tee down, revealing faint scratches on his chest. "I got this during the game he had against the Jersey Stompers three years ago. The crowd was throwing soda and chips and popcorn on him after he annihilated the Jersey team. And I leaned out and screamed, 'Novikov! You suck!' And he *slashed* me with those eight-inch hybrid claws he's got!" Phil leaned back in his chair, appearing way too smug. "And I totally survived."

Horrified, Blayne said, "What are you two bragging about? Abusing fans is not appropriate behavior." Blayne pointed at Phil. "And if you didn't like him, why are you so excited about him physically assaulting you?"

"Who said I didn't like him?"

"*You* said you screamed at him that he sucked."

"Because I'm his *toughest* fan." Phil lifted his hands up as if what he was telling her was somehow obvious to the entire universe. "Which is way better than being just his most loyal or whatever. Right, Mitch?"

"Absolutely."

Disgusted, Blayne said, "The man is a total asshole. He fights with his own teammates. During a game! Who does that?"

"I don't care if he beats his entire team to death," Mitch said, disgusting Blayne even more, which she didn't think was possible. "As long as he keeps winning for teams I support."

"This isn't about Dallas again, is it?"

"He should have never joined that team. It was the ultimate betrayal."

Blayne looked down the table at Jess, crossing her eyes, because, yes, she'd lived through this ridiculous Philly Shifter argument before.

"Hey," Mitch leaned in. "Since you know the guy, maybe you can hook me up with a signed jersey."

"I don't know the guy and I'm not getting you shit."

"It's like you don't love me at all."

"I don't."

"Fine. Be that way. But you can still get me a jersey."

"Two," Phil added. "*Two* signed jerseys."

"I'm not getting either of you anything."

"Why the hell not?"

"Because Bo Novikov represents everything that's wrong in shifter sports." She began to count off on her fingers, "No sportsmanship. No team spirit. No mentoring rookie or young players."

"You're so naïve!" Mitch cried out in his usual dramatic fashion. "High morals don't make you a champion. And," he added, "it's because of this attitude that Gwenie's probably going to make you second string for the championship bout against the Texas Longfangs, so she can bring in Pussies Galore from the Jamaica Me Howlers."

Her hands dropping into her lap, Blayne asked, "What?"

Mitch, most likely realizing how quiet everyone had suddenly become, looked around the table before focusing on Blayne. "Gwen, uh, did mention that to you, didn't she?"

Phil relaxed back in his chair. "I'm guessing not."

Blayne shoved her chair back and stood, Mitch grabbing her arm. "Wait! I'm probably wrong. I'm sure—"

"It isn't that she would make that decision," Blayne snarled, yanking her arm out of Mitch's grip, "it's that she would talk to *you* about it before me." She swiped up her backpack and spun to leave, pulling the straps of her bag over her shoulder at the same time. And, yeah, she kind of knew she hit Mitch in the process, sending him flying into the middle of the dining table. Too bad she couldn't bring herself to care!

Ignoring the wild dogs calling her back to the table, she went to the front door and yanked it open. The grizzly on the other side jerked back.

"Oh. Hey, Blayne." Lock MacRyrie smiled down at her. "I brought Sabina her damn chest of drawers so I don't have to hear her asking me for it anymore."

"Gwen with you?"

Lock's smile faded and he motioned behind him. "Yeah. She's—"

Blayne pushed past the bear and went down the front stairs to the still running pickup Lock used to deliver his handmade furniture. She knocked on the window and Gwen, grinning, rolled down the window.

"Hey, girl! I didn't know you were going to be here today."

"Wild dog brunch."

"You and your breakfast food obsession." Gwen rested her arm on the window. "So what's up?"

"So . . . Pussies Galore as your blocker, huh?"

Gwen's gold eyes grew wide, her expression stunned. "Blayne, wait. It's just—"

"No. No. No need to explain. She rocks. I've seen her play."

"Blayne—"

"And the Longfangs are really tough. Tougher than me, apparently. So I understand."

"Blayne, we're not replacing you, but this is the championships, hon. We need a little bit of an edge."

"An edge I don't have."

"You're too damn nice," Gwen stated bluntly. "You're constantly apologizing to the other team, and you hold yourself back because you don't want to hurt anybody. So yeah," she said, getting pissed, "I guess you don't have that edge we need."

Blayne stepped back from the truck. She knew she couldn't say anything at the moment because she'd start what her dad called, "All that goddamn blubbering."

"Blayne, wait."

Gwen unlocked the door and pushed it open, but Blayne rushed off. She needed to figure out what she was going to do next. She may be "nice"—something she refused to see as a curse—but that didn't mean she was weak. And she would never give up something she'd worked so hard to get.

No. There had to be a way to prove them all wrong. To prove that she wasn't just the Babes resident "cheerleader." A title she'd loved until this very moment.

Yeah. She'd prove them *all* wrong.

CHAPTER 4

B o glanced at his watch. Eight a.m. Time to hit the treadmill.
He left the ice, waving at a couple of the maintenance guys
who knew him by name and went to the locker room. He
changed out of his hockey gear and into sweats and sneakers.
Locking up everything, he checked his watch again and jogged
out of the locker room and down several floors. Bo pushed the
door open, waved at a couple of other maintenance men who
knew him by name, and headed to the massive gym that every
team player, no matter the sport or whether they were on a
minor or major league team, had access to. He wasn't rushing
his run since this was a warm-up but was about to pick up the
speed before charging into the gym and jumping on a treadmill,
when a frustrated groan and a sniffle caught his attention. So did
the scent.

He spun around and jogged back and through the open doorway. He was surprised to find it open. The center had several
smaller stadiums for the minor and junior leagues that didn't get
the size of crowds that the pro teams did. This particular stadium had become the domain of the tri-state derby teams that
had become quite popular, and the space was rarely open this
early since their games and training only happened in the evenings
or on weekends.

Bo jogged to a stop and watched as Blayne picked herself up

off the track. She readjusted her helmet, since it was currently blocking her eyes, and let out another frustrated breath. Then she wiped her cheeks with the back of her hands and he realized she was crying. Wow, she either hit the floor really hard or she needed to toughen up a bit.

He thought for sure she was about to quit, but she suddenly squared her shoulders, crouched down, her hands fisted, her arms bent at the elbow, and after a brief moment, shot off again.

She was fast. Really fast. She was doing well, too, until she sort of . . . wiped out. He had no idea what she'd done, but she went down hard, flipping head over ass in a jumble of long legs, arms, and skates.

Bo grimaced, wondering if he'd have to take her to the health services floor. He stepped forward, and that's when she suddenly bounced back up. Her shoulder looked a little off until she grabbed it with her opposite hand, gritted her teeth, and jerked it back into place. The crack of bones echoed in the empty room, and Bo grimaced again.

He stepped in closer and, keeping his voice even and calm, asked, "Are you okay?"

Blayne spun around, startled even though he'd tried not to startle her. But once she recognized him, Blayne nailed him with a look so loathing, he was sure she still thought he was a serial killer.

"You," she hissed at him. "This is *your* fault!"

Shocked, Bo asked, "What did I do?"

"You're an asshole!"

"You don't even know me."

"On the ice. You're an asshole on the ice. And now everyone wants to be assholes! That's expected now!" She rolled closer. "And because I'm not an asshole, I'm suffering! Your fault!"

Not used to having people accuse him of something so stupid before, Bo said, "Okay," turned, and walked out. He was halfway to the gym when he turned back around and returned to the derby track. Blayne had her arms on the railing and her head resting on them when he walked back in. She stood tall when she saw him.

"What?" she asked when he stood in front of her.

"You know, instead of standing here and crying and blaming me, maybe you should do something to fix whatever your problem is. I have no idea what your particular problem is, but I feel pretty confident it's not my fault."

"It *is* your fault. Because of you and your bizarre ideas about sportsmanship, everyone has to become an asshole or you're considered the weak link on your team. The one who has to be replaced because no one thinks you can handle the Texas Long-fangs. The one who needs to be replaced because maybe once, or sixteen times, you've said sorry when you've accidentally harmed someone during rigorous game play." She folded her arms over her chest. "Have *you* ever said you're sorry after accidentally harming someone during rigorous game play?"

"No. Of course, I've never accidentally harmed someone during a game. I have, however, purposely harmed someone during . . . what was it? Rigorous game play?"

"And that doesn't bother you?"

"No."

She let out a sigh, her whole body sort of deflating. "I'm doomed."

"But," he added, "you don't have to be an asshole to be a winner. I'm an asshole in the rink because that's just how I am when I'm out there. I've known other, really good players who were nice guys."

"Like who?"

"Like Nice Guy Malone. He was extremely nice. And that first time I played against him, when he cross-checked me into the stands, giving me a concussion and a laceration that took forty-two stitches to close, if I remember correctly, he apologized."

"What did he say?"

" 'Sorry, kid.' But more importantly . . . he meant that 'sorry, kid.' "

"Okay."

"I'm guessing, though, that being nice is not your problem."

"But Gwen said—"

"It may look like it's your problem, but it's not your problem."

"Fine. Then what is my problem?"

Bo gestured to the track. "Why did you end up falling?"

"Which time?"

Bo frowned at the question. "Do you fall so often you need clarification of timeline?"

"Sometimes. And sometimes I'm thrown, tripped, slammed, flung, battered—"

"Okay," he cut in, sensing she could keep going. "Five minutes ago before we started this conversation, you wiped out. Why?"

"I don't know."

"Did you trip? Lose your balance?"

"I said, I don't—"

"Don't get frustrated. Answer my question."

She looked back at the track. "I was skating, everything was fine, and then . . ."

"And then," he pushed when her voice trailed off.

"And then I started thinking about how unfair this all was and how no one was giving me a chance and then I realized I was being unfair and I needed to stop feeling sorry for myself and then I realized I was hungry and I would need to get something before I get to work and then when I realized I still had to go to work, I knew I'd have to see Gwen and she'd want to talk and any time Gwen wants to talk it's like a form of torture because there's no subtle with her, you know what I mean, she's just like in your face just like my dad and then I thought, 'Oh, great, I'll need to tell Mr. I Told You You'd Never Be Good At Derby that I was being bumped for a Howler,' a full She-wolf no less and I knew that conversation would get—"

"Stop!" Bo put his hands over his ears and gaped down at her. "Good God, woman. Hit the brakes on the freight train that is your mouth."

*   *   *

How pathetic. She was getting "assistance"—and she was using that term lightly—from the most assholey of all pro athletes. It was kind of like Mother Teresa asking Stalin for advice on the best way to handle difficult lepers.

And now he was telling her to shut up. Like she hadn't heard that enough over the years. The only person who had never told her to shut up had been her mother. Blayne could talk for hours, nonstop, and her mother never said a word or complained. Of course, the party was over once Cranky Old Wolf got home, but that was something to be dealt with in therapy.

Novikov lowered his hands and let out an overly dramatic breath. "I didn't think it would be this easy, but I know what your problem is. You think too much."

"I can say with all honesty," she said flatly, "you are perhaps the only person who's ever said that to me. At least without a definite note of sarcasm."

"Do you know what I think about when I'm on the ice?"

"Something like, 'Will I have to go to hell for what I just did to that guy's face?' "

"No. That never crosses my mind."

"Shocking." Dropping her hands to her hips, she asked, "So what are you thinking when you're on the ice?"

"My puck."

Blayne waited for more. She waited at least two full minutes for more, but Bo didn't say anything else, and for two full minutes they stared at each other until she couldn't stand the silence any longer. "That's it?"

"That's it."

" 'My puck'? You don't think about anything else? Like strategy or what your teammates are doing or time on the clock or—"

"I'm aware of all that, but I'm thinking 'My puck.' "

"How . . . one note."

"It works."

He had a point. Novikov had brought nearly any team he'd been on to championship, was the all-time scorer in the league, and was considered one of the best players of all time. As much as Blayne hated his lack of fair play, she couldn't ignore the fact that the man was a winner.

Something Blayne wanted to be, she just didn't know until this moment how much.

And as she stared up at the seven-one, nearly four-hundred-pound descendent of Genghis Khan himself, it suddenly occurred to her that the one person who could help her become a winner was standing right in front of her.

That's when, for the first time since Sunday brunch, Blayne smiled.

Why was she smiling at him like that? It wasn't that big, sweet smile she usually had. What he secretly called her "doggie grin." No, this was the wolf in her coming out, and the cat in him didn't like it one damn bit.

"What?"

"Nothing." She skated closer. "So, do you train every day?"

"Of course. Don't you?"

"Not really."

"You should."

"Okay." She moved around him. "Are you here every morning?"

"Except Sundays."

"I guess you get in bright and early, huh?"

"Yeah."

"Like . . . what? Five thirty? Or six?"

"Six."

"You start at the rink or the gym first?"

"Rink. That way I can—" Bo's eyes narrowed. "Wait."

She skated to stop in front of him, and her smile had turned decidedly false and misleading.

"Not in this lifetime." Bo turned away from her, but she zipped in front of him, proving she was as fast as she'd seemed on the track.

"You haven't heard my offer."

Bo took a step back. "You're not going to offer me sex, are you?"

Blayne scowled. "No. I wasn't. But I'm not sure I like the look of obvious disgust on your face." She slammed her hands onto her hips. "Are you saying you wouldn't want to have sex with me? Because you were the one who asked me out. And I don't appreciate—"

"Freight train. Brakes."

She snorted at him. Like a bull.

"If you're going to offer sex," he went on, "I just think it should be for something life or death. Or money." He thought on that a moment, nodded. "Yeah. Life-or-death situation or money. But for a chick hobby? That's a little beneath you, don't you think?"

"A *chick* hobby?" she spit at him.

Bo wiped his chin. "What would you call it?"

"A sport! A valid sport!"

"Oh, come on."

"Great. Another guy afraid of women in sports."

"I'm not afraid of women in sports. Wait. I'm lying."

"A-ha!"

"The sows on the Kodiak hockey team . . . I'm afraid of them. They're mean."

Her anger slipped away as quickly as it had come. Now she seemed fascinated. "There are women in the hockey league?"

"Yeah. It's just . . . kind of hard to tell sometimes."

"I had no idea."

"Hockey league is coed. And if you saw the women play, you'd understand why." She slapped his arm. "Ow."

"You respect the sows in the hockey league—"

"And She-wolves."

"—but you don't respect derby?"

He laughed and bam! Her anger was back.

"What's so damn funny?"

"It's like comparing Queen Boadicea to Pam Anderson."

"Don't make up words and think you can distract me."

"I didn't make up—"

"Look, the bottom line is, I need your help. I need an edge. We've made it into the National Championships next month, but we'll be going up against the Texas Longfangs. And the rumor is, part of their training is slaughtering cattle with their bare hands—while human. You've gotta help me."

"I don't know anything about derby. In fact, I don't even respect derby as a sport. So how can *I* help you?"

"Name the last guy who cross-checked you into the stands?"

Bo couldn't help but smirk. "Nice Guy Malone."

"Exactly." She gave a little laugh. "See? I need you to show me how to be less good, moral, loving Blayne and more evil, sadistic, asshole Marauder."

Deciding not to see that statement as an insult, he instead argued, "But I don't really have time to help you." He pointed at his watch. "I have a schedule."

"You can't fit me in for like . . . an hour, a couple of times a week?"

"No. No, I can't."

"You're serious?"

"Yeah." He tapped his watch again. "Schedule."

"Right. A schedule, which can be changed to do the right thing. Yes?"

"No. No, no, no. You can't go around changing schedules. What's the point of a schedule if you're changing it all the time?"

"But schedules should be flexible."

"No. Not flexible." What was this craziness she was spouting? "Schedules can't be flexible. Flexible leads to disorder. Disorder leads to sloppiness. Sloppiness leads to failure. And failure is another word for losing."

Blayne glided a few feet back from him. "You're really not joking . . . are you?"

"I'm not really a jokey kind of guy, but when it comes to schedules and time—I don't joke."

"Oooo-kay. Um . . ." She pulled off her helmet and scratched her head. "How do you . . ."

"How do I what?"

"Well, I always hear about you at the latest shifter-only club openings—"

"I don't go to clubs."

"—or taking out another supermodel—"

"Supermodels have issues with time I'm not comfortable with."

"Or traveling the world to exotic locations?"

"Only when there's a game there. Like the Tahiti World Play-offs. But God it was hot outside the rink. So miserably, miserably hot."

"But I don't understand. I mean . . . how do you . . . when do you . . . ?" Her eyes grew wide and she briefly covered her mouth with her hand. "Are you a virgin?" she whispered.

"What? No!"

"But when do you find time with that rigid schedule of yours? I mean prisoners at Rikers have more freedom!"

"I get along just fine. I've had girlfriends."

"Did they last?"

Bo shrugged. "They were mostly feline so . . . no."

"Yeah. Most felines I know aren't gettin' up at the break of dawn—on purpose."

"I'm aware of that, you know, *now*."

"I have to tell you something," she said, putting her helmet back on. "I am *fascinated* by you. And I now realize that not only do I need you, but you need me."

"Are we discussing sex again?"

"No." She glided closer. "Let's clear the air about that right now. I no longer have boyfriends."

"Oh." Bo raised a brow. "So you're with one of the Babes now?"

"No. You Visigoth."

"You know Visigoth, but you don't know Boadicea?"

"Again, no making up words. Anyway, I no longer have boy-friends."

"Why?"

"My last one was, tragically, a bit of a sociopath. When we went away on a weekend trip to Atlantic City and he said it was on his mother, I thought she had knowingly paid for it. Not that he had stripped her savings account bare."

"Oh."

"Yeah. Nothing really ruins a romantic weekend away with the boyfriend like cops arresting you both. So no more boyfriends."

"So you're celibate?"

"Yeah, I tried that, too, and that didn't really work. So now I have gentlemen callers. And with the gentlemen callers, I have arrangements."

"What's the difference between a boyfriend and a gentleman caller?"

"There's a difference."

"What difference?"

"A difference. Don't judge."

"I'm not judging. I'm just at a loss for logic."

Blayne pointed her finger at him. "Do you want my help or not?"

"Wait a minute. You need *my* help."

"As I said, we need to help each other."

"Not really."

"No, really. You need a social life."

"No. I don't."

"You do. You're almost thirty. A couple more years you'll be a broken down old sports guy, alone, bitter, unloved; some hooker or Vegas showgirl will marry you just for your money and eventually kill you in your sleep. Is that what you want?"

"Not when you put it that way."

"Of course you don't. That's what I'm here for. To ensure your life is not spent in misery and despair. And you're here to ensure that I rock this year's championship. Dude, this is a win-win situation."

"Don't call me dude. And is it really that hard to rock the derby circuit?"

"As a matter of fact—"

"Are your shorts not short enough? Do you need a push-up bra?"

"I'm trying to help you here."

"I'm still not sure I need your help."

"Oh, you do." She placed her hand to her upper chest. "And because I'm a kind, giving person, that's what I'm going to do. Help you."

"How?"

"I'm working on that. But until I figure you out, we can work on me."

Bo looked at his watch, cringing when he realized he'd already lost twenty-eight minutes sitting here talking to her. "Blayne, I really don't have time to—"

"Come on. An hour in the mornings? One hour? It isn't like this will be forever, either. Just until the championships."

Bo went over the schedule in his head.

She placed both hands on his forearm and looked up at him. "Please?"

Christ, how could he turn that face down, complete with big puppy dog eyes? He couldn't. He couldn't turn that face down. "One hour. From seven to eight. But that's it."

"Yay!" Without a running start, Blayne leaped up and wrapped her arms around his neck. "Thank you! This is great!" She hugged him but let go before he could get his arms around her. *Dammit!*

She wiggled on her skates. "I am *so* excited!"

"Be on time, Blayne," he told her.

"Yeah, sure."

"No, no." He caught hold of her arm. "You're still wearing this stupid watch."

"It's pretty."

"But it doesn't tell the time. How are you going to be on time if you don't have a working watch?"

"I'll be on time. I promise!" She suddenly hugged him again, her arms around his waist. "Oh!" She leaned back, looking up at him. "Speaking of which, what time is it?"

"Eight thirty."

"Shit! I'm so fucking late!" She skated away from him.

"This does not fill me with confidence, Blayne."

"I'll be here. Tomorrow at seven. I'll be on time! I promise!"

She skated away from him and over to a pile of . . . stuff. She viciously shoved all that stuff into a backpack—without even a modicum of attempting to organize it first—and pulled the straps onto her shoulders. "Thank you . . . uh . . ."

"You don't know my name?"

"I know your name! I just don't know what to call you. Do I call you Novikov or Coach or Mr. Novikov or The Marauder?"

"Bo. Call me Bo."

"I like Novikov." And he wondered why she'd bothered asking him in the first place. "And you can call me Blayne."

"Like I've been doing?"

"Exactly!"

She headed off for the door.

"Are you skating to work?"

She stopped, looked down at her skates. "Oops," she said with a laugh. "I guess I am now." She looked back at him and shrugged. "If I'm late to the office, Gwen's gonna have my ass. Oh! And I'm not speaking to her today anyway. Ha! Take that, feline who thinks I'm too weak for the Babes!"

Then she was gone and Bo wondered what the hell he'd just gotten himself into.

Dee was heading toward the sports center when Blayne Thorpe suddenly shot out the doors and skated off down the street.

Dee's hands turned into fists and she growled, making the full-humans on their way to work skirt away from her.

That girl! That damn girl! She bounced around the world like a jumping bean. Here, there, every damn where! How were Dee and her team supposed to keep a constant eye on the little idiot when she kept bouncing around?

It was bad enough Dee was forced to do this at all. It was bad enough that the Van Holtz men who ran the Group, the organization she currently worked for, insisted that one wolfdog needed this level of protection. It was bad enough that every time Dee came face to face with Blayne Thorpe, the woman yelled out her name like they were on opposite ends of the earth. But for Dee to have to lower herself to protect a female she was positive was simply a teacup poodle in disguise rather than a predator worth stealing was the height of insult.

For the past two months, Dee had been begging Niles Van Holtz to release her from this bullshit duty. To let her off-leash on more important things than the safety and care of one energy-infused idiot. But did he listen? No. At least he didn't listen to her. Instead he listened to that nephew/cousin/direct bloodline—whatever the hell he called him, Ulrich Van Holtz. And Ulrich was all sorts of concerned about Blayne Thorpe, Useless Girl.

Normally, Dee would have quit this bitch by now. She didn't need money this badly. But the Group had potential for giving her what she wanted in the long term. Dee was all about big picture thinking, and she'd already started moving on her plans to start her own division. But until someone—anyone!—snatched Blayne Thorpe merely because she was a hybrid so the Group could catch those full-humans in the act and take them down, Dee was trapped watching after this . . . this . . . poodle!

Cracking her neck and letting out a breath, Dee followed after Blayne, almost crashing into her on the corner when it turned out the wolfdog had gone down the wrong street—again. Of course, Blayne didn't even see Dee. Didn't scent her. Didn't know she was being followed. She was blissfully oblivious as always.

"Useless teacup poodle," Dee snarled, watching the idiot skate off through the busy city crowd.

Then, resigned to what she had to do, Dee followed after her.

Chapter 5

Blayne skated into the office. Sitting on her desk was an enormous cup from her favorite smoothie place and a cardboard box most likely filled with her favorite nonsugar donuts from the Healthy Eating Bakery two doors down. A place Gwen said she wouldn't go into with a gun to her head because she hated, "All those damn hippies." In Gwen's mind, anyone who didn't eat meat was a hippie. But Blayne went to the bakery for yummy treats made without sugar.

It hadn't taken Blayne long to figure out that sugar and/or caffeine in her system was a one-way ticket to a night in jail. For most people it was liquor or hard drugs, but Blayne had additional issues, so she avoided all of them as much as possible, especially on workdays.

Gwen sat at her desk, and Mitch, half awake and probably not happy about having to be at their office so early, sat in the only other guest chair they could fit in the room.

"Hi, Blayne." Gwen smiled at her. "How's it going?"

"Fine," she muttered, keeping her head down. Was Blayne milking the fact her friend felt awful about what she said for all it was worth? Um . . . yeah!

"Look, Blayne." Gwen stood and walked over to her while Blayne dropped her bag to the floor and began digging through it to get out her work clothes. "I'm really sorry about yesterday. Of course the Babes aren't trading you or removing you or replacing you or anything. Cherry won't hear of it."

Blayne shrugged—pathetically, she thought—and kept pulling out clothes trying to find her cargo pants.

"And Mitch is sorry, too. Right, Mitchell?" Gwen asked through clenched teeth.

"What? Oh, yeah. Yeah. I'm sorry, Blayne. I should have kept my mouth shut."

"It's no big deal," Blayne said, standing.

"It is," Gwen said. "You know I'm loyal to you, Blayne. And I think if we train together until the championships, outside team trainings, it'll be fine. It'll be better than fine. It'll be great."

"That won't be necessary."

"Come on, Blayne. You know I don't mind and it'll be good for me, too. We can practice before work in the mornings."

Stealing from Novikov, Blayne said, "I'm not sure I can fit that into my current schedule."

"Schedule? What schedule? When have you ever had a schedule except the work one I give you every morning?"

"I'm talking about the schedule I now have that allows me to train with Bo Novikov. In the mornings, before work. You know, to help toughen me up so I'm not such a weak link for the team."

Feeling smug but working really hard not to show it, Blayne stood, her work clothes in her hand. Gwen blinked at her, confused, while Mitch had his mouth open, his eyes wide. "I've gotta change. Got that job over at that barbershop on Twenty-eighth. Backed up sinks, I think." She nodded, looked between the two siblings, and said, "Okay. See ya."

She skated out of the office and to the first-floor bathrooms. By the time she'd changed into her work clothes, Blayne was grinning ear to ear. She simply couldn't help it. She hadn't had that much fun in a while.

Giggling to herself, Blayne walked out of the bathroom, squealing a little when Mitch latched on to her arm and dragged her into one of the first-floor conference rooms. They weren't alone, though. Now the wild dogs were involved. Of course, it was their building that B&G Plumbing had their offices in but, more important, she *loved* when the wild dogs were involved. Everything took on a whole new level of crazy when they were!

Mitch dragged her to the front of the room before he released her. "Have you lost your mind?" he demanded.

"You'll have to be more specific."

Jess, the only one sitting, her large belly keeping her far back from the conference table, ducked her head and began to rub her nose.

"Mitch—" Gwen said, trying to end this quickly, but Mitch was on a roll and it wasn't even nine a.m. yet. He held his hand up to cut his sister off.

"Blayne." And he said her name with all types of concern. "This is Bo Novikov we're talking about here. The Marauder. He doesn't train anyone."

"Except me."

"Yeah, sweetie." He placed his hand on her shoulder, and a small part of her—a small part she had control of after lots of anger management classes—wanted to bite his fingers clean off. "But at what price?"

"I'm going to help him."

"Help him with what? Orgasms?"

Blayne curled her hand into a fist under the sweat clothes she still held. She made sure to dig her fingers into her palm so that she didn't laugh. When she knew she had control, she asked, "He didn't say that specifically, but there was some mention of a morning protein drink. I said, 'I hope you like strawberry!'"

"Blayne!"

She waved away his concern. "Look, he's actually really nice."

"See, you already have me worried, Blayne. The Marauder is *not* nice. He's what our mom would call a motherfucker. He's a motherfucker on the ice and, from what I've seen and heard, a motherfucker off it."

"I heard he threw a guy off a building once," Phil added in for no reason that Blayne could see.

"We'll be underground at the Sports Center," she clarified, making Jess and Gwen snort.

"I heard he went after a fan with his hockey stick," Danny tossed in. "And I mean his hockey stick. Hockey stick isn't a euphemism for penis."

Yup! She loved the wild dogs!

"Would you two shut up?" Mitch snapped.

"Watch mouth, cat," Sabina warned, "or I remove your tongue."

"Don't you see, Blaynie." Mitch put his arm around her shoulders. "You're like an illegitimate little sister that I never wanted."

"Thanks?"

"And I want to keep you safe and sound, not sexually abused by sports stars." He pulled her in close, cutting off her ability to breathe. "Novikov isn't going to help you, Blayne. He's going to use you."

"But Gwenie said I should do whatever I have to when it comes to the team."

"I'm sure she didn't mean—"

"If the rest of us," Gwen cut in, "can put out to get our team to the next level, I don't see why Blayne can't."

Jess had to turn her chair around so she wasn't facing Mitch, and Mitch looked seconds from his head exploding off his body.

"*What the hell are you talking about?*"

"Don't yell," Gwen said. "No need to yell. Blayne just understands what she has to do. For the team. Right, Blayne?"

"Right!"

"Now come on. We've got to get to work."

"Wait a minute!" Mitch yelled. "You can't just walk away! This conversation isn't done!"

Ulrich Van Holtz rolled out of bed and, scratching his head and yawning, made his way out of his bedroom, down his hallway, and into his living room, grabbing the remote off the coffee table. Morning news and fresh coffee would get his day started, so he could face the lunch rush at the restaurant and hockey practice with the team that night.

About to press the button that would turn on all the different pieces of equipment that made up his home theater, Ric jumped instead, barely keeping his grip on the sleek device in his hand when he heard, "You wanted to see me?"

Ric closed his eyes and waited until his heart rate slowed down. As with all Van Holtz pups, Ric had been trained from birth to be aware of three things: When filet mignon was a perfect medium-rare, when it was the right time to sell stocks, and when a predator was lurking around one's home. As his restaurant reviews and personal financial portfolio revealed, Ric had mastered the first two. And he'd always felt he'd mastered the third as well.

Until he met Dee-Ann Smith.

He'd met some "lurky types," as Blayne liked to call them, nearly every day, but none had compared with the thirty-four-year-old She-wolf who didn't seem to let little things like titanium doors, heavily armed guards, or lethal laser protection get in her way of entering wherever she felt the need to enter. And since his penthouse suite at the top of the Van Holtz towers had lesser versions of that level of security, he guessed he shouldn't continually be surprised by her sudden appearances in his home.

Feeling calmer, Ric faced Dee-Ann. Like most shifters, he slept naked, but Dee-Ann never seemed to notice, so he didn't bother scrambling to put on clothes. As far as Ric was concerned, it was the risk she took if she was going to just show up in people's houses unannounced.

"I did want to see you . . . two days ago."

"Busy. Watcha want?"

"I wanted to check in about—"

"Teacup?"

"I prefer we call her Blayne, but yes."

The six-two She-wolf shoved her hands into the front pockets of her jeans. It was cold out, mid-February, which meant that Dee-Ann's jeans, Coors T-shirts, and cowboy boots had turned into jeans, a Led Zeppelin sweatshirt, and cowboy boots with an oversized leather bomber jacket, EGGIE sewn in on the front, in case the near-freezing temperatures made Dee chilly.

"We're wastin' our time on her."

"Yes. You've said this before. Many, many, *many* times. But as far as the Group and *I* are concerned, she's a prime target."

"No one's taking that girl." Dee rolled her eyes. "She wouldn't even be good for breedin'."

As much as Ric worshipped the ground Dee-Ann Smith walked on, he still refused to take her shit on this one issue.

A few months back, Dee-Ann had found out that Blayne's name had been sold to a fighting ring that liked to use shifter hybrids for their events. In the past six months, they'd found more than two dozen bodies all over the tri-state area. Some of them were still in shifted form, some human, all of them chewed up and spit out. A few still wearing their thick leather collars, complete with spikes. A few had died during the fight; others had been put down after. All of them had been male, but females had been taken.

Some assumed they'd been taken for breeding, but Ric didn't think it was that simple. It wasn't like breeding pit bulls or rott-weilers, where the puppies grew up into fighting dogs within a year or two. The pups of shifters wouldn't be useful for years, their ability to shift not happening until they hit puberty. The only ones with fighting potential at a young age were the hyenas. They were the only shifters born with their fangs, but the young were kept close to home just for this reason. And no one with two working brain cells was going to try to get into a hyena den to grab up a few of their young. Absolutely no one was that stupid.

No, Ric didn't think they wanted the female hybrids for breeding. He felt they wanted them for fighting, she-predators in general being more vicious than males. They had to be. Often, they weren't merely protecting themselves but their young as well.

And a small fortune had been given to the scumbag who'd sold Blayne's name, so Ric refused to believe anyone was giving up on her now.

"You know when I signed up for this, Niles Van Holtz said I wasn't going to be hemmed in."

"I'm not hemming you in, Dee-Ann. I'm telling you to do your job. I'm not telling you how to do it, just to do it. You and Uncle Van decided not to tell Blayne she was a target, but that means you and your team have to work harder to protect her because she doesn't know to protect herself."

"That was your uncle's idea, not mine."

Actually, Niles Van Holtz, Uncle Van, was his older cousin, but that was neither here nor there at the moment.

"I'll make this simple for you. I want regular updates on Blayne. Where she is, what she's doing, and who she's doing it with. I want you to do your job, Dee-Ann. It's that simple."

Perfect full lips briefly pursed, before Dee said, "As you like." It was her nice Southern way of saying, "I'll do it, but fuck you," but if it got Ric what he wanted, he'd overlook the tone.

He faced his home theater again and used the remote to turn it on. "You want breakfast?" he offered, ready to ease her anger with food. But when he looked over his shoulder at where she'd been standing, she was already gone.

"On three. One, two . . . three."

Gwen and Blayne pulled, yanking the warped door open. The dank smell of mold and damaged plumbing hit them, and the pair turned their heads. "Okay," Gwen said when she could speak without gagging, "maybe we should have listened to my mother about joining the family business."

Blayne laughed. "The smell's not that bad, princess."

"You are such a canine about scents."

"I'll take that as a compliment."

Gwen motioned to the hallway behind them with a tip of her head. "Anyone around?"

Blayne looked, then sniffed. "Nope."

Without a witnessing audience, Gwen walked into the pitch-black room without using the flashlight she had with her. Why waste the batteries when she could see just fine without it?

Gwen found the water-damaged wall that was right beneath where the barbershop and hair salon had their sinks. "Found it."

Blayne nodded. "Yep. That looks kind of long term, huh?"

"Pretty much." Gwen dropped her tool bags onto the floor and reached into one to pull out her sledgehammer. Blayne did the same, the friends standing beside each other. Gwen started, swinging the sledgehammer over her head and into the wall. As she pulled back, Blayne swung. They kept this up until they'd destroyed a good portion of the wall, revealing very old pipes that were dripping from several spots and pouring from others.

"Okay," Gwen said, studying the damage. "Now torturing Mitch aside, what's the real deal with Novikov?"

Blayne gave a little laugh. "I kind of railroaded the guy."

"You, Blayne?" Gwen said with mock shock. "Never!"

"Well he was standing there, being all judgmental about derby—and me!—and I figured why couldn't he help me out since he'd put me into this situation?"

"And how did he do that?"

"By being everything that I am against when it comes to sports and—"

"Please stop. I can't hear that speech again."

"Hey, look!"

"Blayne, wait—"

Too late. Blayne reached into the crevice and pulled out something breathing.

"A possum!"

"It looks like a giant rat."

"It's not a rat. It's a possum. It's so obvious you've never been to the South."

"What's down there but chitlins and giant rats they've renamed possum?"

Grinning, Blayne scratched the disgusting looking thing under the neck. "Isn't he cute?"

"Not even a little. And are you really going to be okay with Novikov? I mean, for once, Mitch does have a point. The Marauder's reputation is for shit."

Blayne snorted. "I can handle him."

Gwen had no idea why Blayne felt so confident about that, but Gwen knew there was no point in arguing with her about it, either. Blayne could be unbelievably stubborn when she dug her feet in. And, hell, if the hockey player could give Blayne even a few useful tips, Gwen wouldn't complain. The wolfdog had tons of potential, but the team could no longer ignore the fact that unless Blayne was pushed into a corner—something that made her homicidal—she was too damn nice.

And of all the things Gwen had heard about Bo Novikov over the years, she'd never heard the word "nice" used.

"Are you going to put that thing down, or am I fixing this by myself?"

Blayne frowned. "He seems awfully small. Maybe we should feed him."

Feed him? Any other predator would be thinking of eating him. But Gwen knew better than to say that because that way lay tears and mucus and hysterical screams of, "*How could you even suggest that?*"

Not in the mood for any of that bullshit, Gwen offered, "Maybe it's just a baby or something."

"You think?" Blayne leaned into the crevice again.

"Blayne, please be careful. Remember last—"

"Badger!"

"Ow!" Blayne glared at the She-wolf nurse standing behind her, forcing the hypodermic into the skin beside her right shoulder blade. "Painful!" she snapped.

"Then maybe, brilliance, you shouldn't get into fights with rats. You wouldn't need this precaution to prevent infections if you just did that."

"It was a badger," Blayne ground out, her teeth clenched tight. "Not a rat. And how was I to know that there was a possum *and* a badger in that hole?"

"How many times is that now anyway?" The She-wolf snapped

the needle off the hypodermic before disposal. "That you've ended up on the wrong side of a badger fight?"

"It's not my fault. It's the badgers' fault. They're out to get me. All of them. They hate me."

The nurse stood in front of her. She hated this woman, when Blayne hated so few.

"Badgers . . . hate you?" she asked with that condescending tone that made Blayne want to rip her throat out.

"Yes."

"Uh-huh. I see why you're always current on your rabies vaccines. You're a walking disaster."

"How is this good bedside manner? I'm almost positive this is what I'd call *bad* bedside manner."

Blayne didn't understand why every time she had to come into the emergency room of this hospital, she had to deal with Nurse Mengele. Blayne didn't know if the She-wolf hated dogs so much or just hybrids in general, but their conversations had gotten pretty hostile lately.

"Why are you still in my ER, stray?" Nurse Fun demanded. "Don't you have to go beg for treats or something?"

Her good nature gone, Blayne snapped back, "Are those the real size of your thighs or do you stuff your pants to distract everyone from your face?"

Fangs burst from gums and the two canines snarled and snapped at each other until a bear walked into the room.

"What the hell is going on?"

Nurse Death stepped back. "Nothing, Doctor. But we have people who need the room and someone isn't leaving."

"I'm guessing that someone is you." The doctor motioned across the hall. "They need you in room six."

"Yes, Doctor."

The She-wolf glared and Blayne sneered back.

The doctor raised a brow at Blayne after Nurse McBitchyson was gone. "I can't leave you alone for two seconds."

"She started it!"

Doctor Iona MacRyrie, Lock's older sister and amazing sow, shook her head and laughed. "You say that every time." Placing her hands under Blayne's chin, she lifted her face. "Honestly, Blayne. A rat did this?"

"It was a badger."

"The badgers have made a return I see. For a while it was . . . what was it again?"

"Squirrels."

"Ah, yes. Squirrels were out to get you."

"Just one. But he was crafty . . . and mean."

"Perhaps, Blayne, and this is just a suggestion, you should leave the small-prey animals alone unless you plan to eat them."

Iona turned Blayne's head one way and another. "I'll give you something to put on these lacerations on your face."

"Okay."

Blayne had first met the doctor at a small dinner party thrown by Iona's parents announcing the engagement of her brother to Gwen. But they didn't really speak, Iona spending most of her time trying to control her cubs. A week later, though, they'd met again when Blayne had ended up in the ER after a vicious run-in with an alley cat. Not a lioness Blayne was insulting by calling an alley cat . . . an actual alley cat. Iona wasn't the ER doctor when Blayne came in, but a neurosurgeon at the shifter-run McMillian Presbyterian Hospital that happened to be on her way home for the night when she'd passed a bleeding Blayne trying to remove the psychotic animal still attached to the back of her head.

Twelve visits later, they had become quite chummy.

"What did Nurse Fun give me a shot for?" Blayne asked, the spot where the needle had entered beginning to hurt.

"I have no idea. Tetanus, perhaps?"

"I got that a while ago and it went into my thigh. You know I'm up on all my shots. That should be in my chart."

"I'm sure it was preventative." Iona stepped back. "I don't know what it is about you two, but I doubt she's trying to poison you."

Blayne wasn't so sure. "Can I go?"

"Yes." Iona pulled out a prescription pad from her doctor's coat and scribbled something down. "Put this on your face after washing. Keep the area clean. It takes longer for your lacerations to heal, so keep that in mind."

"Okay." Blayne took the prescription. "Thanks."

"You're welcome. You need a lift home? I'm off in a few minutes."

"Gwen can take me."

Iona folded her arms over her chest and stared down at Blayne, one brow raised.

"She deserted me, didn't she?"

"She accuses me of being 'one of those butchers' and refers to this hospital as a death trap. So what do you think, Blayne?"

"I'd think that when she said 'Good luck surviving that death trap' after throwing me out of the truck that she would have stayed around to *ensure* that I survived the death trap!"

The team left the ice, the sound of their skates marching back to their locker room echoing through the halls.

Ric stopped and looked back at the rink. He shook his head and glanced over at Lock who stood next to him.

"He's a fucking machine," Lock muttered. "He never stops."

Truer words had never been spoken.

Together the friends watched the hybrid continue to run drills. They watched for about five minutes, then they headed to the locker room and left Bo "The Marauder" Novikov alone on the ice—exactly where he seemed to belong.

CHAPTER 6

Bo shot through the goal crease and slammed the puck into the net.

"Morning!"

That voice cut through his focus, and without breaking his stride, Bo changed direction and skated over to the rink entrance. He stopped hard, ice spraying out from his skates, and stood in front of the wolfdog.

He stared down at her and she stared up at him. She kept smiling even when he didn't. Finally he asked, "What time did we agree on?"

"Seven," she replied with a cheery note that put his teeth on edge.

"And what time is it?"

"Uh . . ." She dug into her jeans and pulled out a cell phone. The fact that she still had on that damn, useless watch made his head want to explode. How did one function—as an adult any-way—without a goddamn watch?

Grinning so that he could see all those perfectly aligned teeth, she said, "Six forty-five!"

"And what time did we agree on?"

She blinked and her smile faded. After a moment, "Seven."

"Is it seven?"

"No." When he only continued to stare at her, she softly asked, "Want to meet me at the track at seven?"

He continued to stare at her until she nodded and said, "Okay."

She walked out and Bo went back to work.

Fifteen minutes later, Bo walked into the small arena. Blayne, looking comfortable in dark blue leggings, sweatshirt, and skates, turned to face him. He expected her to be mad at him or, even worse, for her to get that wounded look he often got from people when he was blatantly direct. But having to deal with either of those scenarios was a price Bo was always willing to pay to ensure that the people in his life understood how he worked from the beginning. This way, there were no surprises later. It was called "boundaries," and he read about it in a book.

Yet when Blayne saw him, she grinned and held up a Starbucks cup. "Coffee," she said when he got close. "I got you the house brand because I had no idea what you would like. And they had cinnamon twists, so I got you a few of those."

He took the coffee, watching her close. Where was it? The anger? The resentment? Was she plotting something?

Blayne held the bag of sweets out for him and Bo took them. "Thank you," he said, still suspicious even as he sipped his perfectly brewed coffee.

"You're welcome." And there went that grin again. Big and brighter than the damn sun. "And I get it. Seven means seven. Eight means eight, et cetera, et cetera. Got it and I'm on it. It won't happen again." She said all that without a trace of bitterness or annoyance, dazzling Bo with her understanding more than she'd dazzled him with those legs.

"So." She put her hands on her hips. "What do you want me to do first?"

Marry me? Wait. No, no. Incorrect response. It'll just weird her out and make her run again. Normal. Be normal. You can do this. You're not just a great skater. You're a normal *great skater.*

When Bo knew he had his shit together, he said, "Let's work on your focus first. And, um, should I ask what happened to your face?" She had a bunch of cuts on her cheeks. Gouges. Like something small had pawed at her.

"Nope!" she chirped, pulling off her sweatshirt. She wore a worn blue T-shirt underneath with B&G PLUMBING scrawled across it. With sweatshirt in hand, Blayne skated over to the bleachers, stopped, shook her head, skated over to another section of bleachers, stopped, looked at the sweatshirt, turned around, and skated over to the railing. "I should leave it here," she explained. "In case I get chilly."

It occurred to Bo he'd just lost two minutes of his life watching her try to figure out where to place a damn sweatshirt. Two minutes that he'd never get back.

"Woo-hoo!" she called out once she hit the track. "Let's go!"

She was skating backward as she urged him to join her with both hands.

He pointed behind her. "Watch the—"

"Ow!"

"—pole."

Christ, what had he gotten himself into?

Christ almighty, what had she gotten herself into?

Twenty minutes in and she wanted to smash the man's head against a wall. She wanted to go back in time and kick the shit out of Genghis Khan before turning on his brothers, Larry and Moe. Okay. That wasn't their names but she could barely remember Genghis's name on a good day, how the hell was she supposed to remember his brothers'? But whatever the Khan kin's names may be, Blayne wanted to hurt them all for cursing her world with this . . . this . . . Visigoth!

Even worse, she knew he didn't even take what she did seriously. He insisted on calling it a chick sport. If he were a sexist pig across the board, Blayne could overlook it as a mere flaw in his upbringing. But, she soon discovered, Novikov had a very high degree of respect for female athletes . . . as long as they were athletes and not just "hot chicks in cute outfits, roughing each other up. All you guys need is some hot oil or mud and you'd have a real moneymaker on your hands."

And yet, even while he didn't respect her sport as a sport, he still worked her like he was getting her ready for the Olympics.

After thirty minutes, she wanted nothing more but to lie on her side and pant. She doubted the hybrid would let her get away with that, though.

Shooting around the track, Blayne got stopped again in a way that she was finding extremely annoying—he grabbed her by the head with that big hand of his and held her in place.

He shoved her back with one good push, and Blayne fought not to fall on her ass at that speed. When someone shoved her like that, they were usually pissed. He wasn't.

"I need to see something," he said, still nursing that cup of coffee. He'd finished off the cinnamon twists in less than five minutes while she was warming up. "Come at me as hard as you can."

"Are you sure?" she asked, looking him over. He didn't have any of his protective gear on, somehow managing to change into sweatpants and T-shirt and still make it down to the track exactly at seven. "I don't want to hurt you," she told him honestly.

The laughter that followed, however, made her think she did want to hurt him. She wanted to hurt him a lot. When he realized she wasn't laughing with him—or, in this case, laughing at *herself* since he was obviously laughing *at* her—Novikov blinked and said, "Oh. You're not kidding."

"No. I'm not kidding."

"Oh. Oh! Um . . . I'll be fine. Hit me with your best shot."

"Like Pat Benatar?" she joked, but when he only stared at her, she said, "Forget it."

Blayne sized up the behemoth in front of her and decided to move back a few more feet so she could get a really fast start. She got into position and took one more scrutinizing look. It was a skill her father had taught her. To size up weakness. Whether the weakness of a person or a building or whatever. Of course, Blayne often used this skill for good, finding out someone's weakness and then working to help them overcome it. Her father, however, used it to destroy.

Lowering her body, Blayne took a breath, tightened her fists, and took off. She lost some speed on the turn but picked it up as she cut inside. As Blayne approached Novikov, she sized him up one more time as he stood there casually, sipping his coffee and watching her move around the track. Based on that last assessing look, she slightly adjusted her position and slammed into him with everything she had.

And, yeah, she knocked herself out cold, but it was totally worth it when the behemoth went down with her.

Bo had been hit by four-hundred-plus-pound guys since he joined his high school team. He'd had guys who literally wanted him dead slam into him with the force of a rampaging herd of cattle. A few had managed to take him down. A couple had managed to ring his bell. But none, absolutely *none*, had managed to catch him off guard.

She'd been coming at him one way and, as he sipped his coffee and let his mind readjust his schedule for the day to allow for this hour of non-personal-training, she'd abruptly changed direction, hitting him on his weaker right side—and dumping him right on his ass.

The remainder of his coffee sprayed across the track, the back of his head hit the ground hard, and Bo suddenly remembered what it was like to see the world from this position.

It took him a moment to shake himself out of that stupor that comes with shock. And he wished he could dismiss it as merely a "lucky shot." But he knew intent when he saw it. She'd wanted to knock him on his ass and she had. A tiny wolfdog had done what guys who had trained for years had been unable to do.

Worried she'd really hurt herself in the process, Bo released the empty cup he was still holding and brought his hands up to grip Blayne's shoulders.

"Blayne? Blayne, can you hear me?"

She groaned and he let out a relieved sigh. She placed her hands on his chest and slowly levered herself up. What he found most disturbing, though, was that when she did, he heard what could only be called a series of snapping noises that did nothing but kind of weird him out.

Blayne gritted her teeth as the noises continued and let out a breath when they stopped. She shook her head, glanced around.

"Blayne?" Big brown eyes focused on him. "Are you okay?"

"Uh-huh." Her head tilted to the side. "Why are you on the floor?"

"Because this is where you put me."

"Where I . . ." She shook her head again. "What?"

"You dropped me like a ton of bricks, Blayne."

"Me? I . . . I did this?"

"Yeah."

"Are you serious? Or are you just being nice?"

"Nice?" he asked. "Is that a real word or did you just make that up? I'm not familiar with this word . . . nice. Is it French?"

She sat up straight, her hands covering her mouth. "Oh, my . . . oh, my God!"

She scrambled off him and got to her feet, shooting around the track with her arms high in the air. And, not surprising since she was from Philly, she began singing the "Rocky" theme, but she didn't know the words so it pretty much consisted of, "Something, something now! Getting something, something now!"

He should be livid or, at the very least, morbidly embarrassed. He wasn't. He couldn't remember ever making someone so happy before, and it had to be the most pleasant experience he'd had in a very long time.

Bo sat up and watched her. "Blayne?"

"Something high now!"

"Blayne, watch out for the—"

"*Ow!*"

"—pole."

CHAPTER 7

"This was great," Blayne said, rolling back and forth in front of Bo. "I learned so much."

Bo relaxed against the railing, watching Blayne move. *God, she's pretty.* "Good," he muttered, not really sure what he was responding to and not really caring.

"So we'll do this again tomorrow?"

"Uh-huh."

"Great! I'll meet you here at seven."

"Wait . . . what?" What had he just agreed to? Why was he not paying attention? But before he could tell her no she skated up to him and put her arms around him, shocking him into silence.

"I really appreciate this help."

"Oh. Uh. You're welcome." Where was his strength of will? Where was his focus? When did he become so goddamn weak?

"I'm gonna be so ready for the championship." She grinned up at him. "And it'll be all down to you. My hero."

Eh. Strength of will was overrated.

"Do you know the time?" she asked.

Of course he did but that wasn't the point. "I see you're still wearing your fake Prada."

She unwrapped herself from him so she could smile down at it.

"Actually, this is my Cha-Chanel. And it's working!" She studied it. "Sort of. But isn't it pretty?"

"Pretty useless."

She rolled her eyes but didn't seem insulted. "Don't start that again. And what time is it? I need to be somewhere by eight thirty."

Bo glanced at his watch, then couldn't look away. He'd scheduled only an hour with Blayne. One hour. No more, no less. But . . . but . . .

"It's . . . it's eight twenty," he said.

Blayne smiled. "Oh, okay. Thanks."

"Eight twenty," he said again.

"Yeah. I got that. Wait. Is there a subtext to the number? Like two eleven on *X-Files*?"

"What?" Bo shook his head. "We should have been done twenty minutes ago." He reached into his pocket and pulled out the list. "See? I have it written down."

"You actually have a list written down?"

"Lists are important."

"See? This is what I mean. This can't be healthy for you. Living on this rigid, ridiculous schedule."

That's when Bo asked, "Didn't you say you had to be somewhere by eight thirty?"

"Yup!" She smiled and Bo gawked at her. He gawked until her eyes got big and she blurted out, *"Oh, shit!"* She lifted herself up and over the railing with one arm. He would have enjoyed it more if she didn't aim her skates right at his head, but he knew she was panicking and he was fast enough to get out of her way. He watched her skate out the door only to return twenty seconds later. "I never went to the locker room," she said, sliding to a stop by a backpack and a haphazard pile of clothes on the floor.

She started to pull her clothes off right there in the stadium, and Bo rushed over to her and quickly grabbed her hands. "Not in here."

"Why?"

"We're not alone."

"Huh?"

He motioned to the top bleachers in the far corner of the room. The maintenance guys who kept the entire sports center running like a well-oiled machine were eating their breakfast and watching the pair. They often watched Bo in the mornings over their breakfast, but they had somehow found their way down to the derby stadium. Bo didn't mind, but he wasn't about to let them have a free show of a naked, panicked Blayne.

"Hey, guys!" Blayne raised her arm and waved.

The males waved back. "Hi, Blayne!"

She smirked. "You guys wouldn't have watched me change without letting me know you were there, now would you?"

"You're kidding, right?" one of them answered back.

"Bad shifters!" she teasingly chastised. "Bad, bad, bad!"

Sensing she'd already forgotten how late it was, Bo grabbed a handful of Blayne's crap. "Come on."

She gazed at him calmly. "What's the rush?"

"It's now eight twenty-four," he announced.

"Shit!" She grabbed the rest of her things and tore out of the stadium, Bo following after her.

One of the maintenance crew tossed out, "Good luck with that one, Marauder."

Followed by another's, "You're gonna need it!"

With a snort that some might consider a laugh, Bo tracked Blayne down in the nearby ladies' locker room. Bo set down what he had by the stuff she'd thrown on the floor. What he didn't understand was why she had so many clothes if she were only going to work? He could hear her in the showers and, unable to ignore the pile of stuff she had lying around, he began to pick up and organize everything.

"Shit!" she called out, not seeming bothered by the fact he was in the locker room with her.

"What?" he asked while he folded her clothes.

"Forgot to take off my skates before I got in here."

"How did you—" No. *It was better not to ask.*

Taking the quickest shower in history—for a woman—Blayne ran back out in nothing but a towel, her skates and practice clothes in her hand.

Bo took the skates and sweaty clothes and handed her a pair of gray cargo pants, a black sweatshirt, and a matching set of sports bra and panties, all neatly folded.

"Thanks!" She went around to the other side of the lockers for privacy, and Bo found a plastic bag to put her dirty clothes in and packed it into her backpack along with her skates—after drying them off and wrapping the wheels in a plastic bag.

Blayne ran back out, now dressed, and reached for her bag. Bo put his hand over it and said, "Shoes."

"Oh!" She spun in a full circle looking for her sneakers, so he held them up to her face.

"Here."

"Oh. Thanks!"

"Sit."

She sat down and undid the laces on her sneakers. At least she tried. Instead she made knots. That's when her cell phone started to ring. She looked at it with something as close to fear as Bo had ever seen. He reached for it and she shook her head. "It's gonna be Gwen," she whispered. "She'll kick my ass."

"Why are you whispering?" he whispered back. "I'm sure she can't hear you."

"You don't know Gwen."

He tossed her the phone and grabbed her sneakers. "Answer it."

She did. "Hello?" She immediately winced. "I know I'm late. I'll be there in a few minutes. Where am I?" Her eyes moved around the room, and he wondered what she was looking for. An acceptable lie?

"I'm, uh, stuck on Fifth. Why am I on Fifth?"

Bo kneeled in front of her to put her sneakers on but stopped long enough to cover the phone and say, "You stopped to get her breakfast."

"I did?"

"You did now."

"Oh!" She smiled. "Thanks." Clearing her throat, she said into the phone, "I stopped to get you breakfast, but I didn't know traffic would be this bad. Is it a good breakfast?" Blayne looked at him and he nodded.

"Best in Manhattan," he whispered.

"Best in Manhattan, apparently." She smiled, now relieved. "Yes. The coffee will be hot. If it's not hot, I'll get some more at a Starbucks or something. Okay. Won't be long."

She disconnected the call. "I hate lying."

"Probably because you're really bad at it."

"I know."

"If she'd been standing in the room, you'd have been screwed."

"Thanks for the pep talk."

Bo put her sneakers on her feet and tied the laces. "There." He reached over and grabbed her backpack. "I've packed up everything."

Blayne took the bag. "That is so sweet. Thank you."

"Yeah, yeah." He stood. "Got a pen?"

"Yeah." She dug into her cargo pants and pulled out a pen. Bo took her hand and wrote on her palm, "This is where you're going to get your breakfast for the two of you. It's shifter run and not far from here. Best Danish in Manhattan. Tell Mike I sent you. I'll call him and tell him you're coming." When Blayne only gazed up at him, he added, "You go wherever you're going without food and/or coffee and that tigon's going to rip your face off."

"Good point." She slung the backpack over her shoulder. "Thanks for all this."

"No problem. And get a new watch."

"I will . . . eventually." She took off out the locker room door, and as Bo came out behind her, Blayne was running back. He wondered if her life was made up of U-turns.

"Wrong way," she said with a laugh.

"I know." He sighed. "And seven tomorrow. Here."

She tripped to a stop. "Seven tomorrow here for what?"

"Blayne . . ."

"Oh." She laughed. "Totally forgot." She pointed at her head. "Thank God it's attached." Without warning, she suddenly sprung up—again without a running start—and kissed his cheek. "Thank you so much! See you tomorrow!"

"And you better be on time!" he yelled after her. "And don't forget the Danish!"

"He was right," Gwen said around a mouthful of Danish. "This *is* the best Danish in Manhattan."

Blayne nodded her head and ate. She was already in love with the bakery because she found treats that were sweetened with honey rather than sugar. When she reached for her third Danish, she said to Gwen, "How did you know I was lying anyway?"

"I always know when you're lying. And those dramatic pauses certainly didn't help."

"I know, I gotta work on the pauses."

"So how did training go with the great Novikov?"

"It went really well. Apparently I don't have enough focus."

"Someone's Captain Obvious."

"What does that mean?"

"It means that everyone knows you don't have enough focus. Even you know."

Blayne couldn't even find the energy to argue that point. "Okay, yeah. I know. But you know, he's really not that bad a guy. In fact—"

"Don't do it, Blayne."

"—I feel bad for the guy."

"And here we go!"

"What does that mean?"

"He doesn't need to be fixed, Blayne."

"I'm not trying to fix him." She took another bite of Danish, chewed it thoroughly, swallowed, and said, "But he could be a much happier person."

Gwen's head dropped forward, a large sigh escaping.

"What?" Blayne demanded. "What did I say?"

"You cannot keep treating every male you meet as some sort of wounded puppy you found on the street."

"I don't—"

"And now you're doing it with Bo Novikov of all people. He's rich, famous, not bad looking, and has had a bevy of females to ride his cock. But you need to believe, for some reason, that he's secretly miserable."

"Well, he can't be happy."

"Why do you say that? Because he's not running around hugging everyone? Because he's been known to beat up a few fans? Make a few kids cry? Get into fistfights with his teammates on and off the ice?"

"That's part of it."

"Not everyone is like you, Blayne. There has been nothing to indicate, at least to me, that Bo Novikov is an unhappy person."

"Oh, really?" Blayne grabbed her backpack and pulled it open, laying it down in front of Gwen. "And what about this?"

The tigon stared at the bag for a long moment. "He did that?"

"You didn't think it was me, did you?"

"Good God. It's so . . . organized."

"He folded my extra sets of panties . . . who folds panties?"

"Maybe he's secretly perverted. He wanted to feel your panties—"

"So he organized my entire bag while I was in the shower? There's not even one pair missing. Gwen, this overly organized bag is a cry for help."

"Or he's happily gay. Gay men, for the most part, are very tidy and very happy they don't have to deal with women's bullshit."

"I thought about that, but I don't think we have that situation here. Look what's missing from this high level of coordination . . ."

"It's not color coordinated."

"Nope. It's alphabetical and in rigid boring lines."

"In other words, something your dad would appreciate."

"Exactly. And I can't let anyone live like that, Gwen. Not anyone!"

Gwen laughed. "That poor guy. He has no idea what he's in for."

Ric skated over to Lock, leaning against the rink wall and protective glass. "Who is that?" he demanded.

Lock glanced across the rink. Novikov stood talking to a hot little fox. She had to be an Arctic fox—she had on shorts. It was below zero outside! "Arctic fox," Lock said while busy readjusting the tape he'd wrapped around his hockey stick.

"Yeah, but what's he doing talking to her?"

"It's probably *his* Arctic fox."

"*His* Arctic fox? What does that mean?"

"It means she's his Arctic fox." Lock didn't know how he could be any clearer.

Reece Lee Reed, who'd moved up from the minors nearly a month ago and was part of the Smith Pack, slammed to a stop in front of Lock and Ric.

"Did he buy her on the black market?" Reed asked with what Gwen insisted on calling "That hick, backwoods Smith accent."

"He doesn't have to."

"Are you saying they're going out?" Ric demanded.

"Is there a reason you sound so upset?" Lock asked.

"You kinda sweet on him, Van Holtz?"

Ric ignored Reed and said, "I heard he was with Blayne this morning."

"God," Reed sighed. "That man is becoming my hero."

"He was helping her with derby," Lock clarified. "According to Blayne via Gwen he was really nice and completely hands off."

"Nice? He was nice? Novikov?"

"I'm telling you what I heard."

Reed chuckled. "Blayne would think Satan himself was just misunderstood."

Lock couldn't even argue.

"What if she likes him?" Ric asked. "What if she's hoping it goes beyond some ludicrous derby training?"

"I still don't see why you're so worried?"

"Good God, man. Look at her!" He gestured to the fox with a tilt of his head. "She's like the porn version of Nanook of the North."

"Nanook does the North," Reed muttered . . . then he laughed at his own joke. He was a self-contained wolf, finding entertainment wherever he wanted.

"I doubt they're having sex. She's his fox," Lock explained again.

Bert, a black bear, skated over and, leaning in, said, "Word in the Center . . . Blayne Thorpe dropped the great Bo Novikov on his ass during derby training."

"Bullshit," Reed said. "Little thing like that. She couldn't drop my sister." Lock had to agree. He knew Reed's sister, Ronnie Lee. She could easily play for the Chicago Bears as a fullback, where Blayne looked like she belonged on the cheerleading squad.

"My source," Bert added, "impeccable."

"Maintenance guys?" Lock guessed.

"Yep."

"Did she really drop him, or was he just trying to get her on the floor and that was the easiest way?" Reed asked.

"Really dropped him."

"Just what I thought. He's weak. A few years of the good life and he's lettin' little gals like Blayne Thorpe drop him."

Ric looked up at Lock before answering, "You're right, you know. Novikov is weak. Completely at the end of his game."

Reed nodded. "That's what I thought. Looks like it's time for some new blood." He skated onto the rink to warm up with the rest of the team.

Bert shook his head. "That was just mean, canine."

In answer, Ric smiled.

Running late for her dinner date, Blayne rushed into the hockey rink, stepping aside as the medical team took out a battered Reece Reed on a stretcher.

"Hey, Reece."

She cringed when he managed to wave and give her a smile

that could only be called blood filled. Blayne looked back at Gwen, but she didn't seem to notice or care as she made the medical team move around her.

"I told you we weren't late," Gwen said.

"We're late, but their practice is running long."

"That's the same thing."

"No it's not. And how come when I'm late, it's the end of the world, but when you're late everyone just has to wait for you?"

"Why do you think?" Gwen walked to the end of the entrance to the rink. They'd both dressed up for the night since they were having dinner out and then going to the Kuznetsov Pack's new downtown club. Blayne couldn't wait. There was gaming to be had at the club. She wasn't very good at gaming, but she loved playing with the Kuznetsov Pack because they didn't care she wasn't very good.

The team headed in, and Blayne and Gwen stepped aside to let them through. Lock skated over first, grinning down at his fiancée. "You look gorgeous."

"I know."

Lock stepped off the rink and into Gwen, and she quickly stepped back. "Stop. You'll get sweat and blood all over me."

"And?"

She laughed and dodged behind Blayne.

"Why am I in the middle of this?" Blayne demanded.

"My human shield."

Ric came up behind Lock. "Good evening." He took Blayne's hand and kissed the back of it. "You look wonderful."

"Thank you." And Ric didn't look half bad himself. She didn't know how it was fair a man as handsome as Ulrich Van Holtz would look even better sweaty and in a battered goalie uniform, but he did.

"We won't be long getting ready." He tapped Lock's shoulder and motioned to the locker room. "I don't know about the rest of you, but I'm starving."

While they all discussed dinner plans, Blayne stood outside the rink and watched Bo Novikov skate alone. His team may be done for the night, but clearly he wasn't. Yet she couldn't help but feel bad for him. Out there. All alone.

Blayne turned and said to Ric and Lock, "We should invite Novikov out with us."

The two men gaped at her before adamantly answering, "No."

Surprised, she asked, "Why not?"

"We want to have a nice time."

"Who's to say we won't?" When they only gaped at her more, she added, "It's a nice thing to do."

Now they looked confused.

"For christsake," Gwen snapped. She walked around Blayne. "We'll invite him to meet us at the club. Does that work for everybody?"

"Yes!"

"No."

Blayne glared at the two men. "You're being mean!"

Ignoring them all, Gwen stepped on the ice and brought her fingers to her mouth. She whistled and, looking more annoyed than usual, Novikov stopped skating and scowled in her direction. Again, Gwen didn't seem to notice or care. She motioned him over with a wave of her hand.

Once she had the hybrid next to her, she said something to him. With that same expression he wore every moment of every day, he looked up and right at Blayne. She wanted to run but instead smiled and gave a small wave. It wasn't easy, especially when it only seemed to make him scowl more.

"Okay?" she heard Gwen ask.

"Yeah."

He skated off and Gwen walked back over.

"How did you manage the ice in those heels?" Blayne asked.

"Why aren't you getting ready?" Gwen demanded of the men.

Lock planted his hockey stick against the floor. "I wasn't leaving you alone with *him*."

"I'm getting cranky from hunger." Gwen pointed toward the locker rooms. "Go."

They did, but they grumbled as they went.

When they were gone, Gwen put her arm through Blayne's and together they walked out of the training rink.

"What happened?" Blayne asked.

"Nothing. I simply suggested to Bo Novikov that he may want to meet us at the club tonight."

"And why would he want to do that?"

"Because otherwise you were going to stay out too late with Ric and be late for your training session tomorrow. Personally, I think it was the Ric mention that upset him the most."

Blayne snorted. "And I'd bet cash that it was the thought of me being late."

CHAPTER 8

Bo walked around his truck and looked up at the club buried behind a few buildings. To a full-human it probably looked like some crackhouse, complete with scary drug-dealer protection out front. But Bo could feel the music vibrating through the ground and into his feet, could smell the different breeds housed inside the building, and could see the shifters easing out of a side door and disappearing into the surrounding darkness. Plus the fact that the scary protection guys out front had eyes that reflected in the darkness pretty much screamed "not-quite-human gathering inside."

Sami and Sander stood on either side of him, also staring up at the building.

"This is gonna be fun," Sander said, rubbing his hands together.

"Let's go," Sami added.

Bo grabbed them by the back of their thin leather jackets and yanked them back to his side. "A few rules," he said.

"Don't be such a drag," Sander whined.

"We haven't even done anything yet," Sami added.

"But you will . . . unless I make rules. So here they are. No stealing. That includes wallets, credit cards, cell phones, smart phones, PDAs, or any other small phone-like items that you think are shiny and pretty. You are also not to take anyone's identity; I don't care how much you think they deserve it. The only cash you'll be using will be yours or mine. I find out anything has gone missing, I start breaking fingers."

"Fine."

"Fine."

They started to walk off, and Bo yanked them back again. "There will be no cons."

"But—"

"No long cons, no short cons. No 'my grandmother is dying and I need money for the hospital'; no 'I was robbed at Penn Station and lost everything'; definitely no 'I have this great idea that just needs a few backers and a plane ticket to South America but only if you want to double your money in less than a week.' Absolutely no pretending either you or Sander are prostitutes, so you can roll someone in the parking lot. No getting anyone drunk and taking inappropriate pictures of them to use later. I don't care if they are mated to someone else and you think they deserve it."

"Okay! Fine."

The pair started to walk off again and Bo yanked them back. "No having sex in the one place you'll definitely be caught—"

"Oh, now come on!"

Sami stamped her foot. "You're killing our fun!"

"Agree or we leave."

"Fine. We agree."

They approached the club, and the foxes immediately caught the attention of the bouncers. Not surprising. Not only were they foxes—therefore not to be trusted—but with their smaller shifter size, they stuck out among their kind.

The bouncers watched the pair closely as they walked by, but when Bo got closer, he saw the recognition in the males' eyes. He got the usual reaction, too, when that sort of thing happened. One male smiled and couldn't let Bo in fast enough, and the other snarled and muttered "no-talent asshole" under his breath as Bo walked into the club. Something he'd become so used to that he didn't even bother to react anymore. Besides, he didn't want to see Blayne with bloody knuckles.

Once inside, the foxes caught everyone's attention first. The females checking out Sander, the males checking out Sami, and those who were flexible either way, checking out both. The pair of them dressed for attention—Sami in her "New York winters are for wimps" leather bikini top, leather shorts, fur boots, and thin leather jacket; Sander in his leather pants, designer silk T-shirt that fit his narrow frame perfectly, and thin leather jacket. Bo knew they looked like Euro trash. Hell, Sami and Sander knew they looked like Euro trash. That was the point. That's what made them so good at what they liked to do when Bo wasn't around to make his strict rules. They enticed to manipulate, but their loyalty to each other was something Bo never questioned.

The club was big and packed. He saw stairs leading to another floor, and a sign next to the stairs that read GAMES UP with an arrow. This floor had several bars and tech music. Not his favorite music, but he could tolerate it.

The trio walked over to the closest bar. Sami ordered them three beers before planting herself on a stool. She faced away from the bar so she could check out the room.

"You think she's here?" Sami asked, removing her jacket.

Bo lifted his nose, sniffed the air. "She's here."

"Then you better track her down and make your move," Sander said.

Bo's eyes narrowed. Sander was being a little too eager, so he reached into his back pocket and pulled out the two sheets of perfectly folded paper. He flicked them open and held one page out to each. "Here are tonight's rules."

Sander stared at the printed page in front of him. "You wrote it down?"

"I find putting the rules in writing cuts down on the morning-after 'But you never saids.' You know I hate the 'You never saids.'"

Mumbling under his breath, Sander snatched the sheet from

Bo and shoved it into his front pocket. Sami took the sheet and carefully refolded it before slipping it into the top of her boot. "Okay," she said, reaching behind her to grab the beers from the bar while Bo handed cash to the bartender. "Let's go find your wolfdog."

Ric, quite comfortable on the end of the U-shaped couch he'd reserved for the four of them, was about to go looking for Blayne when she suddenly dropped into his lap and announced to them all, "I heard people fucking in the bathroom!"

Not sure how to respond to that, Ric simply reached for his German ale.

"Good fucking or bad fucking?" Gwen asked.

Blayne thought a moment, her eyes focused on the ceiling. She finally answered, "*Drunk* fucking."

"Ahhh."

Ric laughed. Blayne always made him laugh, which was why he cared so much about protecting her. His cousin and Dee-Ann may think it was perfectly acceptable to use Blayne as bait, but Ric didn't like it. Yet he admitted, at least to himself, that he did worry that if Blayne knew the truth, she might start doing things that would only put her in more danger. Or maybe she'd cower in her apartment, afraid to ever come out. Or maybe she'd do nothing at all. It was the wild card factor that made telling Blayne anything about this a risk. So, against his better judgment, he told her nothing and hoped that Dee-Ann was as good at her job as his cousin believed she was.

"Did you stand there and listen?" Ric had to ask.

"Of course not!" She reached down, fussed with the heel of her very sexy shoes. "But I did have to pee," she admitted.

"Hey, Blayne," Gwen murmured from the comfort of Lock's lap. "Two o'clock."

Before Ric could stop her, Blayne turned in his lap and rose up on her knees. She raised her arm in the air and began to wave while screaming, "Dee-Ann! Dee! *Ann!* Over here! *Sit here!*"

Ric winced, knowing he'd hear about this later. If there was one thing Dee-Ann Smith couldn't stand, it was being the center of attention.

Glaring at Ric across the packed new club, the She-wolf walked over to the couch.

"Hey, y'all," she said in that enticing Southern accent.

"Dee!" Then Blayne was up, her arms around Dee. Blayne hugged Dee like they were long-lost friends. Although based on the way Dee was currently scowling, Ric doubted that would ever happen.

"Get her off me," Dee mouthed at him. "Now!"

"I didn't know you were coming tonight," Blayne went on, oblivious as always. "I'm so glad you're here!"

When Ric saw Dee's hand reach around to her back, where he knew she had some illegal weapon stashed, he quickly grabbed Blayne around the waist and pulled her onto his lap while snapping under his breath at Dee, "Don't even!"

Dee snarled, her empty hand dropping at her side as he sat Blayne down, both of his arms around her waist.

"Why don't you join us, Dee?" he asked.

"Nah."

"Oh, come on, Dee!" Blayne cheered happily. "Have a drink. Or let's dance!" Blayne tried to stand up again, but Ric held her in place. "How about I introduce you around!" She tried to stand again, but Ric yanked the overeager wolfdog right back to his lap.

With an annoyed growl and a flash of fang, Dee walked off, disappearing into the crowd.

"Don't go, Dee!" Blayne yelled after her. "Dee! *Deeeeee!*" she bellowed one last time before settling back down against Ric's chest. Blayne gave a little pout. "She never hangs out with us anymore. I wonder why."

Ric caught Lock's gaze, but they both quickly looked away, both males afraid of being the ones to say something to make sweet, innocent, completely clueless Blayne Thorpe cry.

* * *

Blayne caught Gwen's gaze, but they quickly looked away from each other, both females afraid of laughing so hard they might piss themselves.

Did Dee-Ann Smith really think Blayne was that stupid? Okay. Blayne had her moments. She'd admit it. But she knew when some heifer was following her. Hard not to be close to the O'Neill Pride and not pick up certain skills. Because of the O'Neills, Blayne knew when she was being shadowed. Of course, she also knew how to hot-wire a car, launder money, and get guns into Northern Ireland. Not that she'd ever do any of those things. She wouldn't. But that didn't mean she lacked the skill or brains to do them.

Yet for whatever reason, Dee-Ann Smith was following her. Constantly.

Blayne had the feeling Ric must have hired her. He worried about Blayne. She knew that hybrids had been taken, their bodies found weeks or months later with their throats or other major arteries torn out and their corpses covered in scars. Although full-blood shifters like bears and lions were often used for hunting by men with more money than sense, hybrids had always been the ignored. Until now. Until someone had decided it was a good idea to turn them into pit bulls.

So, did Blayne mind the protection? Not at all. A little protection from some Southern She-wolf was a hell of a lot better than ending up on the wrong side of a pit fight. But what Blayne didn't understand, and what made her toy with Dee-Ann and Ric so much, was why they wouldn't just tell her the truth?

Maybe Ric was worried Blayne wouldn't feel comfortable basically taking money from him. And normally, she wouldn't. But again, taking a little charity from a friend or ending up in the middle of a pit fight? The answer was a no-brainer for Blayne Thorpe. Yet she didn't like the tricky way they were going about it. She especially didn't like that Ric, someone she considered one of her best friends, wasn't being honest with her.

Was it cruel to mess with them? Maybe.

Would Blayne stop? Doubtful.

At least not until they told her the truth. Besides, it took so little to get on the She-wolf's nerves. All Blayne had to do was be herself, but with a dose of proverbial amphetamine added to really amp it up. She did love amping it up. She'd been amping it up since she'd realized it embarrassed the hell out of her father.

Honestly, the military types were so damn easy.

A shadow fell over them and she sat up, grinning, thinking Dee had returned. But when the shadow kept growing, she knew it wasn't Dee. It was Novikov.

"Hey!" she cheered, glad to see that he'd made the effort to come. "You're here!"

"Hey," Novikov said while staring intently at Blayne. She'd have to work on him with that staring thing. A lot of females would be put off by it, and if he wanted to date a She-wolf, he was risking his eyes. She-wolves loathed the staring game.

Yet once Blayne got past his intense stare, she noticed that he had a beer gripped in his hand and a female hanging around his neck.

Okay. She'd admit that she didn't expect him to bring a date. But she didn't mind. Nope. Not at all. She wanted to help the guy get out and have fun . . . even if that meant dating an obvious porn star.

And isn't she kind of cold in that outfit? Wait. Did he make her wear that outfit?

The group fell into an awkward silence, neither Lock nor Ric bothering to attempt even the basic politeness. She'd have to talk to them later about that. How could she teach Novikov to be polite when two of the most polite guys she knew weren't acting polite? It was a conundrum!

After the silence went on for way too long, Gwen finally asked the question Blayne was dying to know the answer to.

"What is that?" Gwen asked from the safety of Lock's lap, pointing at the fox.

And, to Novikov's credit, he did appear truly perplexed by her question. "What's what?"

Gwen frowned. "Around your neck."

He glanced over, shrugged, and replied, "This is my fox. Sami."

"Hiya," Sami said, looking quite comfortable. She was a cute little thing. An Arctic fox from what Blayne could tell with white hair that reached to her shoulders. But her brown skin and the shape of her eyes suggested she was Eskimo. Wait. *Is that the politically correct term?* Blayne didn't know, and now she felt guilty. What if it wasn't the correct term? What if calling Sami Eskimo was the same as the old guy in Little Italy last week who'd called Blayne that "nice colored girl"?

"So," Novikov went on, oblivious to Blayne's struggle with finding the correct terminology to describe the human side of his fox, "what are you guys doing?"

"Nothing," Lock said, and boy, could he make that one word sound more grudgingly given?

"I'm sorry, no." Gwen, not nearly done with her side of the conversation, leaned forward a little bit on Lock's lap and said, "I can't just let this go. What do you mean she's *your* fox?"

"I don't know how to make it clearer." At one time, Blayne would have thought Novikov was being rude, but now she knew that was just the way he spoke. That was the way his mind formed things. Directness without any venom attached. It was his way . . . and something she'd have to work on with him.

Of course, whether she thought he was being rude or not, Gwen didn't care as she kept digging. Kind of like that hole Blayne dug in her dad's backyard a few months back that he still yelled at her about. "Well," Gwen pushed, "is she your girlfriend?"

"Gwen," Blayne warned, but Gwen only raised her hand to shut Blayne up.

"No," Novikov said simply.

"Your lover?" Gwen went on. "Your fuck-buddy? Any of those terms fit here?"

Novikov and the fox eyed each other, then both shook their heads. "No."

"Then I'm unclear what you mean by she's *your* fox."

"Polars have foxes," Lock explained, but Gwen and Blayne still didn't get what that was supposed to mean.

"What?" Gwen demanded.

"Why don't we just let this go?" Blayne asked, trying to keep everyone calm and sort of rational. But Gwen had already had three Guinnesses on top of her four Sprites at dinner. All that sugar and liquor was making for quite the O'Neill volcano.

"Let it go?" Gwen again pointed at the fox. "She comes in here looking like a future *Playboy* spread, and you want to let it go?"

The fox released her grip on Novikov's neck and took the long drop to the ground. She couldn't be more than five-three and maybe a hundred pounds, if that. And the fact that it was the middle of a cold New York City winter didn't seem to faze her either, since she was decked out in the black leather version of a bikini top and shorts. Something Blayne wore in the summer when she and Gwen hit the Jersey Shore, at least the denim version of that outfit, but for winter? Not in this lifetime.

"You got a problem, feline?" the fox demanded.

Gwen tried to shoot off Lock's lap, but the grizzly knew his woman. He tightened his grip on her, holding her with one arm while he continued to drink his beer with his free hand.

"Let me go," Gwen ordered. "I'm going to tear the little twat's face off!"

Lock chuckled. "That is so not going to happen."

Blayne, always hating when anyone fought, jumped off Ric's lap and got between the two. They weren't close, but they'd locked gazes. And although the fox was tiny, even by human standards, Blayne knew better than to underestimate them. Small, foxes may be . . . but mean. Sometimes, they were really mean.

"Okay," Blayne ordered. "That is *it*." She glared at Gwen. "This is the opening to our friend's club, and you are not going to start a fight." Gwen hissed a little, but she settled back onto Lock's lap.

Blayne faced the fox, held out her hand. "Hi. I'm Blayne. Nice to meet you."

The fox blinked painfully bright gold eyes in surprise. "Um . . .

hi." She gazed at Blayne's hand and, finally, took it. It was a short shake, but Blayne meant it. "I'm Sami. Nice to meet you, too."

"Would you like to join us for drinks?"

Studying Blayne closely, the fox suddenly grinned and shook her head. "You know, I'm going to check on my mate. But I'm sure that Bo would love to stay for drinks." Somehow her smile grew. "It's been really nice meeting you, Blayne."

"You, too."

The fox sashayed off, patting Novikov's arm as she passed. Gwen's eyes narrowed as she watched her, and Blayne said, "What part of 'let it go' are we not grasping?"

"I don't like her. And I'm in the mood for a good fight."

"No more Guinness for you," Blayne said, snatching the half-drunk glass away from her friend.

"Do you want to lose that paw, canine?"

"*Be nice!*" Blayne bellowed.

It was grudging, but Gwen settled down even while the rest of the predators around them watched Blayne closely. *Sure. The drunk tigon is no threat, but the sober wolfdog—watch out!*

Annoyed by the hypocrisy, Blayne tossed the glass onto a tray held by a passing waitress before dropping onto the couch next to Ric. Relaxing back, she realized Novikov was still standing there. And—still staring.

"Sit," she said, motioning to an empty spot on the U-shaped couch. And yes, she did expect him to take the spot she pointed out. Especially since he didn't seem to be one of those purposely contrary types. But what she didn't expect was to suddenly have a tight bear-cat ass shoving its way between her and Ric.

Once Bo had forced his way between Blayne and Van Holtz, he felt much better. He didn't appreciate the way the wolf and Blayne had sat so close together, Van Holtz's arm around the back of her portion of the couch. A little too proprietary in Bo's estimation. So he sat between them.

Blayne squeaked a little as she moved out of his way, and Van

Holtz hit the floor since he'd been sitting right on the edge. The wolf glared up at him and Bo gazed back, sipping his beer. He figured that was the end of it until Blayne punched his shoulder.

"Apologize," she ordered him.

"For what?"

"You knocked him on the floor. Are you really that rude?"

"It seems that the answer to that would be yes."

"I'm fine, Blayne." Van Holtz managed to get to his own big wolf feet without any help from Bo. "I think I'll get another drink. I'll be back."

He walked off and Blayne hit Bo again.

"What now?"

"This is your fault."

"What's my fault?"

"Ric being upset."

"It's not like he ran off to the girls' room crying."

"Would you care if he had?"

"Other than to laugh? Probably not."

Blayne turned on the couch to face him, pulling her legs up so she sat on her knees. "How can I help you if you act this way?"

"Help me? Help me with what?"

"Help with *you*." She waved her hand around his face. "The poor, pathetic, lonely, rich superstar athlete that *you* are."

Bo glanced over at the grizzly and tigon sitting across from them. "She's serious," the tigon mouthed to him, making Bo sigh.

"I'm a good person," Blayne said earnestly, pressing her hand to her chest. "And because I'm a good person, I have friends. And I want you to have friends. But that won't happen if you go around knocking wolves to the floor. Wolves are not to be toyed with just because you can." She held up her finger, "Hold that thought," and spun around on her knees so that she faced the back of the couch. "Hey, Dee-Ann!" Blayne screeched across the club. "*Dee-Ann! You're not leaving already are you? Sit here! Here! We still have room! Dee! Annnnn!*"

With his left ear ringing, Bo watched as some She-wolf stalked off into the crowd while Blayne returned to her original position, facing Bo. "Now . . . where was I?"

"If I want to be a good person like you, I can't toy with wolves just because I can."

"Right!" Again she pressed her palm to her chest, appearing superbly innocent. "I'm here to help you. Let me."

"Dee-Ann, wait!"

Dee-Ann kept walking until a strong hand grabbed her arm, pulling her back. "Please."

"I'm done, hoss. I am *done*."

"It's not that easy and we both know that."

"Find somebody else. I can't deal with her." She tried to walk out the front exit, but Van Holtz pulled her down a hallway and into a private room, recently vacated from the heavy scent of feline sex still lingering.

"You can't walk away from this," Van Holtz told her once he'd closed the door. "Blayne needs you."

"What that wolfdog needs is heavy medication."

"Look, let's just talk. Okay? For a second."

Van Holtz sat down on the couch, and Dee said, "Whoever was on that couch before ya just fucked there."

The wolf stood right back up. "So we'll stand." He took a breath. "You can't let her get to you like this. You know Blayne. She just wants everyone to have a good time. To be happy."

What would make Dee-Ann happy was Blayne Thorpe's head over her daddy's mantel next to the twelve-point buck he'd taken down in his younger days. *That* would make Dee-Ann happy. Continually discussing one pain-in-the-ass wolfdog, however, would not.

Lord, if they were all like Blayne, Dee-Ann wouldn't help one of them. But thankfully, they weren't all like Blayne. In fact, she'd been meeting some real interesting ones lately. Hybrids with real potential who didn't waste her time by being idiotic and embarrassing in public.

"Don't need Blayne Thorpe to make me happy. Just need her to shut her mouth and wait quietly to be snatched up by scumbags. Don't think I'm askin' too much here."

"I think we both know it won't be that easy."

"Well, I can't take much more of her craziness."

"I know. I know. We'll discuss it at the next team meeting. Okay?"

"As ya like. But I guess I don't know why you don't just take her home with you. Make her yours and she falls under the protection of your kin. Nothing they can do about it."

The wolf gazed at her a long moment before he finally asked, "Make Blayne mine? You mean . . . you mean mark Blayne?"

Dee-Ann did what her daddy always did when asked a stupid question. Said nothing and waited until the person figured out on their own they asked a stupid question. And, sure enough, the wolf caught on quick, his whole body going kind of tense.

"I can't mark Blayne. She's like a sister to me."

"Uh-huh."

"I can assure you, Dee-Ann, my interest in Blayne is strictly friendship. I have . . . other interests."

Whatever that meant. Although Dee-Ann didn't care one way or the other. Her biggest concern right now was getting Blayne Thorpe off her radar for good. But until that happened, she had a way around being Blayne's daily watchdog. Normally, Dee-Ann would inform her commanding officers of changes she'd made, but the Group wasn't the Marines and Ulrich Van Holtz wasn't her commanding officer. He was just a rich boy with a powerful uncle who liked him. So Dee would do what she'd been doing for months . . . running the show her way without bothering to let Van Holtz know about it. Why bother? The boy was as useless as tits on a bull, but he still made sure she got paid on time, and she did like getting that money. It was more than she'd thought and much more than she needed, even in this ridiculous city, but it was nice actually having a retirement fund. Especially since she'd never had one before.

"Understand?" he asked.

"Yeah. Sure." *Whatever.* She didn't understand males. He didn't seem to mind that Blayne was a hybrid and they made a cute couple. Besides, if he wasn't careful, that big buck of a hockey player would snatch little Blayne right out from under Mr. Society. One look and Dee-Ann could tell that Novikov didn't play by anyone's rules but his own. And the way he watched that little gal . . . well, when Dee's daddy thought no one was looking he still stared at her momma the same way Novikov was watching Blayne.

But in the long scheme of things, it wasn't Dee's problem. If Van Holtz wanted to lose out on his chance with that idiot that was his problem.

Figuring the conversation was over, Dee walked out, ignoring the "Where the hell did she go?" that followed.

When the two boars stared at each other for way too long in Blayne's estimation, she grabbed Novikov's hand and pulled him away from the couch and Lock MacRyrie.

To her surprise, he followed her without complaint, and she led him up two floors until she got to the "Mood Room" level. Mellow tech music and low lights for those who had no tolerance for the exact opposite, Blayne had a feeling this was the perfect place for Bo Novikov. He didn't seem remotely comfortable near the dance floor, and she doubted he'd do much better on the gaming floor or in the karaoke room where she knew she'd find the entire Kuznetsov Pack. It was clear Jess didn't come to the opening. If she had, she'd be working every floor to make sure the event went off without the slightest hitch. But she was seriously pregnant and kind of miserable at the moment, so the opening of a Manhattan shifter club was not a good idea for her. She was much better off home and comfortable with her mate.

Thankfully, though, it looked as if the club was off to an excellent start, and giving shifters choices like the Mood Room was a very smart move.

Still holding Novikov's hand, Blayne went deep into the Mood Room, trying to find a table or booth. Everything was taken at the moment, and when she arrived at the last booth at the very end of the room, she stopped and glanced at the three male lions sitting in it. She was trying to guesstimate when they might be done and leave when the three males gazed past her and up. Blayne looked up at Novikov just as he tilted his head toward the exit. It was a slight move, barely noticeable if she hadn't been looking right at him, but holy shit did those lions move! Blayne stepped back as the felines took their drinks and escaped, their gazes now focused on the floor in front of them.

Blayne let out a sigh. "That wasn't necessary."

"I didn't want to stand here all night." He pressed his palm against her back, urging her to sit in the booth, but Blayne couldn't believe the size of that hand touching her through her knockoff designer dress. *Like the size of a crater on the moon.*

Okay. A bit of an exaggeration, but Blayne was known to exaggerate when it helped get her point across.

She sat in the booth and, again, thought he'd sit on the other side, but no. He squeezed in next to her. But Blayne wasn't having it this time.

"Over there!" she yelped when he tried pushing her over when she wouldn't move out of his way. "Over! *There!*"

Her demand worked, because he sat down on the other side.

"I need space," she blurted out, her arms going wide to help illustrate her point. "Personal space! I'm a wolfdog. Getting crowded into corners makes us mental! Space!" Annoyed in general, she went on. "And stop scaring people to get them to move out of your way. And don't try and stare down your teammates. That's just rude! You're on the same team. You should be working together, buddies to the end." She flopped back into the booth. "I have so much work to do with you." When Novikov didn't say anything, she demanded, "Well?"

"What if I bought you a new watch?"

"Oh, my God!" she blurted out. "Are we back here again?"

"It irritates me." And his calmness was pissing her off more than she could say.

"This watch goes perfectly with this outfit," she argued.

"But you wore it during training and with your cargo pants to work."

"Let the watch go!" she bellowed, startling the full-human waitress who wore the mark of some wolf on the bare shoulder peeking out from under a sleeveless club T-shirt. Blayne cleared her throat. "Diet Coke please."

The waitress nodded, focused on Novikov. "Bottle water," he said, handing her his half-full beer. "Thank you."

After the waitress walked away, Novikov said, "You know, Blayne, I'm pretty happy with the way my life is right now."

"You can't possibly be happy."

"Why? Because I'm not like you?"

Blayne snorted. "You couldn't handle being me." She swirled her forefingers around her head and admitted, "All that goes on inside this head at any given time . . . would destroy you."

She didn't know who was startled more when Novikov suddenly laughed, but it was something that she would remember for a very long time because it was something that everyone had said he never did. You know, unless he was laughing *at* you.

The laugh took him by surprise. It wasn't that he didn't find things funny, but he usually found things funny later. After he thought about it for a few hours and analyzed what funny was in context.

But in whatever context there was, even Bo knew Blayne was funny. Even when she was angry or annoyed, she knew how to keep her sense of humor. He admired that because he knew few people who had that skill.

Yet his problem with Blayne was that she wanted to "fix him." Personally, he didn't think he needed fixing, but she seemed real determined about it.

The waitress placed their drinks down. Blayne downed half of her Diet Coke before Bo had even picked up his tiny bottle of Italian water that he was sure would cost twenty bucks.

"So this is what I'm thinking," she said when she slammed the bottle down. "Personality makeover."

"No."

"You're being unreasonable."

"I think you're being ridiculous. That makes us even, doesn't it?"

"I say a personality makeover because externally, you're not half bad."

Gee, thanks.

"I mean, you're cute, especially with those freaky blue eyes."

"Freaky?"

"The white hair alone would kill the look but the brown mane under it totally pulls it together. Although you may want to think about upgrading your conditioner." She suddenly rose up on her knees and reached across the table, grabbing his hair and studying the ends. "I don't think these are split ends, but they are a bit frizzy. A good conditioner will help you with that."

"Blayne—"

She sat back. "And your wardrobe isn't bad at all. Which just leaves your personality. And if you let me, I can help you fix that."

"It doesn't need to be fixed. This is who I am; I've accepted that. Maybe you should."

"I don't have a problem with you."

"Then why—"

"Explain the foxes to me," she said, looking very professorial all of a sudden.

"Why?"

"Who are they? Where did they come from? She said she has a mate; does he mind her lounging on you?" She leaned in close again. "Or does he get to lounge, too? Do you guys all sleep in the same bed?" She practically jumped out of the booth. "Are you bi? Oh, my God! That would be so cool!"

"Hey, hey, hey!" He held up his hands to ward off her insane eagerness. "It's not like that! It's never been like that."

She dropped back into her seat. "Oh."

"Sorry you're so disappointed."

"No, no. Not disappointed . . . per se."

And Bo heard himself laugh again, Blayne joining him.

"I'm just trying to understand the dynamic. Were they assigned to you? Or did you choose them like you would a puppy from the pound?"

"I guess they kind of chose me. The first day of school when I moved to Ursus County, they sort of attached themselves to me. Followed me back to my uncle's house. I thought he'd make them leave, but instead he fed them and told me to 'get used to it.' I guess it makes sense. In the wild, full foxes attach themselves to polars and eat what's left over from the polars' kills, which is very logical because polars mostly only eat blubber—"

"Ew."

"—leaving the meat and bone for everyone else."

Her face scrunched up. "Lovely."

"You asked."

"So basically they're like parasites."

"I think Sami and Sander prefer 'scavengers.' "

"But they do live off you, right? Eating your food? Stealing your money?"

"They've never stolen from me. Sami will just walk in and say, 'I'm taking money out of your wallet' and I say, 'Okay.' "

"Nice."

"But they always have some scam going, and haven't gotten money from me in a while. I just make sure I have cash for bail or, ya know, mob types. When they get in over their heads."

Blayne pressed her hands to her head. "I have *so* much work."

"How ya figure?"

"What? You think some lioness or She-wolf will put up with your hot fox wandering in and out of your house, taking cash out of your wallet? They won't be okay with that."

He studied Blayne a moment before asking, "What about you? Would you be okay with it?"

"Well . . . my best friend can turn her head a hundred and eighty degrees when the mood strikes her, her entire family has

Irish mob ties, and my father used to run with a motorcycle club masquerading as a Pack—so I'd have to say I don't know if I'd have room to judge. But I'm me. I'm unique."

Yeah. Blayne was definitely that.

"But we're not talking about me. We're talking about getting you a nice girl."

"Then we're ruling out She-lions and wolves. I mean . . . if we're going for *nice* girls."

Her grin huge, she leaned across the table and punched him lightly in the ribs. "Look at you with the joking."

Feeling pretty good about making her laugh, Bo was annoyed to see MacRyrie lumber up to their table.

"Normally I wouldn't say anything so you could suffer," the grizzly stated with no preamble, "but Gwen said Blayne would be mad at me if I didn't tell you. And I like Blayne."

"Tell me what?"

"Your foxes are getting arrested."

Bo winced and rubbed his forehead. "Dammit."

"What did they do?" Blayne asked.

"It's probably an old warrant," Bo explained, dropping his hand to the table. When Blayne did nothing but watch him with a sad expression on her face, Bo guessed, "We're back at the personality makeover again, aren't we?"

"I'm merely suggesting that with a little help from me you might actually get friends you can go out with that *won't* get arrested for old warrants." She held her hands up. "Merely a suggestion."

Not in the mood to argue this point, Bo eased out of the booth and stood. The grizzly was just shy of seven feet, so they locked gazes again.

"Friends being arrested," Blayne reminded him. "Boar-on-boar violence or helping your friends. Your choice."

Dammit. She was right. Bo moved his gaze over to Blayne. "Tomorrow. Seven a.m. Do not be early or late. Just be on time."

"Will do."

Unsure of how he would look back on this evening, Bo headed off in the hope of preventing his friends from going to jail for the night.

Blayne shook her head. "That man."

"What's going on with you two?" Lock asked and Blayne couldn't help but notice he appeared concerned. *So sweet!*

"I'm trying to help him become a better person. Better person, means a happier person."

"Maybe you should have given yourself an easier challenge first. Like moving the Empire State Building to Jersey with your teeth. Or closing off an active volcano with a pebble and a bottle of water."

"I could be wrong, Lock MacRyrie, but I'm sensing sarcasm."

Bo dragged the two foxes out of the club by the backs of their necks, after he made them return every wallet, watch, purse, and piece of jewelry they'd "grabbed," as they liked to call it. Since foxes always believed that "stealing" had such an ugly connotation.

Thankfully, the two undercover cops who'd busted them were shifters and let the pair off with a warning as long as they returned everything.

"I give you people lists," Bo snarled, throwing them into the backseat of his truck, "and you completely ignore them!"

He slammed the door closed and stormed around to the other side of the truck. He got in and turned the motor over.

"We needed the cash," Sami explained. "We're heading to Thailand tomorrow."

"You know I would have paid for your trip."

"We don't want you to think we're living off you."

"You *are* living off me."

"Yeah . . . but we don't want you to think it."

Bo glared at the couple over his shoulder, muttering, "Maybe she's right."

"Maybe who's right? About what?"

"Blayne. She seems to think I need a personality makeover."

"What's wrong with your personality?"

"I apparently only attract criminals."

"Oh."

Neither fox argued that point, allowing Bo to face straight ahead and ask out loud, "I don't know what she's doing. She's insisting she wants to *help* me."

"Because she likes you," Sami explained, "she's compartmentalizing you. Putting you in a safe zone."

"I don't want to be in a safe zone."

"Then keep doing what you've been doing."

"How does that help me?"

"First off, don't look for logic. You've picked the most illogical hybrid on the planet. Second, she's one of those chicks who has to be 'friends'"—she raised her hands and made air quotes—"with a guy before he can hope to get close, but by then he's already moved on to a girl who doesn't need that and he's already thinking about the wolfdog like a sister. Trust me, she's got thousands of buddies and brothers throughout the tri-state area. If you want more than that, you'll have to work for it."

"I don't mind working for it. It's just . . ."

"Just what?"

"Her lack of time management really worries me."

Sander sat forward, placing his hand on Bo's shoulder. "Will you give a shit about her lack of time management when she's got those insanely long legs wrapped around your head?"

Bo thought on that for a moment, then answered honestly, "No."

"Then why are we still sitting here discussing this?"

The fox had a point.

CHAPTER 9

"We can't keep her here."

After less than three hours of sleep, Dee wasn't in the mood for New York City rudeness. And she heard rudeness.

"Why not?"

"I'll show you." The coyote led Dee down to the main offices, away from where she thought he was taking her, which the rest of the Group called "The Pound." A nickname she didn't much appreciate, but didn't bother arguing about.

They reached one of the communication centers, and the coyote gestured through the glass that offered a clear view into the room.

"Good Lord."

"Exactly."

For months now Dee had been bringing strays she'd found on the street. Hybrid kids with no pack, pride, or clan of their own. If they were really young, she sent them off to a home were they could go to school and at least live a modicum of a normal life while learning how to take down deer, control their fangs and claws, and not snarl at strangers on the street. But the older kids who had potential, she'd been bringing them here. They got free room and board in exchange for going to school, making decent grades, and getting daily training in combat techniques. Dee was convinced she could not only give these kids a new life, but she could also get herself a fierce little combat unit that would be hers and hers alone.

So far it had all been going great, except for the first hybrid she'd brought in a few months back. Abby. Abby never shifted to her human form, she ate off the floor, and she had a thing about running in circles for hours. But this . . . this was a problem.

"How long did it take her to do this?"

"Patrol walked by around three a.m. this morning. When he swung back around three forty—it looked mostly like this.

Abby had ripped through that command center like a damn hurricane, tearing into equipment and furniture with the force of a pit bull on meth. Abby hadn't even left the scene of her crime, either. Instead she was in the middle of the room . . . running in circles.

"She can't stay here," the coyote said again. "She sets the other kids off and she's—"

"I know. I know." Dee just wished she could figure her out. "Has she actually hurt anyone? Or tried?"

"Nope."

Good. That helped.

Dee walked into the room, keeping the door open with her foot. "Abby," she called out. "Abby!"

Abby Vega stopped in mid-run and focused on Dee-Ann. Panting, stumbling a little, the kid stared at her. No, Dee wasn't ready to give up on her yet, but she needed some help.

"Come on, kid. We're headin' out."

With a gleeful bark, Abby charged past, slammed into the wall outside the room, used it to turn her entire body, and charged off down the hallway toward the exit. Sighing, Dee followed after her.

For a week they had been training every morning. And for a week, Blayne was learning that not everyone was as easy to fix as she thought they should be. It seemed that Bo Novikov simply didn't understand he had a problem.

True, in the last Carnivores home game that past Sunday, it

was Bo's skill that won them not only the game but the Carnivores' first time in the Cup playoffs in years. Something Bo should be rightfully proud of, and yet he showed nothing but that scowl as he'd skated off the ice while his own team cheered and hugged each other, the loyal New York crowd chanting Bo's nickname for nearly twenty minutes. If any of that mattered to him, Blayne couldn't see it.

And when she silently noted that throwing overeager fans into the wall when they came at him to sign something—often a body part—seemed normal to him; that not speaking to girls who were clearly putting out "I'd like to know you better" signals because he was running late on his all-day schedule was considered acceptable behavior; and complaining every time Blayne was one or two minutes late for their training rather than going with the flow of life . . . Well, Blayne kept coming back to the same conclusion. The man didn't know he had a problem. And he had *huge* problems!

It was sad really. A relatively decent person who just didn't get that Blayne could help him. Bo never dismissed her completely when she made subtle suggestions about how he could handle things better. Instead he asked what he liked to call "follow-up questions."

For instance, "How do you know he didn't want me to throw him into the wall? He was bragging to his friends about it." Or, "Why should I talk to someone who's on the cover of Japanese *Vogue* when I've got you standing here with your Hello Kitty earmuffs on? Who can beat that for hot fashion?"

These types of questions did nothing but confuse Blayne. She couldn't tell if he was being snarky because he seemed so serious when he asked.

As for time management and enjoying life, they seemed to be at an "agree to disagree" stage. But Blayne was trying really hard to be on time for their sessions. She didn't want to be one of those girls who took her friends for granted.

Blayne looked at herself in her bathroom mirror, her electric toothbrush "wurrring" away in her mouth. Was Bo Novikov a friend of hers? Seriously? She had to think on that a moment. She didn't take in friends lightly. She may have a lot of them, but they had all proved themselves to be good, reliable human beings.

Was Bo Novikov a good, reliable human being? Well . . . he was reliable. Like the watch he wore, that man was extremely reliable. A good human being, though . . . ? Okay, first off, he wasn't a bad human being. So that was something right there. But really, he had to be a good human being if he was spending an hour every morning with her. He hadn't made a move on her, hadn't acted inappropriately, and although she still did find him staring at her occasionally, he didn't make her feel like running for the exits anymore.

In fact, if she were to be honest with herself—and at five thirty in the morning, she could be nothing but honest—she kind of liked when he stared at her.

Which in Blayne's *Big Book of Logic* added up to Bo Novikov being a friend. She chuckled. Who knew that would happen?

Smiling, she went back to dutifully brushing her teeth.

She'd just spit out her toothpaste when her cell phone rang. She ran into the bedroom, tripping over a box she'd left out with old tax papers in it and slamming into a chair she'd moved the night before when she'd gone on a search for a magazine she wanted to read. Limping now, she went to her bed and ended up pulling off all the bedding until she found her cell phone. The ringing stopped but started again a few seconds later because her close friends knew she could never find her phone.

"Hello?" The phone rang in her ear and Blayne realized she hadn't actually connected the call.

"Hello?" she said again once the call had been connected.

"Hi, Blayne? It's Jess."

"Hey, Jess. Whasup?"

"We have a little emergency and could really use your help."

"I'll be right there." Blayne disconnected the call and dashed around the room trying to find clean clothes. She hadn't asked what Jess's problem was because she knew the wild dogs wouldn't bother her unless it was something important. They were a very self-contained group and usually handled stuff themselves. Besides, it was probably a plumbing problem and she didn't want to waste time. If she hurried, she'd be at their house, help them out, and still make it to the training on time with Novikov. *Easy-peasy*.

At least that's what she thought until she stood in the Kuznetsov Pack's frozen backyard.

"How long has she been doing that?"

"Since Dee brought her here about an hour ago. When she wouldn't stop, we panicked."

Blayne could see why. "She hasn't stopped at all?"

"Not once."

Blayne motioned the Kuznetsov Pack's Top Five, as she liked to call them, back into the house. The Top Five included Jess, Sabina, May, Phil, and Danny. The first members of the Kuznetsov Pack and, as Blayne liked to joke, the power behind the throne.

"Explain to me again why Dee's bringing new kids over to your house?"

"Dee says the pup needed some place to stay and would we mind."

And of course, they didn't. The Pack's oldest pup was Kristan, a wolfdog. Because of her, the Kuznetsovs were much more sympathetic to the wolfdogs than most, something Blayne was quite grateful for.

"Poor thing's been living on the streets," May said. "Before that with full-humans in some foster home."

"She needs mental hospital," Sabina said, and based on everyone's reaction, she'd been saying it all morning. "Or drugs."

"No," Blayne said. "No drugs, unless you really want to see her flip her shit."

"So what do we do?"

Blayne grabbed Jess's arm and looked at the humongous watch she always had on. This was probably the kind of watch Novikov wished Blayne had, but the damn thing looked like it weighed a ton. *How is that comfortable?*

"Okay. I have some time."

"Time for what?"

Blayne shifted, shook off her clothes, and ran to the back door. Danny opened it for her and she shot down the stairs and into the backyard. She ran around the pup until she'd caught her attention. The younger dog stumbled to a stop and watched Blayne. That's when Blayne jumped over her, landed on the opposite side, and went into a play bow. Confused, the pup watched her but didn't move. At first. But after Blayne pounced back and forth in front of her a few times, the pup jumped forward, then back, then forward again. By the time they were chasing each other around the backyard, a good portion of the Pack had come out of the house to join them.

Bobby Ray Smith, or Smitty to his friends and the entire U.S. Navy, handed Dee a cup of fresh-brewed coffee while they continued to watch the wild dog Pack play with their newest resident. "See?" he asked between sips. "Told ya Blayne would know what to do."

"Are you telling me all that girl needed was some playtime?"

"Looks that way."

"She won't shift to human. At least she hasn't since I've had her."

"Your daddy don't like to shift to human, so I don't know why you have that judgmental tone."

Dee-Ann gave a shrug, and Smitty knew that would be the only answer he'd get on that particular topic.

"Sure you don't mind me leaving her here?"

"Don't make me no never mind. And you know Jessie Ann will take any ol' stray off the street." He looked down at the mixed mutt lounging at his feet. "Ain't that right, Shit-starter?"

"Well, I appreciate it."

"When did you start taking in strays anyway, Dee-Ann? Dee-Ann?" Smitty turned in a circle, finding himself completely alone in the room. "How the hell does she *do that*?

* * *

Blayne was running for the front door, knowing that no matter how hard or fast she ran, she was going to be way late for her morning training with Novikov, when she slammed right into a She-wolf walking toward the same front door. As they hit the floor, Blayne realized too late that instead of trying to call Novikov on her cell phone—and realizing she didn't actually have his number programmed into her cell phone—she should have been paying attention. It was something her father complained about constantly. That she didn't pay attention or she focused on the wrong thing at the wrong time. And staring down into the glaring face of a Southern She-wolf, Blayne knew her father had been right yet again.

"Uh . . . hi, Dee." True, most days Blayne loved to torture the uptight female, but with all her vital organs within claw distance, she knew it would not be a good time to play that little game. Nope. Not a good time at all.

"You're on me," Dee replied. *She must not be a morning person.*

"Yeah. Sorry about that."

"Off."

"Um, sure. Sorry about—"

"Off, off, *off!*" Blayne stumbled away from the barking She-wolf.

Dee-Ann got to her giant feet, glaring at Blayne the entire time. Really, if Blayne hadn't heard someone coming down the stairs, she'd have run to the kitchen and grabbed a knife to fend the bitch off.

"What's going on?" Smitty demanded when he hit that last step.

"Nothing," Dee snarled.

She yanked the front door open and stormed out, slamming the door behind her.

"You all right, darlin'?" Smitty sweetly asked, his arm slipping around her shoulders.

"She hates me, doesn't she?"

"Hate's kind of a strong word. You're probably better off with loathes or detests."

"Gee . . . thanks."

"Now don't feel bad. Dee don't like most people."

"But everyone likes me. I'm so endearing."

"True, but you should be used to the unfriendly types after a whole week working with that hockey player."

"Yeah. I guess you're—oh, my God!" she burst out, startling Smitty to move away from her. *"Novikov!"*

Bo had been on the treadmill for twenty minutes when she suddenly appeared in front of him. His MP3 player was pounding out The Who, so he couldn't hear a word she said. He could only see her mouth moving. A beautiful mouth, for sure. But not worth the trouble if she couldn't respect his schedule!

She kept talking, but when he didn't say anything, she finally slammed her hand down on the treadmill console. Thankfully, it didn't stop cold, since he was going about fifty miles an hour. Of course the cheetah on the other side of him was going about seventy, but whatever. That cheetah was always showing off.

Once the treadmill eased to a stop, Bo pulled the earplug out of his right ear.

"—ing to me?" she said.

"What?"

"I said, are you listening to me?"

"No." He went to put the earplug back in, but she caught his arm.

"Bo, I'm sorry."

"Oh, I'm Bo now?"

"That is your name . . ." She frowned, obviously not quite sure. "Right?"

"Yes. It is my name. But you've been calling me Novikov . . . until this second when you want me to overlook your total and complete disregard for my time. But don't worry . . . that won't happen again. I won't let it."

"I know you mean that in a really bad way."

"I do. Now can I get back to work?"

Bo reached for the controls, but Blayne scrambled on top of the treadmill and threw herself over the console.

Stunned, he demanded, "What the hell are you doing?"

"Blocking you from getting your workout until you listen to me."

"Why do I need to listen to you? It won't change anything."

"I had a reason. I swear."

"People like you always have a reason."

"People like me?"

"Yeah. People with no sense of time or commitment. Who just float through life knowing they can talk their way out of or into any situation because they're that damn charming. And although I admire that, I'm not that easy. I've gotten this far because I'm a total and complete asshole. Forgetting that, Blayne, was your biggest mistake. Now get off my treadmill or I'm throwing you off."

She gasped. "You wouldn't dare!"

Dammit. She was right. He wouldn't.

"Fair enough." He stepped off his treadmill and over to the one next to him. He grabbed the cheetah by the back of his sweat-soaked T-shirt and yanked him off.

"Hey!"

Bo ignored him, slowed down the tread to fifty miles per hour, and jumped on. He was pumping hard when Bo suddenly had a weight around his neck and hanging down his back.

Letting out a really annoyed sigh, he slowed the treadmill and stopped it. As he stood there, the cheetah now on the other tread-mill giving him the finger, Bo asked, "What are you doing?"

"Trying to get you to listen to me," Blayne said.

"I'm not training with you again."

"Fine. Whatever. But I still want us to be friends."

She did? "Why?"

"Because I like you."

"Blayne, no one likes me. Because I'm an asshole."

"Oh, my God, he's *such* an asshole," the cheetah sneered.

"Unless you want me to beat you to death with that treadmill, you'll shut the fuck up, basketball player."

"Can we talk about this outside?"

Knowing she'd stay wrapped around him through the entire conversation if he didn't do as she asked, Bo stepped off the treadmill and walked into the hallway. "What, Blayne?"

"I wasn't blowing you off. My friends called me with a slight emergency, and it took longer than I thought it would."

"A slight emergency?"

"When it's pup related, it's always a major emergency to wild dogs. But when I got there it was much less major and more slight."

"Okay."

"So you understand?"

"Sure."

"And I'm forgiven?"

"No."

She sighed. "Why not?"

"I know this is all fun and games for you, Blayne, but it's not for me. I'm rigid about my workouts because that's what keeps me in shape, keeps me sharp. I don't have time to sit around waiting to see if you'll show up."

"I know. And I'm sorry. I did try and call you to let you know I'd be late."

"Then why didn't you?"

"Don't actually have your phone number."

Bo blinked. "You don't?"

"Nope. And I tried calling Ric, figuring he'd have your number, but he wasn't answering. Probably because he thought it was his dad. They have issues. So I called Lock, and he did answer but I kept asking him for your number and he kept saying, 'It's in the river with the honey-covered salmon. I love honey-covered salmon, don't you?' And I have to admit, I got a little freaked out, and disconnected that call. And mind you, I'm doing all this while running because I wasn't sure a cab could get me here fast enough."

The more he thought about it, the more he realized he hadn't given her his number. Yet Bo hated giving second chances. People always blew second chances. But she was still wrapped around his neck, her body hanging down his back, and he realized he wanted to give her a second chance.

"I can't meet you tomorrow," he said. "I have a breakfast meeting with my agent. But I can meet you tonight. No team practice tonight."

"We don't have to keep training if you don't want to. That isn't what this is about."

"I know. But I made a promise. Just don't blow it, Blayne."

"I won't."

"You need help getting down, don't you?"

"I am a little high."

Knowing she could get down herself if she wanted to, Bo still reached around, hooking his arm around her waist, and lowering her to the ground.

He held his hand out. "Phone."

She dropped her backpack and desperately dug through it, tossing stuff out of it, until she found the phone at the very bottom.

"It's always at the bottom of my bag," she muttered, handing it to him.

Bo quickly programmed his cell and landline numbers into her phone. Plus his e-mail address.

"I can get text messages, too," he explained.

"Can't everybody?"

"I used to block them, but that irritated my foxes, so I accept them now."

"All right then."

"I don't like distractions," he complained, handing her back the phone. "So don't *abuse* the text messaging."

"And trying to type with those big fingers probably isn't easy, either." When he snarled a little, she held her hands up. "Just kidding. Just kidding."

"Tonight," he told her. "At seven. Understand? Not a second late."

"I promise." She smiled and Christ, it was like the entire hallway got brighter. "You're not as much of an asshole as you keep saying you are."

Yes, he was.

"You're actually a sweetheart." She leaped up and kissed his cheek. When she landed, she said, "Tonight. At seven."

He nodded and turned away while she crouched down to shove everything into her bag. To be honest, he couldn't watch her handle that mess, so he went back into the gym. The cheetah was still on his favorite treadmill, so Bo yanked him off, slowed the treadmill down, and got on.

"You asshole!" the cheetah hissed behind him.

But Bo just gave him the finger and kept on running, feeling *much* better.

Sitting comfortably on top of the tall stepladder, Blayne used the claw part of her hammer to pull away whatever weird crap the old owner had wrapped around the ancient pipes. It amazed her what people would do to stop a leak rather than call a plumber. In the end, they had to call a plumber anyway, but the damage had been done and Blayne was forced to charge an arm and a leg to fix the problem they'd created themselves.

"What is that?" Gwen asked about what was wrapped around the pipe and shoveled another donut in her mouth.

"I'm not sure." Blayne admitted. "And to be honest, I don't want to ask."

"What if it's something gross?"

"I'm wearing my gloves and this stupid mask. Besides, I'm in denial. How about leaving me there?"

Gwen chuckled and continued eating while watching Blayne work. "So you really have Novikov's numbers in your cell?"

"Yep. And I'd really appreciate it if you didn't tell your brother about it."

"Are you kidding? Mitch has no boundaries in general, but when it comes to sports stars, he's even worse."

"He should have joined one of the shifter football teams."

"By the time the pro teams really took off and became legit, he was already a cop. But I think part of him will always regret that he didn't go the other route."

"Yeah."

"So are you two dating?"

"Me and Mitch?"

"No, you idiot. You and Novikov?"

"God, no. Why?"

"He likes you."

"We're friends."

Gwen shook her head and reached for another donut. "Don't be an idiot, Blayne. The man waited, according to what you told me he said, for fifteen minutes for you to arrive. He's Bo Novikov. He doesn't have to wait for anybody. Then, not only does he forgive you for making him wait, he gives you all his numbers."

Blayne lowered the hammer. "You're over-thinking this."

"And you're not thinking at all."

"You act like that's new." She went back to working on the encrusted pipe. "He's not, nor will he be, one of my gentlemen callers."

"Ignoring the fact you keep using that stupid term, *why* won't he be one of your gentlemen callers?"

"He's too uptight. Always telling me to get a new watch."

"You need a new watch."

"And he has an unhealthy obsession over his schedule."

"You mean because he actually follows his schedule rather than randomly changing it when the mood suits him?"

"That's exactly what I mean. He won't be happy with a woman unless she's as uptight and narrow minded as he is. Thank you, but I like my hippy-dippy ways."

Gwen wiped her sugar- and chocolate-stained hands with a napkin. "You could try this new thing called 'compromise.' It's all the rage."

"I know guys like him. I was raised by a guy like him. There is no compromise in his world; there is only submission or death."

"I knew somehow we'd end up back at your father." She tapped Blayne's foot. "And it seems to me Novikov has already compromised where you're concerned."

"He's hoping for a shot at the goodies. Once he gets it, we'll be heading back to Submission Town, USA, where there is no compromise."

Gwen's eyes crossed. "My God, you're weird."

"Don't sound so shocked. You already knew this."

Blayne finished cleaning off the material around the pipe and hung the hammer from a loop on her pants. Taking hold of the pipe, Blayne twisted and pulled, but the metal was too rusted to the connecting pipe that led into the building. She motioned to Gwen. "Anyone around?"

Gwen walked to the garage entrance and did a quick visual search. Shaking her head, she walked back over. "Nope. It's clear. And we're not done talking about this."

"Let it go." Blayne twisted hard, her natural strength tearing the pipe away from the other pipe. If the full-human owner had been around, she'd have had to get it off the hard, and much more boring, way.

Holding the pipe in her hands, Blayne glanced at Gwen.

"What?" Gwen asked.

"It's heavy." She turned the pipe over and looked inside.

"Be careful, Blayne. Let's not have a repeat of—"

"*Badger!*"

CHAPTER 10

B o banged on the door again, seconds away from tearing it off its hinges when Blayne opened it. Without waiting to be invited, he pushed past her, throwing down his gym bag. He couldn't remember being this angry before. And, man, was he angry.

"Do you think," he snarled, "that I offer to help everybody? Do you think my time is so meaningless that I can just sit around at the sports center waiting for you or *anyone* to show up? I know your concept of time is different from the rest of the universe but I am on a *schedule*. Do you even know what that means?" He turned around to face her. *"Do you?"*

One brown eye slowly blinked up at him from a face half covered by an icepack. Surprised, Bo took a step back. "What happened to your face?"

"Badger."

She'd mumbled so he was hoping he had heard wrong. "Badger? What about a badger?"

"I was assaulted by one."

"By a badger?"

"Yes. By a badger." She stepped around him and sat down on a loveseat she was pretending was a couch. Not surprising when the apartment was so small and—*Christ almighty!*—so messy. Bo looked around and wondered how she even managed to move her body around the room.

"Are you using a slang term I've never heard before regarding your assailant or do you mean an actual badger?" he pushed, trying not to think too hard about the horror that was her apartment.

"I mean a badger!" she yelled; then she moaned and curled up on her couch. "Go away, Bo. I want to be miserable alone."

Instead of listening to her, he crouched beside her and reached for the icepack.

"What are you doing?" she asked, weakly slapping at his hand.

"Taking a look." He lifted the icepack, cringed, and gingerly placed it back down on her wounded face. "We're taking you to a hospital."

"I'll be fine. It's just a little swelling."

It was more than a little swelling. "How did this happen?"

"I was on a job, and when I removed this pipe a badger was lying in wait."

Lying in wait? "Are you suggesting it targeted you?"

"Yessss," she hissed. "The badgers hate me."

"I didn't know plumbing was such a dangerous business."

"It is for me."

"How long have you been like this?"

"Not long. Gwen wanted me to go to the hospital, but I felt fine. Finished work, came home to change and get something to eat so I could meet you, and then suddenly I didn't feel so good."

"Let me take you to the hospital, Blayne."

"No. I'll have to deal with that goddamn ER nurse again, and I'm not in the mood to be mocked."

"The nurse made fun of you?"

"She's a bigot."

"I'd like to think you're talking about race, but you aren't, are you?"

"She's a breedist. Now go away. I'll be fine in the morning."

Not wanting to take that risk, Bo reached into his back pocket and pulled out his phone. He had tons of numbers programmed in it, but he barely used any of them. But he still liked having the information because he never knew when he'd need them. Like now.

After a quick search, a voice he knew so well but hadn't heard in years answered on the other end. "This is Dr. Luntz."

"I somehow knew you'd still be in your office."

There was a long pause and then, "Oh, my God. Bold?"

"Hi, Dr. Luntz."

"Bold! Oh, Bold. I'm so glad to hear from you. How are you? Are you okay? I'm so proud of you. Do you know how proud of you I am?"

Bo couldn't help but smile. There were just some people in the world who were naturally amazing. Marci Luntz, M.D. was one of those people.

"Thanks, Dr. Luntz."

"Marci. I don't know why you won't ever call me Marci." Because it felt weird? "So what's up? I'm sure you're not calling me this late in the evening for no reason."

"I need your advice, if you don't mind."

"Bold Novikov, you know I don't mind. If you ever need anything from me, all you have to do is ask. What's going on?"

"I have a friend—"

"A girlfriend?"

"Dr. Luntz."

"Sorry. Sorry. Go on."

"She had a run in with a badger, now her face is swollen."

"Is she grizzly, polar, or black?"

"Actually, she's wolfdog."

"Ohhh!" And he could hear the excitement in Dr. Luntz's voice. Not surprising when she only handled bears and foxes on a daily basis that she would find the hybrids fascinating. "A wolf-dog? Really? Well, well. Now that *is* interesting. Okay. First, tell me what you see. Lacerations? Bites? What?"

Bo moved the icepack again, trying not to cringe this time. "Her face has definite bite marks." He lowered the icepack and checked the areas of her body he could see. "And scratches on her hands. She seemed to have attempted to put up some kind of weak, sad little fight."

Blayne gave him the finger while Dr. Luntz giggled. "Bold Novikov, stop that. Now, what's swelling on her?"

"Just her face."

"Around the bites?"

"Yes."

"Wolfdog, right? Has she had her rabies shots?"

Bo tapped Blayne's shoulder. "Did you have your rabies shots?"

"Yes. I've had all my shots."

"Yes. She's had all her shots."

"Excellent. Then she probably just has an infection. Badgers are nasty little bastards, you know."

"Should I take her to a hospital?"

"No, I don't think that'll be necessary. What she needs is antibiotics and sleep. I can call in a script for you. She will need to take half the pills as soon as you get them, followed by at least three eight-ounce glasses of water. She'll sleep then. It'll probably look like a coma, but she'll just be sleeping. If she wakes up in three hours, she's clear. Give her the rest of the pills and she'll be right as rain by sunup. If she doesn't wake up within four to five hours—take her to one of our hospitals."

"Okay."

"Don't worry, Bo. I'm sure she'll be fine. Hybrids have amazing immune systems as you well know."

"I'll e-mail you the info for a local pharmacy that's run by a leopard. So no worries about dosage."

"Excellent. I'll need her weight, height, age, and wolf breed, also."

"Her wolf breed?"

"Gray wolf," Blayne piped up. To be honest, he'd thought she'd already passed out. "Daddy's a gray wolf. And my metabolism is sixteen times that of other wolf shifters."

"Oh, my," Dr. Luntz said, overhearing the conversation. "That is *fascinating*."

"I'm glad we're entertaining you."

"Very funny. Get me the rest of the info and I'll write her a script based on that. And I'm so glad you called, Bold, even if it was for your sick friend. Now maybe you can get around to calling your uncle."

"Phones go both ways."

"I swear," she sighed out. "You two."

"Bye, Dr. Luntz."

"Bye, Bold. Take care of yourself."

He disconnected the call and quickly began texting her the rest of Blayne's info.

"What's your weight?" he asked.

"I'll die before I tell you that," Blayne muttered.

Not in the mood to argue, Bo put his phone in his mouth—not hygienic but necessary—and lifted Blayne up. He raised her up and down a few times to get a good read on her weight, then placed her back down and finished texting Dr. Luntz that and the pharmacy information. Once done, he called into the pharmacy to give them a heads up and to make sure they could have the meds delivered right away. Everything handled, he sat on the floor beside the couch. Blayne was sleeping now, but she made small whimpering sounds and frowned deeply, which told him she was in pain. He touched the icepack and realized it was no longer cold. Hoping she had another one in her freezer, he picked up the pack and stood. That's when he took a good long look at the pit she had the nerve to call a home.

"How does she live like this?" he asked the air, and that's when he immediately decided she *couldn't* live like this.

Chapter 11

Blayne slept hard. So hard, she only remembered someone waking her once to shove several big pills down her throat, followed by an attempt at drowning her. The next time she woke up, she felt much better and was starving.

Yawning, she sat up and stretched. Her migraine was gone, her face no longer felt ten times bigger than her entire body, and she could now see out of both eyes. It was still dark out, but she had no clue what time it was. She glanced at her watch, but quickly remembered it didn't work. Okay, so Bo was right about *that*. She did need a new watch . . . a task she'd get around to eventually.

She stood and headed to the bathroom, her need to pee overriding her need to eat. She took care of that, washed her hands, and walked back into the living room. That's when she stopped and gawked.

"What . . . wait . . . where's . . . uh . . ."

"Are you well enough to be up?"

Blayne looked over her shoulder. Bo Novikov stood in her kitchen doorway. He was actually kind of stooping a bit because he was too tall for her doorways. To be honest, she'd forgotten he'd come over. Questions like why and how did he know where she lived in Brooklyn faded away as it hit her that she hadn't been robbed by very neat thieves.

She pointed at her living room. "What did you do?"

"Cleaned up. Looks much better, don't you think?"

Blayne walked farther into the living room. "Where's all my stuff?"

"You mean all that trash?"

Blayne faced the insolent beast in her apartment. "Trash? Did you call my stuff *trash*?"

"Isn't it?"

"No! It's not trash. It's my stuff!"

"Which was trash."

Annoyed by his calm but self-righteous attitude, Blayne pointed an accusing finger. "You threw it out, didn't you?"

"Well—"

"Because *you* think it was trash. But it wasn't trash. It was *my* stuff."

"Blayne—"

"Mine!" she bellowed. "Not yours. *Mine, mine, mine!*"

"Blayne—"

"Who do you think you are? Coming into *my* apartment? Taking *my* shit! Throwing *my* shit out!"

At this point, Blayne was good and frothy, but when Bo rolled his eyes at her and let out some kind of soul-weary, put-upon sigh, she'd had enough!

"*Out!*" she barked. "Get out of my house! *Now!*" She turned to make the short trip over to the front door so she could dramatically throw it open, but he caught hold of her sweatshirt and swung her around. For a brief moment, she thought he was about to pummel her, but instead of spinning her around to face him, he spun her around to face the wall behind the couch. The wall with the bookcases she'd originally tossed stuff up onto when she was unpacking and had been meaning to reorganize once she had a chance. Sadly, that "chance" had never made an appearance.

Not only had the three sets of floor-to-ceiling bookshelves been reorganized, but all the books and magazines Blayne had laying on the floor were now on the bookshelves. And not only were the items organized alphabetically, they were organized alphabetically by author within subgroups that were broken down by topic. And yeah, the topics were also in alphabetical order. He'd even found time to do a makeshift binding of her magazines by year and label them so she knew which magazine they were without having to pull them down and look.

"Oh," she said. "Oh, that's nice—eek!"

He swung her around again and this time she faced the kitchen. The spotless kitchen with all the dishes, pots, and pans put away, the counter and stovetop scrubbed clean, and the four bags of trash she'd been meaning to throw in the Dumpster downstairs for the past two weeks finally gone. And she was sure, if she wanted to, she could *eat* off that kitchen floor.

"Wow—"

Another swing and she was looking into her bedroom. All the clothes that had been on the floor were now in the hamper—*I have a hamper?*—and the pile of clean clothes she had in her laundry basket were gone, leading her to believe they'd been folded and put in her chest of drawers. A few had been hung up and put in her closet, which had also been organized, the clothes aligned by size. The shoes, sneakers, and boots she'd tossed into the bottom of her closet—and then spent an hour every morning trying to find a matching pair—were organized on the closet floor. First her work boots, then her sneakers, then her skates, and finally a very small row of dress shoes and heels.

Okay, so he hadn't thrown everything out in a fit of manly I-know-what's-good-for-you-ism but, instead, he'd merely organized all her crap so that she had a clean apartment and actually knew that her carpet was a festive plum color. And he'd managed to do all that in a few hours.

Blayne briefly gnawed her bottom lip, much like that badger had gnawed on her face, but she knew she couldn't avoid it. She had to apologize and say thank you. All in the same sentence preferably. To Bo Novikov.

Suck it up, Thorpe. He's done in four hours what would have taken you three years and an official threat from National Health Services.

Taking in a deep breath, "Bo—"

That's when he swung her around again. Now she was staring at the small dining table that was in her living room because she didn't really have a dining room. Of course, even if she had a dining room, she wouldn't have used the table to eat on because usually it was covered with old and new bills, business paper-work she'd been promising for a month—*or was it two?*—to get finished for Gwen, and the empty family photo album and box of family photos she'd been trying to put together since she'd moved in for her dad's upcoming birthday. Yet all that stuff was neatly piled and arranged on a side table—the urgent bills in their scary pink envelopes right on top of everything with a large piece of paper that had written on it, "Pay these now!" taped across—so those things weren't completely out of sight, which meant they would not be out of mind.

So what was on the table now? Dinner plates and glasses—*I remember those plates and glasses!*—chopsticks, and a rather large quantity of Chinese food from her favorite twenty-four-hour place on the corner.

"Oh . . . wow. I—"

And that's when she heard her front door slam shut.

Blayne cringed and looked over her shoulder. And yeah. She was completely alone. "Dammit!"

Bo was at his truck when he stopped, his head lifting. He sniffed the air and snarled when he realized it was wolf he smelled. She-wolf. Already in a bad mood, he turned toward the scent coming from an alley across the street, but before he could go find out why a She-wolf was lurking around Blayne's apartment, Blayne leaped in front of him, her arms outstretched, her legs straddling the curb. He knew it was her rather pathetic attempt at blocking him from going any farther.

Considering she couldn't fight off a badger, Bo had to admire her moxy.

"I'm sorry," she said. "I'm sorry, I'm sorry, I'm sorry!"

To be honest, he didn't expect her to apologize. At least not right away. And if she did apologize, he didn't expect her to mean it. But she did mean it. He could tell.

"Please don't go," she begged. "I was a total bitch. I know. And I'm sorry."

If she could be an adult about this, then so could he. "And I'm sorry if I freaked you out. I was only trying to help."

"I know. I know." She pressed her hands on his chest and, um, that felt awfully nice. "And I really appreciate it. I just freaked out because one time me and my dad got into it about my 'pig sty' as he liked to call it. And he threw out all my shit. With me standing there! I was fourteen at the time, but I'm sensing now that I've never recovered from the trauma of that event."

Bo wanted to laugh, but he knew she was serious. "He just threw it out?"

"According to him he didn't have time for my lazy ass to shift into motion and do what I needed to do, which meant now, not later, and not when I felt like it. *You hear me, little miss?*" she demanded in a much lower and bellowing voice, most likely imitating her father.

Bo cleared his throat, held back a smile. "Your old man wasn't a Marine, was he?"

Her smile was resigned but still loving. "Navy."

"I figured. My uncle was a Marine. He raised me after my parents died. I recognized the . . . uh . . . tone."

"That explains everything," she said with a rush of cheeriness he'd never seen from any predator before in his life. "Military parents or guardians raise two types of kids. Either the super-orderly kid, which is you. Or the rebellious messy one, which is me."

"So I'm boring?"

"I didn't say that!"

"But you're the rebel and I'm the orderly one."

"Yes. But I bet you can find whatever you need whenever you need it."

"This is true. Which I guess explains why I kept finding four or five packages of the same products lying around?"

She cringed. "You mean like plastic sandwich bags?"

"You had sixteen boxes of those. Most of them unopened or with only a few baggies used."

The cringing grew worse. "Dammit!"

Chuckling and relieved she'd simply forgotten about those bags and wasn't using them for some kind of illegal-drug business, Bo asked, "Did you take the rest of the antibiotics? You need to take the rest of them now that you're up."

She peered up at him with those gorgeous brown eyes. "I'll take 'em, if you come back with me and have some of that Chinese food that I am *dying* to eat. I'm starving," she whispered.

"And if I don't come back in with you?"

"I don't take the meds and then the infection returns, I die a horrible and sad death in my spotless apartment, and it'll be all on your head."

"You really go there, don't you?"

"I do. Can't help myself." She grabbed his forearm with both her hands. "You can't let me die all by myself because I was an impossible bitch."

"When you put it like that . . ."

"Chinese food," she reminded him. "Who can resist the allure of the mighty Chinese food? I know I can't. Why should you?"

How could he turn her down? Especially when she was so damn cute?

"All right. But the dumplings are mine. I'm not sharing."

"Rude and stingy," she said, tugging on his arm until he began to walk, letting her lead him inside. "But I'll let you off the hook this time."

"That's very big of you," he said dryly, making Blayne laugh.

Using the dining table as a dining table lasted all of two minutes before Blayne couldn't stand feeling so constricted and quickly set up the living room floor for an impromptu picnic. Bo didn't complain, but he seemed baffled by it.

"I don't like constrictions," she'd explained. If he understood, she couldn't tell because he simply stared at her before grabbing his wonton soup and taking it over to the blanket she'd laid out.

To be honest, Blayne wasn't sure how a meal would go with Bo Novikov. It was one thing to spend time with him when she was training since most of the conversation involved him telling her what to do. But dinner conversation required a back-and-forth Blayne adored, and it often dictated who became her long-term friends and who she only saw when she happened to pass them on the street. Until now, Blayne had been pretty certain that Bo would end up in the "happened to pass him" pool. He didn't do much that didn't involve hockey, so what exactly would they talk about? Her living room floor seemed an excellent place for a meal because her remote control and twenty-seven-inch plasma was right there for emergency viewing should the silence grow painful.

After two hours, she hadn't reached for the remote once.

"This," she said, handing over the picture, "is my mom."

Bo's smile was wide, his laugh genuine. "Your mom is rockin' the 'fro."

Blayne made her little rock-and-roll sign—that the nuns called devil's horns—with both hands, pinky and index fingers up, middle and ring fingers down and held by thumbs. "Damn right she did. She used to call it her dog mane, which annoyed every lion in a ten-mile hearing range."

"How come you don't work the 'fro?"

"Because my hair grows out like Pippy Longstocking, which is not a look that works for me." She motioned with her hands. "Okay. Your turn. You got a picture of your parents?"

"Yeah." Rolling his eyes like the big geek he was, Bo pulled out his wallet and slipped the small picture out, handing it to her.

The Asian female was almost an atypical lioness, her unblinking gold stare capturing the camera's eye, the small smirk on her full lips appearing mocking and dangerous at the same time. Her cheekbones sharp and her nose wide and rather flat, like her son's. And who was brave enough to cuddle up next to her? The white-haired polar bear with bright brown eyes and an adorable smile standing behind her. Bo's genetic makeup was clearly a fifty-fifty mix of his parents, but he obviously favored the bear side. Not that Blayne could blame him since it was the bears who'd taken him in, who had raised him.

"They look happy."

"They were mostly. They argued a lot, but I think they liked to argue a lot."

"For some couples that really works." She asked what she'd been wondering for a while, "What happened?"

Bo shrugged those massive shoulders. "Drunk driver caused a pileup on the freeway. We were in the first few cars, and Dad didn't hit his brakes in time and the cars behind us didn't, either."

"You were with them?"

He nodded. "In the backseat. All I remember is the sound of grinding brakes and then metal on metal—then I woke up in the hospital. A couple days later my uncle came and got me, and we buried my parents a few days after that in Maine."

Blayne didn't tell him she was sorry; she knew he didn't want to hear it.

"What about your mom?" he asked.

"She was hunted."

Bo turned, his arm resting against her couch rather than his back, his bright blue eyes focused on her. "What?"

"Daddy was stationed in Japan at the time, and Mom was in London. She was a translator for the Embassy."

"Where were you?"

Her eyes crossed. "With the *family* in Georgia. My dad's family. They never really took to me, although Mom tried to make that happen. I was supposed to be there for the summer."

"Do you know what happened?"

"Not really. Daddy won't discuss it, and one uncle that got good and drunk and tried to tell me about it after the funeral—not realizing Daddy was right behind him—found out that tire irons to the head . . . really do hurt."

Bo chuckled. "Don't feel bad. My aunts missed my parents'

funeral but did make it in time to demand the return of their mother's jewelry."

"Rude."

"And stupid. Mom was welcome in town because she came with Dad. I was welcome because I'm half bear. But full She-lions strolling into Ursus County? That's all kinds of stupid. The sows had a field day."

"I have always wanted to go to an all-bear town," Blayne sighed.

"Why?"

"I don't know. I keep thinking the streets would be flowing with honey and the streams with salmon."

"Grizzlies aren't the only ones who live there, ya know. I'm not a big honey fan."

"How can you not like honey? How can anyone not like honey? That's crazy talk!"

"Even though you *know* what grizzlies are, you still think of them as cute teddy bears, don't you?"

"I do."

Bo began to shake his head but ended up yawning.

"I've kept you up too late."

"Nah." He glanced at his watch, eyes going wide. "Okay. Maybe a little. I better go."

"Sleep here."

The way his whole body tensed and he didn't look at her made Blayne realize how that probably sounded.

"On the couch," she quickly added.

They both looked at the oversized loveseat she kept telling people was a couch. "It is a tad small, huh?"

"It'll be fine. But I need to be up at five thirty. I have that breakfast with my agent at six fifteen."

Blayne jumped up and ran into her room, quickly programming her digital alarm clock. She checked it twice, headed back to the living room, ran back and checked it again. She wanted to make sure she would not be the cause of him being late to any meetings.

"All done," she said, walking back out with a pillow and several blankets. He took the pillow and stared at the blankets. "Oh. I turn the heat down at night, so my bill's not so high."

"Thank you, 'cause I'm melting right now."

"Oh! I'm sorry. Right . . . polar."

He dropped the pillow on the couch. "Don't worry. Polar shifters can adjust to any temperature if we have to; we're just more comfortable in the cold."

"Well, no worries. I'll turn the heat down and there's ice water or whatever in the fridge."

"I know. I cleaned the fridge out. It's like you had experiments going on in some of that Tupperware."

"Are we back to that?" she asked, using one of Gwen's favorite sayings. "Really?"

"I'm just saying if you took care of those things on a weekly basis—"

"Sha-sha-sha." She covered his face with the blankets. "Don't make me hate you."

"I thought you liked me," he said around the blankets, so she lowered them since they didn't seem to be quite effective.

"I do." She leaned in, using her "fierce" expression. "But that can change on a dime, mister."

Seemingly unimpressed with her fierceness—and she'd worked hard on that look for years!—he said, "I'll keep that in mind."

"See you in the morning," she said after turning down the heat as much as she dared without risking hypothermia for herself.

"Night, Blayne."

Blayne closed her bedroom door and quickly changed into thermal underwear, sweatpants, sweatshirt, and extra thick wool socks. She loaded up her bed with blankets and burrowed beneath them.

And, as she sat in the dark, and stared out her window at the brick building next door, it suddenly occurred to her that she had a guy she didn't know very well asleep in her living room—and that she'd never felt safer.

That night, Blayne fell asleep smiling.

Chapter 12

Bo's eyes opened exactly at five twenty-five a.m., but unlike most days when he woke up five minutes before his alarm went off . . . things were different. Not "I'm staying in a hotel due to an out-of-town game" different but "there's a wolfdog clinging to me" different.

Without moving his body, Bo studied where he was, which would be the floor. He didn't normally sleep on the floor, but he was definitely on the floor. He was also fully clothed, as was Blayne. In fact, she had on so many clothes, he felt confident in ruling out a wild night of sexual abandon that he couldn't remember.

A good thing, too, since Bo liked remembering past sexual encounters. Less chance of the awkward morning-after moment where one doesn't remember his or her partner's name.

Still, none of that explained why he was sleeping on the floor with Blayne . . . or why they were cuddling.

It was definitely cuddling, too. He had his arms around her and she had her head buried in his chest. They were on their side, facing each other, so he'd wrapped one leg around hers. He'd had sex with women and still never woke up in this position before. He didn't mind waking up this way, it was just not knowing how they got here that was worrying him.

An alarm went off in the bedroom and Blayne groaned, drew her arm back, and slapped Bo right in the face.

Lying there, wondering what he'd done to deserve that, Blayne snarled and said, "Off!" Then she hit him again. When that didn't seem to shut off the alarm that was in another room, Blayne lifted her head. Her eyes blinked wide when she saw him.

"Oh, God . . . was that you I hit?"

"Twice."

"Oh. Oh! I'm so . . ." Then she burst out laughing.

Unable to take the sound of that damn alarm clock anymore, Bo pulled away from Blayne and stood. He went into her bedroom and turned it off. Letting out a sigh, he went back to the living room. And, yeah, she was still laughing.

"Get up," he said. "Get showered, get dressed. We'll go into the city together." He reached down and lifted her off the floor. "The longer you take, the more you're screwing with my schedule."

"Okay, okay. No need to get snippy." She reached up again, and Bo immediately moved away from her, which only made her laugh more. "I wasn't going to hit you again. I promise. And I am sorry about your face. Really." She slid her palm across his cheek. "Did I hurt you?"

"Only my feelings."

She laughed again, leaning into him.

"It wasn't that funny," he complained, even while he enjoyed making her laugh. "Now go get dressed. Time." He tapped his watch for emphasis.

"Okay, okay."

A half hour later, after Bo had pushed and prodded the woman to have some purpose in her step, they got into his truck.

"Is this thing even legal?"

"It's not like I can fit into a two-door Ferrari."

"But I feel like I'm in a military transport plane."

"Don't talk to me in the mornings," he told her. "Not until I get some ice time. Or, at the very least, coffee."

Bo pulled into traffic, and they drove in silence for a while until he heard himself ask, "Can you explain to me how we ended up on the floor . . . snuggling?"

"Sure, I can explain it," she said with that natural cheeriness she had at all hours of the day. He now understood why he'd known she was sicker than she was letting on the night before. She'd been surly, rude, and intolerant. In other words, she'd been acting like every other predator he'd known, but she hadn't been acting like Blayne.

He waited for her to explain what happened, but she kept smiling and staring out the window.

"Can you explain it to me before the end of this millennium?"

"Of course!"

Again Bo waited and again nothing.

Yeah. She was a Navy brat all right. She had the malicious obedience so ingrained in her system, she didn't even realize when she was doing it.

Taking a breath and wishing he'd had some coffee, Bo tried a different tack. "You and me, snuggling on the floor . . . explain it. Now."

"I was thirsty."

Man, she was good. But Bo was determined and raised by a Marine. He could handle this.

He could handle *her*.

"You were thirsty . . . so you came out of your room for a glass of water."

"Right!"

"And you saw me lying there . . ."

"On the couch. You looked uncomfortable. All balled up."

"It was too small."

"It's a loveseat," she reminded him.

"Right. So to help me be more comfortable you . . ."

"Rolled you onto the floor."

Bo waited to turn at a corner. "Did I wake up?"

"Sort of. You kind of snarled. I thought you might maul me."

"So to calm me down you . . ."

"Petted your shoulder and said, 'It's okay. It's me.'"

"And I . . ."

"Smiled and grabbed me around the waist. Did you know you have a really nice smile?"

"Thank you."

"You should use it more often."

"I'll keep that in mind. So after I grabbed you, I . . ."

"Wouldn't let go. And I was tired anyway, and you were so warm and comfortable that I just curled up next to you and went to sleep."

Bo pulled into the underground parking garage of the sports center. He parked in his reserved spot and cut off the engine.

"You have your own parking spot?" she demanded, suddenly not so cheery.

"Yep."

"How is that fair?"

"It's fair because it's to my benefit. If it wasn't, then it would be unfair. Now let's go, I've got to meet him in the managers' restaurant upstairs."

They got out of the truck, and Bo remotely released the rear door so they could grab their bags. He looked at his watch, grimaced.

"You get to go to the managers' restaurant?"

"Can't you?"

When she only scowled at him, he decided discussing it further was to no one's benefit.

Together they walked to the elevators that would take them to the main floor. From there they would take the stairs to the first floor of the shifter-only part of the building deep under the city streets. It was a lot of ups, downs, and sideways, but necessary to protect who they were.

They stepped into the elevator, and Bo pushed the button for the main floor. His foot tapped as the elevator slowly creaked closed.

"Are you always like this?" she asked.

He didn't ask her what she meant because he already knew. "Yes."

"You'll be dead before you're forty."

"The great excuse for every lazy ass I've ever known."

"We're not talking about my issues with time."

"Of course not."

"We're not even talking about your issues with time. We're talking about your . . . intensity."

"My intensity, as you call it, is what makes me the player I am."

"Except you don't seem like you're having any fun."

"Fun? It's a job."

"A job you hate?"

"No."

"Then it should be fun. Otherwise what's the point?"

"What's the point? Millions of dollars and the freedom to do what I want."

"That sounds *great*!" she cheered. "Which would have much more impact if you weren't getting tense and being an asshole because there's the slimmest of chances you might be late to a breakfast meeting with your agent."

"Wouldn't it be rude for me to be late?"

"Well—"

"And don't you hate rude people?"

She sniffed a little. "Touché, Monsieur Bear-cat."

"Do not start calling me that."

"I think it's cute!"

"No."

"Whatever. So when was the last time you went on vacation?"

"Vacation?"

"You know? To someplace relaxing and fun, where work has nothing to do with it?"

"When?"

"Yeah. When was the last time you went on vacation?"

"Never."

Blayne moved in front of him. "What do you mean never? You've *never* been on vacation? Ever?"

"That's often what never means. But I travel a lot for business meetings and stuff. That counts."

"No. It doesn't."

"It does to me. Now can we drop it?"

The elevator doors opened and she jumped out. "Fine. I'm going to practice."

He watched her walk off—in the wrong direction. Her skates were hanging from her half-closed bag, threatening to fall out and be lost forever; the shoelaces on her right sneaker were untied; and she had a piece of blue duct tape randomly stuck to her jacket and a piece of white duct tape stuck to the back of her black cargo pants.

It suddenly hit him that he was not only sexually attracted to this mess of a wolfdog with bad time management skills, but he really liked her. More than he liked almost anyone.

Bo stepped out of the elevator and waited. Sure enough, Blayne stopped, looked around, threw up her hands, and spun back toward him. "Wrong way!" she laughed as she marched by him. "I swear, if the head wasn't attached . . ."

He grabbed her backpack before she could shoot past. "Come on."

"Where?"

"With me. You haven't had breakfast. Your blood sugar will drop on you after ten minutes. I don't want to find you sobbing again."

"That was *one time*! Why do you have to keep bringing it up?"

Ric, busy butchering a gazelle for the day's lunch special, stepped back, the bone saw in his hand. "Badger?" he asked the She-wolf standing on the other side of the island in the middle of his recently redesigned restaurant kitchen.

Dee-Ann shrugged.

Placing the saw down, Ric quickly washed his hands and then went to one of the steel refrigerators they had in the restaurant's kitchen. He pulled out a tray of fresh fruit and grabbed a basket of croissants he'd brought in with him. He put that in front of Dee where she leaned against the counter.

"Ya always try and feed me."

"You look tired. And your jeans are falling off."

"I got a belt."

"She-wolves shouldn't be emaciated." He gave her several napkins. "Eat."

She did eat and studied her phone. Ric went back to his gazelle.

"Did she go to the hospital again?" he asked, removing a leg.

"Nope. Gwen wrestled that badger off her." She shook her head. "I swear, that badger went after your teacup poodle like she owed it money."

Ric laughed, and Dee went on. "Gwen cleaned her up and they finished the job, went to two others, and then headed back to the office, and then she went home. I thought she'd head out to the sports center, but she didn't. Then Novikov showed up."

Stopping in midswing, Ric looked over his shoulder at Dee. "What?"

"You heard me."

"Bo Novikov was at her apartment last night?"

"Yep. He tried leavin', too, but she came runnin' after him just like a puppy, beggin' him to stay. Kind of sad, really. When a man says no, he usually means no."

"When did he leave?"

"Not before Keith showed up to take over so I could come over here, which I guess would mean he was in there all night." She chewed on a piece of fruit before adding, "Yep. Alllll night long."

No. Ric didn't like the sound of that at all.

Bernie Lawman checked his watch again. In the ten years he'd been the agent for Bo Novikov, not once had Bernie ever arrived *before* the hybrid—like he did today. And Novikov had never been late, but it was six thirty-one. That was late. Late for Bo

Novikov. Pulling his phone out, he'd only punched in nine-one-one, when Novikov rushed up to their private table in the back of the members-only club restaurant in the sports center. You had to be a member or friends with a member to get in—and yes, it was something Bernie took great delight in lauding over his family members that none of them had access.

"Sorry I'm late," Bo told him as he dropped his duffel bag off to the side. "It's her fault."

That's when Bernie noticed her. It wasn't the first time some female had tagged along with Bo to one of their breakfast meetings, but it was usually a well-dressed feline Bernie had just seen on the cover of some international fashion magazine. And although this female was pretty, her wardrobe left a lot to be desired and she'd never end up on the cover of any magazine with those thighs. Except maybe one of those weightlifter or running mags.

"Two minutes," she argued with Bo. "You're two minutes late. Not two hours. Such a drama bear!"

She dismissed him with a wave and started to walk off, but Bo grabbed the back of her pack and pulled her over to the table. "You're gonna eat."

"I'm not hungry."

When he only stared at her, she said, "Fine. I'll eat." She pulled off her pack and dropped into the chair. She smiled at Bernie. "Hiya. I'm Blayne."

"Bernie Lawman."

"Nice to meet you."

The waitress came over to take their orders. After Bo and Bernie put in theirs and while the canine put in hers, Bernie motioned to Bo. They leaned in close, and Bernie asked, "What's going on?"

"I want to make sure she eats."

Giggling a little, Bernie said, "Didn't I always teach you to pay them and get rid of them *before* breakfast?"

It was a joke Bernie had tossed at Bo before, usually getting him one of the hybrid's blank stares, but this time the brows lowered and the colors of his eyes flickered from blue to gold the tiniest bit, making Bernie's giggle a hell of a lot worse.

"Did you just call her a whore?" Bo asked, and Bernie knew the guy was serious. Deadly serious.

"I prefer courtesan," the canine cut in, distracting both males. They glanced over and she was buttering up a piece of bread. "It sounds much more romantic, don't you think?"

"You're not my courtesan," Bo argued.

"Well, it's better than being your whore." She leaned in and whispered, "Whore implies you can't get laid without an active credit card or cash. Courtesan implies villas and champagne provided by your vast wealth. You want a courtesan."

"I do not—why are we arguing about this?"

"I didn't think we were arguing." She held the slice of bread up to his mouth.

"What? You're feeding me now?"

"Isn't that what courtesans do?"

"You're trying to irritate me."

"Not really hard when you're being such a cranky ass." She ended up eating the bread herself.

In the end, Bernie didn't mind the wolfdog's presence. Not when she had the singular ability to keep Bo Novikov from ripping Bernie's head off.

When a phone began to ring, both males looked at Blayne, but she only gazed back. Finally, Bo asked, "Do you really think I'd have 'Wake Me Up Before You Go-Go' as my ringtone?"

"Oh! That's Jess's ring." She pulled that mountain climbing–size backpack onto her lap and proceeded to dig through it, dropping all sorts of items on the table while she searched.

"I just organized that for you," Bo snarled.

"Don't start. I know it's in here somewhere. Ah-ha!" She held up the phone triumphantly. "Told ya."

"What do you have the side pockets for, if you're not going to use them?"

She waved him off and answered her phone. "Jess? Hey. What's up?"

The waitress returned with their food, staring at the junk-covered table. Bo grabbed the wolfdog's bag and carefully placed all the items inside, giving the waitress the much needed room for all their food.

The wolfdog didn't even seem to notice, diving into her double order of waffles, ham, and bacon while grunting in answer to whoever was on the phone until she suddenly asked, "I don't understand, Jess, is there shit backing up into your tub?"

Scrambled eggs dripping with ketchup and hot sauce, hovering near his mouth, Bernie glanced over at Bo, but he was still organizing the wolfdog's bag, shaking his head, and making that disgusted noise he often did with rookie players.

"So it's not your tub? Or that's already fixed? There's shit backing up in your sink? What?"

Bernie glanced around, and not surprisingly since the room was filled with predators who had above-average hearing, everyone was scowling at them.

"Well, don't cry, sweetie. I'll fix it. Just let me finish my breakfast. Jess, I've gotta eat. Apparently it's an order. Okay, sobbing over a backed-up sink seems excessive." The wolfdog briefly leaned away from the phone. "And the raging isn't better. So you just calm down right now, missy! Okay." The wolfdog grinned. "Love you, too!"

She disconnected the call and went back to eating. Bo placed the bag against her chair, sighing heavily. "Is there a reason you have a Boba Fett action figure in your bag? Is there a use for it other than more goddamn clutter?"

"I don't know which will upset you more," she replied. "Telling you it's nothing but clutter or confessing that I often take it out and play 'I am Boba Fett' when I don't think anyone can see me."

Her phone rang again. This time the tune was Adam and the Ants' "Dog Eat Dog."

"Christ, it's Phil. She must be freaking them out. I've gotta go." She chugged back her orange juice, put the rest of her bacon and ham on her last remaining Belgian waffle, folded the waffle, and stuffed it into the linen napkin. "I'll bring the napkin back later after practice tonight. See ya!" She grabbed her backpack and charged out of the restaurant, only to return two minutes later, diving into Bo's lap and throwing her arms around his neck.

"Did I thank you?" she asked.

"Not really."

"Well, I promise I'll *totally* get around to it."

"No you won't. You'll forget and leave me hanging."

"I may forget to say the words, but I never forget when someone covers my ass." She hugged him, and to Bernie's surprise, Bo hugged her back. "I'll see you later." She kissed his cheek and took off again, dashing around the bustling wait staff with ease.

"She's a derby girl, isn't she?"

"Yep."

Bernie could tell by the way she moved. "She hugged you, and you didn't push her off you."

"Nope."

"Are you going to invite me to the wedding?"

"After calling her a whore, I'm thinking no."

"I thought we agreed on courtesan?"

Chapter 13

Blayne pulled out the shredded doll from the pipe and shimmied out from under the sink.

"Found your culprit." She handed the remnants over to Jess.

Eyes narrow, the wild dog shook the doll. "Damn kids!"

Blayne got to her feet and pulled off her gloves. She quickly put her arm around Jess's shoulder and hugged her close. "It's okay. I'll take care of it. By the time I'm done, your plumbing will sing. Arias. Now just breathe. Breathe. Now."

Jess let out a puff of air, but eventually, normal breathing did commence.

"There. All better." Blayne plucked the shredded toy from Jess's grip. "We'll just toss this." She walked across the enormous kitchen to the trash can. She stepped on the peddle, lifting the top, and asked, "How about some hot chocolate?"

"I had to lay off the chocolate."

Blayne froze, the toy still trapped in her hand. "Pardon?"

"I had to lay off chocolate. Doctor's orders. Until the baby's born. Caffeine's not good for 'em and the doc wants to make sure she can tolerate chocolate. Apparently there are some issues with wolfdogs and chocolate?"

Blayne swallowed, her hand trembling. "Uh . . . sometimes. Like full canines, some wolfdogs don't handle chocolate well."

Dropping the toy into the trash, Blayne quickly searched out exits in the room, should she have to make a run for it. There were few things that truly scared her, but a wild dog without chocolate was no different—or less deadly—than a starving grizzly.

And a *pregnant* wild dog? *Oy.*

Blayne's father still had scars on his back from what he referred to as "Your mother's sudden distaste for my red beans and rice."

"What about you?" Jess asked, and Blayne realized that the female now stood beside her.

Swallowing, "What about me?"

"Can you eat chocolate?"

Blayne licked her lips. They were so dry now. "Uh . . . I can. But my problem is sugar. Too much of it, with my metabolism and all . . . not a good thing."

The wild dog stepped closer until the only thing separating them was Jess's giant stomach. "Uh-huh."

Blayne instinctively kept her eyes on the ceiling or on the floor or anywhere that wasn't in or near Jess's cold gaze and did what she always did with her dad when things got really tense between them. She said, "I love you, Jess."

A lot quicker than her dad ever reacted to it, Jess replied, "Awww. I love you, too, Blayne." She threw her arms around Blayne and hugged her tight. Blayne let out a silent relieved breath, and that's when she saw Jess's friends standing in the backyard, watching the females through the kitchen window.

Blayne mouthed, "Get in here!" And got back quick shakes of four heads. "Now!"

Rolling their eyes and sighing, the wusses headed to the sliding glass doors in the back of the house and Jess pulled back and smiled up at Blayne, seconds before she burst into tears.

Bo finished his drills. They were the same drills he'd been practicing since he was five years old and his father put his first hockey stick in his hands. He did more repetitions now than he did then, but he still did them and it was the one thing out of his schedule that he knew he couldn't bypass. A situation he'd had to evaluate since his usual daily non-game-day schedule had been destroyed because of Blayne Thorpe.

He'd also come to the conclusion that Blayne was a vortex. A black hole where schedules and basic time management were lost forever.

Not only did she destroy her own schedules, but she destroyed the schedules of others. In fact for the first time since, from his high chair, Bo had pointed at the clock in his parents' kitchen and silently indicated to his astonished mother that she was late with his breakfast, had Bo not been aware of time. It was something internal, something that he could do without much thought. It was like he could feel the tick-tick of a clock inside him, giving him a down-to-the-second idea of what time it was. That is, until he'd spent time in the Blayne vortex.

In retrospect, perhaps it was a good thing she'd run away from him that first time they'd met. If he'd gotten trapped in her vortex at nineteen, he may have not gotten out of the minor league. Instead he'd still be "No Name" Novikov, playing for some barely-paying-me-enough-for-my-seal-steaks team instead of where he was today.

It was definitely something to keep in mind if he was going to continue spending time with Blayne. Maybe he needed to limit his time with her like some guys needed to limit their time with alcohol. "I'll only see Blayne Friday and Saturday, so I can sleep in on Sunday to get over my hangover." Or, in this case, Blayne-over.

The thought made Bo snort to himself as he skated over to the bench where he'd put his towel and a couple of gallons of water, slowing down as he reached it.

He blinked at the wolf watching him, holding out a towel. "You practice every day like that?"

"Don't you?" Bo asked the wolf who'd hired him. Van Holtz wasn't a bad goalie, but he could always be better. He had a lot of potential.

"No," Van Holtz replied. "I don't."

"Explaining so much," Bo muttered while pulling off his helmet. He grabbed a gallon of water, bent over at the waist, and dumped half of it over his head. He stood tall and did a once-over shake, making sure to saturate Van Holtz in the process.

Raking his hand through his wet hair, Bo smiled at Van Holtz. "There. Much better."

The wolf did his own mini-shake, wolf eyes glaring.

"Is there a reason you're here, Van Holtz?" Bo asked. "Shouldn't you be mixing a sauce or creating a fondue or something?"

"I'm here about Blayne."

Bo picked up another gallon of water and took a swig. He swished the water around his mouth, then spit it out at the wolf's feet. The wolf didn't even budge. "What about her?"

"She's a very good friend of mine. Like a sister."

"And?"

"Must we really discuss your reputation in detail?"

Although Bo's game reputation was nearly close to fact, his personal one was a joke. If he'd done half the things he was accused of, he'd never get any practice in. He definitely wouldn't be able to keep up with his schedule. An annoyance many of his past lovers had been unable to overlook. Bo used to wonder where all the stories came from and then it dawned on him it was probably from Bernie, but he didn't really care enough one way or another about it. If people wanted to believe that crap that was on them. If they didn't, also on them. It didn't matter to him.

Yet, for the first time, it did matter to him because this was Blayne. And what Bo didn't need was some sanctimonious tail-chaser acting like he had to protect Blayne from the big bad Marauder. Did this little runt think he was going to warn Bo off? Push him away from Blayne so that . . . what? He could have his shot at her? Was that what all this was about? A way for this canine to get his grubby, flea-infested paws on Blayne by acting like her protective hero/guard dog?

Even worse, now Bo couldn't get the thought of Blayne with some ball-licker out of his mind. That's when Bo felt that unmistakable itch at his hairline, and he knew from that and the way the runt took a step away that his mane was growing. It was a rare occurrence and something unique to him because of his mixed blood. But the idiot had woken up the lion male that had been characteristically sleeping during Bo's daily training session, and now Van Holtz would just have to deal with it . . .

It was the cherry pie that saved them all. Jess couldn't have chocolate, but she could have many non-chocolate baked goods like cakes and pies and cookies. *Thank you, God!*

But she'd still been weepy, so Blayne did what she always did when faced with someone else's sadness . . . she talked. A lot. Perhaps, as Gwen often said, too much. She talked and talked and talked until she finally said something stupid.

"So I had breakfast this morning with Bo and his agent . . ."

The way everyone froze in the middle of pie eating or coffee drinking or texting on their cell phones or typing into their tiny notebook computers was more than surreal. It was downright creepy. And she knew in that second, she should have kept her mouth shut.

"Bo . . . Novikov?" Danny asked.

"Wait—"

"You had *breakfast* with Bo Novikov?" Phil asked. "Were you naked? Or just wearing one of his oversized shirts and looking kind of tousled, you saucy wench you?"

"No, no. It's not like that," Blayne said desperately. "He's not one of my gentleman callers."

"Then what is he?"

"A friend!"

And that's when they all started laughing at her. Nothing like having a bunch of dogs laughing *at* you rather than with you. The wolf in her wasn't appreciating it one bit.

"You can't be that stupid," Sabina said. "A Russian bear like Novikov has no friends."

"He's also feline and Asian. I have a way with Asian felines."

"One! And she does weird thing with neck. You're only friend she can make," Sabina added.

"That's not true," Blayne argued, feeling protective of her best friend. "Don't talk shit about Gwenie. It just pisses me off."

"Why are you so upset?" Sabina asked. "I don't care who you fuck."

"I am *not* doing anything of the sort with him!" Blayne could feel her face getting red. It wasn't that she was shy, but still there were some things not to be discussed in large groups of people. And who she was or was not fucking was definitely high on that list.

"Yet," Sabina went on, "he is Marauder. He will get what he wants."

"No, he will not. I'm not some groupie-whore."

"Then, darlin', what were you doing with him?" May asked. "Because from what I understand, he only sleeps with groupie-whores."

Fed up, Blayne screamed, *"I am not sleeping with Bo Novikov!"*

The wild dogs silently gawked at her until their gazes moved past her and toward the kitchen door behind her. Cringing, terrified at what she may see, Blayne looked over her shoulder and into the bright, gold eyes of Mitch Shaw.

"You"—he said softly—"and *Bo Novikov?*"

"Mitchell, do not blow this out of—"

"I *knew* he'd take advantage of you!" Mitch roared, his lion's mane swirling around his face. "I'll kill him!"

He shot out the door, and Blayne went after him. She was way faster than him and slammed into him before he got ten feet from the kitchen. The problem wasn't catching him, it was taking him down. She wrapped her arms around his head and her legs around his chest.

"Stay away from him!" she screeched. "It's not what you think!"

"Like hell it's not! I'm gonna rip that fucker's lungs out! No one takes advantage of my Blaynie!"

Blayne knew Mitch was serious. Knew he planned to go over to the sports center and confront a man who could crush him with his pinky.

So Blayne did what she had to do. What she always had to do when it came to fighting Mitch O'Neill Shaw.

"No, Blayne! No! Not the hair! Good God, woman! Not the hair!"

Spending most of his time in a house filled with wild dogs had taught Smitty a few things: Dogs never shut up; there was not enough chocolate in the world to satisfy them; why speak quietly when you can yell your conversation; they all howled—badly—when any fire trucks went by; and anytime of the day or night, if there was weirdness to be found, the dogs would find it right in their own kitchen.

This time, however, he found it in the hallway outside the kitchen. And although the wild dogs weren't at the heart of it, like usual, he wasn't surprised to see who was.

"In retrospect," he said to his baby sister, her pretty little face buried in her hands as she stood next to him, "do you think you should have rethought picking yourself an actual wolf to be your mate?"

She didn't answer, but Sissy Mae didn't have to. Then again, where would Smitty find his fun if not for the big-haired lion male desperately trying to pry a crazed wolfdog off his back? It still amazed him how the Smiths had such a bad reputation when, in fact, they were probably the sanest among the packs, prides, and clans. Then again, when they went outside their own to mate, this is what happened.

He got a sobbing female who, while pregnant, couldn't have any sharp objects within five feet of her, and his sister got a lion who couldn't bat off the unwanted attention of an incredibly sweet wolfdog.

"Get her off me!" Mitch yelled. "Get her off me!"

Since no one else was doing anything and Smitty knew he'd eventually need to learn to handle these kind of wolfdog issues on his own for when his baby wolfdog was born, he walked up to the tusslin' pair and grabbed Blayne Thorpe around the waist, holding her nice and tight.

A month back, Smitty had gone with Jessie Ann to a birthday party thrown for Blayne. He'd been thinking he'd rather set himself on fire, but it turned out to be a really nice affair at a Van Holtz restaurant. At the party he'd met Blayne's daddy, Ezra Thorpe. Also a former Navy man, they got to talkin', and Smitty had immediately liked the older wolf. And Petty Officer Thorpe was nothing but helpful once he realized that not only was Smitty's mate a wild dog but that she was about to have their first child. A daughter. Smitty had learned a lot from the man in a few hours. And the most important thing he'd learned was that "No matter what anyone says, wolfdogs don't suddenly go postal and attack for no reason. The reason may not seem logical," he'd added, "but they've got a reason. As long as you know that much, you can control the situation before law enforcement has to get involved."

Keeping that firmly in mind, Smitty said, "What did you do to her, Shaw?"

As soon as Smitty asked that, Blayne released the death grip she had on Mitch's hair.

The lion, now free, spun around and said, "*Me?* I didn't do anything!"

"You all right, Blayne?"

"I am not having sex with Bo Novikov!"

Not the answer Smitty had been expecting, but . . . all right then.

"I see." Smitty placed her on the floor. "And you're telling me that because . . ."

"Because he's about to do something really stupid!" Not exactly new for Mitch Shaw.

Massaging his damaged scalp, Mitch moved away from Blayne and hid behind Sissy like a two-year-old. "I was only going over there to talk to him. I was bringing Sissy for protection."

Sissy's eyes crossed, and Blayne said, "I know you, Mitchell Shaw. First you tell Sissy. Then Ronnie and Bren—then your mother."

"We only want to protect you."

"I don't need protection from Bo Novikov. You guys just misunderstand him. He's really sweet!"

Oh, Lord.

"See?" Mitch crowed. "Do you see?"

"Shut up, Mitch! He's been great. Helping me with derby, making sure I eat—he even cleaned my apartment."

Smitty immediately locked gazes with his sister. They'd always been close and understood what the other was thinking without actually having to say the words.

"Um . . ." Sissy began. "Why now did he clean your apartment?"

"It might have been a little messy . . . and I was passed out on the couch."

Suddenly getting worried, Smitty asked, "What do you mean you were passed out on the couch?"

"It was after the badger attack—"

Sissy raised her hand, cutting Blayne off. "Badger attack?"

"They're trying to destroy me."

Sissy's entire body jerked. *"Badgers?"*

"Don't judge me!" Blayne yelled seconds before she burst into tears and ran back into the kitchen, the wild dogs following after her.

Sissy turned on her mate, slapping him in the back of the head. "This is your fault, Mitchell Shaw!"

"My fault? I wasn't the one subtly questioning her wolf prowess by repeating the word badger over and over again!"

"I'm not talking to you anymore!" Sissy yelled, heading off to the kitchen and a sobbing Blayne.

Mitch was right behind her, too. "Yeah, right. How long will that nirvana last?"

Smitty sat down on the third step of the stairs. He sighed and said to the wolfdog pup Dee had left at the house a few days before, "I understand more and more every day why you won't shift to human."

Abby made a little whining sound and kindly dropped a Milkbone into Smitty's lap. "Aww, thanks, darlin'."

* * *

Lock was cutting through the practice rink, hoping they could get done with practice early today, when he stopped midstride. Lock focused his gaze on the ground and wondered if he'd seen what he thought he'd seen. Deciding it was best to check before moving into the team's locker room, he looked up at the support beam that went from the very basement of the building and straight up into the full-human portion until it reached the roof. Although, in this instance, Lock didn't really need to see the entire pillar. What he saw was quite enough since that was the portion his best friend and team captain was attached to.

Frowning in confusion, Lock asked, "Are you up there for a reason?"

"I'm up here for a reason," Ric calmly replied, "but I'm not up here on purpose."

"If you're not up there on purpose, then why are you up there?"

"Because some hybrids have issues with rage."

"You made Blayne mad?" That seemed strange. Blayne had an incredibly high tolerance for other people's issues. However, when she did hit a wall, she hit it with all the power she had and usually took the wall down.

"No, no. Not Blayne. Another hybrid." Ric glanced over at the ice, and Lock followed his gaze to Bo Novikov skating backward around the rink while he worked on his drills. That shifter was on the ice every day whether they had a practice planned or not. If he wasn't on the ice, he was in the gym. He really worked to be as good as he was, making Lock feel a little lazy for not working nearly as hard. Then again, he saw hockey as a fun diversion that helped pay for his studio and woodworking equipment. If he never got on the ice again, Lock wouldn't lose any sleep. Novikov, on the other hand, seemed like the kind of guy who would play hockey on some backwoods frozen lake somewhere until he died of old age.

"What did you say to him?"

"I simply asked about his intentions toward Blayne. He told me it was none of my business; I strongly suggested it was; and it was downhill from there."

"Downhill or uphill?"

"Lachlan."

"All right. All right. No need to get hysterical."

"I'm not hysterical." He wasn't. Not even a little, but it was fun to act like he was. "I'm just uncomfortable."

"He has a hell of an aim to get you right on that hook, too."

"Yes. We're all impressed by Novikov's aim."

"How long have you been up there?"

"Long enough."

"I can't believe you let him put you up there."

"What can I say? I was weak, didn't even put up much of a fight as you can see from the bruises on my face and knuckles. Yeah, I just *let* the seven-one, nearly four-hundred-pound, bear-lion hybrid descended from the very loins of Genghis Khan *toss me onto this goddamn hook*!"

"*Now* you're kind of hysterical."

"*I know!*" Ric took a breath. "Now are you getting me down or not?"

"I would, but I can't climb very well. Maybe if I was still ten—"

"*Lachlan!*"

"Calm down. Calm down."

Lock sized up the teammates walking by him and tapped the arm of one. "Hey. Bert. Can you help us out?"

Bert lumbered over to his side. "Sure. Whatcha need?"

"Can you get our mighty team captain down?"

Bert looked up. "Huh. I didn't know wolves could climb that high."

"They can't. The polar-lion tossed him up there."

"What's he doing fighting a guy six times bigger than him?"

"Got me." Lock leaned against the pole. "Hey, Ric. Bert wants to know—"

"*Would you two just get me down?*"

"The yelling seems unnecessary," Bert observed.

"That was my thought." Lock stepped back from the pole. "Can you get him down?"

"Yeah. Sure." Bert handed Lock his duffel bag and grabbed the beam. He climbed it easily, not even breaking a sweat, but he was a black bear. And an almost atypical one, too. He didn't have much height at six feet but he made up for it in width. Lock remembered Gwen softly stating one day that Bert was, "a low wall that skates."

Bert reached Ric in seconds and gripped the beam with one arm and both legs while using his free hand to lift the annoyed wolf off the hook he'd been tossed onto. "I'm sending him down," Bert called out.

"Okay." Lock stepped back a little farther and blinked when Ric hit the ground.

"I thought you were going to catch him," Bert said.

"You didn't say I needed to catch him. You said you were sending him down. You should have been more specific."

"You're right. That was a hell of a drop, though, for a little dog." Still gripping the beam, Bert leaned over. "You all right, little dog? Can you hear me?"

Ric muttered something, but Lock couldn't really understand him with his face smashed into the floor like that, so he lifted him up.

"What did you say?"

"I said, I hate all of you."

"Why? We didn't toss you up there."

"Exactly," Bert agreed as he came down the beam. He took his bag back from Lock. "We were the ones who helped you. We could have left you up there."

"Yep. You should be grateful."

Ric limped away, muttering something about "bastard bears."

"Canines are so moody," Bert commented as they walked toward the team locker room.

"And totally ungrateful."

*   *   *

Practice ended early, most likely because the team captain kept going on and on about how his face hurt from that thirty-foot drop he'd taken. *Whiner.* And with the team gone, Bo once again had the ice to himself.

Using his stick, he kept the puck in front of him and skated a figure-eight pattern, looping around and behind the goals, picking up speed as he went along. To be honest, he never tired of this. He could stay on the ice for days at a time and he'd be happy.

Speeding into the goal crease, seconds from sending the puck down to the opposite end, Bo almost rammed into the net when he saw Blayne skate through the doors. She had on her helmet, elbow and knee pads, and fingerless leather gloves. The kind Bo used when he did weight training.

Forgetting the puck—perhaps for the first time in his life—Bo skated over to her.

"Hi. What happened to your face?" She had a cut open on the side of her head and a line of blood trickling down her jaw.

"Huh?" She touched her face. "Oh. That. It's nothing. I got it during team practice."

"Not paying attention again?"

"Can we talk about that later?"

"Okay. So what's up?"

"Uh . . . there's a strong possibility lion males may be coming to kill you. Okay . . . bye!" She turned to skate off, and Bo grabbed the back of her sweatshirt. She kept skating for about a minute before she gave up completely, arms falling limply at her sides.

"Are you going to tell me why lion males are trying to kill me?"

"I didn't say are. I said maybe." She faced him. "For them to rally up enough energy to get off their lazy asses and drive up here . . . I'd be more concerned if it were the females. Then I'd just tell ya to get out of town."

"Blayne."

"Yeah?"

"What's going on?"

That's when she exploded with, "I'm sorry!"

"Okay."

"I am so, so, *so* sorry!"

The workings of the Blayne Thorpe mind. If he wanted a straight answer, he'd have to ask her for one. "Maybe you should tell me what happened first before you apologize any more, otherwise I'm sensing we'll be here all night."

"It's Mitch's fault," she began.

"Okay." He waited a few seconds, then asked, "Who's Mitch again?"

"Gwen's brother."

"Okay."

"He's a big fan."

"Okay."

"Except that year you were with Dallas. He hated you that year."

"He wouldn't be the first from Philly to feel that way. And so Mitch . . ." he pushed when she remained silent.

"Oh. Right. See, this is what happened. I was over at Jess's house and she's pregnant and kinda feeling down because you know it's never easy and I think she's just really tired and feels left out and this is her first pup so I'm sure it'll be better when she has a few more, which apparently she and Smitty are planning to do and anyway, I was trying to make her feel better, which is a definite problem of mine, not the making feel better thing but what I do to make people feel better, which is talk . . . a lot . . . and before I knew it I told her and the rest of her Pack about us having breakfast this morning with Bernie and they immediately began to think we were going out and I was telling them that you are not one of my gentleman callers but they didn't believe me and while I was trying to explain that no, you weren't, in comes Mitch and he hears just enough to blow it all out of proportion and I tried to stop him before he came over here and got himself killed, and I had him in my jaws of death hold but he's a male lion and it wasn't as effective on him as it is on his sister and I told him to keep his mouth shut but he didn't and now everyone in Philly thinks you're taking advantage of me and all the O'Neill males are in a rage because I'm like family, and I'm really sorry about all this."

Nope. He'd never heard anyone talk that fast while creating the longest run-on sentence in human history—and doing it all in one breath. Bo was fascinated.

"You're not saying anything," she observed.

"After all that, what is there to say—"

"I understand."

"—other than . . . exactly how many gentlemen callers do you have that I'm not actually *one* of them?"

"Currently, I don't have any gentlemen callers, but I could at any moment. However, it is not a title given out lightly."

"And what does one have to do to be one of your gentlemen callers?"

"Why are you asking?"

"Just makes sense. If we start going out, I can't actually be taking advantage of you."

Blayne straightened up. "Going out? You mean like on a date?"

"Whatever you call your time out with gentlemen callers. Date works."

"You want to go out on a date with me?"

Bo shrugged. "Might as well."

Might as well? Was that the best the man could do? Might as well?

Before Blayne could show him exactly what she thought about his level of enthusiasm—or lack thereof—Bo continued, "I've already got lions coming after me and that idiot Van Holtz getting in my face."

"Ric knows? *Already?* Who the hell told him?"

"Got me. But I got the feeling he knew I'd spent the night at your apartment last night."

"Of course he knows," she said, relaxing. "He probably heard about it from Dee-Ann."

"And she'd know because . . ."

"I'm pretty sure he hired her to follow me."

Now Bo stood straight. "What do you mean he's following you?"

"Ric's not following me. Dee-Ann is. I'm just sure Ric hired her."

"Blayne," he said, oh-so-calmly, "it's not normal for a man to follow or have you followed. It's called stalking and you need a restraining order."

"Ric Van Holtz is not stalking me," she said, unable to envision her favorite wolf stalking anyone, much less her. "Besides, he's in love with Dee-Ann."

"Which one is Dee-Ann?"

"The She-wolf I screamed at in the club the other night."

"Still have no clue."

"It doesn't matter. Ric thinks he's protecting me."

"From what?"

"Pit fights."

"I have to say it's never boring talking to you."

"You've heard about what's going on with hybrids, haven't you?" When he shrugged, she said, "They're snatching hybrids off the streets and using us like pit bulls and rotties. They've been finding bodies all over the city and Jersey."

"We're not even worth hunting now?"

"Nope. They're still going to the pure breeds for that."

"Great. Something else I have to worry about."

"I'm guessing it wouldn't be easy to take you down."

"Since only hockey players have ever tried, I have no answer for you. Then again, you did pretty well for yourself."

"True, but that's from Daddy-given skills. Few have those."

Bo looked at his watch. "It's late. I'll take you home."

Blayne snorted. "What for?"

"You tell me there's someone out to get you and you ask me that?"

"I didn't tell you that. What I said was that Ric was trying to protect me *and* that hybrids were being grabbed. That does not translate into Blayne has a bounty on her head. Ric's just being 'overprotective but I have lots of money so I can be' guy. Trust me, if I were in any danger, someone would have told me by now."

"I don't like it."

"I don't care." She grabbed his arm and looked at his watch. "Okay. I've gotta get back to practice."

"Yeah, but—"

"See ya!"

And she heard the frustration in his voice when he yelled after her, "And I can't believe you're still wearing that useless god-damn watch!"

CHAPTER 14

Waiting in the diner across from the sports center, Lock watched his best friend not eat. Instead he gazed out the window.

"This isn't about Novikov, is it?"

Ric frowned. "Novikov?"

"And Blayne? The reason you were hanging thirty or so feet from the ground?"

"Oh! Right." Ric picked up a fry. "What about them now?"

"What is going on with you?" Lock demanded. God, he hoped Ric wasn't still mooning over Dee. That She-wolf was so out of reach for Ric, she could be on Mars.

"Nothing. Why?"

"Why? Because you're getting into fights with guys four times your size. When did you turn into your brother?"

"I don't want him taking advantage of Blayne."

"Blayne can handle herself."

Ric shrugged and again gazed out the window. "I guess."

"Are you sure there's nothing else bothering you? You seem kind of . . . anxious."

Ric looked at Lock again. "What now?"

Blayne dragged her backpack onto her shoulders. She was feeling really good right now. She was doing better. Everyone was saying so. The training from Bo was definitely paying off. Now, if she could manage to keep him off her back and out of her social calendar until the championships, she'd be golden.

"Night, guys!" she said, waving.

"Night, Blayne!"

Gwen met her at the door. "You sure you don't want to come to the diner with me?"

"Nah. It's been a long day. I'm exhausted."

"The fight with Mitch took a lot out of you?"

Blayne growled and pushed the locker room door open. "He's lucky I didn't yank his nuts off." Blayne froze right outside the hallway. "What are you doing here?"

Bo leaned back against the opposite wall. He'd showered and changed into black jeans, a blue T-shirt, and work boots. His duffel bag was nowhere to be found and she knew he'd been waiting for her.

"I'm here to take you home."

She rolled her eyes. "I already told you—"

"Wait. I'm here to take you home after I take you out. To dinner. Tonight."

"I am *not* going out with you." Especially when he had that tone.

"You want to save my life, don't you?"

"What?"

"You've got lion males trying to kill me."

"I said maybe. They *may* be trying to kill you."

"Right. But if we're going out, if we're *dating,* I can't be taking advantage of you. Isn't that right, Gwen?"

"Absolutely!"

Blayne shoved Gwen back into the locker room with one good push, and Bo nodded his head in approval. "Nice."

"This," Blayne said after closing the locker room door, "is bullshit."

"Why? What's a little date and a drive home between two people who've already slept together?"

Even though Blayne knew what Bo meant, she still snarled

when she heard that collective, "Ooooooooooooooh!" Followed by several "Told ya so" and "Ride it, Blaynie!" tossed in to really make her crazy.

To show her annoyance, Blayne brought her foot back against the door and heard several barks of pain.

"She mule-kicked the door!" someone yelled.

"I don't get what's going on," she told him. "I don't know what you're doing."

Bo stepped closer until he towered over her. "I'm backing you in a corner, blocking you in, trapping you. But it's your fault I'm doing that."

"*My* fault?"

"Because you've put me in danger, I have no choice. Poor little me against all those big scary Irish male lions." He placed his hands against the door on either side of her head. "And, yeah, it's all your fault."

"How do you live with yourself?"

"I can tell you that over dinner or we can stand here arguing the same damn point for the next ten thousand hours with your entire team listening at the door. Choose which is worse."

"Fine. Dinner and you take me home. And then you are never to speak to me again."

"Let's move that particular threat until after the championships, Blayne!" Gwen yelled through the door.

"Shut up!"

Bo hauled himself into the driver's seat, slammed the door, and started his truck. He put on the heat, trying not to look too embarrassed when it sputtered to life since he never used the heat in his truck, even in the middle of the coldest winter. But Blayne was too busy seething at him to notice or care.

Yet Bo had learned a lot about Blayne in the last couple of weeks, and if there was one thing he now knew, it was easy to distract her from nearly anything. Normally that aspect of her personality drove him nuts, but now he needed it.

Reaching into the back of his truck, he pulled out the small bag.

"I bought you something," he said. He took the box out of the bag and placed it in her lap. She didn't even look at it, so Bo opened the box for her—and waited.

It took about thirty seconds for her curiosity to get the better of her, and she glanced down at the box. Two seconds later, angry brown eyes locked onto him.

"A watch?" she demanded. "You bought me a watch?"

"Don't get mad," he said. "This is just something to help you manage your time before you drive me to drink."

"Because I keep looking at your watch when I need the time, or because I was a few minutes late a couple of times?"

"*Fifteen* minutes late. Fifteen is not a few." He raised his finger. "Don't throw it." He grabbed the box back and pulled the watch out. "Let's see how it looks on you."

"I can't take this watch."

"Why not?" He pulled off the stupid, useless watch on her wrist, flinging it into the very back of his truck while ignoring her outraged gasp, and placed the new one he'd picked up that evening from a bear-run jeweler a few blocks from the sports center.

"Bo, it's too expensive."

"What makes you think that?"

"You want me to believe that you got this from some street vendor?" Instead of answering, Bo stared at her until Blayne blinked and looked back down at the watch. "You got this from a street vendor?" He kept staring since it worked the first time. "For how much?"

"Fifty," he said vaguely.

"Fifty? For this?" She gave a little snort. "I would have haggled them down to thirty-five bucks at least. It's not even a name knockoff. Meirston? What's that a play on?"

"I have no idea." Actually it was the brand name of a very old and very powerful bear dynasty that had been creating and sell-ing jewelry since the time of Moses. At least that's what it said on its marketing materials. "It's nice though, huh?"

"Yeah."

"It can take a lot of abuse."

Her lips pursed. "Which means what, exactly?"

"Do you really want me to spell out your clumsiness?"

"No. That won't be necessary."

"Good." He rested his hand on the gearshift. "You still mad?"

"Livid." But then she smiled at him. "But I'm thinking I can get over it if the meal's good."

"It'll be the best," he said, pulling out of his spot. "I promise."

"There she is," the kid next to him said, pointing at the truck pulling out of the parking lot. "She's with—"

"Don't care." He patted the shoulder of the driver. "Keep close, but don't spook 'em." The van followed after the couple, and he walked back to be with the rest of his team. He'd only been doing this job for six months, but it paid better than what he used to do for twenty years. Mercenary work was unstable and ten times more dangerous. Yet once a man acknowledged that he was dealing with animals, not humans, the rest of this gig was easy.

He lit a cigarette and gripped one of the poles so he could keep standing.

"Are we ready?" he asked the tech who handled the tranquilizers.

"Yep." He handed over the gun that was used to tranq elephants. That would be for the hybrid's boyfriend. They had a second, smaller tranq rifle for the hybrid, but they'd be better off nailing her up close with the syringe instead, and grabbing her at the same time. Of all the hybrids they'd taken down, the wolfdogs were the hardest. None of them seemed to have the same internal systems. Put in too much medication and they could die on you. Put in too little . . .

He scratched the wounds on his neck.

But they'd been watching the energetic little wolfdog for

months now. Their tranq tech positive she had the right dosage for someone of the freak's size and weight.

Still, he knew better than to count on that. Once the team got her in the van, they'd chain her up and keep her that way until they made the trip up north to what everyone called the Fight Farm. So even if the tranq wasn't enough for her, no problem. The wolfdogs, although tough to manage, were still dogs. Once he learned how to handle a female with actual claws, the rest was a walk in the park. Because unlike real dogs and cats, the humans knew what that gun to the head or knife to the throat actually meant.

Making his job so much easier.

They were in Brooklyn, sitting at a stoplight, when Bo realized that little Miss Short Attention Span was playing with her watch. "What are you doing?"

"Nothing," she said, her head down and her finger pushing at the different buttons.

Bo glanced back at the four-hundred-thirty page user's guide that came with that particular series of Meirston watches. A version sized for the cubs. Besides wanting to help her manage her time, he wanted her to have a level of protection that even average shifters didn't have. Bear protection.

Normally, Bo would hand over the directions at the same time he gave Blayne the watch, but he knew if he gave her the directions now, she'd figure out it was the real deal and had cost him a hell of a lot more than fifty bucks. But still . . . if she hit the wrong button, he'd be paying that hundred-grand tab that came from accidental alerts because he knew from Blayne's tiny apartment she couldn't handle that financial hit.

"Uh"—he scrambled—"you know what's cool about this watch?"

"What?"

"There's an emergency beacon."

"An emergency beacon? In a knockoff?"

"It's a really good knockoff." *Or whatever.*

"What's the beacon supposed to do?"

Bo stopped at another light and leaned over, grasping her wrist. "When you're in trouble, you pop this open and pull this little piece out, and press this button. It will send out a beacon signal that can be traced by certain military types."

"*Certain* military types?"

"*Our* military types."

He internally sighed in relief when she pulled her hand away from the watch rather than continue playing with it. "What kind of trouble do I need to be in?"

Even better, she was asking questions about it. Good. Excellent. "Trapped in the Andes and forced to eat your friends because there's no way out is a good example. Missing the downtown bus and needing to make a dentist appointment . . . bad example."

She gave a little laugh as he moved ahead. "In other words, follow my dad's rules on when to bother him and when not to. Skinned knee, suck it up and take it like a Thorpe. Skin hanging off your face after wiping out on your Harley, then definitely call but don't expect sympathy."

Bo nodded. "Kind of like my uncle's rule. Unless body parts are actually detached, he doesn't want to hear about it."

Blayne smiled. "I guess your family must be proud of you, huh? You being a big hockey player and all."

Bo shrugged. "I have no idea. I haven't spoken to them in a while."

"What's a while?"

"Since I left."

She turned a little in her seat so she could look at him with wide brown eyes. "Since you left? You mean ten years ago?"

"Yeah, I guess."

"Why haven't you spoken to them in so long?"

He shrugged, not sure why she seemed so upset. "I don't know. I was busy."

Her mouth dropped open and she gawked at him.

"Okay, why are you looking at me like that?"

"How do you not stay in touch with your family?"

"By not picking up the phone and dialing the number?"

"That's . . . disheartening."

"Disheartening?"

"Disheartening."

"Why?"

"Because you need family. Everybody needs family."

He shrugged, still not sure why she seemed so upset about it. "I guess I'm lucky then."

"I guess." She didn't say anything for a long time after that, simply stared out the window. He wondered what she was looking at, thinking about. Was she thinking about him? His lack of family? Or was she still angry at him? Maybe her mind had jumped to another topic all together? The world? Society? Politics?

What was the name of that actor in "Godfather Part Two"? I know I saw him in that old episode of "Law & Order" last night, but I can't remember his damn name. It's going to drive me crazy until I remember!

They were less than a mile from the restaurant they were going to. Bo had already called ahead, and the owner would have his best table set up and waiting for them. But first Bo had to get something out of the way, so he pulled over at a corner on a deserted street.

She looked around. "Why are we stopping?"

He let out a breath. "I'm sorry."

Her eyes narrowed. "This watch is totally *not* fake, is it?"

"That's not what I'm talking about, Blayne." He turned a little in the seat so he could face her. "First off, I'm sorry I ambushed you earlier."

"You should be. There has to be an easier way for you to get a date."

"With anyone else, but you weren't giving me much choice."

Her hands dropped in her lap. "What does that mean?"

"It means . . . it means . . ." Bo shook his head. He couldn't think straight. Not with her so close. "Fuck it. Who cares what it means?"

"If you're going to get all pissy about it—what are you doing?"

And that's when Bo kissed her, his mouth pressing warm and firm against hers, his tongue easing its way between her lips.

The contact startled her simply because she really hadn't been expecting it. But not expecting it didn't mean it wasn't welcome. And goddamn if the man could kiss as well as he played hockey.

Blayne tilted her head to the side so they could both more easily enjoy the other's mouth and tongue. God, she was so enjoying. He tasted good, his tongue stroking hers in a way that made her think of oral sex. She didn't know why, but she wondered what he could do when they got around to that . . .

Wait. *If* they got around to that. If. The man wasn't in yet. Right? Right, Blayne?

Huh?

Bo suddenly pulled back from her, his tongue licking his lips as if he were still tasting her, his eyes locked on her mouth. Had he closed his eyes at all when he'd kissed her? "I'll be honest," he murmured. "I'm not sure if that helped the situation or made the rest of the night that much longer if I can't do that again until I take you to your front door."

If she could speak, she'd totally agree with him. Maybe she should forget about all her recent rules about hooking up with a guy. Maybe she should just throw caution to the wind, forget about the pasta, and take the big hybrid home to her way tiny apartment and put her really sturdy bed to use. True, it wasn't like her but . . . but . . .

But God she really wanted to.

Blayne grabbed his hand and said, "Bo—"

The sound of shattering glass filled Bo's way-too-big truck, and the hybrid's big chest and shoulders jerked forward, shoving Blayne back into the passenger side door, Bo's body keeping her pinned there.

Wincing from the sudden pain in her head where her skull had met the door, Blayne pushed at Bo's shoulder. "Bo?" she called out. "Bo? Can you hear me?"

Confused as hell, Blayne leaned up a bit. The window hadn't been destroyed completely. Instead there was a healthy-size hole in it and cracks running through the glass that was left. Looking back down at the hybrid on her, she saw the metal tip of something poking out of his brown-and-white mane. Blayne reached around and gripped it, pulling it out until the dart slid from his skin. She lifted it up and stared.

"Fuck—"

The passenger door flew open, and since Blayne had been leaning on it, she fell back with it. She saw black ski masks and knew she was in trouble.

Someone jammed a needle into her neck, and she felt liquid forced into her veins. She cried out, her first instinct to fight, but she remembered how fast Bo dropped, and she went limp instead, her eyes closing.

Hands grabbed hold of her arms and legs and lifted her out of Bo's truck. She felt her body carried to a running vehicle. She sensed it was a van by the way they were able to haul her in and get in with her without any trouble. She heard a male voice ask, "Kill the other one?"

"No. Leave him."

Blayne felt a moment of relief flood her as they placed her on a bench and the van doors were slammed shut. The van sped off and Blayne worked hard not to panic. She needed to remain calm, to handle this rationally. Not easy when she felt trapped, like the walls of the van were closing in, like they'd already locked her up in a cage.

And if there was one thing Blayne hated, it was feeling trapped.

She was gone. But unlike last time, she hadn't run from him. She'd been taken. And he wanted her back. He wanted her back right now.

Bo Novikov sat up straight in the driver's side seat. He could smell the full-humans who'd taken her from him, and rage at the audacity of what they'd done moved through him, his lip curling back over fangs that were three times larger than any lion or bear bred after the prehistoric era. Shoving the driver's side door open, he stepped out and immediately focused on the van taillights he could see ahead in the darkness. Blayne was in that van. He stepped forward, ready to take off after her when it hit him in the back. He felt it like little shocks he'd feel after sliding through a thick carpet and touching a metal door handle. The feeling annoyed but that was about it.

He turned toward the two males who stood behind him, their van parked lengthwise across the quiet street in case Bo had tried to back his truck up to get away. But he hadn't even known they were there. He'd been so involved with her . . .

He couldn't worry about that now. About how unobservant he'd been. How stupid. Not if he wanted to get her back.

Reaching behind him, he caught hold of the probes attached to his back and ripped them off.

"Jesus Christ," the younger full-human sputtered, stumbling back, the taser falling from his hand. The older one was going for his sidearm. With no time to fight these two, Bo grabbed hold of his truck's back door and ripped it off at the hinges.

The older male had his gun raised and pulled the trigger. The bullet slammed into Bo's shoulder, but all it really managed to do was piss him off even more.

Roaring, his mane growing as the rage coursed through him potent and uncontrollable, he threw the door. It hit the one holding the gun, part of his head taken off in the process. The younger one screamed and ran, not even trying to get back into his van and drive away. He just ran, never once looking back.

With Blayne his only thought, Bo turned and shot off after the other van. Unable to see the taillights anymore, he took a chance and cut through the park that this road swerved around, praying he got there fast enough. Praying they hadn't made it to the expressway. He hadn't bothered with his truck because it limited what he could do. And he was fast enough to keep up with most cars or vans.

As he powered around trees and over benches, Bo caught sight of fast-moving headlights farther ahead. He snarled, his speed increasing as he thought about Blayne alone in that van.

They had her. They had Blayne.

Those who had taken her were chatting comfortably. They'd done this before. So much so, they were busy discussing basketball tickets and plans they had for next weekend. And while they chatted, whatever medication they'd given Blayne to knock her out was pouring out of her pores like sweat. She felt cold, her thick sweater doing little to keep her warm, the liquid soaking into the material. Her teeth began to chatter, but she clenched her jaw tight and held on.

Someone leaned in close. A full-human. They were all full-human.

"Jesus. She's sweating like a pig."

"In this cold?" a female asked.

"Chain her up," a gruff voice from the front of the van ordered.

"But, sir—"

"Do it."

The male sighed, and Blayne felt hands grip her wrists, the cold touch of metal against her skin. She took in a breath, steeling herself for what she had to do next. And that's when the van bucked.

"Jesus Christ!"

"What the hell—"

Blayne heard a roar from overhead and she almost smiled.

Bo.

He'd come for her.

"We should have killed him," the female voice whispered to someone else.

"He's on the roof," someone else said, his words nearly muted from the sound of metal being torn apart by claws.

"Kill him," the gruff voice ordered. "Kill him now."

Blayne opened her eyes and took a quick look around. It was a young male who sat beside her, his attention focused on the van ceiling. She looked him over once and saw the blade he had strapped to his leg. Military issue.

"And lock her up!" the gruff voice snapped. The young male pulled his gaze away from the ceiling and back to Blayne.

She smiled at him. He blinked, startled, and quickly tried to grab her wrists. She yanked them away and slapped him across the face. His head jerked to the side, and Blayne reached down and grabbed hold of his blade.

As she slid it free from its holster, she kept in mind what her father had always told her. "Do something, Blayne. Even if it's wrong, do *something.*"

And that's just what she did.

Bo swiped his claws against the roof again, tearing at it to get inside. He could hear screaming now and, roaring in rage, sure they were hurting Blayne, killing Blayne, he shoved metal aside to get inside to her. To save her. But the shock of what he saw when he looked inside that van caught him off guard; that split second of confusion costing him dearly because the vehicle swerved wildly again, spinning in a circle and tossing him off.

Bo's body flipped through the air until he hit the ground hard, his right forearm shattering from the impact while his body continued to flip again, his ribs banging against unfortunately placed rocks. He rolled a few feet more, finally slowing to a stop that left him in excruciating pain and unable to breathe very well.

Bo stared up at the trees over his head. Everything was silent now, and he knew that the van had crashed while he'd flipped across the park ground. To be honest, he wanted to stay right where he was. He wanted to lie here and try to find a way to breathe without that unfortunate whistling sound. He wanted to die here staring up at the trees and hoping that heaven really was an ice-covered pond where all the best hockey players met daily for a new game.

He knew he couldn't, though. Not because he was determined to live—although he'd definitely like to do that—but because he had to get to Blayne. If there was anything he could do for her, he would.

Bo made his body get up, but it was a new experience in torturous pain. An experience he hoped to never go through again. Forcing himself to see past everything that swimmed before him, Bo stumbled his way over to the van, his shattered right arm tucked tight against his body.

He felt panic sweep through him when he saw that the van had wrapped around a tree, the front and side windows blown out, bodies lying everywhere.

"Blayne?" His voice sounded garbled, and he knew that blood poured out of him. He ignored that and searched among the blood-covered and dressed-in-black bodies, hunting for Blayne.

Panting and trying not to pass out, Bo sniffed the air. His eyesight may be average but his sense of smell . . .

His gaze snapped over to a tree about twenty feet away. He walked/limped over to it, and as he got closer he saw her.

The wolfdog was covered in blood and, even scarier, she was wrapped around her own tree. He crouched beside her and touched her shoulder. Like a broken rag doll, she rolled over, and he could tell from the way her body moved that her bones were broken . . . possibly all of them.

"Oh, God. Blayne." He touched her cheek with the back of his left hand. She still breathed but barely. "Blayne. I'm so sorry."

His legs gave out from under him and he fell back on his ass. He sat there, panting, wishing he could change the entire night. Wishing he could tell Blayne how he really felt before he lost her like he'd lost nearly everyone else that had mattered to him. He wished he could—

Jesus Christ on a cross, you idiot!

Bo glanced around, everything growing hazier by the second. Yet he knew his uncle's voice. He could hear it, like he'd been hearing it since he was ten years old.

Don't sit there being pathetic. Do something, boy. Even if it's wrong—do something!

His uncle was right. Bo had to do something. Anything.

He looked over at Blayne. She still had on the watch he'd given her, his having been ripped off when he tore through the van roof. The outside had been badly damaged, but Bo still held out hope for the inside. And at a cost of nearly fifty grand, the damn thing better survive a monumental crash.

Reaching over, more blood pouring from his mouth in the process—*at least nothing hurts anymore*—Bo grabbed Blayne's watch and pushed the tiny button on the side, releasing the face plate. And thankfully, unlike the outside of the watch, the inside remained in perfect working order. Using the tip of his pinky finger, Bo pulled out the now active antenna and pressed the button built inside.

Letting out a relieved sigh he'd done that much, Bo dropped. The last thing he consciously remembered before everything ended was putting his arm around Blayne and wishing that everything could have been different for them.

Chapter 15

Grigori Novikov woke up snarling.

"It's not my phone," a female voice snapped in the darkness.

Moving away from the warm body he'd been wrapped around, Grigori reached down to his jeans lying on the floor and dug the phone out of his front pocket.

"Yeah?"

"Grigori?"

Grigori had a hard time hearing the voice on the other end. There was a lot of background noise. Sounded like choppers. "Yeah."

"It's your cousin. Yuri."

"Yeah?" Because God knew he had a lot of cousins.

"From Brooklyn. We got a retrieval call."

"Yeah?"

"It's Bold."

Wide awake, Grigori sat up. "Are you sure?"

"We're sure. He's in bad shape."

"Bring him here."

"There's a hospital in the city—"

"That's not prepped for a hybrid bear. Bring him here. We'll be waiting for him."

"Okay. We're moving. One other thing."

"What?"

"There's a female."

"Full-human?"

"No. But if she's not dead, she will be."

But he knew his nephew. If she was with Bold, they at least had to try. "Bring her."

"You got it. I'm sending my son. We've got clean up here."

The call disconnected, Grigori turned and dropped his feet to the floor.

"What is it?"

"It's Bold," he replied to the concerned voice. "He needs us."

Gwen pushed up against Lock's side until he took the hint and put his arm around her. She laughed again at the conversation between the two males. If anyone had told her a year ago she'd be engaged to a geeky bear with a honey fetish, she would have slapped some sense into them. But she was starting to realize that life was always about a little confusion. The more confusion, the more interesting.

"Maybe I should call Blayne," Ric suggested after they'd finished their dessert and he was poured another cup of coffee.

"Why?" Gwen asked, although she already knew the answer.

"I don't know if I trust him." Something Gwen had already figured out, based on the reaction of both males when she told them how the hybrid had trapped Blayne into a dinner date. She thought it was funny and cute. The guys? Not so much.

"He's an asshole," Lock muttered in between sips of his coffee. Considering Lock usually had nothing bad to say about anyone, made it all the funnier when he did.

"I don't know if I'd go that far, but I don't trust him with our Blayne."

This was the problem with Blayne. She became friends with all these guys, turned them into the big brothers she never had, and ended up dateless but well protected from any other male who may have an interest. And who had to fix the problem? Who else? Gwen.

"She'll be fine," Gwen assured both idiots. "Trust me, Blayne knows how to take care of herself."

"Yeah, nothing like a mighty slap fight to throw off a hardened scumbag."

"Slap fights are for her friends. If she was in real trouble, I have no doubts Blayne could handle it." She looked at Ric. "So feel free to call off your pit bull."

Ric choked on his coffee. "What?"

"You know, Ric. Your pit bull—Dee-Ann? You hired her to protect Blayne, yeah? Well, if I'm right, Blayne will soon have her very own hockey star to watch out for her, so you can put your bitch back on her chain."

"I'm not clear what you—"

"You did hire her, didn't you? To watch out for Blayne? Because of all the hybrid attacks? I mean," she added, "I hope you hired her. Otherwise it's just goddamn creepy that she's been hanging around."

Ric blinked. "Yes. Right. Of course. I hired her. To protect Blayne. Exactly."

Lock placed his mug down on the table. "You're lying."

He said it so quietly Gwen knew he wasn't teasing. And she watched Ric's expression go from charmingly muddled to predatory cold in two seconds.

"You are," Lock went on. "Because no one in their right mind would hire Dee-Ann Smith to follow someone as a precaution. So you tell me right now"—and that's when the grizzly boar exploded—*"why the fuck are you following Blayne!"*

The full-humans in the diner jumped a little at Lock's outburst, but Ric's head only dipped a little, bright eyes focusing on the grizzly.

Gwen tapped the table. "Outside. Both of you. Now."

She reached for her backpack to get her wallet, but Ric dropped a small wad of cash on the table to cover the bill and the tip.

Once outside, she pulled the straps of her pack over her shoulders and focused on Ric. "All right, start talking."

"Perhaps we can—"

"Don't hand me that shit, Ric," Lock cut in. "This is Dee-Ann we're talking about. And I know her well enough to know that I'd prefer almost anyone else on the planet to be following Blayne around of her own volition. So what's the deal?"

"I can't discuss it."

"Why the fuck not?" Gwen snapped. "What are you hiding?"

Lock stepped in close to Ric, the two best friends staring each other down. One an angry grizzly, the other a wolf not ready to back down. Gwen held her breath and balled her hands into fists until her nails dug into her palm.

After a long minute of mutual staring, Lock stepped back. "Oh, my God. You stupid son of a bitch."

"What?" Gwen demanded.

"You did it, didn't you?" Lock kept going, ignoring Gwen. "You joined the Group."

Gwen shook her head. "What's the Group?"

Lock gave a very short, brutal laugh. "They're like the National Guard. The Unit handles problems outside the States while the Group likes to handle problems inside."

"What does that have to do with Blayne?"

"Answer her," Lock snapped when Ric didn't respond.

Ric folded his arms over his chest, no longer looking like the sweet, unappreciated wolf she always thought of him and replied, "Blayne's name was sold. For the pit fights."

"Sold?" Gwen tried desperately to understand all this secret agent bullshit. "You mean so she could be taken?"

"Right. Dee-Ann's been watching her to protect her."

"That's a lie," Lock growled. "I know Dee-Ann. She's nobody's babysitter. You've been using Blayne as bait, haven't you?" She knew what Lock said was true when Ric didn't bother denying it. But Lock snapped, not surprising since a lot of his time in the Marines was spent playing the bait for the rich fuckers who hunted their kind.

Lock's grizzly hump began to expand as he grabbed Ric by his leather jacket and lifted the wolf from the ground. *"Haven't you?*" he roared, and the wolf snarled, lips pulling back to reveal two-inch-long fangs.

"*Stop it!*" Gwen yelled, slamming her body into Lock's. "Stop it right now!" When the two didn't move, she said, "Put him down!"

Lock did, dropping the wolf. Ric landed without a stumble, and Gwen stepped between the two, facing Ric. "Did you tell any of this to Blayne?" she asked him.

"No. It was decided that it was best if we didn't."

Gwen briefly closed her eyes. "No, Ric. That was not best. Not with a wolfdog. And not with Blayne Thorpe."

"We've got her protected."

"Dee-Ann's with her Pack tonight," Lock said.

"We have someone else covering her tonight."

Lock sniffed. "Trainees."

"You put trainees on Blayne?" This was getting worse, and Gwen quickly dug into her jeans to retrieve her cell phone.

"She'll be fine. It's not like they're fresh out of high school, Gwen."

"You guys don't understand," she said. "You think you know Blayne . . ." Gwen again shook her head and speed-dialed Blayne's cell. She did it two more times, knowing her friend's phone always ended up at the bottom of her bag. But after the third time of not answering, Gwen knew it was time to worry.

"Well?" Lock asked.

"She's not answering."

"That doesn't mean—"

"*You don't know Blayne!*" she yelled in Ric's face. She paced away from the men. "You don't know her at all."

Christ, they were in so much trouble. Somehow, someway, they'd lost that damn wolfdog. Dee-Ann, also referred to around the Group office as "That Bitch" was going to have their collective asses for this. It would be especially hard to explain away considering Bo Novikov's truck was the size of a small tank and really hard to miss. But they got caught in New York traffic. It wasn't their fault!

"Turn here," she told Tommy. He did, and after less than a mile, he pulled to a stop.

"Fuck."

Gemma got out of the car. She pulled her weapon from the holster and quickly advanced to a damaged van and a full-human missing part of his head.

"This one got off a shot," Tommy told her.

She nodded and walked over to Novikov's black truck. The driver's side window was broken, both doors open. She heard House of Pain's "Jump Around" and knew someone had it as a ringtone. As she stood beside the passenger's side, she could tell it came from the backpack. Blayne Thorpe's backpack, which still had her wallet and credit cards. Nope. Not a robbery.

"I'll call Dee—" she began, but stopped when she saw the look Tommy gave her. Or, should she say, that Tommy gave whatever was behind her.

Gemma sniffed the air and unleashing her fangs, the She-leopard spun around, her claws out. The grizzly caught her by the head and lifted her off the ground. She hissed and snarled, slashing at him with her claws. She heard Tommy roar and then she was flying, right over the truck and right into her tiger partner. They hit the ground hard, rolling on impact. She got up first, and that's when she saw the black bear and the polar lumbering toward them.

Tommy was up, too, but he was about to launch himself at the grizzly. She caught his arm. "Run," she said. And when he only stared at her, she screamed, *"Run!"*

They took off, getting back to their car in seconds. She got in the driver's side, slamming the door and putting the still-running vehicle in reverse as Tommy got into the passenger side.

The car jumped back several feet, but the polar had it by the front, lifting the vehicle off the ground.

"Shit! Get him off!"

Tommy pulled his weapon and opened the window. He leaned out and started firing, hitting the polar in the shoulder and upper chest. It didn't kill him but it sure did piss him off.

He roared and yanked, tearing off the hood. But it freed up the vehicle long enough for Gemma to reverse down the street half a mile. She shifted to drive and spun the car around, heading back the way they came. Tommy relaxed back into his seat, panting, his eyes shifting from gold to brown as he tried to calm down.

"Bears?" she demanded. "Goddamn bears?"

"Not our bears."

She knew that. Although the Group had bear team members, the bear nation, as they liked to call themselves, still did their own thing. It was a very weird and very dangerous relationship between all the breeds. Yet as long as they were left alone, bears never bothered the other shifters. But piss them off or go after one of their own and all hell could break loose.

And, at the moment, it looked as if hell was running free in Brooklyn, New York.

Yuri Novikov looked up as one of his men stood in front of him. A fellow polar, bleeding from gunshot wounds. "Full-humans?" he asked as he crouched beside a dead one.

"Nah. Cats. Military issue weapons."

He knew it couldn't be the Unit. They didn't get involved inside U.S. borders. That left the Group.

"What does the Group have to do with this?" Yuri asked.

"Don't know."

"Did you ask or just attack?"

The polar sniffed. "You know I hate cats."

And wolves and coyotes and hyenas and anything else not bear.

"Your cousin?" the polar asked Yuri while trying to dig out the bullet in his shoulder with his own fingers.

"Heading home. They'll take care of him. And leave that alone." Yuri slapped the idiot's hand away from the worsening wound. "You're worse than my grandkids."

"Those cats may have been looking for that wolfdog."

Then the Group could take that up with Ursus County. The wolfdog, and whether she lived or died, wasn't his problem.

"Look at this," Yuri said, pointing at the full-human body. The polar crouched down.

"Nice cuts," he said.

"All strategic. Major arteries only. Neck, inside thigh, upper inside arms. I haven't seen work like this since the military."

"Your cousin?"

"The kid's a hell of a hockey player and a hell of a predator, but that's about it. Ripped-out throats and torn-out thighs are probably more his style. This . . . this takes skill. And a coldness I've only seen among the Unit."

"The wolfdog?"

"She has no tatts. No serious scars. Kinda tiny. And the Unit doesn't take hybrids. Especially the canines. Too hard to handle. Too unstable."

"Then who?"

"Don't know. But," he pulled out his cell, "I better call Grigori just in case. He hates surprises, and I think he's had enough for one night, don't you?"

Marci Luntz, M.D., watched the chopper touch down. She motioned to her medical team, and they rushed over with two stretchers.

Micah Novikov stepped out of the front passenger seat and closed the chopper door. Marci remembered when the boy came to visit every summer. He'd grown into a good-size polar, but like his own father Yuri, smaller than Grigori.

Feeling sick in her stomach, Marci impatiently waited for her team to bring Bold off the chopper.

Marci had grown up with Bold's father as she'd grown up with Grigori, but she hadn't met Bold until the ten-year-old was brought back to town by his uncle. Both his parents had died, and the silent little cub had very little to say those first few weeks and months. When he left eight years later to embark on his career, she knew she'd see him again. But not like this. She never expected to see him again like this.

Her team rushed him inside, one of them trying to help him

breathe. She started to follow, but Micah caught her arm, holding her back.

"The girl," he said, and tilted his head toward the chopper. "She's still breathing."

Marci's second team only needed one orderly to pull the girl out; Bold had needed four. There was less blood on the girl, but her body looked . . . wrong. The orderly placed her down on the stretcher, and his gaze met Marci's. He shook his head, already giving up on her, but Marci wasn't that easily dissuaded.

"Get her in and find Dr. Yu."

"Marci," Micah said next to her. "That girl . . . something's not right."

"Why? Because it looks as if every bone in her body's been broken?"

"No. Not that. It's something I heard—"

"Micah, we'll talk about this later."

She rushed off, following after the two teams, Grigori right beside her. By the time she reached the emergency room, Dr. Baxter was already working on Bold.

"I've got him, I've got him," Baxter said before she could even walk in. "Check on the girl. She's circling the drain."

"Got it." Marci turned and saw Dr. Yu heading down the hall toward her.

"We have a black female, wolfdog, in suite two." They walked in together, the nurses already prepping the wolfdog. "It looks like catastrophic damage to—"

Both doctors stopped and looked around the room, wondering where that noise came from.

"What was—"

"I don't—"

They heard it again, and this time the nurses jumped back from the patient, one of them snarling in startled panic.

Marci and Yu looked at each other and then back at the wolfdog. Slowly, they stepped closer, each woman leaning in with their right ears close to the girl's body to see if they could catch the sound again . . .

Snap!

"God!" Marci jumped back and right into Michah who stood behind her. "That noise. It . . . it came from her."

Yu, a Harvard- and Princeton-trained surgeon and Great Panda, leaned in closer. More snapping sounds had her standing up straight, the wolfdog's body twisting with each sound.

Eyes wide, black and white hair falling out of her sensible bun, Yu said, "I . . . I think her bones are . . ."

"Snapping back together," Micah finished for her. He looked down at Marci, shrugged in a way that reminded her of Grigori. "I tried to tell you."

"How fast can your uncle get here?"

Ric let out a sigh. When he'd gotten the call from the team watching Blayne, he'd split off from Lock and Gwen—not hard since Lock wasn't speaking to him—and headed into the office. Not even on the elevator yet, and Dee was behind him and asking him questions that did not make him feel comfortable.

"Why?"

"Want the bad news, the worse news, or the good news?"

He sighed again. It did not help Dee-Ann sounded so . . . perky. "Bad news."

"No clue if the wolfdog is dead or alive."

Yes. That was very bad. "Good news?"

"I know where she is."

Okay. That held promise. But still . . . "And the worse news?"

Without actually moving, Dee still managed to shrug her entire body. "She's in Ursus County, Maine."

And when he slammed his head into the wall, hoping to stop the panicked screaming in his brain, Dee-Ann didn't seem at all surprised.

Grigori watched doctors, the boars and sows he'd grown up with, patch up his nephew. He never thought he'd be here again. Not in this physical place, but back in this moment. The last time had been with Grigori's brother, but then it had been full-humans trying to save the polar's life, his feline wife already gone. There had been nothing they could do. Probably nothing a shifter doc could do, either. The damage had been too extensive. When it was over, all that had been left was the boy. His brother's only child. Grigori had been in the Marines at the time, part of the rarely mentioned but well-known shifter-only Unit. He'd received immediate leave to go to his brother's bedside, but Grigori had assumed his remaining older brother would take the boy in.

How wrong he'd been. His eldest brother had sworn he'd never forgive Bold's father for some dumb argument they'd had years and years before, but apparently that had been true. He didn't forgive him. And although he still lived a nice quiet life in Ursus County with four kids and a sow who could have easily handled one more kid who needed the man's family, that would never happen.

Grigori knew that the options for a hybrid cub weren't great. Foster care. Orphanage. Taken in by full-humans. Grigori couldn't stand the thought. So he'd gone to his C.O. and been released from duty. Something that wouldn't have been easy for the full-human Marines, but shifters played by different rules. Sometimes they simply had to when it came to caring for their young. So Grigori had taken on raising the quiet, neat little boy with time issues. It hadn't been easy. Grigori was only twenty-nine at the time, and it was usually the sows who did the bulk of the raising when it came to cubs, but he wouldn't let that stop him. The boy needed him. Because what ten-year-old folded his socks without a C.O. to tell him to? And the boy had that weird thing about time and Christ, the lists! There were so many lists. At first, Grigori worried that the kid had been mentally damaged by the accident. The first few months, he kept looking to see if the kid tortured animals or drew weird pictures that involved killing people. He was just too quiet. Too polite. Too solemn. Especially for a bear or lion cub.

He'd bring the boy in to see Marci Luntz, and she kept telling Grigori not to worry. Then, one day, the boy had walked in on Grigori watching a hockey game on TV. For the first time, the kid sat down beside him without being asked to and watched along with him. He hadn't bothered before with TV, always more a fan of reading, something Grigori had always found boring. But the kid had watched every second of the game, almost smiling when it was over.

The next day, on a hunch, Grigori came home with a pair of hockey skates, stick, and a puck, and took the kid to one of the ponds near his house. Without saying a word, the boy put on his skates, expertly tying them up, wrapped up the handle of his stick with tape, and hit the ice. That's when Grigori saw what the kid had been missing for the few months they'd been living together.

Then, after watching him for a good hour, Grigori realized something else.

The kid would be a superstar. For someone so young, who he guessed hadn't been on the ice in months, Bold Novikov had the most impressive moves Grigori had ever seen, and the kid was only doing drills.

At first, Grigori was the only one who saw it. Even for a ten-year-old, Bold was smaller than any of the other cubs. Quieter, less playful. Grigori worried that pressure from the other kids would make Bold give up, especially when they started calling the kid "Speck." Grigori should have known better. That kid didn't give up on anything. Always smaller than the other bears he played with, Bold never let that hold him back. He never let the reaction he got from the rest of the town for being tough and mean on the ice get to him. The kid had a goal and he went for it with the methodical planning of a war-time dictator.

It was almost a shame the kid had no interest in the military—he'd be a general by the time he was thirty. Or killed by his own troops. It could really go either way.

Dr. Karl Baxter walked out of the surgery. "Okay. We got the bullet out and sewed up what we could and put a cast on his arm. Now we wait and see."

Grigori nodded. "Okay."

The Yellowstone grizzly patted his shoulder. "Why don't you

get some coffee? You'll probably need it. By the time you get back, we'll be able to let you in to see him."

"Okay. Thanks, Karl."

"Of course."

Grigori headed down the hallway toward the elevators that would take him to the cafeteria, but he paused at the doorway of the room where the wolfdog was being treated. While the nurses had refused to go back into the room with the "poppin' and lockin' canine," as she'd been named by the orderlies, Betty Yu and Marci had refused to leave her side. Fascinated by every snap, crackle, and pop coming off the little girl.

"How's she doing?"

Marci glanced up at him and then away, pushing the girl onto her side and focusing on her back. "She's alive but still unconscious. To be honest, I have no idea if she'll ever come out of—" She pointed at the wolfdog's back. "Betty . . . what is this?"

The panda walked around the bed. "What's what?"

"This? It doesn't look like a laceration."

"More glass?" Betty looked at Grigori. "We found glass imbedded in her flesh. Probably from the accident."

Accident. Yeah. Right. From what he'd heard about thirty minutes ago from his cousin, the crash of that van was not a simple accident. Far from it. Especially since Yuri didn't even think that most of the full-human victims had died from the crash. They were dead before it.

"I thought we got all of it," Betty explained after grabbing a clamp-looking thing with long handles and placing it against the wolfdog's flesh, "but we may have missed a piece or two."

She tugged and pulled something from the wolfdog's flesh. It sparkled in the harsh emergency room light, but it wasn't glass.

Yu held it up. "What in holy hell is this?"

Yeah. Grigori would like to know that, too.

CHAPTER 16

Something was choking him. Choking him to death. He grabbed at it, trying to pull it from his throat. Strong arms grabbed his hands, pulled them away. He fought back, struggling against them, knowing they were trying to kill him.

"Bold!" He heard the voice. Recognized it. "Bold! Listen to me! It's Dr. Luntz! Open your eyes, sweetheart! Open them and look at me!"

He did, but it wasn't easy.

It was Dr. Luntz hovering over him, her hands on his face, brushing his cheeks with soft, cool fingers. "You're safe, Bold. You're safe."

He tried to answer, but he choked and coughed, his body trying to expel whatever was trapped in his throat.

"Let's get this out of him," she said to someone off to his left. "Easy, Bold. Easy. You're going to be fine."

Tape was removed from his mouth and the tube pulled from his throat. He quickly rolled to his side, the coughing getting worse as mucus and saliva poured out of him.

"It's all right, Bold. You're fine." She stroked his back, his neck, while someone else wiped his mouth. After the coughing subsided, he was again rolled onto his back.

Marci Luntz smiled at him. That warm smile she used to always give him anytime she saw him in town. "Hi, Bold."

He had to admit he was glad to see her, but there was just one thing . . . Marci Luntz didn't leave town. Not since she'd returned from her residency at Johns Hopkins. To quote her, "What's out there for me? Full-humans? Snobby cats and cranky wolves? Thank you, but I'll stay right here."

Bo looked away from her and around the room, gazed out the window with all that bright morning sun that shed light on all the snow and ice covering the trees. Those trees with the deep gouges ripped into their trunks from hundreds of years' worth of bears.

Christ, he was back. Back in the town he'd moved to after his parents died. The town he'd left eight years later.

He was back in Ursus County, Maine.

But why? Why was he back? And why was he hurt?

He moved his gaze to his arm. He had on a cast, the pain as bone and muscle repaired itself radiating up his arm and throughout his body.

Christ, his arm. He'd broken his arm. When? How? And, more important, would he still be able to play?

Fear shuddered through Bo, helped along by feeling hot and cold all at the same time. The fever. He had the fever. Rationally, he knew that was a good thing. The fever would help repair him. So would Dr. Luntz.

He returned his gaze to her. She smiled. It was that warm smile he remembered so well. He focused on it, immediately feeling calm and centered when he did. He was about to return her smile, something he rarely felt the need to do for anyone when Dr. Luntz was pushed aside and a big, fat, stupid face he remembered all too well moved in close. Too close.

"Speck!" he screamed in Bo's face. "How ya doin', Speck? How ya feelin', buddy?" The polar looked Bo over, grinned. "I see you finally hit your growth spurt, huh? 'Bout friggin' time, I'd say. Right, kid?"

"Fabi—"

"It's okay, doc! Speck here's my cousin, right? You know that. Speck adores me! Don't ya, Speck? Don't ya adore your cousin Fabi?"

Uh . . . no. No, Bo didn't adore his cousin. As always with the idiot, Bo wanted to bat him around like a tennis ball. Yet he could almost hear a voice telling him that wouldn't be right. *He's family,* the voice insisted. *You've gotta have family!*

He knew that voice . . . and that ridiculous sentiment. Blayne. That was Blayne's voice.

Blayne . . .

With his right arm in a cast and still healing, he used his left to grab Fabi Novikov around the throat, his fingers squeezing until his cousin's eyes bulged from his head.

Dr. Luntz grabbed his arm, trying to pry him off. She screamed out the door, "I need help in here! Grigori! Somebody! Now!"

Bo leaned up while pulling Fabi in closer. "Where is she?" he asked, his voice not more than a ragged sound torn from his damaged throat. But that pain didn't stop him from bellowing in Fabi's terrified face, *"Where's Blayne?"*

Grigori walked down the hallway toward his nephew's room. The kid was doing okay. Marci seemed real sure he'd be just fine, and Marci wouldn't lie to him, even if she wanted to. The fever hit the kid hard but that was to be expected. Bold had tossed and turned all night, his big body shifting from human to animal every few minutes, leaving his sheets soaked in sweat and the need to replace the cast on his arm twice. It was hard fitting anything to his shifted form. He'd taken a lot of both his parents and came up with something pretty damn new.

He'd had no intention of leaving the kid this morning, but Marci had sent Grigori off for coffee and the hospital cafeteria's amazing biscuit sandwiches because, and he was quoting here, "I don't know which is annoying me more at the moment. Your face or that pit you call a stomach grumbling every ten seconds."

He still brought her back a couple of honeycomb biscuits. He'd never thank her verbally for helping his nephew, but the biscuits should do the job.

Grigori came around the corner and stopped short. He wasn't

exactly shocked to see his nephew storming down the hospital hallways, yelling out, "Blayne!" Nor was he surprised to see half the staff trying to stop him. But why that dumb ass Fabi got so close that not only could Bold get ahold of his neck but now drag him along as he stalked the halls looking for that freaky little wolfdog was beyond him.

"Don't just stand there," Marci complained from behind Bold. "Do something!"

"Yeah, yeah, yeah." Grigori moved down the hallway until he was about twenty feet from the boy. He planted his feet and barked, *"Bold!"*

Bold stopped, blue eyes narrowing. For a moment, he wasn't sure the boy recognized him. For a moment, he was sure that Bold Novikov was going to charge him. So Grigori added, "Put your cousin down."

Bold looked at the blood relative he had in his left hand. Shaking his head, he returned his gaze to his uncle and raised the hand holding his cousin. Then he shook Fabi a bit. "Where is she? Why won't anyone tell me?"

"I'll tell ya where she is as soon as you put your cousin down. You're crushing his windpipe."

Bold released Fabi. "Where is she?" he demanded again.

Grigori motioned to a room between the two of them. "Right in there. So you can stop acting like a putz."

The boy gave a short snarl and stormed into the room. That's when Marci felt the need to glare at Grigori and he shrugged in response. What had he done?

She wasn't in the bed, but cold relief washed over him when he saw her standing naked by the large picture windows of her hospital room, staring out over the snow and ice outside. He hadn't known what to expect when the horror of the previous night came back to him. When he realized she was not at his side, safe and healthy.

He took a brief moment to look her over. She had lots of lacerations that the docs had sewn up, but it looked to be mostly from glass. And there were a bunch of bruises that were already fading. But still . . . he remembered how her body moved the night before when he'd turned her over. He knew broken bones and spinal damage when he saw it. He knew because he'd caused his fair share of it. And although shifters could heal from the kind of damage she had faster than humans, it would still take months, maybe years to recover.

Yet here she stood, tall and strong.

Swiping a blanket she'd tossed aside from off the floor, Bo walked up behind her and wrapped it around her body. He didn't release her, though, simply held her. Bringing his head down to press against the side of her face, he said, "Blayne?"

"How?" she asked.

"How what?"

"How did you get us to Siberia?"

"Siberia? What makes you think we're in Siberia?"

"An unholy amount of snow and ice and friendly polar bears." She pressed her hand against the glass, and that's when Bo saw the three polar males outside the window. One had his black nose pressed against the glass and that's where Blayne had her hand.

"They're shifters, Blayne."

"They are? But they're so nice."

"They're sub-adults. And I think they were just staring at your breasts."

"Oh. So no Siberia?"

"Nope."

"That's disappointing."

"Sorry."

"Don't be. I still have something to shoot for."

He pressed his lips against her cheek, and Blayne's hand came up and stroked his jaw. "That was a hell of a kiss, Novikov."

He chuckled and hugged her tighter. "Are you okay?"

"I'm still breathing. In my world that's okay." She looked down and gasped. "Oh, God, Bo. Your arm."

"It's okay."

"It's not okay. It's in a cast." She pulled away so she could face him. Her gaze went to his other shoulder and now Bo saw tears. "Your shoulder."

Not knowing what she was talking about he looked down, saw the bandage on his shoulder. Now that he was aware of it, he felt the pain, too. That's right. He'd been shot. He remembered.

"It's okay."

She shook her head, tears streaming down her face. "I've ruined your career. I've ruined you."

Wow. When she went there, she really went there.

"Blayne, you've done nothing wrong."

"I'm so sorry. I'm so sorry I did this to you." She pressed herself into him, sobbing against his bare chest. "God, what did I do?"

Not sure how to handle this, he did what he used to do ten years ago when he was confused. "Dr. Luntz?"

The sow appeared in the doorway, her face concerned. "What is it, Bold?" He motioned to the wolfdog in his arms.

"What on earth . . ." She rushed in, pressed her hand to Blayne's forehead. "What's going on?"

"Uh . . . she thinks she's ruined my career and my life. Apparently this is all her fault."

"Oh, honestly. The Novikov men." She gripped Blayne's shoulders and pulled her away from Bo. "Come on, dear." She took her back to the bed. "You need to calm down. You need to stop crying. You know we can't give you anything to do it for you."

Grigori appeared in the doorway. The sight of him took Bo by surprise. Not because he looked substantially different—he didn't. A little older, definitely a lot more gray in all that white hair, but that wasn't it. It was seeing him at all, after all this time. And to see him looking so . . . concerned.

"What's going on?" he demanded, his eyes on Bo.

"Now I need you to calm down," Dr. Luntz snapped at Grigori. "There's nothing here we can't handle. Right, dear?" she asked Blayne, trying to get her attention.

"I've ruined his life," Blayne said between her sobs. "It's my fault."

"You haven't ruined anything. He'll heal. You both will."

"He'll never be the same. He'll always be flawed. Damaged. Useless."

Shocked, Bo looked at his uncle and Grigori began laughing, making Blayne snap, "It's not funny!"

"Of course it's not funny," Dr. Luntz said, rubbing Blayne's shoulders, and trying her hardest not to laugh as well. "You ignore him, dear. He's an idiot. We've all come to accept that." Dr. Luntz winked at Bo before sitting down beside Blayne.

"Now I want you to listen up—"

Dr. Luntz looked at Bo and he filled in, "Blayne Thorpe."

"—Blayne Thorpe, because I hate repeating myself. Bold Novikov will be just fine. We have the best damn doctors on the Eastern Seaboard here in Ursus County, Maine. Finer than the boy deserves, and that's a fact. But they stitched him up nice and tight and made sure that he'll be back on the ice before you know it. The only thing that will ruin his career will be old age and the fact that he keeps willfully hurting people."

"Only when they get in my way," he tossed in.

"See? Even now he's still as mean as a circus bear. So don't fret. I just want you to breathe in and breathe out, real easy."

Blayne did what she was told, several times, until she'd calmed herself down.

"There. Feel better now?"

Blayne nodded. "Yes, ma'am."

"Good. Until your fever is completely over, we can't have you getting too upset, now can we? And you know why, don't you?"

"Because I'll flip out and you won't be able to calm me down without the risk of killing me."

"Right. So you stay calm and relaxed, for a little while longer. Okay?"

Blayne closed her eyes, waited a beat, before replying, "Yes, ma'am."

"Good. Good. This is how I like things anyway. Nice and calm. Loud noises just irritate me. Now, are you hungry, Blayne?"

"Yes, ma'am."

"All right. I'll get you something to eat." Dr. Luntz began to pull away, gesturing to Bo when she did. When he only gazed at her, unsure what she wanted, she sighed and grabbed his hand. She pulled him toward the bed and pushed at him until he sat beside Blayne.

"I'll bring you both something." She patted his shoulder before walking out, taking Grigori with her, the door closing behind her.

"Who was that?" Blayne asked.

"Dr. Luntz. She was the doc who helped us out after your tragic badger assault."

"Until you know what it's like to be stalked by badgers, don't mock me."

"Wouldn't think of it."

She rested her head against his bicep, and Bo couldn't help but smile a little. She felt wonderful against him.

"Are you sure you're okay?" she asked.

"Yeah."

"You're not lying to me?"

"I'm not good at lying."

"I know. That watch did not cost fifty bucks. More like a grand, right?"

"Uh—"

"It's okay. I'll let you off the hook because it saved our lives, right?"

"You have no idea."

"I do." She looked up at him. "Thank you."

"Stop. You're going to make me all weepy-eyed."

She laughed a little. "Yeah. Right."

Blayne brought her right arm out from under the blanket, and Bo cringed when he saw that at least three of her fingers were badly broken. Her forefinger and ring finger twisted over the middle.

Bo reached for her hand, wondering why Dr. Luntz hadn't fixed this when Blayne was still unconscious, when Blayne grunted and the three fingers gave a loud triple *"Snap!"* And like that, Blayne's fingers were back in place. She made a fist, then stretched out her fingers, and sighed. "I thought those would never pop back."

"Pop back?" Christ, was that what happened to all those broken bones he'd seen last night?

"Yeah. You know."

Not really, but maybe it was best not to ask. As a fellow hybrid, he knew they each had all sorts of good and bad that came with their mixed bloodlines, and to be honest, he was grateful that whatever mix Blayne had, had managed to keep his little wolfdog alive.

"Do you mind if I lay down until she comes back?" she asked. "I'm still sleepy."

"Yeah," he admitted, "me, too."

"Then lay down with me." Blayne gave him a smile he was shockingly grateful to see. She quickly got under the covers of her bear-size hospital bed and pulled the other side back for Bo to get in there with her.

"Uh . . . Blayne, I'm sorta naked here."

"So am I. I won't tell if you won't." Her smile grew, and he knew she was easing out of her fever. "Come on."

Not sure it was the right thing to do but wanting to do it so badly, Bo got under the covers. Blayne turned on her side away from him and then commanded, "Spoon me!"

"Woman, I'm naked!" he said desperately.

"Don't whine, don't call me 'woman,' and just spoon."

Positive this was not the right thing to do but with little choice, Bo moved in behind Blayne. He did, however, try to keep his lower half as far away as possible. Not very effective though when Blayne moved back until her ass pressed against his groin.

"Perfect," she sighed. Then she laughed. "God, Bo. Your cock is huge."

"You're trying to hurt me, aren't you?"

"Nah. I like you too much for that."

Yeah, but did she like him enough? Of course, by the time he worked up the courage to ask she was asleep.

Marci looked up from her plate of honey buns. "What?"

Grigori sat down across from her at one of the cafeteria's booths. "I thought you were bringing them food."

"By now they're out cold. I'll feed them when they wake up again."

"She's a cute little thing, isn't she?"

"Uh-huh." Marci knew where this was going.

"But a wolfdog?"

Typical. Wolfdogs had the worst reputation among the hybrids, but Marci had never thought that was fair. "Seems to me she has more to worry about. Did you see that mane on him when he was looking for her? It grew in sudden, ya know? It wasn't there when we brought him in." She ate a bit of honey bun before asking, "How is Fabi, by the way?"

"I sent his dumb ass home."

"That boy is dumb, Grigori."

"Just like his father."

"Speaking of which—"

"No. He's not coming to visit."

"Dumb. All of 'em."

"Thank you."

"You and Bold don't count."

Grigori stared at her plate. "You going to eat all those honey buns?"

"You don't even like honey."

"We both know I'll eat anything if it's sweet and tasty." Then he grinned, and Marci seriously considered throwing the whole plate at his face.

A barely audible chime had Grigori reaching for his cell. He pulled it off his jeans and answered. "Novikov."

Marci went back to her honey buns, slapping at Grigori's hand as he reached for one. He said little more than "uh-huh" into the phone, but when he hung up, he looked positively bemused.

"What?"

"That was Kerry-Ann. Seems she got a call from Niles Van Holtz."

Alpha Male of the Van Holtz Pack? Calling the superintendent of their town? "What did he want?"

"He's coming here."

"Why?"

"To get the wolfdog."

"You can't tell me that the Van Holtzes would have a hybrid in their Pack." From what Marci knew the Van Holtzes were almost as bad as the Prides when it came to that sort of thing.

"He's on his way from Washington state to New York and then here. Even bringing a bear from Jersey with him. They'll be here tomorrow."

"For protection?" she asked with a laugh.

"Somehow I'm doubting that."

"You think Bold will go back with them?"

Grigori shrugged. "Probably. He's got the Llewellyn Cup finals coming up. He won't want to miss that."

"You know, you could visit him sometime. Maybe watch him play."

The polar grunted. "He could invite me."

"Oh, my God! You two!"

"What are you yelling at me for?" He snatched the last honey bun off her plate. "And I'm taking this because you owe me."

"I don't owe you anything but a swift kick to the ass. Both you and your nephew!"

"If nothing else," Grigori said around that honey bun, "if Van Holtz comes for the wolfdog at least we won't have to worry about protecting her."

That was true. No one in Ursus County was a big fan of wolves, and any hybrid with more than one-eighth wolf blood was considered wolf. The poor child would be a walking target.

"Van Holtz coming here," Marci said, looking out the window. "Won't we need a red carpet for his arrival?"

Grigori laughed and Marci joined him.

*   *   *

Blayne woke up. She immediately became aware that it was now dark out, meaning she'd slept the entire day away, and that her bones had completely healed—and were about ten times stronger than they were before they were damaged—and that she was snuggled in close to Bo Novikov. Her face pressed against his neck, his cock pressed against her inside thigh—and he was sweating.

This was how they'd woken up together the first time, wasn't it? Only there'd been no sweating because they'd both been fully dressed.

What could she say? She liked naked better.

Blayne dragged her hands up Bo's back, enjoying the feel of his skin under her fingers. Slid her leg up his thigh, causing friction against his cock.

She felt his jaw tense against the top of her head, and she knew the sound she'd been hearing was Bo's teeth grinding together. Smiling, she kissed his neck, remembering that interrupted kiss they'd had the night before.

When she made small swirls on his flesh with her tongue, Bo finally said, "Please tell me you're awake."

"Uh-huh." She dragged her tongue up his throat to his tense jaw.

"Okay, okay," he said desperately, "that helps. Um, uh . . . Blayne"—he groaned, his hands caressing her—"maybe we should hold off on this until, uh, you're feeling better."

"I feel great. Fever's gone, bones healed, and I have way more energy than I know what to do with." She rose up enough to look down into his face. "I need you to kiss me again."

He peered at her with those clear blue eyes. "Won't I be taking advantage of you?"

God, he was so cute! "Not even close. Now kiss me."

He did, bringing his head up until their lips touched. Blayne let out a deep sigh, her tongue meeting his. Yeah, she remembered right—their first kiss *had been* that good. She'd worried that she'd blown it out of proportion because of what happened afterward. She hadn't.

Bo's hands slipped into her hair, his fingers digging into her scalp. His body came up off the bed, and Blayne was forced to sit up with him. She gripped his forearms with her hands, the fingers of her right hand taking hold of the plaster from his cast. Their kiss grew more intense, their tongues delving deeper as they fought for breath.

Blayne couldn't believe how amazing this was, and it was only a kiss.

They had to stop. He had to stop. But he couldn't. He couldn't stop. Not when she tasted so wonderful, felt so good against him. He'd been waiting ten years for this, and he didn't want to waste another second. But they weren't in his house or her itty-bitty Brooklyn apartment. They were in the Ursus County Memorial Hospital, with the risk of nurses and doctors—good God! Or his uncle or Dr. Luntz!—wandering in whenever they damn well felt like it.

He pulled out of their kiss, his eyes shut tight because he knew he couldn't look into those big brown eyes. "Blayne, we have to stop."

Instead of stopping, she reached down and grabbed hold of his cock, her grip squeezing and stroking at the same time.

Vixen! Evil, cruel vixen!

"You need to"—he shuddered—"stop."

She kissed his neck, jaw, mouth. "Don't want to." She pressed her mouth to his ear. "I want to watch you come."

His eyes crossed and Bo knew he was running out of will-power here. They both knew it. One more stroke from her hand and he was a goner, not stopping until she was pregnant and wearing a wedding ring.

Knowing full well this was not a good time to make life-altering decisions; Bo did the one thing he knew would stop Blayne. He said, "Blayne . . . I saw you."

"Saw me where?" she asked, nipping at his shoulder.

"In the van. I saw what you did in the van."

Her lips and hand stopped moving and, slowly, Blayne leaned back to look into his face.

"Oh," she said. "Okay." Then she bolted.

Bo caught her arm and hauled Blayne back on the bed. "Don't run on me," he ordered.

Of course she was going to run. Did he really expect her to stay? But his grip was firm and he was one of the few who Blayne didn't think would be affected by her Windmill Claws of Mauling technique.

So she did the next best thing. She lied. "I don't remember anything," she said. Her father, always a planner for the inevitable, had told her that could be her excuse in almost any awkward situation. And this was awkward.

"Are you worried I'll tell?" he asked, brushing the fingers of his free hand against her cheek.

Tell, have me put down . . . whatever.

"I won't tell what I saw, Blayne. I'll never tell. It's our secret."

She wanted to believe him but—

"I promise." He gripped her chin and forced her to look him in the eye. She'd had no idea she'd looked away. "I swear to you I'll never say a word."

"It was Daddy," she blurted. "After what happened to Mom . . . he wanted to make sure I could—"

"Defend yourself. I'm glad. I'm glad he did that."

She gave a panic-tinged laugh. "It wasn't him, though. Who taught me, I mean. Daddy's not the best fighter as human. Except in a general brawling, biker gang sense. But he has a lot of friends. From the Unit, the Corps, the Navy . . . and a couple of wild dog friends of my mom's who were in the Israeli Army." She chewed her lip, her body shaking. "Only Gwenie knows."

"Not a word, Blayne. Not from me. Not ever."

She swallowed and took a breath. She realized that like Gwen, Bo understood what could happen if he did tell. Wolfdogs were considered unstable and dangerous. Add in well-trained abilities with weapons and that fear from other shifters doubled. Some pure-bred shifters wouldn't care. The ones who'd trained her never had. But there were others . . . others who'd make it their goal to wipe her from the planet.

That wasn't Bo. That would never be Bo. He'd keep her secret. She knew that.

She wrapped her arms around his neck and hugged him, her speeding heart returning to its more normal rate.

Bo hugged her back, his hands rubbing against her back.

After she stopped shaking, Blayne moved off. Hot and kinky ideas about sex wiped clean, she took hold of his cast-covered arm. "How's the arm? Really?"

Bo felt around the cast with his free hand. After a moment, he ripped into it with his claw, easily destroying the plaster. He wiped off any clinging material and moved his arm around a bit. "It feels good. Won't really know, though, until I get back on the ice."

"I'm up to heading back later today, if you are?"

"Good." His hand cupped her chin. "We've got some unfinished business to get to."

She felt a sharp thrill, knowing he wanted her. "Yeah. We do."

"Besides, I don't want to spend any longer here than I have to."

"Why?" He made a sound and Blayne asked, "Did you just grunt at me?"

"I don't want to talk about it."

"The grunting or why you don't want to be here? Because I have more concerns over you grunting at me."

"Blayne."

"Is that your getting-tough-with-me tone?"

He shrugged. "Kinda."

"It's pretty weak. You're tougher when we're training." She poked at his wounded shoulder with her finger. "Does that hurt?"

"No."

Blayne went up on her knees, placed her hand over his mouth with one hand and yanked the bandage off with the other. Bo roared in agony, but she ignored all that to get a closer look at the damage. "They'll need to take these stitches out before we leave."

"Thank you, Dr. Butcher!"

She laughed, leaning in closer to examine the nearly healed wound. "Any idea what caliber?"

"Looked like a forty-five."

"A forty-five to stop a mighty bear-cat? Foolish full-humans."

"Stop calling me that." He moved his shoulder around. "You hungry?"

"Starving," she admitted.

"At this hour, we have two choices in Ursus County. The hospital cafeteria or . . ." He motioned to the window, and Blayne focused her gaze outside at the snow-covered land—and the small family of deer walking past. She grinned, her stomach growling in approval.

"I'm for the 'or,'" she said. "Definitely the 'or.' Besides," she clapped her hands together, "I want to see what you look like when you're shifted!" She was amazed what nature could come up with when species combined! She couldn't wait, but Bo looked a little freaked out about it. "What's wrong?"

"Nothing. But you can't laugh."

"Laugh? Why would I laugh?"

Instead of answering, Bo shifted. Right there on the bed. Blayne didn't laugh, although, she did squeal, forced to jump off the bed by the sheer size of Bo Novikov's animal form.

An animal form that was, basically, a sixteen-hundred-pound, twelve-foot-long . . . white lion male. His front paws were like all lion's but his hind paws were polar and the size of dinner plates. White fur covered those paws, each with nine-inch-long black claws. His ears were too small for what had grown into an absolute *giant* mane, and his face was clearly feline with the flat black muzzle rather than the longer polar snout.

Yet what fascinated Blayne the most were his fangs. Openly ogling them, she could only think of prehistoric saber-toothed cats. Easily two inches thick and seven and a half inches long, they were dangerously sharp, the front incisors stretched past his bottom lip to beneath his chin.

When human he may be more bear, but when he shifted he was just one giant cat, bigger and longer than a liger and, she bet, all the male-lion aggression one could fit into him.

He watched her closely, probably worried she'd try and run on him again. But she was too fascinated!

Blayne sprung back on the bed and bounced right on top of him. Laughing, she pulled her hands through his mane and down his body. Eager to see him move and hunt, she scrambled off him again and dashed to the window. She pulled it open, ignoring the blistering cold that tore in, and shifted. She dashed outside and quickly turned so she could watch him.

Bo dived off the bed and right through the window, not even touching the floor. For all his size, he moved as liquid as a feline. And she knew as she ran after him that she was in big trouble. Because she'd never seen anything more beautiful before in her life than a shifted Bo Novikov. The intensity of it was so powerful it reminded her of something her mother once told her when she was way too young to really get it. "I loathed your father until I saw him take down an elk. That combined with him on his Harley—I was lost, baby. Lost."

Yep. She finally got it.

CHAPTER 17

Blayne sensed a presence in front of her. She knew it wasn't Bo. He was behind her and had been the entire night, holding her in his big arms, those razor-sharp claws near extremely vital organs, but she never once felt unsafe. Not with Bo. Not ever again. But someone else in their human form was coming at them from the front, leaning in close. Blayne didn't even open her eyes before she wrapped her mouth around the face close to her and bit down.

It was a male, and he went down screaming, trying to throw her off.

"Fabi found 'em," someone said off in the distance.

"Get her off me! Get her off me!" She guessed the one called Fabi screamed.

Large, human arms wrapped around her and pulled her back. Since she knew those arms belonged to Bo, she released the male she had a good hold of.

More bears in human form showed up, surrounding them. Some on snowmobiles and some on foot. They all wore T-shirts that read URSUS COUNTY POLICE. The older polar Blayne had met the night before walked up to them. He was the only one not wearing any police department gear.

"We've been looking everywhere for you two. Get back to the hospital and get dressed. Her people are coming for her."

Her people? Blayne didn't have any people but her father, and good God, she hoped that he didn't know anything about this. He still hadn't let her live down when she'd gotten lost in a department store when she was ten. So for her to get caught off guard and picked off by trackers? Christ, Mr. CrankyWolf would make sure to have it put on his tombstone to ensure she'd never forget.

"She nearly bit my nose off!" Poor Fabi. But who sticks their face near the muzzle of a sleeping wolfdog? Why not just put your arm in their mouth or try and take their food? Either of these would make as much sense.

"You shouldn't have gotten so close, you idiot," Bo said in that friendly way he had. But how he wasn't freezing to death, she'd never know. Then again, how could any of them not be freezing to death? The grizzlies and black bears had on long sleeve tees and jeans while some of the polars had on T-shirts and shorts.

Even with fur, Blayne was cold, and she knew she'd be colder if she weren't being held by Bo. Even human his body kept her warm.

"I see you haven't changed, Speck," the polar she'd bitten shot back at Bo.

And without Bo saying a word, Blayne sensed his change. Felt his body become tense, his attitude darken. She immediately responded to that change, her own body tensing, a low growl rolling past her muzzle.

Fabi stepped back and the older polar watched her close.

"I don't know," Fabi said. "Seems to me she has enough wolf in her that we should put her down now."

Blayne didn't have a chance at a good bout of panic over that particular statement before Bo dropped her, shifted, and leaped at the polar. He took him down, Fabi shifting in the process, but his twelve hundred pounds and average, mundane fangs were nothing compared to Bo's bear-cat sexiness—and yes, that's how she thought of his shifted form.

Bo landed on top of Fabi, keeping the polar pinned to the ground with his weight alone, leaned in, and roared. The sound echoed and the rest of the bears began to move nervously, their jaws popping, their fangs coming out. All except for the older polar. He rolled his eyes and said, "Let him go, Bo. He ain't worth the trouble, and he's your cousin." Yet Bo didn't move; he didn't back down. Finally the older polar added, "You've got my word, I won't let anything happen to the wolfdog. Promise."

That seemed to be enough for Bo. He nodded and stepped off his cousin—*His cousin calls him Speck? Not okay*—moving back and back until he had Blayne pinned against the tree with his big bear butt. She swiped at him, yelped, and she felt his body shake. Laughing at her! He was laughing at her! What a bastard! She caught hold of his long cat tail with her teeth, tugging at it. With a snort, Bo walked off, dragging a tugging, growling, completely ineffectual Blayne behind him.

Oh, but she'd show him. She never gave up. Even when it made complete sense to give up and run away, she wouldn't.

They made it back to the hospital with Blayne attached to Bo's tail the entire way. It amazed him those were the same teeth that had torn into a deer the night before with such gusto. Maybe she was going easy on him, because he didn't feel a thing. He climbed back into the window he'd gone out of, Blayne right behind him since she still held on to his tail. He lifted his tail and placed her on the bed, whipping his tail around until she released him. She rolled off, shifting from wolfdog to naked hottie in seconds, laughing as she rolled across the bed.

Bo shifted and quickly shut the window, knowing how cold it was to everyone else not born and raised in Ursus County, Maine.

"I can't believe you bit his face," he laughed.

"I can't believe that asshole is your cousin. And Speck?"

"The town nickname because I was so small."

"Small? In whose world are you small? And your shifted form?" She rolled to her stomach and rested her chin on her fists. "Wow," she said. "Just . . . wow."

"You're making fun of me, aren't you?"

"No way." Blayne scrambled to her knees. If she remembered

she was naked, she didn't seem to care. "Bo, I think you're amazing."

"I have tusks, Blayne."

"Those aren't tusks. Those are fangs. Like the mighty saber-toothed cats of prehistoric times. If I had those, I'd never be human. I'd run around with my cool, über-long fangs, daring anyone to fuck with the mighty Blayne of the Thorpe Dynasty."

"You have a dynasty?"

"I would if I had those cool fangs!"

Bo grinned, surprising himself. He'd never discussed his fangs before without getting in a fight or walking away hurt, swearing never to shift again. He grew out of that stage, though, and simply stopped shifting unless he was by himself. But he couldn't ignore Blayne's enthusiasm. She really should represent all hybrids. She loved each of them, with all their quirks and foibles and unholy-size body parts, individually. He had to admire that.

"We better get dressed," he said, noticing the pile of clothes someone had put out for them.

"You don't think my father's coming to get me, do you?" And she winced when she asked, making him a little worried.

"I don't know. My uncle is the king of the unclear."

Still kneeling on the bed, Blayne sat back on her haunches. "Wait . . . that was your uncle? The big polar?"

"Yep." The clothes put out for Bo were also his uncle's. He recognized the scent. He nearly smiled again. For the first time, he'd be able to wear his uncle's clothes and not swim in them.

A pillow hit him in the back of the head, and, startled, Bo faced Blayne. "What was that for?"

"Your uncle? Who you haven't seen in ten years? And you don't hug him or kiss him or show him any affection? Because unlike *Flabby*"—and that totally made Bo laugh—"he was nice to you. And seemed concerned."

"The Novikovs don't hug, Blayne."

"Neither do the Thorpes, but that never stopped me before, much to my father's annoyance. No wonder your uncle looked so hurt," she said.

"Hurt? About what?"

"An ungrateful nephew!"

"I didn't see him trying to kiss me or hug me or anything else."

"So?"

"What do you mean, so?"

"Sometimes, you idiot, you have to show affection to get it. Sometimes, you have to suck it up, be a man, and show the people you care about that you actually do care!"

Marci lingered outside the hospital door, listening with avid interest to the argument going on inside. Normally, she'd never be this nosey, but that wolfdog was saying all the things she'd never been able to say before to either idiot, er, Novikov. For years she'd watched them play the "Novikovs don't show emotion" game and for years she'd watched them never get as close as she knew they not only could but should.

And she knew what it was, too. Bold had convinced himself that his uncle was only doing what he morally felt he should do, not that he loved the boy more than he could ever put into words. And Grigori had convinced himself that Bold was so stand-offish because he didn't like him, let alone love him, and that he'd been biding his time waiting to get away from him rather than the entire town who still called him Speck. They were both foolish and incredibly stubborn males who never listened to anyone, and although Marci still tried when she could to get both past all this, she'd given up hope.

Until this very moment. Until this very wolfdog.

"Why are you yelling at me?" Bo asked, and as usual, he didn't sound hurt or angry, merely confused. Male bears . . . the most confused of any carnivore on the planet!

"Because family is all, Bo. You should stay," she suddenly said.

"I am *not* staying."

"I'll go back with whoever is coming to pick me up and you can stay a couple of extra days."

"I'm not staying, Blayne. So forget it."

"Do we really need to have the 'when was the last time you went on vacation' discussion again?"

"The Cup Finals begin in two weeks. Do you really think that I'd miss one day of training before Finals?"

"You know what I just heard? 'Blah blah blah blah blah . . . finals.'"

Marci quickly covered her mouth with her hand and bit the inside of her cheek to keep from laughing.

"You need to stay and see your family."

"No."

"You're being unreasonable."

"And you need to get dressed unless you want me to drag you on that transport naked. And don't you dare cry!"

Marci heard the wolfdog sniff loudly and dramatically three times before saying, "Fine. Be that way. Alone, bitter, friendless."

"Don't alone and friendless kind of go together?" Marci heard something crash, then Bo growl, "And stop throwing things at my head!"

Straightening her clothes and trying to wipe the smile off her face, Marci stepped in front of the doorway and knocked.

Blayne was still seething when the doctor from yesterday knocked and stepped into the room.

"Morning," she said, looking kind of serious.

"Morning," both Blayne and Bo mumbled.

Blayne knew Bo was pissed at her, but she didn't really care. Family was family, in her mind, and unless they were stealing from you or abusing you, a body just had to put up with them. That's what being blood meant. Most hybrids didn't even know their families; shunned from birth, their birth parents forced out, they often ended up living a hard life if anything happened to the ones who raised them. Blayne knew she was lucky that her father had decided to keep her and raise her. Others, unable to survive without their pride, pack, or clan, often deserted their young pups and cubs who then ended up roughing it in the system. It was hard enough being a shifter in a world of nonshifters, but to be a hybrid . . . Blayne couldn't imagine it and didn't really want to. And like her, whether he realized it or not, Bo was one of the lucky ones. He may have lost his parents, but to find a family member willing to take him in was no small feat. So the fact that he didn't slather that polar with love and adoration stuck in her sensitive paw like little else could.

"How are you both feeling?" the doctor asked, stepping farther into the room until she stood between the bed and the side table where someone had put out clothes.

"Fine," Bo mumbled.

"Much better," Blayne said.

"Good." She clapped her hands together, startling Blayne and Bo, causing both of them to snarl a little, but if she noticed, she didn't show it. "So I guess Grigori told you that Blayne's people are coming for her. In fact, they may already be here."

Blayne couldn't help but wince. "My father?"

"Your father is a Van Holtz?"

Blayne not only laughed out of relief, but the thought that some "born with that stick up his ass"—as her dad put it—Van Holtz would deign to claim any wolfdog as their child made her fall back on the bed.

Bo threw clothes at her, his anger already gone as he watched her. "Put some clothes on, Giggles."

"Hey! I could be a Van—"

"Don't even," he cut in, already smiling, which was good because she was laughing again. "Just get dressed."

"I guess the answer to your question then, Blayne, is it's not your father."

Blayne pulled on thermal underwear, sweatpants, and a sweatshirt.

"Hmmm," the doc said. "I was afraid of that." She motioned for Blayne to stand on the bed, and she examined the bottom of the sweats. "These are fox cut pants, but, as I feared, they're too short for you."

"We'll be here another half hour. Tops. She can suck up the shortness."

Before Blayne could point out that no one had asked his damn opinion, the doc did it for her.

"And who asked you, Bold Novikov?" Marci said, tossing shiny black and gray hair off her forehead.

"Bold?" Blayne giggled. "Did you call him Bold?"

"That's his name."

"Dude, your name is Bold?"

"First off, stop calling me dude. And second, you got a problem with my name?"

"Not if you were on the cover of one of my mom's old romance novels."

"Bold is actually a very old and respected Mongolian name," the doctor interjected. "It means steel, and as you know the early Mongolians were all about the power of steel."

"Steel Novikov," Blayne said, ignoring Bo's head dropping forward in defeat. "How *cool is that?*"

"Do not run around telling people my name is Steel or Bold or anything else."

"But—"

"No."

"But—"

"No."

"Just let me—"

"No."

"Someone's Mr. No Fun!"

Laughing, the doctor headed toward the door. "I'll come back for you when Grigori shows up to take you to town. I can't miss the chance of meeting an actual Van Holtz," she said, a teasing smile on her face.

Before walking out, she stopped in the doorway and said, "Oh. One other thing." She walked back to Blayne, pulling something out of her hospital coat and putting it in Blayne's palm.

Staring down at the tiny electronic item, Blayne asked, "What's this?"

"A microchip. It was in your back, right beneath your shoulder blade. Your body was trying to expel it. Probably why you had such a harsh reaction from that last badger attack Bold told me about."

"I don't understand. Microchip?"

"You know," the sow said as she walked to the door. "The kind you'd use to microchip your pet dog or cat. I had the lab check it out, and this one actually has a homing beacon. The lab technician said someone could track you for up to three hundred miles. I'll be back in a few," she promised before walking out the door, leaving Blayne to stare at the chip in her hand.

No way. No. *Way.*

They wouldn't, would they? They wouldn't actually . . . *microchip* Blayne, would they?

But the way she went to sit on the bed, missed it completely, and ended up with her butt on the floor, Bo knew that, at the very least, that's what Blayne thought.

He went down on one knee in front of her, his hand on her shoulder. "Blayne?"

"Ric . . . *microchipped* me? Like a house pet?"

The jealous, devious side of him—he liked to call that the lion side—wanted to scream, "Yes! That bastard microchipped you, and you should never see him again! Or I can kill him for you! Let me kill him for you!" But the expression on her face tore into Bo more than her fangs had torn into Fabi's face. So the nicer bear side replied, "I doubt that. And, if he did, I'm sure he did it for a good reason." That last part made Bo want to retch, but he said it anyway. Although he did adore the look on Blayne's face when she raised her head: her brows pulled in, one corner of her top lip lifted, and she gawked at him as if he'd lost his mind.

"Grigori's here," Dr. Luntz said, walking back in the room. She'd taken off her lab coat and wore a Boston Bruins sweatshirt and a Boston Bruins knit cap. "We better get moving. Storm's coming."

Bo nodded and focused back on Blayne. "You ready?"

She let out a breath and stood. "I'm ready."

And he had to say, the coldness coming off her rivaled any storm coming off the Atlantic that this town had experienced in the last hundred years or so.

Ric paced restlessly in front of Niles Van Holtz until Van finally grabbed his cousin by the arm and held him in place. The nervous pacing didn't bother him, of course, but it sure did bother the twenty bears standing around waiting for nothing more than for them to leave. They'd even brought Ric's friend Lock to accompany them, but the bears seemed to care less about the Van Holtz's grizzly escort. These bears didn't like wolves and they really didn't like Van Holtzes, so they wanted nothing more than to see the back of them.

They waited outside the police chief's office, the bears unwilling to allow them to even sit and wait for Blayne's appearance in a warm room. Whatever. Van could do nothing but smirk at all the bullshit from the uptight bears. His wife used to ask him why he rolled his eyes anytime someone mentioned bears, and as he always said, "Because they don't matter nearly as much as they think they do."

"Ric," Lock said, and both Van and Ric turned, watching the big SUV turning the corner and pulling to a stop a few feet away. A polar boar and a black sow stepped out from the vehicle, followed by the Marauder, a player who had always impressed Van with his unparalleled ruthlessness on the ice and his unwavering lack of approachability off it. And, apparently nothing had changed, his always-there scowl locking on Ric with something akin to a homicidal intent Van found a little unsettling, considering.

Then after all of them came the small wolfdog. She had her eyes down and didn't look at all like the Blayne he'd met in late October of the previous year. That wolfdog had been full of life and laughter, but this Blayne, beyond the bruises and healing wounds littering her face and neck, seemed miserable. Devastated. Christ, what had those full-humans done to her? Or was it these bears who'd hurt her?

He knew his cousin was thinking the same thing as he seemed to grow taller, his back snapping ramrod straight, his head dipping down, and a low growl easing out of him. Lock stepped up beside him, showing whose side he was on should things get ugly and protecting his friend all at the same time.

The small group walked up to them and, after taking a calming breath, Ric asked, "Blayne? Are you all right?"

"Yeah," she said softly. "Yeah. I am."

Lock's gaze moved around the group of bears that, Van abruptly noticed, had grown in number.

"Let's get you both back home," Lock said.

"Yes," Ric agreed, his gaze still on Blayne while she continued to stare at the ground. "Let's get you home, Blayne. Home and safe."

And that's when Miss Thorpe's dark brown eyes fastened on Ric, her gaze ripping into him with a rage that nearly took Van's breath away.

"Blayne?" Ric asked softly, taking a small step toward her.

Growling, Blayne stalked away from all of them. Ric began to go after her, but Grigori Novikov stepped in front of him, blocking him.

The Marauder followed after her instead, the pair stopping once they reached the corner.

Van didn't know what the hell was going on, but he knew it wasn't good. Not even close to good.

"I don't want to go back," she said simply.

Bo blinked, surprised. So this was what Blayne was like when she was really mad. Good to know. "Okay." He wouldn't force her to go back. "Where do you want to go? I have houses in Tahiti, Paris, London, Edinburgh—"

She looked around. "I want to stay here."

"Here . . . where?"

"Here. In Ursus County." She took another look around. "I like it here."

"You can't stay here, Blayne."

"Why not?"

"You can't stay here, Blayne," Bo repeated. "Trust me on this."

Grigori strode up to them, the wolves and MacRyrie waiting for them at the end of the block. "What's going on?"

"Nothing I can't handle," Bo told him.

"Can I stay here?" Blayne asked, and Grigori appeared as stunned as Bo felt when she'd first told him she wanted to stay. Never before, in the history of the town—and it had a very long history—had any non-bear or non-fox not mated to an Ursus County resident ever wanted to stay.

"Stay . . . here?" Grigori's low voice even cracked a little on that question.

Blayne sniffed once, then again. "You . . . you don't want me to stay?"

"Uh . . ."

"That's all right. I understand." A lone tear trailed down her cheek. "If I were you, I wouldn't want me around, either."

"No, no," Grigori rushed to explain, panicking. "Don't misunderstand. It's just—"

"What is going on?" Dr. Luntz demanded as she stomped over. "Those wolves are getting snarly."

Grigori turned to Dr. Luntz. "Blayne wants to stay."

Dr. Luntz watched Grigori for a moment, focused on Bo, and finally focused on Blayne.

"You want to stay here?"

"Not forever. It's just—"

"Of course you can stay, Blayne."

"*What?*" Both Bo and Grigori said at the same time.

"We're not turning this poor, sweet girl away. Besides, it's not forever. Right, Blayne?"

Blayne nodded quickly, recognizing an ally when she found one. "No, ma'am. Not forever."

"Just until these rude bastards learn a lesson about how to treat you. Right?"

Blayne threw her arms around Dr. Luntz's shoulders, going up on her toes to reach them, and hugged her tight.

Dr. Luntz chuckled and hugged her back. "You can stay at Grigori's house." She winked at Grigori. "He won't mind."

Knowing his uncle, Bo was sure Grigori was about to argue that particular point, but Blayne released Dr. Luntz and looked up at Grigori with those wide, imploring eyes. Not wolf eyes. Dog eyes. And who, with a soul, could turn down dog eyes? Bo couldn't, and he now realized, neither could a polar he would have thought was as hard-hearted as they came.

Grigori sighed, big and heavy, before saying, "Of course you can stay, Blayne Thorpe. Wouldn't be right to turn you away, now would it?"

The smile she unleashed nearly knocked all three of them on their asses, it was so bright and wide, and her eyes filled with tears again. This time from gratitude. "I promise, Mr. Novikov, I won't get in your way or bother you or anything."

"Grigori's the name, and I don't think you'll get in my way. Little thing like you."

"You sure about this, Blayne?" Bo asked. "You sure you want to stay?"

"Just until I feel . . . better about going back."

"What's better for you? Groveling or crawling through glass?"

"Anyone can grovel," she grumbled.

"Broken glass it is." Bo shrugged at his uncle and said, "Guess you better get my old room and the guest room ready for us, and I'll tell Van Holtz."

"You can't," Blayne said.

"But I look forward to telling Van Holtz. I'm really hoping on sobbing so I can point at him and laugh."

"I don't mean you can't tell him. Actually, you *can* tell him because I'm not talking to him ever again . . . or until I get over it, which may or may not be ever or even longer."

Grigori and Dr. Luntz exchanged confused glances, but what really freaked Bo out was that he now understood exactly what Blayne meant.

"I mean," she went on, "that you can't stay."

"I'm not leaving you in Ursus County alone."

"I won't be alone." She leaned against Grigori, resting her head against his arm. "Grigori will take care of me."

Dr. Luntz snorted, quickly looking off, while Grigori raised a brow at his nephew.

"Like I'll let that happen," Bo told him, and to Blayne he said, "I'm staying."

"Llewellyn Cup Finals."

Then Bo Novikov said something he never thought he'd ever say. "The Cup Finals will be there next year."

Blayne knew her mouth was hanging open but . . . but . . . he was willing to miss Cup Finals? For her? Had the world gone off its axis? Were volcanoes erupting while rivers and lakes overflowed? Had the world ended? She looked up at the sky. Nope. No pigs flying overhead, either.

"What's that look for?" he asked.

"You're willing to miss the finals . . . for me?"

"I attacked a van for you."

"But that didn't interfere with your schedule."

When Dr. Luntz and Bo's uncle burst out laughing, Blayne knew Bo had always been this way. And for some reason, that made him cuter.

"I'm staying, Blayne."

"Yeah, but—"

"You wanted me to have a vacation. *This* will be my vacation."

"All right. But I don't want any whining about it later. Or any latent bitterness used against me when you're at your lowest."

"Where do you come up with this shit?"

"The *Dr. Phil* show."

"I like that you admit you watch it."

"I'm brave that way."

"Sorry to interrupt the mutual weirdness of you two," Grigori cut in. "But the wolves and that grizzly are getting anxious."

"You want to tell Van Holtz? Or me?"

"*I'm* not speaking to him." She folded her arms over her chest. "So you tell him."

"You've got it." She got the feeling he'd enjoy it, too.

Bo started to walk back over to Ric and the others when Blayne grabbed his arm, thinking of one more thing that could really make this hell on earth for Ulrich Van Holtz.

"You need to tell him one other thing."

"Will it make him even more miserable?"

She laughed. "Oh . . . yeah."

"She's laughing," Lock said next to him. "That's a good sign. Right?"

Ric didn't know. Blayne wasn't acting like Blayne. She was closed off from him. He expected a lot of things from Blayne but that hadn't been it. And he definitely didn't expect her to walk away from him. That last look she'd given him . . . it was like she wanted to rip out his throat. Did she blame him for this? For being taken? For being dragged to Ursus Fucking County of all places?

Maybe she did. And maybe she should.

Although part of him was grateful to the bears for taking her in and patching her up, he also couldn't believe they simply hadn't taken her to the closest shifter-run hospital right there in Brooklyn. They'd transported her out of the state and away from those who'd protect her and didn't see her as "nearly too much wolf to tolerate" as one recently mauled boar with facial lacerations had muttered.

Well, whether she blamed him or not, and whether she was right to blame him or not didn't matter. All that mattered at this very moment was getting Blayne Thorpe back to the city and absolute safety.

"They're heading back," Lock said low, and Ric turned to face them.

That idiot Novikov led the way, and Ric was kicking himself he'd hired the prick for the team. Sure, they were heading to the

Cup Finals because of said prick, but that wasn't the point. He was much too close to Blayne for Ric and Lock's liking, and once they had her back home, Ric was going to put a stop to all the bullshit.

Novikov walked up to him, looked him over, and said, "We're not going back."

Ric waited for some kind of punch line, some kind of indication the big oaf was joking. Unfortunately, Ric kept waiting.

Lock, however, didn't wait. "What do you mean she's not going back?"

Like Ric, Lock could give a flying fuck what Novikov did or didn't do and who he did or didn't do it with, but Blayne was another story all together.

"Was I not clear in my word usage?" Novikov asked with a condescension worthy of British royalty. "Should I simply use smaller words or speak slower to help you understand?"

Lock stepped into Novikov and Ric quickly got between the two. Something he knew was kind of stupid, but he couldn't help himself. Besides, he didn't have time for their boar-posturing bullshit.

"Are you telling us," Ric said, trying to pretend that two males much bigger than him were not snarling and snapping at each other over his head, "that Blayne isn't coming back ever?"

"No. That's not what I'm telling you. But Blayne doesn't feel safe in New York. She feels safe here. And I'm on vacation. I need a vacation."

"Blayne feels safer in Ursus County?" He couldn't help but take a quick glance at all the bears standing around . . . scowling. "Did she hit her head?"

"Heh. Funny," said the man with absolutely no sense of humor.

"Blayne's coming home with me, Novikov."

"No, Van Holtz. She's not. But," he said before Ric could put up a worthy fight, "she will go back to New York when her father comes to pick her up."

Now Ric was completely confused. He immediately looked at Lock, and the grizzly had the same expression on his face.

"Her father? Blayne's father? Ezra Thorpe?"

"Does she have more than one father?"

"I . . . I didn't think you'd want him to know," he said to Blayne who stood behind Novikov and it hurt that she'd feel safer behind the asshole who was known for smashing players' heads into the ice than Ric who'd been watching her back for the last few months.

"She does now," Novikov replied for Blayne. And even that seemed wrong! Had they brainwashed the woman? A woman who barely let anyone speak even when it was their turn? A woman who talked so much that she'd been known to almost pass out from lack of oxygen. *That* Blayne Thorpe was letting this idiot speak *for* her?

What in holy hell is going on?

"You want Blayne back in New York, you'll need to get Ezra Thorpe to come here and get her. It's that simple."

"Yes, but—"

Novikov turned away from him, dismissing Ric that easily in the middle of his sentence and walking away. As he did, Blayne suddenly moved forward, and for a brief moment, Ric thought she'd gotten her sanity back. She walked up to him but didn't speak. Instead, she held her fist out in front of her body. Not to hit him, he didn't think, but to give him something. He held his hand out, palm up, under her fist and she opened her fingers, something small and nearly weightless dropping into it.

Without another word, she turned and walked away, Novikov right with her. The older polar stood in front of them.

"You city folk better get in your chopper and fly away. There's a storm comin'. Hate for you to get caught on the wrong side of that."

Ric closed his hand over what Blayne had given him and said, "I'm not leaving without—"

Van stepped in front of Ric. "Thank you for your hospitality. We'll be in touch."

"As ya like. But don't waste your time coming back here without Blayne's father. We won't like that one bit."

"Of course." Van turned, facing both Ric and Lock. "Let's go, gentlemen."

"You can't be serious," Lock said, stating out loud what Ric had been thinking.

"I rarely am serious, but what I can tell you is these bears *are* serious. Would you like to hang around and wait to find out how serious they are?"

Lock glanced around and, eventually, shook his head. "No. He's right, Ric. We have to go."

Ric nodded, and they all headed back to the rented vehicle they'd picked up at the small airport more than seventy miles away.

Once in the bear-size vehicle and heading out of town, predatory bears of every type watching them from the surrounding forests, Lock asked, "What did Blayne give you anyway?"

Ric realized he'd forgotten all about that and slowly opened his tightly clenched fist so they could look. Lock briefly stopped the SUV, and the three males leaned in and studied what Ric held. It was Van who recognized it first, being that he was one of the rare shifters who, on occasion, enjoyed having pet dogs or cats of his own.

"Holy shit, someone microchipped her."

And as fury washed over Ric, leaving him nearly breathless, he knew there was only one person in the entire universe who'd have the goddamn nerve, the unmitigated gall, to microchip a goddamn shifter.

"I'll kill her!"

CHAPTER 18

Bo stopped the snowmobile in front of the one-story cabin where he'd grown up. It still had the long wraparound porch with those old but comfortable chairs he'd sit in for hours every night and dream about the day he'd get out of here.

Blayne clung to him, her arms tight around his waist, her head resting against his back. If he had to come back here, he couldn't think of a better way than this.

True, he'd expected to be on his way back to the city by now, but he knew Blayne wasn't ready to return. He didn't blame her. At the moment, she didn't know who to trust or what the hell was going on. Maybe if Van Holtz had brought Gwen with him, but bringing the Alpha of his Pack was just... weird. Why would Niles Van Holtz come? Why would he care? Being friends with a packmate didn't make you Pack. At least not as far as the Van Holtzes were concerned.

The thought that Van Holtz was interested in making Blayne his own had crossed Bo's mind more than once, and letting her stay in Ursus County until her old man showed up seemed like a better and better idea the more he thought about it. Besides, time alone with Blayne would give Bo a chance that, as far as he was concerned, Van Holtz hadn't earned. Of course, he would have preferred taking this shot with Blayne at one of his other homes.

Especially since he had them set up perfectly, including access to free-range hunting.

Not to say he didn't like his uncle's more modest yet sizable house. Bo actually loved this place, not realizing that fact until he'd left.

He opened the always unlocked front door and stepped inside, Blayne still right behind him, holding on to the back of his uncle's denim jacket. The house still smelled the same, looked the same. Yet Bo was shocked at the sense of tranquility he felt stepping inside. He knew immediately that keeping Blayne here, at least for the time being, was the best idea all around.

Once inside, Bo went down the hall and into the living room. He walked over to the giant sectional. A big "L" shape, the couch took up most of the room, allowing up to two polars to sleep on either section as human or as bear.

Bo reached behind and caught hold of Blayne's wrist, tugging her around until she stood in front of him. "I'll be back. Okay?"

She nodded and sat down on the edge of the couch before glancing around. "I feel like I'm in a home for giants."

Feeling a little playful and wanting to put her at ease, he patted her head and said, "Don't worry, tiny little female. We only eat uninvited canines."

She slapped his hand off. "Very funny."

Chuckling, Bo walked away from her, out of the living room and into the hallway. If he went left, he'd find his uncle's bedroom. If he went right, he'd find a guest bedroom, a bathroom, and his old room. That's the way he went first. The door was open and Bo walked inside, but he stopped halfway in, shocked to find that his room was exactly how he'd left it. His desk, with the framed pictures of his parents, still had his last list that included what he'd need to pack and the time he'd need to leave his uncle's house to catch his ride to Philly and his future. His senior year school books, conveniently placed on his desk for easy access during homework time, were still expertly aligned, along with his pencils, pens, and extremely heavy laptop where he'd typed up all his papers. His framed hockey posters were still aligned on the wall, his books were still aligned and grouped according to subject on his bookshelves, and his closet was still neatly arranged with the clothes he'd left behind.

There was one new addition, though. His senior hockey jersey from his final winning game. It had been framed and placed on the wall by the head of his bed. Since he'd never had a headboard, the jersey sort of served in that role.

It seemed so strange to see that his uncle had done that. Not once, in the ten years he'd lived with the man, had Grigori mentioned Bo's hockey obsession other than to say every morning when Bo was heading out to the ice pond, "Skating again?" And Bo would always reply back, "Yep."

Not sure what any of this was supposed to mean or if he needed to think about it too much, Bo started to back up, but a hand against his back stopped him, and he watched Blayne slip around him and walk into the room.

"This place is kind of freaky big but I think I sort of love it. It's very manly with all the wood and everything."

She plopped onto his bed, bouncing several times. "Wow. You had a king-size bed when you were in high school?"

"That's considered a double."

"Oh."

He had the feeling it was finally starting to dawn on her what she'd put herself into. Not everyone could handle living among bears.

"This is all your neatness, isn't it?" she asked, her avid gaze taking everything in.

"How can you tell?"

"The type of organization you use. The almost Nazi regime alignment you've got going here."

"You're comparing my love of things being organized to Nazi Germany?"

"Yeah," she answered simply. She saw the jersey and rolled her eyes. "I can't believe you put up your own jersey."

"I didn't."

"Really?" She pursed her lips and watched Bo for a long moment. "So your uncle did it?"

Bo stuck his hands in the back pockets of his jeans. "Yeah. I guess."

"Uh-huh. The uncle you haven't spoken to in ten years."

"The phones work both ways."

"Well that's some lame-shit excuse-making you've got going there." She dropped back on the bed. "So where am I sleeping?"

"Here."

"Someone's getting a tad cocky."

"I'll be in the guest room, little Miss Assumption."

"I can take the guest room. You know . . . since I am the guest."

"Nope. You'll stay here." He liked the thought of her being in his bed whether he was with her or not. He liked it a lot.

"Are you insisting on that so your sports jersey can subconsciously influence my feelings about you?"

Bo shook his head. "You are so weird."

"So says Mr. Alignment. Or should I call you Herr Alignment?"

"Funny."

Blayne suddenly sat up. "I want to go running."

"Running? Running where?"

"Anywhere. I need to go running."

"You've been through a lot. Can't you just relax?"

"Running is relaxing."

"Wolfdog or human?"

"Either."

"There's a storm coming."

"Is it a nor'easter?"

Again Bo shook his head, turned to walk out, but found his uncle standing behind him. "I wish you wouldn't do that."

"I wish you'd be more observant." He motioned to Blayne with his chin. "Adams is coming over here to talk to your wolfdog."

"The name's Blayne," she said while studying Bo's bookshelves. "Feel free to use it."

"Quiet, sassy." Grigori leaned in and whispered low, "You better talk to her."

"Talk to me about what?" When his uncle glared in her direction, Blayne tapped her ear. "Wild dog hearing."

"Great. Adams will be here in about five minutes," he told Bo. "Get her ready."

"Yep." Bo stepped back in the room and found Blayne walking across the floor on her hands. Although he appreciated the view of her long legs, he still had to ask, "What are you doing?"

"What does it look like I'm doing?" She forward flipped, landing right in front of him. "I need to go running," she said again, and he was starting to realize she didn't mean it in the "I had too many funnel cakes and I need to burn them off" sense.

"Why do you *need* to go running?"

"Because I have a lot of energy built up, and if I don't work it off, I won't be held responsible."

"That kind of sounds like a threat."

"It kind of is."

Bo quickly looked her over. "You can't go running in those clothes."

"I know. These boots are way too big and the pants way too small." She leaned around him and gazed into his closet. "Do you have anything I can borrow?" When he snorted, she added, "From when you were a kid?"

"Sure." Bo went to his closet and pulled out one of his old jerseys. He tugged it over her head, pulled her arms through the sleeves, and let the jersey drop.

"I can't run in a dress," she said, not even looking at what he'd put on her.

"It's not a dress, which I haven't worn since the baptism." He pulled her to his dresser mirror. "That's my junior high hockey jersey. I wore this when I was twelve."

"I sense you're trying to tell me something."

"I am. I'll need to buy you clothes. If we can find them in your size."

"That's okay. I'll pay you back when this is over."

"No."

"No?"

"If you have to pay me back, it'll limit what I can buy you and how much. I don't like limits. Therefore . . ."

"Therefore?"

"Therefore you will take what I give you and thank me for it by saying 'thank you.' Since I know you'll assume it—sex will not be required for said clothes."

"You sure you never went to college?"

"Nope. I just read a lot of books. You should try it."

"Books . . . so endlessly boring!" Lifting up the sides of his jersey as if it were a gown, Blayne twisted from side to side like a little girl showing off her newest birthday dress. "How about you buy me what you want and I'll make you dinner when we get back. I'll even throw in my killer chocolate mousse. Because I'm that giving."

"I'll agree if you use my kitchen."

"You've cleaned my kitchen, so it's totally ready for food service."

"It's too small. You can use mine."

"You've scrubbed that kitchen within an inch of its life, haven't you?"

"Actually, no. I don't have that kind of time anymore. So I hire people to do it for me. But they've passed my white glove inspection and that's all that matters to me."

Blayne laughed, relaxing back so her head rested against his chest. She smiled at him in the mirror. "Your sense of humor is not for everyone, but I have to say it's growing on me. Like an out-of-control fungus."

"That's lovely."

Her head tilted to the side. "I hear a truck."

"That's the police chief, so I'll make this quick. You don't remember anything from the attack after they dragged you out of my truck."

"I don't?"

"No."

"Why not?"

"Remember how worried you were about my reaction to what I saw in the van?"

"Yeah?"

"Use that logic here. Wolfdogs have a reputation, Blayne. Combine that reputation with trained skills instilled in a daughter by her loving father, and we have worried bears. Worried bears lead to easily startled bears, which leads to tragic maulings. Let's keep those to a minimum."

"I don't understand. Are you telling me that everyone knows or doesn't know about what happened in that van?"

"I think they're not sure. You not remembering protects both of us. What works in your favor is that everyone here considers you small"—he pressed his hand over her head and pushed a little until she bent her knees—"and kind of goofy." He swooshed her around a bit.

"This is humiliating," she complained, trying to knock his hand off.

"All their misconceptions work in our favor. You being confused and with some memory loss covers us until we leave." He released her. "Speaking of which, any ballpark on when your father might get here?"

"My father? Oh. That would be never."

"Sorry?"

"My father will never come here to get me unless you're releasing my body. And that would be only so he could yell at my corpse for being an idiot at getting caught by trappers."

"Your father's going to blame *you* for this?"

"If my father could, he'd blame me for World War Two and the disappearance of the Aztecs."

"You two have a very odd relationship."

"We do."

"Then I'm unclear on why you sent Van Holtz to him."

"So when he realizes how little my father cares, he'll feel guilty and come back here *on his knees*." She tossed her hair over her shoulder. "*Then* I'll go back. But not before."

They heard a knock at the door, and Blayne headed out of the bedroom. She stopped briefly in the doorway. "Can I keep this jersey?"

"No."

"Thank you!" She skipped out of the room. Were grown adults supposed to skip?

"I said 'no,'" he called after her. "It was definitely and unequivocally a 'no.'"

"And I'm definitely and unequivocally ignoring your 'no,'" she called back.

And for some damn reason that reply made him smile.

Gwen paced incessantly in the small airport's main room, the staff that handled all the transport for wealthy shifters watching her closely, ready to bolt at any second. She, however, didn't care. She only knew she wanted Blayne back.

The doors opened and the three males who'd gone after Blayne walked through—alone. Her muscles going tight, Gwen rushed up to Lock. "Where is she?"

"Let's talk over here."

"No. Tell me now."

Lock caught her arm and pulled her toward the corner, but she knew if Blayne wasn't back, it was one man's fault.

Knowing that she'd never be able to get away from Lock without causing him damage, she simply turned her head to scowl at the male she blamed for all this. He and his cousin or uncle or whatever the hell Niles Van Holtz was to Ric stopped walking and the cousin or uncle or whatever suddenly screamed, *"Jesus Christ! How does she do that with her neck?"*

"Where's my Blayne!" she bellowed over the other one. *"What did you do, Van Holtz?"*

Lock picked her up and carried her to the closest bathroom. Once inside, he said, "You need to calm down."

"I'll calm down when I have Blayne back. Where's Blayne?"

"She won't leave Ursus County."

It was Lock's wording that caught Gwen's attention, and she

immediately calmed down. "What do you mean, she won't leave?"

"She says she won't leave."

"What did those bears do to her? Is this some kind of Munchausen syndrome or something?"

"You mean Stockholm Syndrome. And it's Munchausen or Munchausen by proxy, which is completely different from—"

"Lachlan!"

"Okay, okay." He blew out a breath. "Blayne's really upset right now because someone microchipped her, so she's not coming back."

Gwen felt her anger spike again. "Ric microchipped Blayne?"

"No. Of course he didn't."

And if it wasn't Ric, then it had to be . . . *"That She-whore!"*

Gwen flung the door open to walk out and find the heifer who'd done this to her friend when Lock's big hand slammed the door closed before she could leave.

"You're not going anywhere."

"Like hell I'm not."

"Let Ric handle this."

"Do you really expect me to leave my friend alone in bear country while these bureaucrats screw around with Blayne's life?"

"Gwen, she's got the protection of someone I know will watch out for her. He's a former Unit commander and Novikov's uncle. No one's going to hurt Blayne."

"She's not planning to stay there forever is she?" Although Gwen wouldn't put it past Blayne. Actually, she wouldn't put *anything* past Blayne when she was pissed off enough. And microchipping her . . . oy.

"Of course she's not. She simply wants her father to come for her. Probably to ensure it's safe enough to come home." The snort was past her nose before she could rein it in, and Lock's eyes immediately narrowed. "What?"

Gwen shook her head. "Nothing. So is Ric going to, uh, *talk* to Petty Officer Thorpe?"

"Probably his Uncle Van."

"Okay then." Gwen turned, grabbed the handle to the bathroom door, and pulled it open.

But, again, Lock shoved it closed with his hand.

"What aren't you telling me?"

"What makes you think I'm not telling you something?"

"Maybe because you answered me with a question?"

"Maybe you're reading questions that aren't there?"

"Gwendolyn—"

"I'm positive that Blayne's father will do what is in the best interest of his daughter."

"Really?"

"Absolutely." She grinned because it helped her to stop from laughing hysterically. "Because if there's one thing I know, Lock, is how much that man loves his baby girl."

"I don't remember what they were wearing."

"You said earlier they were wearing ski masks. So which is it? You don't remember or they were wearing ski masks?"

Dammit! This was why Blayne avoided lying. She simply wasn't very good at it. It took too much to remember what she'd said and what the truth was and what she could tell and what she couldn't. So she handled the gruff, less-than-friendly black bear police chief, Ray Adams, the way she was often forced to handle her dad when he found her crawling into her bedroom window after curfew . . .

Blayne burst into tears.

The police chief's entire body jerked in surprise, and Grigori hit him in the shoulder. "What the hell's the matter with you?"

"*Me?*"

"Apologize."

"Fine. Miss Thorpe, I'm—where did she go?"

She heard Bo clear his throat. "She's under the couch."

"Under the . . ."

She watched as three sets of enormously large feet appeared in front of her, followed by three faces, two that appeared fascinated, another that was trying not to laugh. Blayne made sure more tears and snot-filled sobs followed.

"Good God, she is under the couch."

"You frightened me!"

Adams's body jerked again, and Grigori again slugged his shoulder. "You frightened her."

"Frightened her," Bo said, shaking his head sadly.

"I didn't mean to. I was just asking some questions." They stood up and she got another view of those feet. Like the Spanish Armada those feet.

"Look," she heard the police chief bark, "I'm not trying to frighten her—"

"And yet you are."

"You are," Bo repeated.

"She's hiding under my couch . . . sobbing!"

"Sobbing," Bo repeated, and Blayne had to put her hand over her mouth to stop from laughing.

"How do you live with yourself, Adams?"

"Yeah. How do you?"

"Would you shut up!" Adams snapped, and she knew it was directed at Bo.

"I think you've asked her enough questions," Grigori said, and the feet moved away from her line of sight. A few seconds later, the front door opened and closed, and when the sound of the truck roared to life, the feet returned.

"You think we should leave her under there?"

"We could. She could scare off the dust bunnies."

"Very funny." She stuck her hands out. "Help please."

Big hands grabbed her and carefully pulled her from under the couch, placing her on her feet.

"Are you all right?" Grigori asked.

"I'm fine. Sorry I had to Plan B it."

"It worked."

"How worried do I have to be?" she asked.

"Not at all. Adams is just being nosey."

"And I make him nervous."

Grigori gave her a small smile. "Wolves make us cranky, but you're under my protection, Blayne Thorpe. So you have nothing to worry about." He leaned down a bit, his face close. "But that, little girl, means no knives."

She shook her head. "No, sir. I, uh, just get a little testy when I'm backed into corners."

"I'll keep that in mind and make sure everyone else is clear on it. Fair enough?"

"Yes, sir."

He stood tall. "Then we have an understanding. And while you're here"—he gestured to Bo—"you can keep him out of trouble."

"Me? What did I do?"

Grigori grunted and walked off.

"More like I'll need to keep *you* out of trouble," Bo muttered to himself.

"Not if I can go running!" She ran in place, giving him a big cheesy smile. "Exercise is good for the soul. At least that's what my anger management therapist in tenth grade told me. Wait. Don't walk away. She gave me great info that helps all hybrids!"

CHAPTER 19

Van stood at the front door of the Queens, New York, house and knocked again. When no one answered, he walked down the front porch steps and briefly debated what to do next. He had the man's cell phone and home number, but this wasn't something one told over the phone or left a message about.

Deciding to wait in his limo until Thorpe showed up, Van headed down the front path. But he stopped, turned his head. His ears twitched, and he knew he heard something coming from the back of the small house. He followed the sound until he reached a metal fence. A black man in his fifties, wearing a Harley Davidson sweatshirt and grime-covered jeans worked in the near freezing cold on a cycle that even Van would have to say was gorgeous. Of course, he knew nothing about motorcycles. The Van Holtz Pack liked to get around in more conventional vehicles. Cars, private planes, hovercrafts.

The Magnus Pack, however . . .

And although Ezra Thorpe hadn't been part of that Pack in a number of years, it seemed his love of motorcycles had not faded.

Van unclipped the metal gate and walked into the backyard. He moved cautiously until he stood behind the wolf; then he waited.

Thorpe, his hands deftly untwisting something from the bike, didn't turn around when he said, "Explain to me why some stray is in my backyard?"

"Mr. Thorpe. I'm Niles Van Holtz."

Thorpe looked over his shoulder, his cold, light amber gaze swept Van from his feet to his head. "Yeah. You certainly are." He focused back on his bike. "So explain to me why some Van Holtz is in my backyard."

"It's about your daughter, Mr. Thorpe."

"What did she do now?"

Van didn't know why the wolf would ask that question, but he answered him anyway. "Nothing."

"She must have done something for you to be here. That girl can find trouble in an empty milk carton."

"Full-humans snatched your daughter last night in Brooklyn."

Van would admit, he expected a modicum of panic from that sentence. The wolf didn't even tense up. And he kept fixing his bike.

"What does that have to do with the Van Holtz Pack? I wasn't aware you let in hybrids."

They didn't but Van was working on that.

When Van didn't respond, Thorpe asked, "So where's the body? Shouldn't I be identifying something?"

Van worked hard not to judge people's actions against his own. His wife was a good example. Many found her cold, but he knew better. So maybe he was just not reading the wolf right.

"There is no body, and your daughter is quite alive."

"Then what do you want?"

"She's currently in Ursus County. We'd like you to come with us to retrieve her."

Thorpe's hands stopped moving, and slowly, he looked over his shoulder again at Van. "Why?"

"She's requested your presence."

"Why?"

Getting frustrated, "Could you just come with us to get your daughter please?"

Thorpe grabbed a rag and wiped his hands while getting to his feet. "Why don't you just tell me what's going on?"

"Full-humans have been snatching hybrids and using them to fight. Like pit bulls. Your daughter's name was sold a few months back, and we've been watching her ever since, hoping she'd lead us to them."

"I see." He studied Van again. "The Group, right? You work for them."

He ran them, but he wasn't sure admitting that would help him right now.

"You know, something doesn't make sense," Thorpe went on. "My daughter is all about helping. She gives strangers on the street food, helps out at the pound, and runs—while not being chased, mind you—in marathons to help different charities. That's just her way. So, I see her being all over this particular situation like a bad rash . . . if she knew. So my question to you, Van Holtz—did my daughter know?"

"No."

"So you were using her as bait? And Christ knows, my daughter hates to be lied to," he laughed. "So she stuck you with me. Right? This was her brilliant idea?"

Feeling a small sense of relief that the man understood the situation better than Van could hope and, more important, seemed to be taking it so well, Van nodded. "You could say that."

Thorpe chuckled a little more. "That girl. Look, why don't I make this easy for you and me?" Thorpe tossed the rag to the ground and placed his hands on his hips. The sleeves of his sweatshirt were rolled up to the elbow, and Van saw the anchor tattooed on Thorpe's right forearm, but it was the tattoo on his left forearm that was far more telling. It was his daughter's name and her birthdate.

"Blayne likes to feel we have a rough-and-tumble acrimonious relationship, and I let her. Because in a bizarre, Blayne-like way it makes her feel more normal when, in fact, my girl's weird. I know she's weird. Her friends know she's weird. And we all accept it because she's weird, but she's also amazing. And I want my weird but amazing girl safe. So this is what you're going to do. You're going to track down the fuckers who grabbed her and you're going to do what the Group does best, which is wipe their full-human asses from the planet. You're going to do this in a timely manner and then, when it's safe, I'll go with you to bring my girl back." He stepped in closer. "And, even after staying with those goddamn bears in Ursus County—who, by the way, hate wolves and are terrified of wolfdogs—my girl better be as annoyingly perky and helpful as she was when she was grabbed, or I'll raze Van Holtz territory to the ground from here to the West Coast, leaving nothing but craters the size of the Atlantic Ocean when I'm done."

Shocked, Van stuttered, "I'm . . . I'm sorry?"

"Didn't anyone tell you? That's what I used to do in the Navy. I was an engineer. Worked with the SEALS. I can take an amount of plastique that would barely blow up a squirrel and level a city block with it. It's all about placement, really. Find the right weak spot and I can destroy anything. So you're gonna make sure my kid is safe, since you put her in this position. Or you can start telling your wife and kids now how much you'll miss them when they're gone."

A shocking burst of anger shot through Van's system, and his chest slammed into Thorpe's, but the lone wolf only laughed.

"Come on," he said, showing a smile he'd often seen from the wolf's daughter. "You're gonna fuck up that nice cashmere coat? And if it makes you feel any better, I'm sure when we get Blayne back, she'll forgive you. Even if I won't."

The wolf turned his back on Van, and Van knew that Thorpe felt no fear from him. A true lone wolf. There were some that were nervous freaks, terrified by every sound or strange look. Then there were the ones like Thorpe. They'd sneak into a camp full of sleeping humans and drag one of the smaller adults or teenagers off into the night for food. Why? Because they didn't give a fuck.

As Van returned to his waiting limo, he knew that they'd have to do exactly what Thorpe had demanded. They had no choice. Not just for the Van Holtz Pack's safety but for the safety of everyone who might come in contact with the wolfdog's father.

There were some very dangerous men in the world who were completely safe to be around . . . until something happened to the one person in their lives who kept them happy. Clearly, as irritating as he said he found her, Blayne kept her father happy. And if something happened to that wolfdog while she was living among all those unstable bears, then there would be nothing else for that lone wolf to give a fuck about—and to Van that meant everyone else would pay.

"What do you have on your feet?"

Blayne lifted up her leg, grabbed her foot in the palm of her hand, and brought it up until she could easily see what she had on her feet. The Babes didn't call her "Flexi" for nothing. "In common vernacular, I'd say they were shoes. Of the sneaker variety."

Bo's gaze flickered over her stretched leg. She knew she heard a little growl, but she pretended she didn't. She liked giving the hybrid her infamous blank stare. She could tell it drove him nuts.

"These aren't the sneakers Norm recommended," he said.

"Those were expensive and these are on sale. And they're cute!"

His gaze continued to move along the length of her leg. "You have a very pronounced arch."

"Years of ballet and gymnastics." To illustrate, she went up on her toes with the leg she still had on the ground.

And there goes that growl again.

Okay, she'd admit it. She was having the best time. The absolute best! Blayne knew she shouldn't be. She knew she was in huge denial over being betrayed by a very close friend or possibly friends, but playing with Bo was making all that much easier to deal with. Why? Because he took everything so seriously! Honestly . . . sneakers? He was upset over sneakers? He almost made it too easy to toy with him.

"If you're going to run around here," he said, trying desperately not to look at any of the hockey equipment taunting him from across the room, "with all this packed snow and ice, you should take Norm's recommendations."

"He makes *expensive* recommendations. I've put myself on a budget because I won't abuse our friendship."

"Why don't you just admit you're always cheap."

"Not cheap. Thrifty! I love getting deals."

"A Prah-Duhhhh watch is not a deal."

"It was pink and sparkly."

"And couldn't tell time."

"Are we back here again?"

Bo stood and grabbed Blayne by the ankle, flipping her over. "Hey!" Carrying her by her one leg he took her back over to Norm Blackmon, local Maine sloth bear and sports supplier.

The inconsiderate hybrid held her up in front of Norm, ignoring her hysterical giggles. "These aren't going to work for her."

"I know," Norm grumbled. He talked in a grumble, Blayne had noticed, all the time. "Tried to tell her. She kept looking for cheaper. Cheaper ain't always better, Miss Blayne Thorpe."

"But these are cuter," she reminded them both. "And how come everybody in Maine uses my full name?"

"Get her the other ones." Bo yanked off the sneakers she wore and handed them back to Norm. "A few pairs, different colors. I have no idea how long we'll be here."

"Yep."

"You're ignoring my wants and needs."

"Quiet." He held her upside down until Norm returned with the sneakers. Bo flipped her over and placed her on her feet. After allowing her a short dizzy spell from all the blood rushing back and forth between both ends, he took the shoebox from Norm and crouched in front of her.

"That pair's a bit bigger in the toe 'cause she's wearing the thick thermal socks I gave her. Those will keep her feet warm when she's running or just walking around."

"Good. You better give me twenty more pairs of those, too. She's not real good with doing laundry."

"Hey!"

Bo finished lacing up and tying her sneakers. "How does that feel?"

"Like I may lose toes due to lack of circulation."

"Oh." He undid the laces and retied them, this time without causing her acute pain. "Better?"

"Yep."

He stood, forcing Blayne to drop her head back to see him.

"You have everything you need?" he asked.

"And more."

He grunted—she decided to take it as a verbal agreement—and held his hand out to the salesgirl who worked for Norm. "Here." He attached a small MP3 player to her new, insulated vest, dropping the earplugs into her palm. "I had them download some music for you."

"How do you know what I like?"

"I cleaned that pit you call an apartment. Not hard to figure out what you like from that. And you have very eclectic taste in music."

"I bore easily." Blayne smiled. "Thank you for this." She touched the very expensive player that even refurbished and online, she couldn't find a reasonable price she was willing to spend to get one. "That was very sweet."

"Uh-huh."

Grigori walked into the store carrying a medium-size bag from a jewelry store. "Here," he said, reaching into the bag and pulling out a square box. He handed it to his nephew. Even if Blayne didn't know what it was from the shape and dimension of the gift box, she'd have known from Bo's reaction. Like a drug addict about to get a long-needed fix, he tore open the gift box and took out a big, silver watch. He put it on his wrist and sighed happily.

When Blayne looked up at Grigori, he quickly said, "It wasn't me. According to his mother, he was born this way."

Grigori took out another box and opened it, taking out a

smaller version of Bo's watch and placing it on Blayne's wrist. "Anytime you're out of the house or away from me and Bo, you wear this, Blayne. You understand? Any problems, you use this button here to open the face and push the button inside to send out an alert. This signal goes directly to the county's police department, so someone will come right for ya. Okay?"

"Where's the one Bo gave me?" she asked.

"It's not going to be easy to fix."

"That's okay. I just want it back."

Bo scowled. "So you can have even *more* crap in your apartment?"

"I want it!" she yelled, making all the bears close by jump and look at her. "For sentimental reasons," she finished softly.

"It's broken. What sentimental reasons could it—ow!" He covered his arm where she'd pinched him. "What was that for?"

"For pissing me off." She pointed at the new watch. "And exactly how much did this one cost? And don't lie to me."

"I choose not to say."

"You choose not to say?"

"Yeah. You don't want me lying, so I'm not going to tell you."

She turned to Grigori, and he instantly put up his hands. "Watch me not get in the middle of this."

"Did it cost more than the other one?" she demanded.

"I'm not saying."

She stomped her foot, getting frustrated with Bo. "The other one cost too much."

"It saved our lives. I don't know about you, but I can't put a price tag on that."

"I can't take this." She tried to get it off, but the clasp wouldn't open. She looked up at Bo and he shrugged.

"It's childproof."

"It's what?"

"Only cub sizes will fit you, so I told the jeweler to make sure it was childproof. That way cubs can't take them off and lose them during the day when they're out playing with other cubs."

"I am *not* a cub."

"No. You're not. But still . . . I'm glad I did it."

She snarled, but Grigori put his hand on her shoulder. "It's for your protection, Blayne."

"You might as well have me handcuffed!" she ranted. "I feel trapped! Tagged like a lion in the wild!"

"On that note . . ." Grigori picked up the gift boxes and paper and headed toward the door. "See ya!" Then he was gone.

Blayne held her arms up to the ceiling. "Don't you understand?" she pleaded. "I'm a wolfdog meant to be free! To roam the hills and roads as I see fit. Not to be held down by your expensive timekeeping devices. *I can't live in this kind of*—ooh! Earmuffs." She walked over to the display and found several really cute pairs that would definitely keep her ears warm. One pair was even made to look like a raccoon head. She put those on first and grinned at Bo. "What do you think?"

When he only let out a frustrated breath and walked away, she shrugged and went back to sorting through the rest.

Bo watched Blayne jog off down the street. He really hoped that running would manage those wildly swinging emotions of hers. True he enjoyed them, but he wasn't sure every other bear in a two-hundred-mile radius would.

Taking one last look at the hockey display in the window, Bo forced himself to walk away. He was on a break. A vacation. He didn't *need* hockey. He could survive without it. And he would. He walked into the local bookstore and checked out the display, grabbing several things to read. When he realized that only took fifteen minutes of his time, he decided his uncle's house needed some sorting out.

A lot of sorting out. Plus, the extra clothes and things Blayne had purchased would need to be organized and put away, and the kitchen could do with a good scrubbing. Yep.

See? He didn't need hockey. Nope. He was fine without it.

Marci slammed down her cup of coffee on the counter. "I don't believe any of you."

"It's true, Marci," Lorna Harper said, leaning over the counter of her tea and coffee shop and lowering her voice. "They say that girl with Speck killed all those full-humans. With her bare hands."

"First off, Lorna Harper," Marci began, trying to control her black bear temper, "stop calling Bold Novikov Speck. And second, trust me when I say that sweet little girl didn't do anything but nearly get killed. It was Bold who came to her rescue."

"Everyone knows wolfdogs are crazy, Marci Luntz," Jezebel Simons, spectacled bear and the town's bookkeeper, said in that imperious way she had. "And from what we've heard, she ain't no different. Nearly bit poor Fabi Novikov's face clean off."

"Actually, it was just his nose," a voice said behind them, causing the three sows to scream, Marci and Jezebel spinning around with bear claws unleashed.

When Marci saw it was Blayne standing behind them, she quickly put her claws away and bumped Jezebel with her hip. "Blayne, dear. We didn't know you were there."

"I saw you through the window and wanted to say 'hi.'" She pointed at her head. "Do you like my new earmuffs?"

They were bright pink—and bunnies. She had bunnies on either side of her head. They were earmuffs Marci had bought her twin granddaughters . . . who were five.

"Adorable."

She grinned, looking quite pleased. "Thank you."

Marci, wanting to give the other sows a moment to catch their breaths and for Lorna to stop popping her jaw in warning, observed, "I see you got yourself a whole new wardrobe."

"Yes. I like to run and Bo wanted me to have the right clothes so I didn't"—she made air quotes with her insulated glove–covered hands and lowered her voice—" 'freeze that cute but dumb ass off.' "

Marci, recognizing all the Novikov men in that imitation, laughed and was glad to hear Lorna and Jezebel joining in.

"That boy," Marci said. "Takes after his uncle."

"I'm waiting for him to walk home," Blayne explained, "so I can go back to the sports store."

"Going to spend a little more of Bold Novikov's money, dear?" Lorna asked, and Marci wanted to slap her.

"Oh, no. Well . . . actually . . . okay, yeah." When the three sows only stared at her, Blayne added, "What I mean is, I'm going to spend more of his money, but for him. He's on this, 'I'm on vacation' kick and so he thinks that means he shouldn't play hockey, but I know and you know and the *universe* knows that if that man doesn't get on some skates soon, all hell will break loose. So once I'm sure he's gone, I'm going to have Mr. Blackmon round up his best equipment for Bo and send it over to his uncle's house. Kind of like when trying to entice a reformed alcoholic to start drinking again. You just leave the bottle of scotch lying around until he finds it."

"That's an interesting . . . comparison," Marci said, working hard not to cringe.

"Anyway, I just came in to say 'hi.' " Blayne waved at them and said, "Hi!"

Marci and the other two sows jumped but all managed to remain calm. Perhaps because their cubs weren't in the room.

Blayne started to walk out but she stopped and faced them again. "I just want you all to know, I'm not here to cause any problems or bring problems or anything. I know I should have probably just gone home with Ric and Lock and Mr. Van Holtz but . . ." she focused on the floor. "I really don't know who to trust right now. Except Bo. He saved my life, and I want to do what I can to make sure he's happy while he's here." She looked off, bit her lip, and said softly, "He's been so wonderful to me. I don't know what I would have done . . ."

Before Marci could move, Jezebel had her arms around Blayne, hugging her tight against her.

"Now don't cry. There's no reason to cry."

"I don't know what's wrong with me." Blayne stepped back, wiping her eyes with her hand. "I'm not usually this emotional."

Uh . . . she's not?

"You've been through so much, sweetheart. Is it any wonder you're a bit upset over the little things?"

Lorna, one of the more tightfisted bears, came around the counter and handed Blayne a cinnamon pastry stick. She knew well enough that Blayne had no money on her, but the thought that Lorna would give anything for free had Marci dazzled.

"You take this, dear heart. You'll need the extra energy if you're going running."

Blayne took the treat and smiled at Lorna. "Thank you, ma'am."

"Now none of that ma'am business. We're not that old! I'm Lorna. And this is Jezebel Simons. Now you need anything, you just let us know, all right?"

"Thank you so much." She gave them a watery smile while enjoying her pastry and walked out the door.

"That poor thing," Lorna said once Blayne was gone.

"I know!" Jezebel agreed, their tones completely changing in the five minutes the girl was in the shop. "I hope that Grigori Novikov is taking good care of her."

"He better be," Lorna said, walking back around her counter. "Or he'll have to answer to me!"

Blayne walked to the end of the street and turned the corner, her knees almost melting from the delicious taste of the pastry in her hand.

"How did it go?" Grigori asked her, leaning up against the building, reminding Blayne of the man's nephew.

If Bo ages this well . . . yowza.

"Just as you said."

"You got the tears, too?"

"I told Gwen working on that tenth-grade production of *Romeo and Juliet* would totally pay off one day."

He grinned. "Good kid. Have a good run." He walked past her and rubbed her head, reminding her she needed to do something with her hair. She'd checked out what Grigori had in his three bathrooms before heading into town, and those two-in-one shampoo-conditioners were considered Satan's plaything among the O'Neill Pride. She'd have to find something better.

"I know I saw a drugstore," she mumbled around the pastry. She did see one. About a block away. She started down the street but froze, slowly turning and facing the store she stood in front of.

After a moment, she walked inside and almost fell to her knees.

"What do you want?" a grizzly sow snapped at her from behind the counter, and Blayne knew she was being rude to her, but she didn't care.

She pointed at the rows and rows of shampoos and conditioners, all—according to the signs out front—made from honey. "Your products . . ."

"What about them?"

"All natural?"

"Of course." And the sow sounded mighty insulted. "No silicones, parabens, sulfates, or anything else you shouldn't be putting on your hair."

Blayne dropped to her knees, real tears this time streaming down her face as she looked up at the suspicious sow. "I've been searching for you all my life!"

When Dee walked into the Van Holtz restaurant, she knew something was off. The waiters were all lingering outside in the main dining room, getting ready for their lunch service. Probably not strange to anyone else, but every time Dee had come in around this time previously, the wait staff was usually hanging out in the kitchen. It seemed like a very laid back place until the crowds stampeded the door and then everyone got serious and got to work. But for all of them to be out in the dining room . . .

As she walked through, heading to the kitchen, she noticed that everyone watched her. She also took that as a bad sign. Of course, Smiths were all about "bad signs."

"It's a wonder you and your daddy ever leave the house, the way y'all keep seein' such bad signs," her momma was known to complain once or twice over the years.

Yet Dee was rarely wrong when it came to these things, so she trusted her instincts and enjoyed the feel of the holstered .45 she had attached to the back of her jeans.

She pushed the kitchen door open and strode inside. Only one person was in there, and that, too, was rare. Usually Ric had a whole staff of chefs and assistant chefs and sous chefs and whatevers a place like this particular restaurant needed. Yet he was all by his lonesome, hacking up some zebra into pieces.

Her lip curled a little. She never could stand the taste of zebra. To her it was an acquired taste . . . like squirrel.

Deciding it was wise to keep the big island where Van Holtz and his staff did most of their prep work between them, Dee rested her arms on the marble and leaned in.

"How did it go?"

"Oh, it went fine," Van Holtz replied back. "Just fine."

When he didn't say anything further, she shrugged and turned toward the door. "Okay," she said, heading out.

True, he could have thrown the meat cleaver he'd been using at her, but he opted for part of that zebra, the hoof slamming into the door with a force and skill she'd had no idea the rich wolf possessed.

She faced him and could see how angry he was by the lack of expression on his face.

"Problem, hoss?"

"You microchipped her?"

Dang. She'd hoped that wouldn't be found out.

"It was an easier way to track her. I did it through my phone. How d'ya think I found her so quick after they took her?"

He glowered at her, long and hard, and she knew what he wanted. Dee sighed and said, "Tell me where she is and I'll apologize to your teacup poodle."

"You can't. Because she's not here."

"She back at her place?" She couldn't help but smirk. "Or should I be checkin' out Novikov's place?"

"She's still in Ursus County. She's refused to return home until her father, someone she trusts, comes to get her."

Good Lord. Is that what all this fuss was about? Because the teacup poodle got her feelings hurt? Did Van Holtz really expect Dee to care? When there were hybrids out there with *real* problems?

"I'm sure he won't mind," she said, unable to hide the boredom she was feeling.

"You microchipped her," he said again.

And, fed up, she replied, "I really don't care."

"Good. Then neither will I. You're fired." He turned his back on her and reached for another sharp cutting tool. But Dee was too startled to merely walk away.

"Pardon?"

"I said you're fired."

"Because of the poodle?"

"Because shoving something into someone's body against his or her will is often called assault. And for that you get fired."

"Fine," she snipped. She could get work anywhere. She didn't need him or the Group or anybody for that matter!

She again turned to the door, but it swung open and Niles Van Holtz walked through. "Oh, good. You're both here."

"I'm leavin'," she said. "Been fired."

"That's been canceled."

The younger Van Holtz spun around. "Like hell it has! We agreed!"

"No. You ranted and I said 'uh-huh' a lot to keep you calm. But we have a bigger issue right now that we need to deal with."

"What now?"

"Spoke to Blayne's father. Ezra. Have either of you met him?"

Dee had seen the man, but she hadn't spoken to him. He seemed like every other Magnus Pack wolf she'd ever seen. Big, unfriendly, with a thing for two-wheelers.

"He's a unique man," Niles Van Holtz went on. "And unless we want him to start doing some real damage, we need to take care of something before he helps us get Blayne out of Ursus County, and we need to take care of it fast."

"Which is?"

"We need to find the ones who grabbed Blayne. Find them

and take care of them." The older Van Holtz looked over at Dee. "That seems right up your alley, wouldn't you say?"

"I guess."

"We don't know where they are," Ric said. "And all our tracking team found was Novikov's truck, and that was gone when we sent a full team out. The area was swept clean by the time our people got there."

"Bears," Dee said, and when both men stared at her, she said again, "Bears. It was bears who took Novikov and the poodle—"

"Stop calling her that!"

"—all the way to Ursus County. The bears cleaned up the place, and those bears aren't getting rid of anything from something like that."

"That makes sense," the older Van Holtz pointed out to his cousin. "Think Lock—"

"He is *not* going to help us anymore." Ric glanced at her. "And he's not talking to *you* at all."

"Did you turn him against me?"

"*Me?*"

"Would you two cut it. We need a contact."

Ric shrugged helplessly. "I know Lock and his parents. And forget his uncles. They *adore* Blayne."

Niles looked at her.

"The only bears I know besides Lock are in Tennessee." She scratched her head. "There is one person who might be able to help." She dug into her leather jacket and retrieved her cell phone. "My cousin Sissy. Her and Ronnie Lee have been fucking bears for years, so they should know somebody."

Niles chuckled as Ric growled and went back to decimating that poor zebra.

Lou Crushek, also known as Crush to those brave enough to call him that to his face, pulled open his front door and gazed through one eye at the full-human female who simply reeked of cat.

"What?"

"And a good afternoon to you, too. Late night?"

"Pretty much." They stared at each other as only fellow cops could. "I guess you want to come in?"

"Thanks for the invite!"

Knowing resistance was an absolute waste of time, Crush stepped back and Dez MacDermott, one of the few full-humans on the force he actually respected, walked into his apartment. He'd known Dez for a lot of years. They'd done some good work together, and more than once, he'd thought about trying to hook up with her, but something had always kept him from bothering. He used to think it was the "shittin' where you eat" aspect of hooking up with a coworker, but he realized later that it was simply because she was, in her heart, a cat lover. Literally.

Closing the door, Crush turned to face her. "So what is it? And make it snappy, twinkles."

"And to think you're still alone." She dropped onto his couch like she owned the place. She must have picked that up from her husband Mace Llewellyn. A more atypical lion male a body wasn't likely to ever meet.

"Anyway, do you know a"—she pulled out her battered notepad from her backpocket and glanced at the name—"Bo Noveeko? Since I'm positive you don't know Blayne Thorpe."

"No-vee-koff," he pronounced for her. "And he's the best damn hockey player you'll never hear about, full-human. What's it to you?"

"He's missing along with Blayne Thorpe."

"What do you mean he's missing?" *And who the hell was Blayne Thorpe?*

Dez opened her mouth, he assumed to respond, but her cell phone went off. She tensed her hands tightening into fists. Softly, she said, "You know I'm a dog person, right?"

"I thought you were more a cat person?"

"Only when it comes to marrying them. Actually having them as friends, I'm all about the canines. But let me tell ya . . . like a goddamn dog with a bone this guy!" Dez's famous short temper snapped, and she yanked her still-ringing phone from her jacket pocket. "What? I'm talkin' to him . . . you know you're startin' to piss me . . ." She held the phone out to him. "Talk to him because I'm about to go Bronx on his ass."

Chuckling, assuming it was that husband of hers, Crush took the phone. "Yeah?"

"Mr. Crushek?"

"Yeah."

"This is Niles Van Holtz."

Placing the phone against his thigh, Crush said to Dez, "You put me on the phone with a Van Holtz?"

"Well, you know what would happen if I kept talking to him."

"Good point." Crush put the phone back to his ear. "What do you want?"

"More bears . . . lovely."

"Do you want something?"

"We need your assistance."

"Who's 'we'?"

"The Group."

"Oh. *That* we."

"Yes. One of your Brooklyn associations handled something last night, and we need access to what was located. As soon as possible."

"Hold." He put the phone against his thigh again and focused on Dez. "What does he want?" Because he couldn't handle the Van Holtz vague speak right now. It was too early for him.

"Last night some scumbags tried to kidnap Blayne Thorpe. She's a wolfdog. Novikov was with her, and a beacon was set off that called in some kind of bear clan out of the Brooklyn woods to finish that tea party that these scumbags started."

See? That was clear . . . at least to him. "You friends with Novikov?"

"I couldn't even pronounce his name."

"But the girl . . ."

"She's a friend. She's a friend of a lot of people. If it was just these rich canines, you know I wouldn't be here. But for Blayne . . ."

"Got it." He lifted the phone. "I'll see what I can do."

"Yes, but—"

Crush disconnected the call, not even wanting to hear the canine's voice for another second. "Wanna go for a ride, MacDermott?"

"You just want me to drive, don't you?"

"I haven't had my coffee. Don't mess with me, woman, when I haven't had my coffee."

Dez stood. "We'll get some on the way."

Grigori walked into his house and immediately wanted to walk out again. The boy! The goddamn boy! He hadn't changed! After ten years he hadn't changed!

"What are you doing?" he demanded.

The boy looked up from wrestling the couch out of the living room. His giant, L-shaped couch.

"Can't clean under the couch properly if it's in my way."

Okay. So he'd have to kill the boy. He could. Grigori had killed before. Never family, but that didn't mean much when the boy was messing with his house.

"I thought you said you were on vacation."

"I am." He started pulling the couch again. It wasn't that Grigori worried the boy would damage the couch or his walls because he knew Bold was too uptight and persnickety to do that. No, for Grigori it was about the principle!

Maybe if he choked the boy out? At least then he'd sleep.

Before he could put his plan into action, he heard a grunt behind him. He turned and saw Norm Blackmon standing there. Even stranger, Irina Zubachev stood behind Norm. A meaner grizzly sow he didn't know. Of course, she was one of the Kamchatka bears. Descended from tough, brutal Russian bears that were known to not only eat humans when they were starving, but even when they merely had the munchies. And although they'd grown up in Ursus County together, Grigori could not think of one time the woman had ever been to his house. Ever.

"What?" he asked both of them.

"This is for Speck," Norm said, walking in with a big box.

"Don't call me that," the boy muttered, finally putting down the couch.

"And this is for Blayne," Irina said, making both Grigori and Bold gape at her. If there was one thing everyone in town knew, it was that the Zubachevs hated, loathed, despised canines and, at their mildest, had merely torn the legs off a few rather than their heads. Grigori wouldn't think about what Zubachevs had done to canines at their worst. "Tell her I'll have that deep conditioner for her tomorrow."

Bold stood next to Grigori now. "Is that all for her hair?"

"And yours. She's right," Irina told the boy flatly. "You got frizz issues. A little conditioner will do you good."

With that Irina walked out and Norm dropped the box at their feet. "Take this. It's from Blayne."

Bold pulled the envelope off the top of the box, opened it, and read out loud, "For my sanity and everyone else's, please use these."

Norm was already grinning, and Grigori joined him when Bold opened the box and pulled out a primo set of skates.

"I'm on vacation," the boy complained, and Grigori looked desperately at the sloth bear standing next to him.

Bo flew head first out of his uncle's house, over the porch, and into the snow. The hockey equipment followed, painfully colliding into his back and skull.

"Are you trying to tell me something?" he yelled at the two older bears before the door slammed shut in his face. "That's just rude!" he quoted Blayne.

Bo sat up. "Fine. They don't want me here. I won't stay here." He stripped to his boxer briefs, put on all the gear except the skates and socks, and walked to the pond on his uncle's property, which was his favorite pond anywhere in the entire world.

And for the eight years he'd lived in Ursus County, this was the pond he'd come to every day in the winter, like clockwork, by six a.m. Summers were tougher, of course, and he was forced to use the indoor rink to practice, but he'd made friends with the maintenance guys, and they'd let him in to practice. Day after day, summer after summer, until Bo had earned a set of his own keys.

He dropped his equipment and sat on the ground to get on his socks and skates. He felt real excitement as he did, already looking forward to some time with just himself, his stick, and the ice.

Bo stepped onto the ice and took in a deep breath. Blayne had been right. He did need this, whether he was on vacation or not.

Grinning, he put his helmet on and started off with a few drills.

Blayne ran up the hill and stopped at the very top. She panted hard, hands on her hips as she looked over the beautiful countryside. This hill was the highest and she could see the ocean on her right. If she looked straight down, she could see one of the huge man-made saltwater lakes, three polars sitting by it, stretched out and quietly contemplating . . . what? The true meaning of life? Mathematical theorems? Some great science experiment?

Bears were so smart, they could be thinking up the next great thing. She bet it was great to have a brain like that, to be able to think like that. Blayne always wanted to be a genius. To be able to spout theorems and equations the same way she could quote bad horror films and every episode of *Seinfeld*. Unfortunately, her brain didn't hold on to things for very long. At least not important things.

Not like bears anyway. Smart, thoughtful, caring bears.

And that's when she saw a seal pop up through a hole in the ice, and one of the bears grabbed it by the head and dragged it out. The seal squealed, but the polar bit into its head, holding it and running because the other two polars came after him. Even more horrifying, she had the feeling they were playing, as opposed to a more typical life-and-death struggle that she might catch on the National Geographic Channel. When they started to play tug with the still breathing but soon-to-be-dead seal, Blayne turned away and started back down the hill. When she got to the bottom, she froze, surprised and concerned.

"Hi, ya," she said, crouching down. It wouldn't approach at

first, watching her closely. "Where did you come from, little guy?" She smiled and opened her arms. "Come on."

That seemed to be all he needed, the mixed dog ran forward and into her arms. She immediately noticed three things. This mixed canine had been through hell and back, his leg had been broken and no one had bothered to fix it, and some brain trust had mixed a pit bull and wolf together. To create what? The ultimate fighting breed?

Having nearly ended up on the wrong side of a similar situation, Blayne immediately felt a kinship to the eighty-pound dog. She hugged him close, careful not to rub against any fresh wounds. But she quickly realized he had no fresh wounds. His scars were all old, his leg long healed to a useless mess. Yet he couldn't be more than a year or two old.

"What's your name, little guy? Did they even give you a name?"

After having been so cautious around her, he now slathered her with wet dog kisses and jumped from side to side, eager to have a friend.

"Oh, my God. You are so cute! Wanna come with me? Wanna go running with me?"

He turned and charged off, stopping to spin around to look at her. Blayne stood and followed. For a basically three-legged dog, he moved fast, but Blayne kept up with him, moderating her gait so that they ran together. She let him take the lead and she followed him up another high hill. They stopped at the top and Blayne looked down, fascinated by what she saw. She held her hand out and her gloved fingers went through a wall of what she could only call a winter storm. Snow and ice laced the other side. When she pulled her hand out, the tips of her glove were frozen together, and the only thing that kept her fingers attached to her hand was the fact that she wasn't completely human.

Shaking her head, she said to the dog standing by her side, "That's amazing, huh? And weird."

Blayne started to turn away, but she stopped and leaned in. Not wanting her nose to freeze off, she didn't get too close, but she wondered about the farmhouse she could see on the other side. A farmhouse with several buildings that looked deserted and was right by the ocean. A nice piece of property except that it was completely cut off from anything and everything, stuck between an American bear town and a Canadian one from what Bo had told her.

Reminding herself to ask about it later, she rubbed the dog's head and then headed off down the hill. They kept going, running through a forest, Blayne stopping when she caught sight of a pond in the distance. She moved a little closer, smiling as she watched Bo Novikov do what he did best—conquer the ice.

"He's amazing, isn't he?" The dog pressed against her leg, tongue hanging out, looking very happy. "If I moved like that, little guy, I'd own the world, too."

The dog ran a circle around her and charged off. Laughing, Blayne followed.

CHAPTER 20

Bo walked up the porch stairs and into his uncle's house. Grigori was coming down the hallway, his big coat on.

"Where you off to?" Bo asked, dropping his equipment by the door just like he used to.

"Storm comin'."

"And?"

"Don't be smart."

Too tired and happily satisfied to argue, Bo walked past his uncle and headed toward the bathroom. But he stopped, looking into the dining room. "What's all this?"

"Neighbors brought food."

"That was nice."

"Yeah." Grigori opened the front door. "Not for you, though. For Blayne Thorpe."

"For Blayne?"

"That's what I said."

"Is she here?"

"No. But I'll look for her while I'm—"

Blayne ran in before Grigori could finish, and she wasn't alone.

"What is *that*?" Grigori demanded.

"My new friend. He doesn't have a name yet. Let me know if you think of one."

"He can't stay here."

Blayne took off her goofy earmuffs. He hated those things. They were creepy little bunny heads. "Why not?" she asked.

"What do you mean why not? Because I don't want him here." Blayne didn't say anything, simply gazed at the much taller and bigger polar. "You heard me," he pushed. "He can't stay here." She kept gazing, and Bo could imagine the big dog eyes his uncle was getting . . . and not from the dog. "You're only a visitor, ya know, Blayne Thorpe. Here because of my goodwill. So don't push your luck." The gazing continued until Grigori snarled, and snapping before he stormed out, "He better be gone when I get home in the morning!"

The door closed and Blayne faced Bo, looking kind of smug for a canine trapped among bears. He motioned to the dining room. "What have you been up to today?"

She walked over and gawked at the dining table. "Wow. Is that all for us?"

"No. That's all for *you*. Apparently everyone seems to think Grigori and I were planning to starve ya to death."

She gave the tiniest snort. "Dude, your accent's coming back."

"I ain't got no accent. And stop callin' me dude." Bo scratched his scalp, ready for his shower. Speaking of which . . .

"That's from Irina Zubachev."

Bo gritted his teeth when Blayne squealed and dashed over to the bags. "I'm so excited to try this stuff!"

"Well, you can try it after my shower. Grigori's shower is out and the other one only has a tub so—"

Bo watched Blayne grab both bags and make a wild run for the only working shower in the house.

"Blayne Thorpe, don't even think about—"

"Ha-ha!" she crowed, slamming the door before he could even finish. Seething, he looked down and watched the mangled dog who'd come in with Blayne back up and into the living room until he found a couch to hide under.

"Good idea," Bo muttered, and glanced at his watch. Okay, okay. How long could she take in the shower anyway? Ten minutes? Maybe fifteen? He could wait.

He walked to the bathroom and stood outside it, his arms folded over his chest and he did just that. He waited.

Blayne couldn't wait until she got Gwen and Mitch to try some of this stuff. The shampoo cleaned her hair without stripping it, and the conditioner currently sitting on her head was absolute perfection! Allowing her to detangle her hair without ripping it completely from her head. She couldn't be happier. While she let the conditioner do its work, she got around to actually showering the rest of her body, humming while she did. To be honest, she had no idea how long she was in but, as usual when it came to her "hair washing time," Blayne didn't notice little things like time.

Too bad some other people currently in her life weren't as comfortable.

"Are you done yet?"

Blayne squeaked. "Are . . . are you in the bathroom with me?"

"What are you doing in there? You're taking too long!"

Gasping in outrage, Blayne snarled, "Fuck off! I'll be done when I'm done!"

"When is that? Another five minutes? Another ten?"

"Can't you take a bath or something?"

"No."

It amazed her how certain he always was. No doubt ever.

"Then I guess you'll have to wait until I'm done."

"Which will be when?"

Now he was pissing her off. "When. I'm. *Done.*"

And that's when the insane hybrid bellowed, *"Too long!"* from the other side of the shower door. Blayne spun around when the door slammed open and watched through the one eye that didn't have honey-infused conditioner in it as Bold Novikov stepped into the shower with her.

"Have you lost your mind?" she screamed, trying to get the conditioner out of her eyes and cover her naked body at the same time.

"You're taking too long!"

"Too long for what? Did we have plans I'm not aware of?"

The shower, an exquisite bit of bathroom engineering, had five showerheads that could be individually adjusted by temperature and water pressure. Yet Blayne only had three going at the moment, each adjusted to what she—and her hair—needed. And the shower that was so wonderful and big was now way too small since it not only had a seven-one cranky polar-lion hybrid in it but his big dick, too!

"Look—" she began.

"Don't 'look' me. I've been standing out there for a good fifteen minutes. More than enough time for a *normal* human being to shower—"

"*Normal?*"

"—but instead of getting in and out you stay in here and abuse the Ursus County water supply!"

"First off"—she yelled over the now *five* pumping showerheads and her exploding rage, busy trying to get all the conditioner out of her hair—"I am as normal as anyone else who can shift into a half African wild dog and half wolf! And second, I wasn't abusing anything! I'm a girl! A girl with a lot of hair that likes to be pampered and loved!"

"Are you giving your hair its own personality?"

"Yessss," she hissed at him as he scrubbed himself clean, attempting to prove how fast he could do it. *Goddamn show off!* "Because my hair is *that* amazing! And third, don't blame me for your obsessive compulsive disorder! You have a schedule to keep—that's on you. Not me! So suck it up, Genghis! This is one peasant who's not running from your OCD boar-rage!" She turned away from him and then spun back. "And use some goddamn conditioner on that *mop*!"

And to help him with that, she threw one of her new and industrial-size, thirty-two-ounce bottles of conditioner at him. The one with the wheat protein added. She had good aim, too. Hit him right in the face.

Blayne knew, too, that if she'd seen anger or rage, she would have run. But there was none of that. No. Instead, she saw that he had the same expression he'd had right before he cross-checked a rookie who'd been moving up behind him during his last game.

She saw determination.

Blayne took a step back and she knew instantly that had been the wrong move. His gaze narrowed, watching her close, his eyes turning from bright, light blue to gold in a split second.

Lion-male gold.

She was no longer Blayne. She was prey. And they both knew it.

Bo watched Blayne's claws unleash from her hands while fangs extended from her gums. She braced her legs apart and waited for him to move first. He liked that. It was bold. Like his name.

In the thirty seconds since that bottle of product slammed into his face with the power of a baseball thrown by a major league pitcher, Bo's mane had grown until it practically covered his eyes and tumbled past his shoulders and to his pecks in an unruly mass of light and dark browns.

Knowing she'd wait, he made a classic hockey move by dropping his head as if he was going to move to his left to circle around her. Blayne saw it and went for the shower door to his right. He caught her there, as he knew he would since no one in the game was as good at "deking" or head-faking, as he was. But he forgot he wasn't dealing with some nonplayer. She may not play hockey, but she was a derby girl. When he had her around the waist, Blayne let her weight come back on him, surprising him. In the process, she brought her elbow down and slammed it into his collar bone. Bo slipped backward and into the opposite wall, Blayne still in his arms, but she twisted and head-butted him. True, she only got him in the jaw, but it rang his bell. Then she was out of his arms and gone.

Slipping and sliding through water and suds, he followed after her. He saw that perfect ass hard-charge into the living room, and he went right for it and her. So focused on his prize, he didn't know she was crouching by that entrance until his brand-new hockey stick slammed into his shins, flipping him head over ass. He landed so hard he took his uncle's prized, handmade coffee table out in the process.

In that second they both froze.

Oh, shit, he thought.

"Oh, shit," Blayne whispered.

He went up on his hands and knees, and Blayne crouched by him, the hockey stick still in her hands.

"He's gonna kill me," Bo whispered.

"He's gonna kill us both!"

Bo looked down at the table. "There's gotta be a way we can fix it."

"How? We just threw four hundred pounds of rampaging male at it. This table is done."

She was right. He knew she was right. And all Bo could do was laugh.

"Bo! It's not funny!"

Yeah. It was. But he couldn't even tell her it was because he was laughing too hard. So instead he wrapped his arms around her waist and pulled her in close, the hockey stick still between them. She had to move it, though, when he pressed his head against her shoulder.

"I hope this isn't nervous-breakdown laughter."

When he snorted, she laughed with him, dropping the stick and putting her arms around his shoulders.

It was the best end he'd ever had to a weird day.

They sat next to each other on the couch. They hadn't bothered to get dressed yet. Instead they sat and they stared at that completely destroyed coffee table. According to Bo, the table had been handmade by some master wood guy, and Grigori had only paid a few hundred for it. Of course now it was worth several thousand. Or, ya know . . . it had been.

She could imagine how bad it would be had this happened with her dad.

"Should we clean it up?" she finally asked. "Or let him see the devastation?"

"I don't know. He'll be home in a few minutes so—"

The phone rang, and they both looked over at it. When it rang for a third time, Blayne nudged him and Bo reached over and picked up the receiver. "Hello?" He looked at Blayne and nodded. "Okay. Sure. No problem. See you later." Bo hung up the phone. "That wind we've been ignoring, coming from outside, is the storm. It's bad and Grigori is going to crash on Dr. Luntz's couch for the night."

Blayne snorted. "Yeah. Right."

"What?"

"Yeah. On her couch. Right."

"What are you talking about?"

"You can't be that naïve."

"Naïve about what?"

"Bo, they're sleeping together. For a while, from what I can tell."

"Dr. Luntz and Grigori? No."

"Yes. He's crazy about her. Can't you tell?"

"No. I can't. And I'm not comfortable with this conversation."

"I think it's sweet. They argue to hide how they feel about each other."

"Since I was brought here those two have been arguing."

"She doesn't want anybody to know." Blayne cringed. "She's not married, is she?"

"Her husband passed away a few years back."

"There you go. She's not ready to deal with a real relationship. But Grigori is waiting for her. It's so sweet."

"Where are you getting this from?" he demanded.

"Instinct. You can't tell when people are madly in love?"

"Apparently not."

"She probably has kids, right?"

"Grown children. One of them is a physician at the hospital."

"Doesn't matter. They still love their father, and I'm sure she thinks this will hurt them. But they're such a cute couple. I bet he's loved her for years," Blayne sighed. "That's so romantic."

"You bruised my shins."

Blayne sighed again, but this time she was annoyed. "Is that all you've got to say?"

"Yes! Because I don't want to talk about this anymore!"

"Fine. We'll both pretend your uncle is an untouched schoolboy and Dr. Luntz is the Virgin Marci and they're not at her house, right now . . . gettin' it on. Bow-chica-bow-wow."

"Okay," Bo said. "Prove it."

"Prove it? You want me to prove fucking?"

"I want you to prove that my uncle and Dr. Luntz are being inappropriate with each other."

"Oh, my God! Is that what you call it?"

"When it involves my uncle and Dr. Luntz, yes! Now prove it!"

"Fine!" Blayne stood up and marched into the hallway. She headed right for Grigori's room. Unlike his nephew, Grigori was neat but not obsessively so, which she was glad to see. She went right to his side table and opened the drawer. Smiling triumphantly, she held up the opened and extremely large box of condoms. "Proving not only that Grigori Novikov is far from an innocent schoolboy but that safe sex is important at any age!"

"Aaah!" Bo turned from her and marched back out of the room. "I can't handle this!"

"What's wrong?" she asked, following after him. She gasped, stopping in her tracks. "Are you in love with Dr. Luntz?"

Bo spun around to face her. "*What?* Eew. No! She's . . . she's like . . ."

"Your mother. Oh, how sweet! You don't want him defiling the woman who's been like a mother to you."

"Why are we having this conversation?"

"Because you freaked out over a half-used box of condoms."

"Because *you* didn't get out of the shower."

"Are we back here again?"

"Yes!" he yelled. "We are!"

"Fine," she said calmly. "Ignore the reality of your situation."

"And what reality is that?"

"That we're alone, naked, and with a half box of condoms." She stood by him now and turned the box over, dumping the condoms at his big, bare feet. "See what you miss when you obsess over bullshit?"

Bo watched Blayne's naked ass walk away. "Don't sashay away from me," he murmured, enjoying the view.

She gasped, stopped. "I do *not* sashay anywhere." She talked with both hands now without facing him. "I may saunter. Even glide. But I do not sashay. That is for ladies of the night."

He liked how she couldn't—or maybe it was she simply wouldn't—say "hookers." Too demeaning for women probably. Too rude. Blayne hated rude.

"I don't know," he said, walking up to her. "Looked like a sashay to me."

Bo brushed his fingers down her back. The damage from the accident was still there. Not nearly as healed up as his wounds were, but they were all superficial. Overall Blayne was healthy and strong, an athlete whose only limits were her own. She talked about his skills, but did she realize what she had?

He moved around her, his fingers sliding over smooth flesh. "So we have a storm outside, a house full of food, and half a box of condoms. What would you suggest we do with our time, Blayne Thorpe?"

"That's easy. We paint each other's toenails while talking about boys and watching John Hughes movies. If we're feeling really adventurous we play the 'stiff as a board, light as a feather' game and then pray we haven't woken up the undead."

"I'm almost positive my uncle doesn't have toenail polish or John Hughes movies and I don't like talking about boys because they use me to do their homework, unaware how gorgeous I am until I take off my glasses and get that complete makeover set to a thumping eighties soundtrack."

Her grin was wide. "Then I'm completely out of ideas."

Bo stepped into her, nudging her back until she was plastered against the wall. "Then goddamnit, Blayne Thorpe, just fucking kiss me."

She squinted up at him as if she were trying to see Jupiter. "I'll need a ladder to make that happen."

He grabbed her around the waist and lifted her up, enjoying her squealed giggles; her arms looping around his neck, her legs around his waist.

"And now?" he demanded.

"And now, I'd have to say, you have me where you want me, Marauder. Genghis would be proud."

"Then you better kiss me quick before I burn your peasant village to the ground and take all your women as my concubines."

"Oh, no," she whispered, staring at his mouth. "I'm trapped between wanting to help my people and keep my innocence. What will I do?"

"What you always do, Blayne," he told her honestly while pressing his body into hers. "Help everyone else."

She leaned in, her hands moving from his shoulders to his face, her fingers stroking his jaw. "My God," she whispered, her sweet breath brushing against his mouth, "the sacrifices I'm forced to make for my people."

Blayne pressed her mouth against his, her lips parting, allowing him to slide his tongue inside and taste her. Their playful teasing stopped, both of them groaning, their hands clutching. Their heads tilting to opposite sides, allowing them to delve deeper inside the other.

Bo's physical reaction to Blayne was immediate and powerful, instantly telling him that the best thing she'd done for either of them that first time they'd met was run from him. Because this feeling was as addictive as it could be destructive when first starting out in life. He'd have ignored everything around him simply so he could enjoy this woman's taste and feel, again and again.

But, ten years later, there'd be no walking away. There'd be no worrying about the what ifs and the if onlys.

He finally had her, and the Marauder had no intention of ever letting her go.

*   *   *

Oh, man, was she in trouble. Huge trouble. "Call the priest for an exorcism, get the pope on the phone, have the police on standby" trouble.

Because this was not the sweet, patient kiss of a gentleman caller. Nor was this the more typical horny gropings of a guy she knew she'd be done with when the sun came up.

In fact, Blayne didn't know what the hell this was, but she did know that "it" and Bo "The Marauder" Novikov were nothing but trouble. The best kind of trouble but trouble nonetheless.

Yet knowing that didn't stop her from gripping him tighter with her legs while digging her hands into his hair. His mane had come back, tumbling down around his shoulders and to his back, and she knew the reappearance of that mane was because of her. And what red-blooded, all-American shifter girl could walk away from that? Not her that was for sure. And why should she? She was no longer the easily panicked seventeen-year-old who saw a lust-filled gaze as an unprovoked serial killer attack. No, this was something Blayne had been waiting for, for a very long time. Maybe even forever. And now that she had it in her hands, she wouldn't turn away. She wouldn't run.

Bo leaned back a bit and those sweet blue eyes were gone, replaced by what she liked to call calculating feline gold eyes.

"Bed," he growled, staring down at her.

Blayne shook her head. "Here." She pulled her arms away and pressed them high up on the wall, giving him a good look at what she was offering him—which was everything. "I want you to fuck me right here."

He hiked her up higher until her breasts were right by his mouth. Closing his lips around one hard nipple, he began playing with her in a way that had Blayne panting and her claws digging into his shoulder. She writhed against the wall, but Bo's big hands had her pinned there, making her crazier. He switched to her other breast and did the same, pulling a choked cry from Blayne. He was doing something to her with his lips that had her confused and turned on so much she could barely think straight. Her body began to shake hard, and she thought he was going to bring her off right then, but he lowered her again and with his grip tight on her with one arm, Bo leaned over and swiped up one of the condoms that had scattered on the floor. He tore the packet open, and she watched him slide the latex over his hard, straining cock, the pre-come leaking from the head. Once he had it on, his hands slid under her ass and he moved back a bit from the wall. He lowered her so her pussy lined up with his cock and he pressed the tip against her.

"Look at me," he ordered her, and taking her time, she tore her gaze away from his cock and moved it up to his face. "You sure about this, Blayne?" And she saw the tips of his fangs peek out from under his top lip. She hoped they didn't grow to the full-size versions he had when shifted, because that would be awkward. "There'll be no going back after this," he warned her. "So you need to be sure."

She didn't know what he was trying to tell her, and she wasn't in the mood to waste time trying to find out. So she said, "If I wasn't sure, I'd be fighting you off and screaming for help." She gripped his shoulders with her fingers and leaned in until she could use the tip of her tongue to lick a line across his chest. "Trust me, Novikov," she said, feeling her own fangs sliding from her gums. "I'm sure."

She grinned, shocking herself that she was still able to tease him. "Although I do think it was very polite of you to ask."

His answering smile was beyond wicked, and he pressed forward, the head of his cock pushing inside her. Blayne's first thought was, "Huh. That feels bigger than it looked." Then Bo rammed it in the rest of the way, and Blayne didn't have any additional thoughts for several long moments. His cock filled her too much. Too much for her to have a cohesive thought. Too much for her to temporarily have *any* thought. Panting, she gripped him tighter and raised herself up a bit until she could press her mouth against his chest.

"Don't move, don't move, don't move," she managed to desperately think.

He moved.

And she had no idea how it went from *Good God! This is too much! Take it out, take it out!* Straight into *Oh, God! I'm coming! I'm coming!* But she was. She was coming hard and fast, and absolutely nothing could stop her.

Claws dug into his shoulders, and he heard a muffled scream against his chest. He could only pray she was coming because he wasn't really sure he could stop. He never thought it would feel *this* good. Sure. He'd imagined it would, but he also imagined he'd like bacon-flavored ice cream because he liked bacon so much. He'd been horribly wrong about the bacon-flavored ice cream. But he hadn't been wrong about Blayne.

With each thrust inside her, he felt more a part of her, the heat of her branding his cock as hers for as long as she may want it. And he really hoped she wanted it for a very long time.

Too soon Bo lost his fight to hold back, but that couldn't be helped. Not with Blayne holding on to him so tight and screaming against his skin. He couldn't hold back. Not another minute, not another second.

When he came, it shot through him like a potent blast of adrenaline, tearing through his veins, into his fingers and toes, and finally out his cock. He wrapped his arms around Blayne and held her against him as each ejaculation ripped through him. By the final one, Bo didn't think he could move anymore. That he'd ever be able to move again.

Shaking, he went down on his knees and then on his ass, Blayne still held tight against him. Unable to do much of anything else, he kissed her sweat-soaked forehead and listened to her hard breathing.

For a long moment, he worried that maybe it had all been too much for her. That he'd been too much. She always seemed so small to him compared to the full-breeds. But then Blayne Thorpe said something that was very Blayne Thorpe and let him know she was just fine.

"Wowski," she sighed.

And Bo smiled, knowing that he'd never hear a better compliment.

Chapter 21

Bo stared up at the ceiling, his hands smoothing up and down Blayne's back. "We're going to have to clean this hallway before my uncle gets home," he murmured. Although, to be honest, not feeling the need to clean at the moment.

He really should feel bad. He'd kept Blayne in this hallway for about two hours. They kept trying to get to a bed or a couch or something a little softer, but they simply couldn't manage it.

If Blayne minded, she certainly didn't show it.

"Later." She sat up, brushing her hair out of her face. It had dried into a mass of curls that she obviously had no control over without a hot iron. "I'm starving."

"We've got food."

"Real food? Or seal blubber?"

"Probably both."

She stood and stretched, and Bo was reaching for her again, his hands on her waist before she realized it and scrambled back.

"No! Food!" She headed off to the bathroom. "I'll be out in a minute." Less than that, as she shot back out again. "Oh, my God."

"What's wrong?"

"We left the shower on."

"That's not good for the town water supply."

"Thanks, Mr. Helpful." She went back into the bathroom, closing the door behind her. Bo dragged himself off the floor, stopping to pick up the empty packets and used condoms he'd tossed around like some heathen, since he assumed all heathens were messy. Unwilling to use the kitchen trash for his used condoms, he walked outside naked to drop them in the big cans his uncle had behind the house. That done, he headed back inside, guessing that the weather was probably a negative twenty Fahrenheit. Weather that was not for the weak or the felines.

Once in the house, he closed the back door and headed to the dining room, passing the living room. That's when he stopped and walked back. Blayne had on one of his high school hockey jerseys and nothing else. Although she didn't need much else since it went past her knees. She'd found his uncle's CD collection. What Bo used to call his "subversive music pile" for no other reason than it pissed the old bastard off.

She'd put on some French alternative band singing about Tokyo and was dancing around his uncle's living room like she hadn't just spent the last two hours with Bo buried either cock first or head first in her lap. Where she got all that energy from, he'd never know.

"Come on," she said, jumping up onto one of the couches. "Dance with me."

"I thought you were hungry."

"I'm never too hungry to dance to pretentious French music!" And only Blayne could make a compliment out of an insult.

"I can't dance to this," Bo told her, walking across the room.

"Are you one of those guys who won't dance?"

"Not everyone has your lack of shame." He dug through his uncle's collection, going for what he had in the back since he knew the CD was his and not Grigori's. He popped it into the player. "After cleaning up that hoarder's nest you call an apartment—"

"Hey!"

"—I know your taste."

Blayne's mouth dropped open when she heard the first bits of the song. It was from a very old movie soundtrack that few people knew about.

"How . . . how did you get this?"

"Bootleg. Not easy to come by."

"I know! I've been trying to find this for years."

If there was one thing Bo always had a weakness for it was sixties music and bad sixties cult movies. "Hot Rods to Hell" or "Riot on Sunset Strip" or anything with hippies and ridiculous drug usage and uptight parents . . . he was there. But "Wild in the Streets" was one of his all-time favorites, and he'd searched with his old computer and even slower modem all through high school for the soundtrack. He somehow knew Blayne was the one person who could appreciate the great get-up-and-riot tune "Fourteen or Fight," and he was right. She not only knew the song, she knew the words to the song.

She crooned the first slowly sang line, and Bo crooned the next one back to her, moving up to her as she stood on his uncle's couch. Something he'd normally never allow simply because it wasn't his couch and they'd already destroyed the man's coffee table. But it was Blayne and . . . and she knew the words to "Fourteen or Fight!"

And when a man found a woman like that, he let her stomp all over his uncle's damn furniture or anywhere else for that matter!

Marci had insisted they check on the kids since they were out for a late-night stroll anyway. Harsh Maine winters didn't bother Ursus County bears, not when you were born and raised here. Although Grigori didn't need much of an excuse to stay the night at Marci's, he also figured his nephew could use a little space. He'd always been a little awkward around girls. Either too gruff, too busy staring, or just too . . . OCD. Most females couldn't handle it.

Still, the boy didn't need a babysitter, but try telling that to Marci Luntz. Grigori didn't bother to argue some things with her. She could be stubborn as any black bear he'd ever met before. The grizzlies and blacks never as relaxed as the polars.

They lumbered up to the house, his belly full of the dying old walrus he'd found on the beach and Marci's face still covered in the honey and pissed-off bees she'd taken from the year-round hives the town kept a few miles away.

Marci was about to go up the stairs and into the house, but Grigori knew better. Using his body, he pushed her toward the side of the house with the big picture window. As they came around the corner, they both froze, their mouths open in shock while they focused on that window and what went on behind it.

Seeing Blayne on his couch didn't bother him a bit. She was a little tiny thing, so it wasn't like she could do any real damage. But seeing his nephew naked and dancing *with* Blayne while they listened to that crappy sixties music the boy loved . . . well, *that* was something Grigori had never seen, never expected to see, and was now kind of freaked out by seeing.

Not because the kid was naked. Not because he was singing— the boy had always been a bit of a hummer when he thought no one was around. But the smiling? The laughing? The pretending he had a mic while Blayne played a hippie backup singer with her long hair covering her face?

That was something Grigori *never* expected to see. At least not without the use of very strong hallucinogens. And the reason why was simple. This was Bold Novikov. The kid who only seemed to come alive when he was on the ice or discovered what he considered a mess somewhere in the house. Otherwise, Bold kept to himself, watched everything, said nothing, and plotted his escape from town.

Grigori didn't think he knew *this* kid and never thought the boy had it in him.

Not wanting to get in the boy's way, he turned to Marci to lead her back to her house. But he found her on her back, in the snow, laughing her black bear ass off. Anyone else, he'd think they were laughing at the boy, and Grigori wouldn't stand for it. But he knew Marci Luntz. She would never laugh at Bold. No. This was pure happiness for a little boy she'd cared for and loved nearly as much as her own cubs, and Grigori could already imagine the conversation he'd have to hear for the rest of the night about how *she* knew that Blayne Thorpe was perfect for "her"

Bold and how long before they figure it out and blah blah blah. He was already dreading it. Nothing worse, sometimes, than chatty sows.

Deciding he wouldn't wait for her to get off her ass, Grigori grabbed her ankle and dragged her back to her house.

She laughed the whole way.

Blayne stared out the window, a hard-driving wind throwing snow and ice against the glass. Normally storms like this depressed her unless it was Christmastime because it usually meant she was trapped at home, bored out of her mind. Although she was rarely trapped for long, being the one person in all of Philly or New York who could track down an open Chinese restaurant when everything else was closed due to the storm. She'd find the food, get it, and bring it back to her father or Gwen's Pride. Whoever she figured would be the most welcoming. Anything was better than being trapped at home by herself with no one to talk to her but, ya know, herself. Which she tried to stop doing when she was thirteen and the nuns kept asking her if she was speaking with Satan.

Big arms looped around Blayne's shoulder and soft lips brushed her cheek.

Nope. This time she wasn't depressed at all.

"Who made the beef stew?" she asked.

"Mrs. Henderson, I think."

"Best. Ever."

"I'll let her know you liked it."

"Nah. I can tell her."

"You know Mrs. Henderson?"

"Met her earlier today. Met lots of people."

"Any problems?"

She laughed. "Stop worrying. Everyone's been really nice to me."

"Let me know if they're not."

"Yeah. Yeah." She turned in his arms and basically climbed him like she would a rock wall. Arms around his shoulders, legs around his waist, she pressed her forehead against his. "Let's fuck!" she exclaimed.

Bo sighed, pulling her in closer and heading toward the bedroom. "Have I mentioned that I *adore* your absolute lack of subtlety?"

Chapter 22

Dez MacDermott knew that if five, ten years ago someone had told her "You'll be sitting in an average office building in downtown Manhattan, that's actually owned by wolf shifters so that you can discuss the hybrid-hunting issue," chances were Dez would have had them put in for a psych eval.

And yet here she was, doing just that.

"What do you mean they won't help us?"

Dez took the cup of coffee handed to her by her husband, Mace. "Thanks, babe," she said around a yawn, before refocusing her attention on a befuddled Niles Van Holtz. *Niles? What kind of name is Niles anyway?*

"They have to help us," he insisted. He was cute when confused.

"Yeah, I tried that logic. So did Crush. They said no. Actually, what they said was, 'Tell 'em to fuck off,' but ya know . . . Brooklyn bears."

She sipped her coffee, badly needing the caffeine. She hated all-nighters, and that's what it turned into because the bears kept her and Crush waiting for hours before they'd talk to them. Although she wasn't positive, Dez had a feeling this thing was blowing up into quite the drama. She normally wouldn't care, but she liked Blayne. She had a lot more energy than Dez could normally handle, but she was always willing to babysit at the last minute and took great care of Dez's son Marcus. But Crush had told Dez that as long as Blayne was protected by that Russian guy, Novi-whatever, she should be fine.

She hoped Crush was right, because she was seriously enjoying the disbelief on Niles Van Holtz's face and the despair on his cousin Ulrich's. And if it turned out Blayne wasn't safe, she'd feel guilty as hell.

"Looks like I'll have to talk to them myself," Niles said, sounding pretty haughty.

"Better bring backup. I sensed they would enjoy hurting you. I have to say . . . bears and wolves? Didn't know about all the hate."

The younger Van Holtz looked across the big conference table at Sissy's cousin Dee-Ann. The She-wolf appearing to care less about Blayne than anyone else in that room. When Ulrich glared at her, she let out an annoyed sigh and dropped her legs off the table, since she'd had them up there through the whole meeting while relaxing back in the expensive chair, sipping coffee and enjoying the donuts someone brought.

"Are you going to do *something*?" Ulrich demanded.

"Yeah," Dee-Ann shot back. "I'm leavin'. See? This is me walkin' out." The door slammed shut behind her, and Mace took the coffee out of Dez's hand as he had a tendency to do and sipped it.

"Just an FYI for you," he said to Ulrich, giving Dez one of his famous smirks. "Dee's been known to wrestle a gator back home in Tennessee when she's bored, so you may want to keep that in mind before you really piss her off, Dog Fancy."

Ulrich stared at Mace for a good minute before he asked, "Who are you again?"

Knowing that not much else could insult her husband, Dez threw her head back and laughed.

Dee-Ann marched down the hallway toward the elevator. Not a lot pissed her off. Unlike the rest of the women in her family, she didn't get angry at every little thing. What was the point? But Ulrich Van Holtz was wearing on her damn nerves.

"You!"

Dee froze when something hard and heavy hit her in the back of the head. Fangs out, she spun around but immediately stopped when she realized it was her cousin's pregnant female. It wasn't the whole kid-glove thing because Jessie Ann was pregnant that kept Dee from slapping the little bitch, it was because wild dogs were known to be highly unstable when pregnant. Defensive, highly emotional, and apparently quick to throw things. And the She-dogs standing behind Jessie looked like they weren't about to get involved unless Dee made the first move. Normally, something Dee-Ann wouldn't give a second thought about. But Smitty had made his demands real clear. No picking on the dogs . . . no matter how much they may be asking for it.

And the good Lord knew that Jessie Ann was asking for it.

"This is *your* fault," Jessie Ann went on, sounding hysterical over a helpless poodle. Did she adopt Blayne, too? How many mutts did the woman need in her life anyway? "Because of you Blayne is trapped in scary bear territory. Because of *you*."

"You need to stay out of this, Jessie Ann."

"It's Jessica, bitch!" Jessie snarled as she stomped forward, her belly leading the way and her She-dogs watching her, knowing that Dee wouldn't do anything to harm her cousin's future child.

Thankfully, though, Sissy Mae and Ronnie Lee jumped in front of Jessie Ann, hands on the She-dog's shoulders.

"Jessie Ann, I thought we talked about this," Ronnie pleaded.

Jessie pointed an accusing finger at Dee. "You! You microchipped her like a . . . a . . ."

"Like the rescue mutt she is?"

Sissy and Ronnie Lee looked at Dee, their eyes wide, and Jessie shoved the pair out of her way, descending on Dee. But before claws, fangs, or fists could connect Smitty was there, grabbing his mate under the arms and carrying her off.

"We'll discuss this later, cousin," he tossed over his shoulder before disappearing into the bathroom with his cursing, spitting mate.

"What?" Dee snapped when she realized Sissy and Ronnie were still staring at her, looking surprisingly disgusted for two females whose whole life goal at one time seemed to be the torturing of Jessie Ann Ward.

"I know that tone isn't directed at me, cousin," Sissy stated, one brow raised. And Dee took it as the challenge it was, stepping forward, but Ronnie Lee quickly got between them.

"No, no, y'all. Not here."

Sissy crossed her arms over her chest. "You better figure out how to fix this, Dee-Ann. Or I'm going to get real fuckin' cranky. That little wolfdog has a lot of friends, and I happen to be one of them."

Great. Someone else blaming her for this mess.

Deciding she was tired of playing nice about all this, Dee headed toward the elevator.

CHAPTER 23

"**A**re *you awake?*" Blayne's eyes opened wide to find a descendent of violent barbarians hanging over her. *"Well?"*

"I'm awake . . . now."

"Good." He kissed her, and Blayne automatically reached for him, her arms slipping around his neck. But before she could get comfortable, he pulled away. "I didn't want to get up before you did."

Why did they have to get up at all? Oh. That's right. Because she'd just spent the entire night fucking the most OCD hockey player ever.

Bo sat on the edge of the bed, scratching his head and yawning. "We slept late."

Hearing someone moving around in the living room, Blayne grabbed Bo's jersey off the floor and tugged it on before glancing at the clock on the nightstand. "You consider seven a.m. as sleeping late?"

"Yes."

Deciding not to worry too much about the man's issues with time, Blayne raised her arms high in the air and took one of her nice long stretches. She was canine after all.

Her muscles were deliciously sore and now that she was up, Blayne felt a rush of energy hit her system. She wanted to run, to play, to . . .

She stared at Bo's back. It was huge. Wide, muscular, and smooth. Like a giant target calling her name.

Grinning and using all the strength and power in her body, Blayne launched herself at The Marauder.

Bo felt something tap his back and he opened his eyes to find arms and legs wrapped around him.

"Yes?"

"I have way too much energy and no way to work it off!"

Bo realized that Blayne wasn't simply hanging off him, she was attempting to Blayne-handle him into submission.

"Well." He grabbed both her hands in one of his. "I have some ideas on how we can work that extra energy off."

"You want to go running with me?"

"Or," he tried, "we can get back in bed and fu—"

The bedroom door flew open. *"Morning, Marines!"*

Bo snarled at his uncle while Blayne pressed her mouth against his shoulder and giggled.

Dressed in one of his old Marine T-shirts and sweatpants, Grigori marched into the room. "So what are we planning for today? Anything interesting?"

"Not anymore," Bo muttered, earning himself a slap to the side of the head. "Ow."

Grigori leaned in, scowling right into Blayne's face. She only giggled more.

"And what are you planning, Daddy's Girl?"

"Running, sir!"

"Running? You know what runs, Daddy's Girl?"

"Is the bellowing really necessary?" Bo complained.

Ignoring Bo, Blayne answered, "Dainty little princesses, sir?"

"Exactly! Dainty, pretty, little princesses. Just like you!"

Bo rolled his eyes. This was just painful.

"What about you, boy? 'Cause you can't just sit around all day, doin' nothin'."

"When have I ever sat around, doing nothing?"

Blayne jumped off the bed. "I'm getting in the shower."

"You're showering *before* you go running?" Bo asked.

"You want me to run while unclean?"

Why did he ask these questions?

Blayne cheered, "Wahoo! Running!" and cartwheeled out of the room.

Grigori smirked at him. "You're letting her wear one of your precious jerseys?"

"Why are you still standing here?"

His uncle leaned back, peering out into the hallway. "I need you to come to town with me," he muttered.

"You're not on my schedule."

His uncle scowled. "I'm not what now?"

"I wrote out a schedule. You're not on it."

"Uh-huh. Can you fit me on the schedule?"

Bo grabbed the notepad off his night table and looked it over. "Well, let's see, maybe I could move—"

Grigori snatched the pad from him and tore it up, throwing the tiny pieces at Bo's head.

Bo stared at him. "You don't think I made a copy?"

"Get dressed," his uncle spit out between clenched teeth.

"I have to shower first, and Blayne's using the only one that works."

"Can't you just take a bath?"

"I don't have a duckie. How can I take a bath without a duckie?"

"It's like you want me to beat you. It's like you're begging me, too. And what happened to my goddamn coffee table?"

"That was Blayne. Blayne did it."

Hands on his hips, his uncle glared at him. "You're blaming your girlfriend for that mess in my living room?"

It wasn't until his uncle said it that Bo realized that Blayne was his girlfriend—even if she didn't know it yet. He grinned and happily answered, "Yeah. I am blaming my girlfriend. My girlfriend Blayne."

They heard the panting behind them and together watched Bo's shifted girlfriend Blayne turn in circles trying to catch her tail. She didn't seem to be in any rush to stop.

"How long can she keep that up?"

"My girlfriend Blayne?"

"You're going to keep calling her that now, aren't you?"

"Yeah, actually, I am. Just to annoy you. As we know my whole goal in life is to annoy you." Bo motioned to the hallway. "She's still going."

"Twenty bucks she throws up."

Bo felt confident in his girlfriend Blayne. "You're on."

It had been a gut feeling that sent her back to the States. That feeling she sometimes got when she knew something was really off. That's what had hit when she'd been sitting in that Thailand bar planning to roll a couple of worthless and rich full-human Aussie males who kept yelling at her slowly because they were sure she couldn't speak English. Why the yelling, she didn't know, and how saying something slowly would help if she really didn't speak English was another way down Lack of Logic Lane, but in the end it hadn't mattered.

Sami had walked away from some easy money—dragging Sander behind her—because she knew something was wrong. And now that she was standing in the middle of Bo's Manhattan apartment, staring down a She-wolf who'd been caught going through his shit, she knew she'd been right.

Sander walked into Bo's office, his nose in the air. "I scent She-bitch," he announced. "Oh," he said when he caught sight of the She-wolf. "Guess that's you."

"Is there a reason you're in our friend's apartment?" Sami asked. "Or are you just stealing?"

"Because that's our job," Sander added, not really helping.

The She-wolf didn't respond, cold amber eyes sizing up both Sami and Sander.

The one thing foxes prided themselves on was being able to spot trouble. Not merely by scent but by a general sense of preservation. Extremely necessary when the smallest of the predators and nearly every breed and species didn't trust you. The only species more loathed than foxes? Hyenas, which was kind of depressing when Sami thought about it too much. Because hyenas were just creepy.

And now that Sami had checked out this She-wolf, she knew that not only was Bo in trouble, he had trouble searching his apartment. This female would kill them and have them in a shallow grave before lunchtime. Actually, she'd probably work up a little appetite for lunch.

When the She-wolf finally spoke, her accent combined with the female's size had both Sami and Sander making sure they could instantly escape out the window or door if necessary. She didn't know what the Smith wolves fed their pups, but Christ they were a *huge* breed of canine!

"You the hybrid's friend?" the She-wolf asked.

Knowing panicking now would only set the female off, Sami answered honestly, "He's our polar."

She frowned a little at Sami's answer, but shook her head. "Whatever. I need information. About the Brooklyn bears. Thought he'd have something here."

"Bo doesn't know anything about the Brooklyn bears."

"They hate him," Sander added.

"'Cause he's a hybrid?"

"No, it was because of that year he played with the Jersey Stompers."

"Yeah. He *stomped* all over that Brooklyn-born bear playing for the Long Island Devourers. They said every one of his vertebrae had been ruptured. Took him years to get back to playing—and he was never the same."

"He shouldn't have taken Bo's puck," Sami argued, like she'd been arguing for five years since it happened.

The She-wolf let out a breath. "I was really hoping I could find something here to help me out."

Sami, always more distrustful than Sander, questioned, "What for?"

"Because I need to help one irritating little wolfdog. That's what for."

Knowing exactly who she was talking about, Sami wondered what the hell she'd been missing since they left town. She dropped into the leather seat across from the desk the She-wolf had been going through. "Why don't you tell me what's going on, and I'll see what information I can get for you."

"You could get me information?"

"There's a lot of foxes in this town, and we give each other information about ongoing cons, the best fences in the city when you need some quick cash, and when someone's bringing in the latest shipment of high-quality diamonds. We're all real friendly with each other—as long as we're not trying to take each other's polar."

"Yeah," Sander agreed, dropping into the other chair. "Because *that* would be wrong."

Blayne was running down a side street of the town when a door opened and she ran face first into it.

Stumbling back, her hands to her forehead, Blayne heard, "Oh! Oh! You poor thing! Blayne, are you all right?"

"Yes, Dr. Luntz." She smiled in an attempt not to wince. "I'm very hard headed."

"Let me see." The sweet sow studied her head closely. "Don't even think it'll leave a dent." She patted Blayne's cheek. "You look . . . cheery."

Blayne raised a brow. "So do you."

The doc's eyes widened, and Blayne whispered, "I won't say a word about you two." Then she gave the sow two thumbs up. Dr. Luntz turned a lovely shade of burgundy and glanced behind Blayne.

"You have a small army following you, dear."

"Yeah. I know." Blayne looked over her shoulder at the small pack of dogs that had been following her since she and the pittie mix left Grigori's house. "Do you know where they're from, Dr. Luntz?"

"Marci, dear. Call me Marci. And"—she shrugged—"I'm not really sure where they come from. They just show up. Don't bother any of us, so we don't bother any of them. Foxes fight with them, though." She frowned. "I doubt they'd do all that damage."

They wouldn't. Coyote shifters maybe, but not the foxes. They were all about the thieving, no time for random dog brawls.

So then where did these dogs come from? They were clearly more escaped fighting dogs like the pittie. Many of them covered in scars, missing one or both of their ears, or had damaged limbs. It broke her heart to see them, but it wasn't the human part of her they responded to. They knew their own kind. Every one of them had been crossed with a wolf. Rotties, pinchers, pits, German shepherds. All power breeds. All dangerous working dogs on their own but add in that part of wolf that had been bred out of them and there was a whole new world of dangerous added to the equation. She refused to believe any of the locals had anything to do with these dogs, but then who did?

"Well, Blayne Thorpe," a voice said beside her. "How are you doing?"

Blayne smiled at the sow. She didn't know her, but she seemed friendly. "Good morning."

"Love the earmuffs," she said.

"Thanks! They're little fake raccoon heads. Bo said they were unholy because he felt like they were staring at him. He's so cute when he's being unreasonable."

The sow examined her carefully before introducing herself. "I'm Superintendent of Ursus County, Kerry-Ann Adams."

"I'm Blayne Thorpe. Plumber," she tacked on, feeling the need to have a title.

Kerry-Ann blinked. "You're a plumber?"

"Blayne has her own business," Marci bragged. And when Blayne looked at her in surprise, she added, "Bo told me. Now exactly what do you want, Kerry-Ann Adams?"

"Do I need permission to talk to her, Marci Luntz?"

"As Blayne's personal physician . . . yeah, ya old sow. You do!"

Sensing a fight but not sure why, Blayne quickly cut in with, "I'm hungry!"

Both sows jumped, eyeing her. Blayne motioned to the tea shop Marci had just exited. "How about an all-natural honey bun. Yum. I love honey buns. Don't you?"

"I don't know, Blayne," Kerry-Ann confessed. "I have been dieting lately."

"Why bother?" Marci sneered. "Nothing will help to make that fat head of yours smaller."

"All right then!" Blayne put her arm around Marci's shoulders, going up on her toes to do so, and practically dragged her "personal physician" into the tea shop. "Yum. Smell those honey buns. Are those fresh?" she asked Lorna Harper.

"Right out of the oven. And," Lorna said, smiling, "sugar-free. Just for you."

"Oh, my God," Blayne said sincerely. "You guys are so sweet." She pointed at a table. "You two sit down, and I'll help Lorna bring everything over."

Snarling at each other, the two sows headed over to the table, but Blayne caught Marci's arm. "Be nice," she whispered.

"But—"

"I get tense when people get pissy. Unless you want me chasing my tail or hiding under that chair over there . . . be nice!"

Marci agreed and walked away, and Blayne leaned over the counter as Lorna placed a tray filled with honey buns and decaffeinated tea—again, just for Blayne—in front of her. "What's going on?" Blayne whispered.

"Knowing that Kerry-Ann, she's about to ask you for a favor. Kind of the same way they do it in *The Godfather,* I imagine."

"Will it involve me killing anyone?"

"Doubtful." Lorna laughed. "But it will probably involve that Bold Novikov." Lorna leaned in closer, Blayne following suit, and she whispered, "She's been bragging around town how she can get your Bold to play with the team against the Canadian bears. Just a friendly game, mind, but that boy never did anything to help anyone but himself."

Blayne wanted to argue with Lorna, but she couldn't. Although after spending a little time in Ursus County she understood why Bo was that way.

"You do know," Blayne felt the need to explain, "he's not *my* Bo?"

"That's not what Marci Luntz told us earlier."

Small towns. Blayne loved visiting them, but she wasn't sure she could live in them full-time. Everyone was in everyone else's business. Something she would never do . . . unless her help was needed. Then, of course, she'd get involved.

Picking up the tray, Blayne walked over to the table.

"Now, dear—" Kerry-Ann began, but Blayne cut her off.

"I'll help you on one condition."

The shrewd She-bear glanced over at Marci as if to say, "Told ya so."

"And what would that one condition be, dear?"

"You stop calling Bo 'Speck.'"

That didn't seem to be the response the sow had been expecting, immediately trying to defend herself and the entire town. "Well, it's just a nickname. We all have them and—"

"He doesn't like it. And it seems kind of mean to me. I hate mean and I don't help mean people. Because mean people upset me." She placed the tray on the table. "You wouldn't want me upset would you, Superintendent?"

The sow slumped back in her chair. "You're a sobber, aren't ya, Blayne Thorpe?"

"I prefer the term sensitive."

"Took you long enough in the bathroom," Grigori complained as they walked into town. "You're like a woman."

"According to my girlfriend, Blayne"—his uncle growled—"I'm supposed to let the conditioner sit for fifteen minutes."

"Conditioner?"

"Yes. According to my girlfriend, Blayne—"

"What are you? Twelve?"

"—I need better conditioner than that combo stuff you use. I need all-natural with no silicones so that I can have a beautiful shiny mane."

"You cannot be my brother's son. You can't be."

"She also says—this is my girlfriend Blayne again—that by putting in a little more effort on my hair, I won't have to worry about that receding hairline that you're currently dealing with."

Bo easily ducked the swipe of that big arm and grinned. "Gettin' a little slow in your dotage."

"And you're becoming a smart ass."

They hit town, heading toward the police chief's office on Main Street. As they walked, the locals passed and each one greeted them with, "Mornin' Grigori . . . Bold."

After the fifth time, Bo stopped, his uncle turning to face him. "What?"

"Why are they all calling me Bold?"

"That's your name, idiot. Or are you starting to forget after too many pucks to the head?"

"I don't forget anything, which is why I know something is up. No one in this town calls me Bold but you and Dr. Luntz."

"Can't you try calling her Marci? She takes it so personally when you don't."

Bo's eye twitched. "When did you start caring about how Dr. Luntz takes anything?"

"That's none of your goddamn business, boy."

"Since when?"

"Why are we arguing about this?" Grigori bellowed.

"I don't know!" Bo bellowed back.

Muttering, his uncle stormed off and Bo followed him. The entire way to the police chief's office everyone went out of their way to greet Bo, some asking after Blayne. It was weird and made him nervous. By the time they arrived at Adam's office, Bo was tense and anxious. Before he knew it, he'd begun to organize the chief's incredibly disorganized desk, ignoring the deputies and his uncle who watched him.

"Sorry," Adams said as he walked in from a back room. "Just

got off the phone with our people in New . . . what's that boy doin'?"

"Ignore him," Grigori said.

"Yeah, but—"

"Ignore him or we'll be here all goddamn day!"

Bo held up a near empty Pepsi can that was warm and had probably been sitting there for three days. "Are you saving this for a reason?"

"No, but—"

He dropped the can in the trash and kept organizing while Adams began talking. Obviously the chief had faced the fact he had two choices here: Let Bo clean—or deal with an anxious, big-fanged hybrid.

"Heard from our people in New York. Those Van Holtz fellas are gettin' pretty anxious about your girl. They were pushing for more info on the ones who caught her."

"Why?"

"They weren't real sure, but they heard it had something to do with her father."

Grigori sniffed. "Probably wants them dead for touching her. Not that I blame the man."

"The bears in New York weren't real helpful to the Van Holtzes or us. They kept saying they had more research to do."

"Research about what?"

"Got me. The one I talked to was acting real sketchy. Don't much like sketchy."

"Me, neither," Grigori agreed. "Think we need to worry?"

"Doubt it. Because we've got the one thing no one—bears or anybody else—wants to risk. We've got the boy. They want him to play for this year's Cup with the Carnivores."

"See, kid?" Grigori asked him while Bo diligently organized the chief's paperwork. "The whole hockey thing is actually paying off."

Blayne had been running for about an hour, avoiding the Kamchatka bear territory like Bo told her to, although she didn't see why. Irina Zubachev had been ever so nice since Blayne had dropped nearly three hundred dollars of Bo's money on hair products from Irina's store.

Turning, Blayne headed toward the ocean.

She couldn't believe the beauty of this place. She wondered what it looked like in the summertime, but right now, in the midst of winter, it was truly a wonderland. Snow was everywhere, and icicles hung from the many trees and buildings she passed. Bears of every type roamed around, often in their shifted form, none of them showing her much interest. And while they had lakes and rivers filled with salmon, they also had a lot of seals. Where they got the seals from, she didn't want to know. How many met an untimely end as a polar meal, she also didn't want to know.

Instead, Blayne kept running, her small pack of dogs behind her.

She saw a small walking bridge and headed for it. As she ran across, she saw her first sign of locals in human form this far away from town. Two males, polars, fishing. She ran up to them and stopped.

"Morning!"

They both jerked a little before turning only their heads to look at her. Their scowls faded and they smiled.

"Blayne Thorpe. What you doing out here?"

"Running!" She patted the dog that pressed up against her side. He was trying to warn her off, but she knew there was nothing to worry about. She'd met Earl and Frank the day before, and they were so nice!

"I only run when chased," Frank muttered.

"Did that trick work?" she asked.

"Like a charm," Earl said, rewarding her with a smile. "Where'd you learn to fish anyway, city girl?"

"Daddy. He took me fishing all the time. He said it was the only way to get me to give him some peace and quiet, otherwise I scared off the fish—and the one who got the biggest fish, didn't have to clean it. I haven't cleaned a fish in eight years."

"Where you off to now?" Frank asked.

"Loop around town. See if I can spot Bo."

The two bears chuckled and nudged each other.

"Would you two grow up?"

"Just be careful. Lot of ladies after that one," said Earl.

"You'll have some competition," Frank added.

"We're friends," she argued.

"Yeah. Friends."

"Is that what they call it these days?" asked Frank.

Shaking her head and laughing, she said, "I give up!"

"You might as well," Earl yelled after her as she took off running. "Once a bear sets his sights on you, it's real hard to get away!"

"Also known as stalking in other parts of the country!" she yelled back.

And she laughed again despite herself when they yelled back, "Only if you're caught!"

Dee didn't realize the greatness of the fox connections until she stood outside the Brooklyn bear's headquarters. Unlike the Group's faux office building, the bears had a five-story brownstone that, from the outside, appeared like a nice family home on a decent piece of land in a quiet Brooklyn suburb. But as she'd gotten closer, Dee spotted the multicamera security system that ringed the property. And, when her eyes strayed to the trees—the black bears sitting in them, keeping watch.

Getting past the bear's external security was not much of a challenge for Dee. She'd been sneaking around the bears of Collintown for years, just like her daddy taught her to. Especially helpful when she was dating the Collintown sheriff's son. Her daddy would have been doing a whole lot of different kind of sneaking if he'd found out about that.

So, yeah, getting past those cameras and tree-sittin' bears—not a problem for Dee. Getting inside the first floor? Also not a problem. But getting to the floor where they had those bodies that the foxes had told Dee still hadn't been destroyed . . . ? That was the challenge.

The first thing Dee did was strip naked, placing her clothes someplace she could get to them easy if she had to make a run for it. Then she pried off the metal grate covering the vent. She placed the grate on the floor, stepped back, shifted to wolf, and leaped inside. She low-crawled her way through and down, desperately trying to keep her claws from scraping against the interior metal. Bears had amazing hearing. Of course, they also had a shit-hot sense of smell, so she had to get in, get out, and get home before they realized they had a wolf in their midst.

Dee reached the lowest level—about fourteen floors underneath the house—and, after pressing her snout against the grate and sniffing carefully, she eased out into the room. She landed and shifted back to human.

The room was pretty damn cold, but that was probably to keep the bodies from decaying. She unzipped the first body bag. A full-human male, in his forties. In fact . . . Dee's head tilted to the side. She knew the guy. Ex-SEAL and a real scumbag. Dee leaned in. Although there was burned skin and broken bones, she could see what killed him. The cut across his throat, opening up the arteries on both sides of his neck. Dee moved to the next table, unzipped the bag. Again the throat was cut but not like the ex-SEAL's. Instead, there were individual cuts at the location of each artery in the throat. Dee moved down and saw the same cuts on the inside of the upper arms and the inside thighs. Very precise and measured cuts. Done by a professional.

Dee thought about the hockey player, Novikov. She'd done a little research. After the death of his parents, he'd been raised by his uncle, a Marine and former Unit member. Although she'd never met him personally, Grigori Novikov had done training with other team members she knew. He was supposed to be really good and could easily have taught his nephew a few things.

Leave it to Blayne Thorpe to land face up, as usual. She gets kidnapped with the one nonmilitary trained male who could protect her. Dee wondered what it was like to be that lucky.

Not bothering to look at the rest of the bodies, Dee moved over to the desktop computer set up in the corner. She tapped the keyboard and the screensaver vanished, revealing a log-in screen. She turned her arm over, the information that male fox had written there in black ink clear and bright against her skin. Leave it to bears to use a twenty-two code password. She had a great memory but for random numbers and letters? Uh, no.

She quickly typed in the password and zipped through the system, finding what she needed faster than she thought she would. Yet as she delved deeper, looked closer, she began to realize that, as usual, Blayne had found her way into more trouble. Honestly, how did that poodle manage to live so long?

Realizing the Group would need to move faster than she originally thought would be necessary, Dee logged off the PC and stepped back—and right into a rather large wall.

"Find what ya needed?"

Dee looked over her shoulder and up. Way up.

"As a matter of fact, I did."

"Good. Hope it was worth it."

And when Dee's head collided with that wall, she wasn't really sure she could say it was.

Bo stared out the big picture window of the police chief's office while his uncle and Adams discussed Blayne.

He didn't understand it. Three days ago, after a call like Adams had just gotten from the bears out of Brooklyn, they would have pushed Blayne to the outskirts of town with the force of every deputy they had. And that would have been if they were in a good mood. But now? Well, now things were different, weren't they?

"They say the Van Holtzes are really pushing to get her back," Adams said. "And they wanted to see the bodies of those full-humans. Even sent some polar to ask."

"And?"

"Told 'em to fuck off."

"Good. They'll get her back when *she's* ready to come back."

Mouth open, Bo again wondered how the woman did it. She'd only been here three days!

"Anything else?" Grigori asked.

"Yeah. We're sure it's because they're attracted by Blayne but, uh . . . I've been getting complaints about all the strays running around town the last couple of days. They're gettin' into trash, shittin' all over the place. What do you want to do?"

"Have Ben Chambers catch 'em and put 'em down. We have it in the town budget."

"Okay. I'll put in a call and—"

"You're going to kill them?"

Bo could actually *feel* the boars behind him cringe at the sound of Blayne's voice coming from the open back door. Biting back his grin, he looked over his shoulder. She stood there in her gray and pink winter running outfit, one of those "strays" sitting patiently at her side, big brown dog eyes—from both canines— staring at the males.

"You . . . you can't just kill them."

"Blayne—" Grigori began and, right on cue, Blayne Thorpe burst into devastated tears.

Dee backed up from the wall, her hand swiping at the blood flowing down her mouth and chin.

She faced the four bears behind her.

"Did you really think we didn't know you were coming here, canine? That it wouldn't spread through the foxes that some She-wolf was looking for a way in, and that that information wouldn't get back to us?"

"Thanks for the naked thing, though," another said, grinning. "That was fun."

The bears unleashed their much larger claws, and Dee asked, "That's it? You're not even going to let me offer sex for a chance to get out of here alive?"

The one who'd tossed her into the wall snorted. "Sweetie, your shoulders are bigger than mine." The grizzly had a point. "Besides, we told your Alphas to stay away. Now the Van Holtzes need to learn a lesson."

Dee smiled. "Oh, darlin', I'm not a Van Holtz . . . I'm a Smith."

The smug smiles faded, along with the bravado, and Dee scented the panic and the rage that only came from bears. Apparently the foxes hadn't told them everything about her after all.

A long arm swung out, claws aiming for her face. Dee caught the grizzly's wrist in both her hands and yanked the bear forward. She unleashed her fangs and bit into his forearm, tearing out flesh, muscle, and possibly some artery when she pulled away.

Roaring, the grizzly snatched his arm away from her while a black bear attacked her from behind. Dee ducked and went under the bear's legs, grabbing the retractable baton he had in his back pocket. Not her bowie knife, but it would do in a pinch. She moved away from the black and into a polar, slamming her fist into the polar's throat. Trachia crushed, the polar dropped to his knees, so Dee planted her foot onto his shoulder and launched herself at the black bear, using his own baton by smashing it into his head.

The last bear was in the middle of shifting when she landed and took him out at both his still-human knees. She was loving this baton!

Laughing at the wounded bears, Dee opened the door to leave—and froze, her laughter dying in her throat. Boars she could handle . . . but sows?

Dee slammed the door shut, shoved a desk in front of it, and sprinted for the vent. She never looked back.

"How could you even think it?" Blayne cried, burying her head into Bo's chest after running into his arms. "They're defenseless! Helpless! Abused!"

"Blayne," Grigori begged, "please calm down."

"I'm just like them! Are you going to do the same to me? The big green needle? *Or just shoot me in the back of the head?*"

"We're not doing anything!" Chief Adams swore loudly. "I promise!"

"Swear it!" she commanded through her tears.

"I swear it, Blayne. We won't touch the dogs."

"Even after I leave?" She glanced back at both bears. "You'll protect them once I'm gone?"

"Blayne—" Grigori began, but Chief Adams cut him off.

"We will. We *both* promise."

Taking in a shaky, tear-filled breath, Blayne again rested her head against Bo's chest.

"I'll take her back to the house," Blayne heard Bo tell his uncle.

"All right. I'll be home in a bit." Really big hands patted her back, almost breaking her nearly unbreakable bones. "Don't worry, Blayne. Everything will be just fine."

She sniffed, nodded, and let Bo take her away from the chief's office and into the woods behind it.

After a few minutes, Blayne straightened up but took Bo's hand as they walked for a while through the woods, snow starting to fall again. When they were about a mile outside of town, Bo asked, "Feeling better?"

She sniffed. "Yeah. Much."

Bo stopped, lifted her hand, and pressed it to her chest. "Blayne?"

"Uh-huh?"

"Did you really expect me to buy that load of shit performance back there?"

Blayne snatched her hand back. "Shut up!"

"Oh," he said in a high voice, "you're going to hurt my dogs? My poor wee brutal fighting dogs? Who will love and protect the brutal fighting dogs who've been taking down the Ursus County deer population for the last month? Who? Who?" Bo laughed and didn't seem able to stop. "That was the best dinner theater I've seen in years!"

Refusing to respond, Blayne grabbed hold of the bottom of Bo's long-sleeve tee and wiped the tears from her eyes. Then she blew her nose in it.

When she pulled back, the look of horror on the hyper-neat

hybrid's face was worth the risk to her life she knew she was taking.

"What?" she asked innocently.

"You disgusting little—"

"I didn't have a tissue!"

"That's not an excuse!"

She giggled. "It is for me."

Bo reached for her, but Blayne squealed and took off running, Bo Novikov right after her.

Okay. She knew it was wrong, but seriously . . . she was having the *best* time!

CHAPTER 24

Ric looked up from his desk. "What?" he asked the leopard standing there.

"We're ready to go."

"Good." He pushed his chair back and walked to the door. The team he'd handpicked for this was waiting and armed to the teeth. They wouldn't waste time with shifter etiquette since this would be full-humans they'd be dealing with.

Ric grabbed his own weapon—a .45—and put it into his holster before he bothered to look at the woman he loved but refused to speak to. Although it was hard to be mad at her with her face looking like that.

"I'm okay," she said again.

Unable to not speak to her for any length of time, Ric said, "Dee . . . they were sows. We both know your ribs took a beating from them." Not to mention her legs, spine, and head, but her ribs took the worst of it.

"I said, I'm okay."

He motioned to one of the team leaders and the lioness led everyone out. When they were alone, Ric said, "You're not going."

"Don't answer to you."

"Actually, you do."

She ignored him, reaching into her locker and pulling out her vest and several weapons he didn't remember placing on the authorization list.

He walked up to her. "Dee?"

When she didn't answer, he placed his hand under her chin and lifted.

"I'm fine." She slapped his hand away.

"You can't even move."

"I can move enough."

He placed his hand on her forehead, and she jerked away, but not fast enough for him to notice another problem. "You've got the fever."

"Probably. But it won't hit good and proper for at least another hour or so. We'll be done by then."

"Dee—"

"I need to be in before the fever has hold of me. Won't be responsible for anything I do if you keep me out. Understand?"

Yeah. He understood. Understood that she was the one who'd gotten the information that was leading them to the New York base of the people who'd grabbed Blayne. Dee wasn't about to let someone else follow that through. Not when she'd been working on it for so long.

And the fact that the bears had known this info since they'd tracked the full-humans' damaged vehicle and their weapons to the location was something he and his Uncle Van would deal with at a later date.

"All right. But when the team's done, we take you to the hospital."

"Fine." She held her vest in one hand and kept her other hand pressed up against her ribs. "Help me get this thing on, will ya?"

It was the first time he'd heard her ask anyone to do anything for her not in the context of ordering food at a restaurant. He decided to take it as a positive sign.

He took the vest from her and turned her so she faced him.

"And no need to look so full of yourself, Van Holtz," she complained.

He was polite enough not to disagree, but he did smirk. It was a Van Holtz thing. He couldn't help himself. At least that's what he said when she snarled at him.

"I need ice time," Bo complained after writing a list of all the things he needed to do that evening in order to reorganize his uncle's library—and burning his soiled shirt in his uncle's backyard pit. "Want to come with me?"

Blayne snorted. Not exactly the answer he was expecting.

Pulling a training jersey over his head, he watched as she fed the dog under his uncle's couch. *When Grigori realizes she's expecting him to keep that dog . . .* "What does that snort mean?"

"It means do you really expect me to be like the other skanks who shine your knob? Sitting around *watching* you play hockey?"

"I don't want you to watch me play. I need training and you're available."

"I can't help you train."

"Because you're a girl?" And he was surprised when that bowl of fresh chicken and steak for the dog *didn't* come flying at his head.

"No, you sexist prick. Because you equated my roller skating ability to a seal moving across land. I somehow doubt my ice skating skill will impress you any more."

He crouched in front of her, the dog under the couch whimpering and moving farther away. Good thing the couch was so big. "This is true, but I'd hate for these to go to waste." He brought around the box he'd been hiding behind his back and placed it on her lap.

She stared down at the box and sighed. "This isn't a clock, is it?"

"No. This isn't a clock. I think you'll like it."

Blayne didn't seem too convinced, but she pulled off the top and moved the tissue paper around until she gasped and grinned. "Oh, my God!"

"They should fit. Norm had to search like crazy to find your size, though."

"They're ice skates."

"They're *hockey* skates."

She held them up. "*Sparkly* red hockey skates."

"They didn't have pink."

"I can't play hockey in pink, isn't that the law?" She dropped the skates in the box, tossed the box aside, and threw her arms around his neck. She hugged him tight, and he'd never been so glad he'd followed a whim before.

"Thank you so much! I love them!"

He hugged her back and kissed her neck. "Good. Now let's get going."

She pulled back. "I'm still not sure what you want me to do. I haven't gone ice skating since I was thirteen when Gwenie decided it was a good idea to teach me some derby moves. That humiliation alone was enough to ensure I never got on ice again."

"Well, I have uses for you and your exemplary stick skills."

"Such as?"

He grinned. "I need a goalie."

What the hell had she been thinking?

"Eek!"

Why did she agree to this?

"Ack!"

Why didn't she just say "no"? Or even "hell no"?

"Ow!"

Like her father had constantly told her, "You don't think before you do, then you're shocked when you end up on the wrong side of a shit pile." As always, the cranky old wolf was right, and she'd ended up on the wrong side of a big, fat shit pile.

Blayne tried to duck, but the hard piece of plastic slammed into the back of her head. "That's it!" she roared, positive her skull must have cracked in several places from that hit. What good was a helmet if it couldn't protect her precious cranium from small, flying, lethal objects? "That is *it*! I'm done!"

She tried to shake off the two different gloves she had to wear, one for blocking and one for catching the puck, but he'd taped the damn things on her with duct tape since they were too big.

After wearing nothing more than elbow and knee pads and some glitter with her derby uniform of tiny shorts and tank tops, she felt completely weighed down by the hockey equipment. Even worse, she had to use Bo's grade school stuff, which was *still* too big for her! Plus she couldn't see with the damn helmet that kept sliding all over the place. Christ! How big was this guy's head anyway? She did, however, have the lovely bright red—and sparkly!—skates he'd gotten for her. She loved the skates. But that was all she loved about this vicious, violent sport!

"I can't do this anymore!" She struggled to get the helmet off, not easy when she couldn't get off the gloves, which meant she couldn't get a grip on the strap holding the helmet in place.

Bo skated by her, not appearing to weigh his just-shy-of four hundred pounds by the way he managed to glide.

"Wuss," he teased as he glided by again.

She snarled, her arms dropping to her sides. "I am not a wuss. I am simply tired of being pummeled by that damn puck." For hours! He'd been torturing her for hours! She was hungry and cranky and covered in little puck-size bruises!

"Just a girl," Bo tossed out as he skated around her in sexy little circles. She couldn't explain why they were sexy, but damn him they were! "Can't play in the man sports. You'll need to stick with your little girly derby."

Blayne swiped up the junior hockey stick and swung at Bo. He caught the curved end of her stick with his own and skated backward, pulling her along with him.

"You," she hissed, "couldn't handle derby. The Babes would eat you alive and you know it."

"Could I wear those shorts?"

She pressed her lips together to keep from laughing. The image of him in the Assault and Battery Park Babes short-shorts would stick with her for eternity.

Bo pulled Blayne around the pond without looking behind him. He'd worked this pond so much as a kid, he instinctively knew its dimensions, so he didn't need to look.

"You trained on this pond, didn't you?" Blayne asked. "When you were a kid?"

"Yup. I came out here every day before school and after, during the winter."

"You miss it, don't you?"

"I guess."

"You should visit more. I'm sure your uncle would love to have you."

"Blayne—"

"I'm just saying."

"Don't."

"Everyone loves having you back. You're the town hero."

"And you know this because . . ."

"Bob Sherman told me."

So startled, Bo almost tripped. "Bob Sherman?" he asked. "Who runs the gas station?"

"Uh-huh."

"Why were you talking to him?"

"I bought bottled water from him this morning during my run—I put it on your account by the way—after I chatted with Craig and Luther Vanders outside of the farmer's market."

"You talked to Craig and Luther?"

"Yeah. They're really nice. Gave me free fruit."

"They *gave* you free fruit?"

"Yup. I offered to run back to Grigori's place to get some money, but they said it wasn't necessary. They really are sweet."

And stingy. Craig and Luther were stingy bears. They didn't give anything away for free. A pear, a strawberry, a peanut. Nothing!

Instead of asking about the Vanders brothers, he asked about Bob Sherman, also referred to as Mean Old Bob Sherman or That Old Bastard Bob Sherman. "You talked to Bob Sherman? And he . . . talked back?"

"Sure."

"Okay."

"Don't feel bad because you can't do that. Not everyone has that skill."

"Can't do what?"

"Be chatty and friendly. I'm a firm believer not everyone *needs* to be, and it really irritates me when people try to force others to do it. Like they're not being normal if they're not talking, talking, talking."

"Uh-huh."

"More important," she went on since nothing ever deterred the woman from her ultimate goal, "if you're staying with your uncle when you visit, you won't have to talk to anyone but him. And the most you two do in the mornings is grunt at each other. So it's a win-win for both of you."

"You're not clear on the whole 'letting it go' concept, are you?"

"Uh . . . Bo?"

"Okay, fine." He didn't want to argue with her. They were having such a good time, why ruin it? And let's face it, if he hadn't snuffed the life from her for blowing her nose on his shirt, he had to be crazy about her. That was the only explanation that made sense to him. Of course, how she felt about him, he still didn't know. "I'll visit Grigori more often." Not hard since he just had to do it more than once in ten years to keep his promise, but those were little details she didn't need to know.

"No, no," she said, frowning. "I don't mean—" She stopped skating, bringing him up short. He was impressed by her technique and about to tell her that when she motioned toward the far side of the pond with a small tilt of her head.

Bo looked across the ice . . . and sighed. "Shit."

They were all standing on the outside of the pond, wearing hockey uniforms from the town's weekend team. A group of locals who got with other locals to play when the mood struck them. Most of them bears that Bo had grown up with. If this were Ursus County's main lake, about ten miles from where they were standing, Bo wouldn't have thought much about the locals showing up. But this pond was on Grigori's territory, and no one would come out here without an invitation because no one wanted to fuck with Grigori.

Snarling a little, Bo glared down at Blayne. "This is your fault, isn't it?"

"I thought they'd give me more time to talk you into it." At least she didn't try to lie to him.

"Is this why everyone's been so nice to me today?"

"It was my only stipulation. But I told them I couldn't promise that you'd definitely do it."

Which was why they were doing it this way. Bears. Sneaky.

"Blayne Thorpe," Raymond Chestnut called out. "Is Mr. Important still up for a little friendly game then? Like you said? Or is the tiny feline ready to run off into the woods and hide?"

Blayne scowled and Bo admitted, "Actually, that's him being nice."

"Oh." Her scowled faded. "All right then." She gazed up at him. "So are you going to play?"

"I really don't want to."

"Think of it this way, Bo, a couple of hours out of your life that they'll remember for the rest of theirs? Is that really too much for you?"

She could have hit him with a crowbar and it wouldn't have slammed into him with the same force the way her simple words did. Because she was right.

He stroked his hand down her cheek and yelled over his shoulder, "The feline is in."

The boys cheered, and the blinding grin he got from Blayne made every second of the next few torturous hours worth it.

"But I'll expect a backrub when we get home," he told her, skating with her over to the snow and ice covered dirt so he could help her get her skates and pads off.

"Okay," she replied, "but only if I can be naked when I'm doing it."

He didn't know why her words caught him off guard, but he ended up face down on the ice anyway. Shocked, Blayne stared down at him for several seconds before she raised both arms in the air and began singing that song from the movie "Rocky" that she *still* didn't know the words to. "Flying somethin' now . . . Feelin' somethin' now . . . lalalala now . . ."

Chestnut skated up behind him and, grabbing hold of the back of Bo's jersey, lifted him to his feet.

"Don't worry, Novikov. If that one there wanted to rub me down naked, I'd have tripped over my own skates, too. Although"—he watched Blayne badly skate around the ice—"I'd insist on no singing, if I were you."

CHAPTER 25

The Canadians showed up to be the opposition. Mostly polars and grizzlies that they'd all known and grown up with over the years.

They decided on positions and agreed to a few basic rules that included no permanent injuries before separating and heading to their team goals.

That was when Bo noticed them. How could he not when it was pretty much the entire town—Ursus County and the local Canadians—sitting around waiting for the game to start. He quickly scanned the crowd and saw Blayne standing by herself. He skated to the edge of the pond and motioned her over.

"What's this?" he asked when she stood in front of him.

"Um . . ."

He took off his helmet and shook out his hair. "No 'um.' What is this?"

"They just showed up."

"Uh-huh."

"I'm not sure I'm appreciating your tone lately."

"My tone?"

"It implies I'm not being truthful."

"Maybe we should ask the chief and my uncle about how truthful you are, she of the crocodile tears."

"You're enjoying that way too much."

"I guess I kinda am. Besides," he leaned down and pressed his forehead against hers, "I like that you have a devious side, Blayne Thorpe."

Blayne grinned. "Your accent's coming back."

"What accent?"

"Now who's not being truthful?" She stepped away from him and turned.

"No kiss?" he called after her as she walked away, catching *everyone's* attention.

Blayne looked at him over her shoulder. "Did you have to yell that?"

"Is that a no?"

"Yes. It's a no. No kiss for you."

"Oh, come on!" everyone called out, startling Bo.

"You can't leave him hanging like that!"

"Kiss him!"

"Go on and kiss him, cutie!"

Then someone began to clap and chant, "Kiss him! Kiss him! Kiss him!" And everyone joined in.

Blayne marched back over to him. "I blame you for this."

"You're the one getting to know everybody. If I had my way, we would have never left my uncle's house." He leaned down and added in a whisper, "Or my bed."

"Don't worry. It'll still be there when we get home tonight."

She reached up, placing her hands on his shoulders, and pulling him down until she could reach him while on the tips of her toes. Blayne kissed him and the whoops and catcalls faded to nothing more than background noise as he pulled her in close and kissed her back.

"They're all staring at us, aren't they?" Blayne asked when they finally separated.

"Pretty much."

"Then it's a good thing I'm not shy." She winked at him and headed over to the residents who had lawn chairs and benches out for everyone to sit on. Marci had saved a seat for her.

"You two are looking happy," she said.

"Not as happy as Grigori was when he got home this morning."

"Uh . . . um . . ." Flustered, Marci immediately turned back to the pond where the two teams were warming up. "This is very exciting," she rambled on. "Very few of us have seen Bold Novikov play in years."

"You guys don't have a professional team nearby?"

"Only minor teams from other bear towns come this far north. The professional teams won't come out here because we're not very welcoming of other species."

"Oh." Blayne thought about that a moment. "But everyone welcomed me."

Marci's smile returned. "That we did." She leaned in and whispered, "The whole town's talking about how you handled Kerry-Ann. She's usually real intimidating."

"Is that because of her beady little eyes?" Blayne asked in a whisper. "Because with a little makeup, I could totally help her with that."

Marci took Blayne's hand between both of hers, "I am learning to adore you, Blayne Thorpe."

His uncle, the only one anyone trusted to be ref of this game since he was too hard on Bo to ever ignore his mistakes, was about to drop the puck when they heard all the laughter. They briefly paused to focus over at the onlookers.

"Seems that tiny girlfriend of yours is fittin' in pretty well, Bold Novikov," Raymond remarked, obviously impressed.

"She does have a way about her."

"It must be the dog in her, because wolves . . ."

Both teams sneered in agreement about wolves until Grigori leaned in and asked, "Are you two girls done talkin' or should we forget all this and start braiding each other's hair instead?"

Bo focused back on the game, doing his best to push Blayne out of his mind. Not easy when he could still taste her on his lips.

His uncle dropped the puck and Bo went for it, trying to get control of it. Bad move. What he should have done was remember how these impromptu pond games were played. If he had, that Canadian polar would have never been able to bash Bo's skull in with his stick before skating off with Bo's puck.

Blayne cringed when she saw Bo go down from that hockey stick to the head.

Looks like dinner tonight will be clear soups. Or straight intravenous feeding.

Bo slowly sat up, shaking his big head. Probably all that ringing in his ears was confusing him. But it didn't last long. His head came up and he snarled, his gaze locking on the polar who took his puck and was busy trying to get past Bo's goalie.

Bo got to his feet.

"Uh-oh," Marci said to the woman beside her. "His tusks are out."

"They're not *tusks*," Blayne argued. "They're fangs. Like the mighty saber-toothed cat of yore."

"Yore?"

"He probably got it from his ancient Mongolian ancestors," Blayne added.

"I doubt it," a sow sitting behind them said. "Saber-toothed cats were from a long-extinct subfamily of cats. Mostly from North and South America. Bold Novikov's lion kin come from ancient China but I believe can be traced back to ancient Africa where the first . . ."

The sow's lecture faded out when Blayne turned around and stared at her.

Grinning, Marci said, "This is my daughter, Rebecca. Did I mention she has her Ph.D. in paleontology?"

Now Blayne stared at Marci.

"Like 'Jurassic Park,' dear."

"Ohhhh. Right." Because that was a movie she'd seen. "Well, whatever. They're fangs, as far as I'm concerned. Not tusks. He's not a walrus."

"Although he's been known to eat walrus."

Blayne shuddered. "Thanks for that, Marci."

"Just involving myself in the conversation, dear."

Right. Sure she was.

Blayne returned her attention to the game, but of course that was around the time she was hit with a splash of blood across her face and neck from whatever Bo did to some poor Canadian polar that got in his way.

Trying hard not to laugh, Marci reached into her large designer bag that was part traveling medical bag and part purse, pulling out a large white cloth.

"You," Marci coughed back a laugh, "poor dear. Let me clean you off."

It's always nice to know that morbid embarrassment follows me wherever I go.

During a timeout, Bo skated over to the sideline where Blayne was waiting.

"Where did all that blood come from?" he asked.

She glared at him, but didn't answer. Since she seemed relatively unharmed, he didn't worry about it.

"Game's going pretty well, huh?"

"Sure."

She didn't sound sure. "What? Say it."

"It's just a suggestion, but maybe you could . . ."

"Could what?"

"Let someone else get a goal."

"Why would I do that?"

She rubbed her forehead with both hands. "Because it'll be very cool to do and you have absolutely nothing to lose?"

"Except my puck."

Her hands turned into fists, and he thought she might try pummeling him, but she looked off, took a breath, and tried again. "Only a truly confident man—"

"Is willing to be a loser?"

That time she did swing, hitting his arm and chest with those tiny wolfdog fists. And his laughing—not helping.

The truth was Bo had never willingly allowed anyone to get his puck, but Blayne did have a point. He had nothing to lose. But there was a bigger issue here.

"Will it make you happy if I do this?" he asked.

"Yes," she hissed, frustrated. "It would make me happy."

"Then I'll do it."

Blayne blinked, her fists unfisting. "Just like that?"

"Yep. I like making you happy."

Her grin—worth any going-against-his-personal-beliefs moment this would cause.

"But don't try this during an actual game where I'm getting paid millions of dollars to win," he added, so boundaries were clear.

She laughed, heading back to her seat. "Like I care what you do at that dog and pony show at the stadium."

Nope. He didn't get her at all, but man did he like her.

Blayne returned to her seat, Marci watching her close.

"What was that about?" she asked.

"Just a little conversation. Nothing to worry yourself about."

"Seems to me like you two are getting serious."

"Getting serious about what?"

The sow dismissed her with a hand wave. "Forget I asked."

"I will." Kerry-Ann, who'd shown up once the game had started, held out a bag of popcorn for Blayne.

"This is going so well, isn't it?"

"You were supposed to give me more time," Blayne reminded her around a mouthful of popcorn.

"I had complete faith in your skills, Blayne Thorpe."

"Uh-huh." Just for that Blayne took another handful of popcorn. "I have a question."

"And what's that, dear?"

"All the stray dogs I keep finding. Where are they coming from?"

Both Kerry-Ann and Marci shrugged.

"Don't know," Kerry-Ann admitted. "We find 'em all the time.

Figure they've been coming from one of the full-human towns. A few of the store owners wanted us to get a team together to hunt them down and . . . uh . . ." She studied Blayne a moment before finishing with, "Take them somewhere they could live forever in happy fields."

Even if Marci hadn't spit out her Sprite, Blayne didn't buy that for a second.

"Contrary to popular belief, Kerry-Ann, dogs aren't stupid. We *know* when we're going to the vet."

"Well, we didn't do it, did we?" Kerry-Ann snapped. "It was just a suggestion anyway."

"Uh-huh." Blayne took more popcorn, now feeling fully entitled to the entire bag. "And what about the farmhouse?"

"What farmhouse?"

"The one near the beach. You have to get through Antarctic Minor to get to it."

Marci chuckled. "She's talking about the old Benson place, Kerry-Ann."

"Gosh. No one's lived there for years. Can't get to it anyway from here because of the storms."

"What are those anyway?"

"They're the reason we don't have any more covens running around Ursus County," Marci murmured.

"They wanted to make the polars comfortable by making certain parts of the area cold year-round. Needless to say, that went badly."

"Even the polars don't feel like going through that freezing weather. It's hell on their coats."

"And the Bensons died without a cub of their own, so that house goes untended."

"But it's a beach property, right? You could sell that, couldn't you?"

"To who? Full-humans? Remember, Blayne, they don't know we're here and we plan to keep it that way."

"Well those dogs have to be coming from somewhere, and it needs to stop."

"I have a few friends in the Humane Society who could look into it," Marci told her. "I'll call them and ask."

Blayne pressed her shoulder into Marci's. "Thank you. Dr. Luntz."

"Oh, stop your foolishness, Blayne Thorpe. And duck."

"What—"

The puck slammed into her head, sending Blayne flipping into the lap of Marci's daughter.

"My fault!" one of the Canadians yelled from the ice.

Marci shook her head at Blayne. "Told you to duck, now didn't I? You don't listen, Blayne Thorpe."

Bo went behind the goal, the entire opposition right on his ass. They'd been riding him for almost the entire game, knowing he was the one they had to stop. He hard-charged around, the other team's winger coming at him from the front, their left defenseman at his back. The rest of Bo's team moving in and the opposition's goalie crouched and ready to block Bo's shot.

Could he get through them all and possibly get the goal? Yeah. He could also get his head cut open in the process and end up spending the rest of the night icing his wounds and taking massive amounts of over-the-counter pain meds to get rid of what would be a monstrous headache rather than playing what had become his favorite game outside of hockey—Making the Naughty Wolfdog Squeal.

Using an overabundance of peripheral vision that gave him almost a 360-degree view of everything around him, Bo saw Raymond Chestnut push past the other team's right winger. Where he was going, Bo didn't know or care. Instead he yelled out, "Chestnut!"

The nearly eight-foot polar stopped on a dime and turned toward him. Bo swung his stick back—hitting someone in the face—then forward, the slap shot sending the puck away from the group and at Raymond. The polar blinked in surprise. He'd played with Bo throughout grade, junior high, and high school, and never once had Bo purposely shot the puck to anyone. He seemed so stunned that Bo was sure he'd let the puck go right by him.

Thankfully, he didn't. Raymond halted the puck with his stick, spun, and sent it off—right past the goalie who'd only seconds ago realized that for once Bo no longer had the damn thing.

The puck sailed into the ratty net that had been used for every inside town game for the past forty years, the goalie diving in after it, his team piling on top of him, trying to help. It was a lost cause. The puck was in and Grigori threw up his arms and blew his whistle. The game was over and Raymond Chestnut had made the winning shot.

The crowd roared in approval, everyone coming off the bench and across the ice. Raymond shook hands and gave hugs while appearing stunned out of his mind. A polar sow threw herself into Raymond's arms as did five cubs. It took Bo a second, but he eventually recognized Meg D'Accosta. Raymond's girlfriend throughout high school and apparently his mate now.

"That was impressive!" Blayne smiled up at him, her hand holding an icepack to her forehead. "I thought you were going to not do it."

"I'll admit, it wasn't easy for me. And how's your head?"

"Oh, you know . . ." A sound like a shot ricocheted around them, and the bears and foxes all fell silent, focusing on Blayne.

Her cheeks bright red, she lowered the icepack and, except for the nasty cut still there, even the swelling was gone. Once again her bones had "snapped" back.

"It's much better," she muttered.

"I see that."

"Huh," Grigori said next to them. "And I thought the boy had the hardest head in Ursus County."

Everyone laughed, and Bo pulled an embarrassed but giggling Blayne against him, hugging her tight.

"We're all going to the Chestnuts' bar for drinks," Dr. Luntz said, her hand patting Bo's back. "You'll come with us."

Bo shook his head. "I can't. I've got stuff to do back at Grigori's house."

His uncle growled, and Blayne stepped away from him. "What stuff?" she asked.

He pulled the list out of his hockey pants and unfolded it. "Let's see—"

Before he could read off the first item, Blayne leaped up and snatched the paper out of his hand, Grigori and Marci laughing.

Bo stared at his empty hand for a moment, shocked, before turning his gaze to Blayne. She held the sheet with two hands, and he could see the evil intent in her eyes.

"Blayne Thorpe, don't you dare—"

Too late. She ripped the paper into shreds and tossed the shreds into the air. "It's snowing!" she cheered.

Unlike before with his uncle, Bo didn't have time to write a copy of this list. His precious, detailed, perfectly timed out list! How could she?

Bo skated toward her, and Blayne squealed and stumbled back from him.

"You're not going to do anything crazy, are you?" she asked.

"That was my list."

"It was too confining!" she argued. "You need to learn to live in the moment."

"And you need a good dousing in Small Bear River." He reached for her, but Raymond Chestnut swept her up in his arms and took off running toward town, the rest of the two teams right behind him, the town cheering them on.

"You want your wolfdog back, Bold Novikov, guess you're going to have to come and get her!" Raymond crowed, everyone applauding in agreement.

Grigori stood beside Bo now. "The boys seem to have taken to your Blayne."

"I don't run after women," he said, still pissed off about his list.

"You shouldn't run after them. None of them deserve it."

"Right."

" 'Course everyone in town knows that Blayne can put whatever she wants on account, in your name. And if you *walk* to town now, those boys can probably damn-near clean out Chestnut's bar long before you get there."

"And," Dr. Luntz tossed in for good measure, "there is something about Blayne Thorpe that just screams, 'Drinks for everybody!' Don't ya think, Bold Novikov?"

With a short, outraged roar, Bo took off running before the damn woman could put him in the poor house.

Chapter 26

Josh Bergman couldn't believe he'd done four years at Penn State to end up being a security guard. But he couldn't ignore the fact that the money was worth every damn second that he sat in this same chair, night after night, staring at TV screens. Especially after his old man cut him off after he'd gotten expelled before his senior finals. He still couldn't believe how that turned out. His own frat brothers turning on him because of what some girl said. Where was the loyalty?

Whatever. Things were already looking up. They'd lost a whole team a few days ago, and he'd already gotten word he'd be going in for training and would be assigned to a team of his own. The money for team members was just damn phenomenal. He already had the car and rims picked out for when he got that first paycheck. But until training started, he had at least another week to kill before he could give this bullshit job up for good.

Josh reached behind him to grab another bottle of water from the small fridge under the desk when something on one of the cameras caught his attention. Forgetting the water, he leaned in and studied the screen. After a moment, a girl walked into camera range. Josh tapped on the keyboard, zooming in. She was cute, he'd give her that but there was something . . .

She turned and her eyes glinted in the one streetlight across from her. They glinted just like a dog's.

Josh keyed the com attached to his ear. "I've got an alert at Door Six. I repeat, an alert at Door Six." He waited for a response, rolling his eyes. Tim probably smoking another joint behind the garages and not paying attention. That guy would have this job forever. "I need a call back, Tim. Are you hearing me?"

"Doubt he's hearing much of anything anymore."

Josh spun his chair around, not thinking, just reacting at the female voice behind him. As the chair turned, there was a flash of metal and he couldn't say he felt anything—even when blood sprayed across the console—but even without that pain, without the feeling, he knew he was dying. Knowing this, however, he still put his hands to his throat, trying to stop the bleeding. The woman, a bitch as big as him and covered with bruises and cuts, was busy with the console and didn't seem to notice or care that he was standing up and stumbling away from the desk.

He staggered over to the emergency exit. Once the doors opened, the alarm would go off and cops and ambulances would swarm this place. People who would keep him alive. He was too important to die. He knew that.

Josh reached the door, and removing one of his precious hands from his throat, he shoved the big metal bar with OPENING DOOR WILL ACTIVATE ALARM written across it. But as the door flew open, there was no alarm. And standing right outside weren't cops and ambulances and people who would keep him alive. But animals. Freaks. The biggest one he'd ever seen, even after working at this place for six months, stepped up to him and grabbed him around the face.

"And where were you going, genius?" the thing laughed, carrying Josh back inside and crushing his entire head with that one hand at the same time.

The She-lion pushed Dee aside, dropping into the seat the bleeding security guard just left. "Could you have gotten more blood on this goddamn keyboard?"

"Speed is your friend right now," Dee snapped. It was one thing to put up with the pretty male lions but she had no patience for the females. And with the pain from her broken ribs as they knitted themselves back together and the fever slowly but surely coming on her, she had no patience for anyone. Male or otherwise.

The She-lion tapped on the keyboard for a few seconds. "We're in."

Dee shoved her a little to get past to join the rest of the team. Thankfully Van Holtz had only chosen the best for this. Good. She hated having to do everything on her own because she didn't trust the ones working with her.

Using only hand gestures, she sent groups down one set of side stairs, another up, and after prying the elevator doors open, took a group with her, all of them climbing up the elevator cables to the top floors.

They waited until the She-lion still on the computer did what she needed to. She shut off all the power in the building. Already past nine o'clock, everything went pitch black. Good thing her team could see in the dark.

Motioning to the grizzly hanging underneath her, she watched him move up so he could pry open the doors. They could hear the full-humans trying to figure out what was going on. Some were laughing, thinking it was funny. But some were concerned, moving cautiously. Grabbing the hand held out to her by the grizzly, Dee let him haul her out of the elevator shaft and onto the floor. Again using only hand signals, she sent her team off to do what they'd been sent to do while Dee walked down the hallway toward big double-doors.

Before she reached them, she scented full-humans moving silently up behind her but ignored them, keeping her focus on reaching that door. She could do this because she knew her team would handle them.

Dee pulled out her bowie knife, the blood from the security guard still on it, and walked up to the double-doors. The bodies of full-humans silently dropped behind her.

Instead of kicking the doors open, she applied a small explosive to each door hinge. She stepped back, turning her face as the hinges blew. The doors fell forward and Dee walked in. Three guards protecting the one important male who ran this place pulled their guns but Dee moved fast and cut throats until she had the important full-human by the neck. Using the back of her hand, she smashed his face, knocking him out, and dragged him out of the office by his collar.

"Move out!" Dee yelled, her team falling in behind her. The grizzly grabbed the full-human Dee was dragging and tossed him over his shoulder. The bear leaped at the elevator cables, his gloved hands and booted feet taking him down to the first floor in seconds. Dee and the rest of the team followed, hitting the exit moments later.

"Go! Go!" she ordered, her team charging for the three trucks waiting for them. Once her team shut the truck doors and rumbled off down the street, Dee motioned with her hand to a dark corner. The first giggle was followed by several others, and the hyenas charged out of the darkness and into the building. Two clans. One spotted, the other striped. They tore into the building, and when the last one ran inside, still laughing, she let the door close and limped over to the Maserati waiting for her at the corner.

She slipped inside and closed the door.

"Hyenas?" Van Holtz asked. "Really?"

"By morning there won't be anything left but an empty building." She leaned her head back, closed her eyes. "Besides, I call them in for a little late-night snacking and they leave my cousin's Pack alone. It's called tit-for-tat."

"Sounds like a deal with the devil to me." Van Holtz pulled onto the street and headed away from where the trucks were going.

"Wait. I need to talk to—"

"Uncle Van will handle that. *You're* going to the hospital. And don't argue with me," he growled when she started to do just that.

"Fine."

"Yeah. Fine."

She glanced around the car. "What about some American muscle?"

"Now you're complaining about my car?"

"Pansy car for rich foreigners. Like yourself."

And when he shifted that pansy car, ripping paint off buildings as they shot by, Dee didn't say anything but . . . okay. She was impressed. If a man could handle a car like this . . . well, maybe he could handle something that many had considered too fast.

Maybe.

With enough liquor, even bears will dance.

And yet, Grigori Novikov never thought that would include his nephew. Who, as a matter of fact, was stone-cold sober. Of course, Blayne had begged to have that sixties psychedelic crap Bo liked put on and the dance floor was so packed that there wasn't much moving going on, so it wasn't like anyone could really break out any fancy moves. But still. His nephew. Dancing. With his girlfriend. Who he kept calling his girlfriend. And his girlfriend who still hadn't caught on yet. Too cute and smart to be that dumb, but there ya go.

Marci dropped down next to him. Unlike Blayne and Bo—Marci had been drinking. A lot. He knew this even before she started singing along with The Supremes' version of "(Love Is Like A) Heat Wave." Thankfully, most of the gossips were drunk off their ass, too. So hopefully he wouldn't have to hear tomorrow how "this was a mistake" and "we should have never" or "I should have never" or whatever else she insisted on saying anytime they were nearly "caught."

Caught? He got his AARP card the other day in the mail, weren't they too old to be "caught" in a relationship? He knew she worried about what her cubs would say. They'd adored their dad and with good reason. But they were all adults with cubs of their own.

That's when he remembered that Rebecca Luntz-Peters hadn't left the bar and as was her way, had been nursing one lone beer all night. He glanced over and, yep. She was gaping, her mouth open. Then she was scrambling for her cell phone. Probably to call her older sister in Boston and her younger sister in Nevada.

Awkward.

Not sure what else to do, Grigori said, "Let's dance."

He grabbed Marci's hand and hauled her drunk ass out away from the table and to the dance floor. He pulled her into his arms and held her against him in an attempt to keep her under control.

"You're going to regret this in the morning," he told her.

"Blayne said I should go for what I want. So I went."

Figures it was that damn wolfdog. In town less than three days and all hell was breaking loose! Wasn't it bad enough she had a dog living under his couch?

"Maybe you should have made that decision while sober."

"I'm not drunk. I'm just fortified. Blayne, however—"

"Has been drinking Shirley Temples all night."

"Yeah. Which are full of sugar."

"So?"

When his black bear only giggled, he had a bad feeling.

Bo watched his uncle close his truck door and walk around it.

"You'll be all right?" he asked Grigori.

"Yeah. I'm just going to drive Marci home."

"I don't need you to drive me home, ya bastid. I'm fine."

Bo would have believed that more if Dr. Luntz was sitting in the passenger seat rather than on the truck floor, and if she had her eyes open rather than closed. And if she weren't slurring her words a bit and calling his uncle "bastid."

"Yeah. Right." Grigori rolled his eyes at his nephew. "I'm gonna make sure she gets settled. So, uh . . ."

Rather than get an explanation that would just freak him out, Bo cut in, "No problem. Take your time."

Grigori nodded at him, got in his truck, and drove off. Bo turned and headed through the woods back to his uncle's house. He stopped, though, when the burden he carried on his left shoulder slid out of his old hockey pants—that were shorts on him when he was twelve but ski pants on Blayne—and hit the ground. Letting out an annoyed sigh, Bo reached down to grab her, but she'd already taken off running.

"You'll so never catch me!" she screamed at him over her shoulder.

This wouldn't be so bad if she were drunk like Dr. Luntz. But Blayne was stone-cold sober and on a caffeine-sugar rush the like the world had never known before.

"Damn you, sugar," Bo yelled at the heavens. "Damn you!"

He'd be better off trying to control a six-year-old after straight sugar had been poured into his mouth, rather than a crazed wolfdog running around Ursus County territory in the snow . . . with no pants on.

"Blayne Thorpe, get back here!"

She laughed and kept going, forcing him to run after her *twice* in one day.

And if Blayne was fast simply from her combined bloodlines, adding sugar and caffeine to that mix made her a jet, shooting through the woods and other bear's territory until she reached his uncle's house. That's when she stopped, waiting for him to catch up.

"Don't move," Bo said as he carefully approached.

He almost had her, too, until she yelled, "Catch me!"

"I don't want to catch you."

"Then I guess you never will!"

She took off again, laughing, and Bo took several steps back, then charged forward. He planted one foot on the stoop and propelled himself to the roof. He charged up and over it, leaping from the base of it and straight down at Blayne who'd turned to head off into the woods behind Grigori's house.

Bo tackled her from behind, his arms going around her and pulling her into his body. She squealed as they sped toward the ground, but he turned and took the brunt of the contact on his shoulder and back.

They landed hard, Bo knowing from experience that his shoulder had probably taken the worst of it. They lay there for a long moment, both panting, Bo flat on his back and Blayne on top of him, facing up at the dark sky.

But they didn't lie there long before Blayne said, "I still wanna run." She tried to pull out of his arms, but Bo held her tight. "I wanna run," she insisted.

"I don't care, Blayne."

"You can't hold me here, you Visigoth!"

"I can. I will."

"Why?"

"Because you'll run and run and run . . . with no flippin' idea of how to get back here. You'll get lost in the snow and then me and the rest of the town will have to track your ass down. It's not happening."

She let out a breath, her body going lax. But Bo wasn't fooled. After less than a minute, she desperately tried to wiggle out of his arms again, snarling and snapping at him. He let her do it. He let her snarl and snap and growl and fight and struggle and anything else she could think of. He let her keep it up for what felt like a good thirty to forty minutes while he held her. Then, panting harder than she had before, she sort of dropped against him. Figuring she'd worked her energy off, he got to his feet, still keeping his arms tight around her waist, and carried her into his uncle's house.

Once inside, and while still holding her, Bo decided she needed some warm milk. That had always helped him sleep when he was a kid. At the very least, it couldn't hurt. While Bo put some milk in a saucepan to warm up and threw some logs into the fireplace along with some newspaper before getting the flames good and roaring, he still carried Blayne around. He simply couldn't risk putting her down yet. Couldn't risk she'd bolt on him. Especially when he heard the wind pick up outside, another storm hitting them.

He poured the milk into a mug and carried it and Blayne back into the living room. Once he had her settled on the couch, he handed the mug to her and she took it. That's when he realized Blayne was shaking, her teeth chattering together. He quickly grabbed one of the blankets off the couch and wrapped it around her legs.

"Better?"

She nodded. "It's so cold."

"Your adrenaline rush wore off. And you're not wearing any pants."

"They were too big. You must have been a freakishly sized child."

"Which is why Fabi still calls me 'Speck'?"

She sipped the milk, scrunched up her face. "Can't I have some chocolate in—"

"Not in this lifetime." Or at the very least not tonight. "No sugar, no caffeine. Chocolate has both. You just drink that as it is and relax."

She pouted and Bo warned, "And don't throw it, either. Just drink it, Blayne. Now."

"I don't like plain milk."

"I don't care. Now drink."

She did, but if he didn't know better he'd swear he was force-feeding her arsenic. When she was done, he took the mug and returned it to the kitchen. He thought about washing it now, and normally he would. But for some reason . . .

By the time Bo made it into the hallway, Blayne had already sprinted out the front door. He didn't go after her this time, though. He simply watched.

Blayne sprinted outside, ready to go for a nice long run. She was soooo bored! She hated being bored. She hated being trapped in one place for too long. She hated being unable to do what she wanted, when she wanted. And she knew, once she got her stride, that Bo "I'm God's gift to the universe and hockey" wouldn't get close to her. She was that fast. The combo wild dog and wolf speed made her nearly as fast as the cheetahs. The only downside was she didn't have the cheetah lung capacity, so sometimes when she ran fast for very long stretches, it felt like her chest was going to explode and she sometimes passed out, not waking up for days—but she'd worry about that tomorrow!

Right now she simply wanted to run and run and run and . . .

Holy shit! It's cold!

The snow came down in one big blanket, and the wind nearly knocked her off the porch. Squealing, she ran back into the house and slammed the door.

Bo leaned against the kitchen doorway, his arms crossed over his chest, a smirk on his face. Haughty! That was the only way she could explain the expression he wore. Haughty and rude!

"A little nippy outside?" he asked.

"Oh, shut up!" She paced by the door, wondering what she would do now. Then she remembered the television.

She had the remote in her hand and aimed at the TV when Bo walked into the living room behind her and said, "Cable's out."

"What?" She turned on the TV anyway, and there was more snow there than outside. "What the hell?"

"Cable usually goes out when it snows like this."

"It's like the Dark Ages!" she yelled, shutting off the TV, unable to stand looking at all that fuzzy white, and brought her arm back.

"Don't throw the remote," Bo said. "You break it and Grigori will lose his mind."

Growling in frustration, she dropped the remote on the couch and began pacing again.

"I am so damn bored!"

"And what are we going to do with you so bored?"

"I don't know!"

He relaxed against the wall. "You could read?"

"Read?" She wanted to spit at him. "Does it look like I can sit and read for a few hours?"

"No TV, no running, and no reading . . . my God, what will you do to get rid of all that excess energy?"

"I don't know!" she wailed, despondent.

"Well, while you think of something, I'm going to bed. Of course, you can join me."

"I'm not tired!"

"Okay. Good luck then. If you need me for anything, I'll be in bed. Naked."

Blayne froze. Naked. Naked Bo. And if she were naked, too . . .

She turned around but he was already gone.

Bastard.

Bo heard something behind him, but when he looked over his shoulder, he only saw the empty hallway. Shrugging, he faced forward again, and immediately stopped.

Blayne stood in front of the bedroom door, one hand pressed against the doorway, the other on her waist. How she got past him . . .

"Yes?" he asked.

"So . . . uh . . . you busy?"

"Just going to bed. I'm tired and the sun's almost up. Mind moving?"

He tried to step around her, but she crowded up in the corner, blocking him. "Are you really tired?"

"Exhausted. Had that game and a really late night at the bar. What's a guy like me to do?"

"Oh, gee, I don't know." She moved into him, wrapping her arms around his chest. "Anything you want?"

"I get that anyway. What are you offering me that makes you special?"

Blayne gasped. "You rude, son of a—"

"That's what I thought." He reached around her, opened the door, and stepped into the room.

"You're just walking away?"

"Not walking away. Stepping away. To my bed."

"Yeah, but—"

"Night, Blayne." He reached behind him and gathered up his jersey, pulling it over his head. When he shook his hair out of his eyes, Blayne stood in front of him and she still wasn't wearing any pants. "Yes?" he asked.

"Let's lay our cards on the table here. Okay? I don't have a lot of options right now and"—she shrugged—"you'll do."

"I'll *do*?"

"Isn't that good enough at the moment?"

"No." He pushed her aside and sat on the bed, removing his boots.

"Oh, come on, Bo. Help a girl out."

He tossed the boots aside and stood. "I could. But what am I getting out of it? It seems one sided, don't you think?"

"One sided? You're getting *me*! And you're damn lucky, too!"

"I guess."

"You *guess*?"

Bo stripped off the rest of his clothes and stretched out on the bed. He placed his hands behind his head and watched her. "You haven't exactly given me anything to change my mind."

"Well, we'll see about that." She went for the boots first, but she must have forgotten that she'd laced them up tight in the front so when Blayne tried to slip the right one off by using her left foot, she ended up sprawled flat on the floor. Bo cringed when he heard her hit the hard wood.

"Blayne?"

"I'm fine. Just shut up!"

He heard her muttering about "goddamn knots," but she eventually got to her now bare feet.

She'd borrowed someone's soft hair band to pull her mass of hair into a high ponytail when they were dancing. She tugged it out with one hand, but ended up cursing as stray hairs were caught between the twisted material. That was another three minutes of Blayne trying to get that loose since she wasn't about to yank it out and risk pulling out what she insisted on calling her "precious tresses" in the process. When she finally got that done, she tossed the hair band aside and shook her hair out. She gave him a small, ridiculously sexy smile, before reaching for the jersey she still had on. She got that off without any problem. And the sweatshirt under that. And the thermal shirt. And the T-shirt because the thermal material made her chest itch.

By then Bo was laughing so hard he was on his side, curled into a ball.

"I give up," she said. "The whole sexy beyond belief thing is just so not me. I'm going to sleep on the couch."

That snapped him out of his hysterical laughter and he was up and reaching for her arm before she even got to the door. He tossed her back on the bed, her panicked squeal making him laugh again.

"Why leave after it took ten hours to finally get you naked."

"Gee. Thanks. How can I turn down *that* offer?"

"You can't."

"Actually, I think I can. I will." She tried to get off the bed but Bo had her around the waist, pulling her up against his chest.

"You can keep running, Blayne. But I'll eventually catch you."

"I'm faster."

"I can hold out longer."

"Barely."

"Enough." He kissed her neck, her shoulder. "Besides. You need help with all this untapped energy. Can't have you running around my uncle's house in circles, now can we?"

"I can chase my tail for a few hours. That'll work."

"I'll chase your tail." He pressed his hand against her groin, forcing her ass to rock back against his hard cock. "You just try not to trip over your own two feet in the process."

Bastard. Now she realized why Marci Luntz kept telling her to "watch yourself with those Novikov boys."

The man had a way of teasing her until she wanted to punch him while making her wet and horny at the same time. How was that fair?

One of Bo's fingers slipped inside her pussy, and Blayne gasped, her hips rocking against his hand while her arms reached back to wrap around his neck. Unable to reach his neck, she settled on his arms and turned her face up so that he could kiss her, his tongue sliding past her lips and invading her mouth. Blayne groaned, her fingers digging into his flesh.

A second finger slid into her and with his other hand, Bo stroked her clit. He took his time, leaning over her shoulder so he could watch as his hands slowly and deftly brought her off.

She panted, her body weakening, as the orgasm tore through her.

Bo's fingers left her, and Blayne went to lie down. That's when he grabbed her legs, lifting her up until her knees rested on his shoulders.

"Hey!"

With her clit still sensitive from the recent orgasm, Blayne winced when Bo's mouth pressed against her pussy, his tongue first teasing her clit, then those goddamn lips.

Blayne squealed. "Wait!" she begged. "Wait!"

Blue eyes changing to gold watched her. The brown mane beneath the white was now longer, reaching past his shoulders.

"Bo!" She tried to twist away from him, but his grip on her thighs was powerful and unrelenting. His lips began to twist and turn her clit, and Blayne's body shook as another orgasm built and built, finally ripping through her. Her neck arched and she screamed out her release, her hands able to reach the ceiling to steady herself.

When the last shudder rocked through her, she was laid out on the bed and Blayne opened her eyes. Bo stared down at her, one hand petting her cheek.

She reached out for him with both arms, but he took hold of her wrists, gripping them in one hand, and pushing them over her head and into the mattress.

"Wait—"

It was too late. He licked his lips, studied her chest for a moment, and then leaned down, licking her nipple. His lips wrapped around it and Bo tugged, pulled, while his free hand was busy invading her pussy again with his fingers.

Blayne, too weak to fight at this point, could only groan and wait for it. She waited and it hit, slamming into her, careening through her system. She came hard, her body writhing beneath Bo's, the sensation that her arms were pinned, increasing the intensity until she exploded around the hybrid who'd done this to her.

*   *   *

Bo released her hands and grabbed a condom from the un-opened box he'd found in his uncle's closet—something he would not discuss further—earlier in the day.

He turned Blayne onto her side with shaking hands, his body unable to wait anymore for her.

Bo bent her knees up, before he leaned into her and pressed his cock against her pussy. He shoved once, hard, and entered her, Blayne showing she wasn't unconscious when she groaned and gripped the bedding.

"Look at me, Blayne," he ordered her.

Her face turned toward him, her brown eyes slowly blinking open. Once he knew he had her attention, he powered into her, taking her with long, strong strokes. She panted and writhed beneath him, moaning his name.

Bo took his time, at first. Thinking he could stay inside her forever and could keep going that long. But his body couldn't handle that ride. Not after watching her come again and again.

Laying his palms flat on either side of Blayne, he raised his upper body over her and picked up the speed of his strokes. He no longer had any control, unable to temper the pace or the strength of what he was doing.

He took her like that, fucking her hard, wanting to claim her as his forever. Waiting for her to show him that she belonged to him. That at least her body knew, if not her mind.

"No," she groaned. "I can't. Not again. I can't."

But she did, her pussy gripping his cock, tearing his orgasm out of him as she came again, her body shuddering beneath his.

As Bo released inside her, his body shaking from the power of it, he buried his face against Blayne's shoulder. And it wasn't until he tasted blood that he realized his—smaller for his human form but still longer than most shifter's—fangs had embedded into Blayne's flesh.

For a brief, hopeful second, he'd hoped that Blayne hadn't noticed. But then her entire body tensed and she said, "What the hell did you just do?"

CHAPTER 27

Ezra Thorpe opened his front door. It wasn't even five yet, but he hadn't slept since the day Niles Van Holtz had shown up at his house.

And here he was again.

"Well?"

"We need to get your daughter out of Ursus County. We need to get her out now."

Ezra had already heard from his buddies and connections that the Group had located and raided the building that housed the people who'd tried to take Blayne. He'd also heard that the hybrids who'd recently been stored in the basement, prepped for transport, had been released. But the hybrids who'd already been through a few fights, their moneymakers awaiting transport to a new location, had been too far gone. They'd been put down at the location. Harsh but necessary.

Yet what did any of that have to do with Blayne or Ursus County?

"Why?"

The wolf scratched his head, glanced up, then finally admitted, "Uh . . . 'cause that's where they've been taking the hybrids to get them ready to fight. Breaking them in, I guess. Anyway, we need to figure out what we're going to do next and, to be honest, we could use your skills."

Ezra let out a sigh and reached for his coat from the stand. Only Blayne, he thought as he followed Niles Van Holtz to his limo.

Bo returned with a washcloth and some antibiotic. He placed everything on the bed and sat down across from her. Instead of reaching over to her to care for the wounds, he gripped her around the waist and pulled her onto his lap patiently waiting until her legs wrapped around his hips.

She stared off over his shoulder and bit the inside of her lip when she felt the first swipe of the cleaning cloth against her brand-new bite marks.

"Blayne?"

"Uh-huh?"

"You're not talking to me."

"Uh-huh."

"Are you mad?"

"Uh-uh."

"But you're not talking to me?"

"Uh-uh."

"I need you to talk to me, Blayne."

She shook her head. *Not a good idea. Not a good idea.*

"I just marked you, Blayne. I won't lie and say I had it planned out, but I can't say that I mind, either. The way I feel about you . . . making you mine just feels right. But I need you to tell me how you feel. I need you to say something. Anything. Please."

Well, if he wanted her to say something . . . "I'm never going to be on time, I'm either going to be twenty minutes late to two hours early, and don't think I can function on that list thing you do, I mean I like lists as much as the next person and they can be quite helpful but I will not live under your Stalin-like schedules, nor will I feel bad if I put something in what I am sure is your frighteningly pristine home out of place—how can anyone relax in that kind of situation? And I don't want to live in fear of you getting a bug up your ass and throwing out what you've affectionately referred to as my 'crap,' and speaking of which, I love the watch, I really do, but at some point I will want to take it off, maybe wear some cheap piece of crap I get for a deal on the street and I don't want you freaking out every time I do, I can't constantly be worrying about time and to be quite blunt . . . I want children, lots and lots of children and you don't even like kids, not only that—"

Bo placed his hand over her mouth. "Brakes. Train."

She glared at him over his fingers.

"To make this easier for me, I'll address each of your points. In order."

In order?

"Number one, you may always be late, but I'll always be on time. And yes, I will bug you if you're running late and it's holding me back as well, but it's not something I'll get hysterical over because I understand that's you and you won't get hysterical when you realize that I give you too-early meeting times since I already know you'll be two hours late." *Wait. What?* "Second, I don't insist anyone keeps or maintains a schedule but me. All I do ask is that you respect the schedule I do have because right now, at this point in my life, it's about hockey and my commitment to the team I'm on. Third, stop comparing my time management skills to dictators. Fourth, I won't throw your stuff out unless it's actually in the trash, but if I start seeing extreme hoarder tendencies, you're going to therapy. Fifth, I don't care if you wear cheap, pretty crap as long as you don't use that cheap crap as an excuse for why you're late. You can't have it both ways. It's not fair. And sixth, I don't hate children, but I'm positive that I'll always consider my kids better than anyone else's because they're mine, which will automatically make them amazing." He paused, nodded his head, and said, "I think I hit all your concerns."

"Every one," she agreed.

"Yeah."

"You actually listened to me, and took me seriously."

"Of course."

Blayne stormed off the bed. "And how, exactly, am I supposed to deal with that?"

Bo leaned back on the bed, his palms flat, his arms keeping him propped up. "At this point . . . *nothing* I say will make you happy, will it?"

"Probably not!"

She would always make him crazy, wouldn't she? Whether they were in bed or out of it, she would always make him feel a little off kilter. A little . . . baffled. He wasn't sure that was a good thing, but he knew he'd never be bored. He'd never wander away from her. The thought of what she'd do while he was gone was simply too terrifying.

She snatched his jersey off the floor and pulled it on before storming out of the room. Deciding he wasn't done with this fight, Bo went after her. She was already walking out the front door, morning light flooding the hallway by the time he turned the corner.

"You're not even wearing shoes," he called after her, relieved to see that at least the storm had blown over.

"Thanks, Mom! I'll keep that in mind."

Grabbing a set of boots she'd left lying on the floor, he followed her out the door.

"Do you want to lose your toes? Do you think that'll be attractive?" She stood at the top of the porch, so he crouched beside her, placing her feet in the boots. "Don't make me mental, Blayne."

"Uh . . . Bo?"

"We can argue. You can walk away."

"Bo."

He tied her boots. "But don't walk away into volcanoes or tsunamis or into the freezing Ursus County cold because you're being a drama queen."

"Bo!"

"What?"

Blayne cleared her throat and said, "Uh . . . Bold Novikov, I'd like you to meet my father. Ezra Louis Thorpe."

Praying she was kidding—but already knowing she wasn't—he looked down the porch stairs. Unsmiling, black, powerfully built, in his fifties, and still wearing a buzz cut that was mere millimeters from bald, Bo knew this was Blayne's father.

"Sir," Bo said before raising his gaze to Blayne's. "I am so naked," he whispered. What kind of first impression could he be making right now?

"I'm almost positive he noticed that," she whispered back. "Although if you go inside and get some pants . . . I don't think he'll mind."

Bo nodded. "Good plan." Then, with as much dignity as he could muster, he stood and walked into his uncle's house.

Blayne waited until Bo had disappeared into the house before she marched down the stairs to her father.

"Why are you here?" she asked, seriously confused.

"I thought you wouldn't come home unless I came here myself to get you."

"Yeah, but . . . I didn't expect you to actually come here. Although a phone call making sure I was okay would have been nice."

Her father flicked her on the forehead, something she'd always hated. "Yeah. I can tell you've been hiding under the couch, waiting to be rescued for days now." It took a lot not to cringe when her father reached over and tugged down the collar of her jersey just enough to see where Bo had marked her.

"Huh," he said. He laid the collar back down, sighed. "I don't want to worry you, but you're still oozing."

"Gee . . . thanks, Dad."

"What do you want me to say?"

"You see that your daughter is marked, and that's the best you can come up with?"

"What would you like to hear then? 'Hope your kids aren't freaks?'"

"Oh, my God!" she exploded. "*You're a such a—*"

A big hand wrapped around her face, cutting off the rest of the sentence that would send father and daughter into one of their screaming matches. "Let's get you dressed," Bo said, shoving her toward the house. "So we can head home."

He pushed her up the porch, down the hallway, and into the bedroom they'd been sharing. He closed the door. "You need to calm down," he told her.

"He called our future children freaks!" she accused.

"We're having children now? Because before he showed up you couldn't handle living under my brutal regime."

"I never said that."

"Really?" he asked, grabbing the clean clothes he'd placed on the bed for her and handing them over. "Because it sounded like you did."

"I don't hate you, you idiot. I'm in love with you. *That's why I'm panicking!*" She marched to the door and yelled, *"And our children will not be freaks!"*

"Except their mother already is," her father yelled back.

Deciding that the old bastard's untimely death was in order, Blayne yanked the door open, but Bo quickly slammed it shut again. He leaned against it and gazed down into her face. "You love me?"

"Do you think I'd put up with your obsessive nature for five seconds if I didn't love you?"

"And I'm sure the multimillion-dollar hockey career has nothing to do with it," her father said through the door.

"When we get home, old man. You are so going to the old folks kennel!"

"Yeah, yeah," her father said. "I look forward to it. Until then, think you can shift that shiftless ass into gear so we can get out of here before those Van Holtz idiots start whining about your goddamn safety—again?"

* * *

They walked into the chief's office, and Blayne squealed, "Lock!" She tore across the room, throwing herself into the grizzly's arms.

Bo's eyes narrowed, and his mane dropped to his shoulders.

"Oh, no," her father said next to him with a level of sarcasm even Bo was finding hard to take. "Your kids won't be freaks at all."

"I love your daughter, sir," Bo said low for Mr. Thorpe's benefit only. "But don't think for a second I won't snap your neck like a twig if you get on my nerves." The wolf looked up at him, brows raised, and Bo added, "No, really."

Laughing, the wolf walked away from him while MacRyrie placed Blayne on her feet.

"I'm sorry I didn't talk to you the last time you were here," she said.

"Don't worry about that. Are you all right?"

"I'm fine. I'm great! And I'm so glad to see you."

Blayne hugged the grizzly again, and MacRyrie patted her back, leaning in a bit. His head dipped low, his nostrils flaring, and that's when his gaze shot up to Bo's. The hybrid raised his arms in clear challenge, a bit of grizzly fang making him snort.

"Blayne?"

Blayne lifted her head from MacRyrie's chest and looked at Van Holtz standing a few feet away. "Blayne, I'm . . . I'm so . . . ."

She unwrapped her arms from MacRyrie's waist and walked up to Van Holtz.

"I am so—"

The slap to his face rang out, startling everyone in the room, even Bo and her father. But Van Holtz took it like a wolf, not even backing away.

"Don't ever lie to me again," she said. "Don't ever betray me again. The next time, I promise you won't get off so easy."

"I know." Van Holtz shrugged. "Now can I have a hug?"

The smile blossomed across Blayne's face, and she leaped into Van Holtz's arms, making Bo sigh. The woman needed Bo in her life if for no other reason than to protect her from these idiots she insisted on befriending.

Van Holtz hugged Blayne tight to him, his nose against her neck. Two seconds of that and, like the grizzly, those eyes shot up to Bo's. This time . . . Bo grinned.

"That's right," he said without saying a goddamn word. "She's mine. Off limits!"

But just as Bo was feeling the need to go ahead and say those words out loud, his uncle stepped in front of him. Whispering, he said, "You should head back now. Take Blayne with you."

Sure, his uncle could be throwing him out because he was tired of him or Blayne or both, but Bo knew better. Something was wrong. He nodded, about to sweetly suggest to Blayne that they leave, but those damn wolfdog ears.

By the time he stepped around his uncle, she was standing in front of Van Holtz, facing them all. "Why do you want us to go?" she asked.

"Blayne—"

"Why, Grigori?"

"Tell her," Ezra Thorpe pushed. "You might as well tell her."

"Tell me what?"

It was Van Holtz who, as usual, did the talking. "The ones who did this to you, who grabbed you, they're part of a bigger organization. A multistate fighting ring. It seems on the East Coast, after they grab the hybrids they hold them for a few weeks or months, to get them ready for the fights before they sell them off to different buyers all over the country."

"Okay. And?"

Grigori shrugged. "You've been asking questions about that old farmhouse near the beach. It seems the town strays have been coming from there. But they're not just raising fighting dogs, Blayne."

Bo, not sure he was hearing correctly asked, "Are you saying they've been running these things on shifter territory all this time?"

"Looks that way. Coming in from the Pacific, using the storms to cover for them."

"How did full-humans know about Ursus County much less that farm?" Bo asked.

"We're working on that," Van Holtz said. "Diligently."

Blayne looked around at the men in the room. Except for Bo and her father, they were all avoiding eye contact.

"What?" she finally asked. "What aren't you telling me?"

When no one stepped up to say anything, Niles Van Holtz did. He'd been standing quietly off in a corner all this time.

"We've not only come here to take you back, Blayne. But we've just sent a team in to take down the entire thing. Right now."

Bo still wasn't sure why everyone was acting so strange though. But one look at her father, had Blayne turning on both Van Holtz males. "You're going to kill them all . . . aren't you?"

"They're full-humans," Bo said. Not in the least bit of mood to see Blayne defend the same assholes who would have used her like meat. "Tell me you're not crying over them."

"Not them," she snapped. "They're going to kill the hybrids."

Bo looked to his uncle and saw the truth of it on his face. He understood why but that didn't make it right. And how could a pure breed ever understand that?

"Blayne, it's for the best," Van Holtz told her in a calm, even tone that made Bo's scalp itch.

Blayne stared at Van Holtz for a very long moment. Bo would admit, he expected her to snap, to cry and kick and scream. That was Blayne. Always fighting for the helpless. But, her head dropping, she only nodded and walked over to her father.

"I understand," she practically whispered.

Van Holtz looked at his Alpha and the older wolf nodded, pulling a two-way transmitter from his pants pocket.

"It's a go," he said into it.

Because none of the weak males in the room wanted to focus too closely on Blayne, they all found other things to do. Lots of bullshit "command center" type chatter. The only one who didn't join in was Bo and Ezra Thorpe. His daughter had moved behind the wolf, her forehead resting on his shoulder. Bo looked at the wolf and that's when Mr. Thorpe motioned to the empty spot next to him.

A little confused but seeing no reason not to do as he wanted, Bo walked over. The wolf stepped closer, their arms almost touching. Mr. Thorpe was only about six feet tall and they must have looked ridiculous standing right next to each other. But when Bo saw Blayne slip out the backdoor, it suddenly all made sense.

Bo glanced down, and the cold-hearted wolf who couldn't stand his daughter and hated everyone—as per Blayne—shrugged and quietly waited for all hell to break loose.

CHAPTER 28

"Where you goin', teacup?"

Dee-Ann watched the wolfdog freeze in her confused tracks. She'd already walked off one way, turned around, and headed another, only to come racing back the other way. Never once noticing, sensing, or scenting that Dee was standing right there watching her.

Of course, Dee knew this would happen. Sure. The males thought they could control the teacup poodle with their overwhelming maleness, but Dee knew Blayne would try to do something stupid about the hybrids who'd been trapped by those full-humans. And it wasn't that Dee didn't understand. She did understand. Hell, she'd been building her own little hybrid team for months now. They were young, but every one had potential. But there was a difference between some streetwise stray and a hybrid that had been through absolute hell for weeks, maybe even months. No. They couldn't bring them back. They couldn't unleash them on New York or even Ursus County. So her team would go in fast and quiet and take care of them all at one time. Just like they'd been trained to do.

But what Dee wouldn't deal with was having anything else happen to this idiotic wolfdog. She was tired of getting blamed for it all; she was tired of people she considered her friends not speaking to her; and she was tired of having to even think about any of it. So, she let the males do their thing and she'd waited out here. She'd waited out here because she knew the wolfdog would come . . . and she did.

"Dee-Ann."

Dee ambled on over to the wolfdog. "I know what you want to do, darlin', but that can't happen."

"It's easy for you, isn't it?" Blayne asked. "Killing? Wiping out your own? Oh. That's right. We're not. We're just mutts. Strays."

"Whatcha think I should do Blayne? Really? Take 'em home with us? Maybe call in that Dog Whisperer guy, see if he can get them under control? Turn 'em into respectable hybrids? And then sit around prayin' that they don't up and tear someone's throat out while they're waiting in line at McDonald's for a Big Mac and fries?"

"I think you at least have to give them the chance. We're not all the same."

"I know. Some of them are even more unstable than you are."

"Insult me all you want, Dee, but I'm going to help them."

Done with this conversation and this irritating little heifer, Dee-Ann grabbed Blayne's arm.

The wolfdog stared down at where Dee's fingers gripped her. "Get off me."

"We can do this easy or not, teacup, up to you."

Blayne raised her gaze to Dee's. "I said let me go."

"I'll let you go when I get you home. Now move, little girl."

Blayne did, too, awkwardly swinging her fist at Dee's already bear-abused face. Bored nearly to tears, Dee caught Blayne's fist and twisted the wolfdog's arm until she had her on her knees.

Turns out that was right around the time Blayne pressed the barrel of the .45 Dee had tucked into her side holster against Dee's inner thigh.

Not doing anything too sudden, Dee slowly glanced down at the weapon Blayne held. The safety was off and Blayne's finger was on the trigger. She didn't even feel the girl pull the weapon from Dee's holster.

"Let's be calm, Blayne."

"Forget about losing a leg here, Smith. I pull this trigger and I blow a major artery. You'll bleed out before they can do a damn thing to help you. So get your fuckin' hands off me."

Dee released Blayne, the wolfdog turning out to be full of all sorts of backbone.

Holding Dee's own weapon on her, Blayne got to her feet and took a step back.

"You used me," Blayne said, not sounding like the teacup poodle Dee had been watching the past few months. "You've been using me all along and then you had the nerve to fucking tag me? Are you kidding me?"

Dee slowly raised her hands and said, "Blayne—"

"All this time you've been waiting for them to grab me. When would you have moved in? After they put me in my first pit fight? Or after they put me in my twelfth? Or would you have not bothered because you don't like me much anyway?"

"You've got this all wrong, Blayne."

"No. I don't." And that's when Blayne punched her. Not some pansy, teacup poodle punch either. But a Muhammad Ali punch with her left hand . . . and Blayne was a righty!

Dee grabbed her freshly healed but now rebroken nose. *"You crazy little whore!"*

"What are you going to do now, bitch?" Blayne demanded. "What are you going to do now?"

It was a rarely seen thing and she'd gotten it from her momma, not her daddy. The Lewis Pack She-wolf rage. She'd grown up hearing how Smith males had always found that rage "sexy," but the Smith males weren't right in the head.

Blayne had the .45 aimed right at Dee. "Pull the trigger, bitch," Dee challenged. "Do it."

And the crazy bitch did! Twice!

One of the bullets grazing Dee's ear before hitting the tree behind her. And something told Dee that Blayne wasn't a bad shot. Not the way she held that weapon, the way she grinned at Dee. Why she'd purposely missed her, Dee couldn't fathom, and she was simply too angry to try.

Hands shaking, Dee grabbed her ear, felt blood on her fingers. Rage tore through her like a wild fire.

"So what are you going to do now, Dee-Ann? Huh? What are you going to do now to your teacup poodle?"

Tossing the gun past her, Blayne laughed and took off running.

And the last thing Dee consciously remembered doing at that moment was tracking her weapon down and charging off into the woods after Blayne Thorpe.

They heard the shots behind the chief's office, and the younger Van Holtz looked past Ezra. "Where the hell is Blayne?"

"Where's Dee-Ann?" Niles Van Holtz wanted to know.

The big buck hybrid who was locked on Ezra's kid like a tick went out the backdoor, the rest of the males running after him. Ezra shook his head and followed, stepping outside in time to see the big She-wolf charging off into the woods after his baby girl.

"The farmhouse is that way," Grigori Novikov told the males.

"If Dee-Ann gets her hands on Blayne—"

"That won't happen," Blayne's hybrid said, and shifted. Shifted into something only Blayne could truly love.

Yep. I'm gonna have freak grandkids.

Grigori Novikov shifted with his nephew and took off after the two females. The black bear police chief charged back to town to put a call out to his deputies. MacRyrie and the younger Van Holtz went to follow after the Novikovs, but Ezra grabbed the males from behind and pulled them back.

"To the chopper," he said.

Ezra knew what his daughter was doing, knew what she was risking. Because that was who she was. He'd accepted that about her a long time ago, but he'd always have her back.

"Let the bears get them from land. We're going by air, gentlemen."

Blayne saw where bear country ended. It was clear because through the snow and ice center, she could see that it was a beautiful, sunny day on the other side. She pushed harder, running straight into that cold pocket that would kill a full-human in his or her tracks. She burst out the other side and right into cold but snow-and-ice-free weather.

Breathing hard, her gloved hands feeling like ice, Blayne kept running. She heard a grunt behind her and knew that Dee had made it through and was coming after her.

Bet she's pissed.

She'd laugh if she had the breath, but she hadn't pissed off a goddamn Smith She-wolf because she was bored with living. She did it because she needed Dee-Ann's help. But Dee-Ann didn't take Blayne seriously. She called her teacup. Rude! So Blayne had taken a page from the Ezra Thorpe philosophy manual on losing friends and irritating enemies. She'd basically instigated a fight.

It had worked, too. She'd pissed off Dee-Ann Smith something fierce. Now Blayne would have to figure out how to live long enough to get her help. But as Blayne made it up that last ridge, strong hands caught hold of her by the shoulders, lifting her off her feet and slamming her into the closest tree. Dee-Ann shoved her forearm against Blayne's throat, pinning her in place.

Fangs out, blood covering her face from broken nose to sweater-covered chest, Dee-Ann was one step from feral. But Blayne knew there was one thing that might get Dee back. One thing that she did care about.

"Look," Blayne spit out, finding it really hard to talk with a forearm against her trachea. "Look," she pushed, using her eyes to gesture to the left since she couldn't with her body. "Please. Look."

Keeping her in place, scowling in distrust, Dee glanced over . . .

Blayne coughed when the forearm moved away, her hand rubbing what she knew would be a big fat bruise. But at least Dee hadn't crushed anything vital. That was something.

"I think they knew you were coming," Blayne said, staring down the ridge.

The full-humans had Dee's team pinned down behind a building. Cut off from their transport near the beach and the land behind the farm. They weren't dead yet, but they would be.

"The whole town will be coming this way," Blayne told Dee.

"I guess there's no point in telling you to go back, is there?"

"I'm getting the hybrids out, Dee. But feel free to kill all the full-humans in between me and them." Blayne grinned when Dee didn't pop her in the face. "You know, since you're so good at that and all."

By the time Bo and his uncle stepped into the middle of the never-ending storm, half the town was with them. The locals came for two reasons. They came because full-humans were using their territory to torture others. And, more important, because Blayne needed them.

As one rampaging clan of bears, they came through the storm and to the other side. They could hear the gunfire now that they were clear of the torrential winds. The team that the Van Holtzes had sent in were in the middle of a firefight. Standing on the ridge, Bo could see Blayne and the Smith She-wolf moving down, using the trees for cover. Bo wouldn't try to stop Blayne. No point. But he could help. They could all help.

He charged down the ridge and up to the first full-human male he found. A full-human who turned quickly, his machine gun tight in both hands. Before he could pull the trigger, Bo slapped the gun down, ripping off one of the full-human's arms in the process.

Oh . . . that was totally an accident. Sorry.

A bullet grazed his side and Bo lowered his head, charging the shooter, accidentally ripping off a leg in the process.

My bad. Sorry.

While the bears stomped and slapped around full-humans and Dee-Ann shot the rest while helping to unpin her team, Blayne found where they kept the hybrids. There was a thick chain and padlock on the doors, but she was able to open the doors enough to slip inside.

Some of the hybrids, probably the newer ones, called out for help. But many simply watched her, their bodies covered in old scars and new wounds, their eyes dead. She didn't care. She was getting them all out.

There was just one problem . . . unlike pure-bred wolves, Blayne wasn't real good with opening locks. At least not without keys.

She tried several times and was about to go looking for a hammer or ax when a disgusted She-wolf grabbed hold of the padlock Blayne held. "Didn't your daddy teach you nothin', teacup?"

"Trust me. He tried."

Tucking her weapon back in its holster, Dee crouched in front of the first cage and began to work on the lock. Blayne stood and looked around. The place was simply inhumane. Cages sat on top of cages, and in each one was a hybrid shifter. Some were badly wounded, some were dead, and some were silent, simply watching them. Something told Blayne that they'd been here for a while. That they'd given up hope of ever being found.

Dee got the first cage open and moved to the next. Blayne helped the shifter out of the cage and led him to the door. "Shift and run," she said. "Head to Canada. Don't look back." Unfortunately, Blayne simply didn't trust that Dee's group would not harm the hybrids, so sending them to Canada was her best option at the moment.

Blayne assisted each shifter that Dee released, the pair getting into an excellent team mode Blayne would have never thought they could manage.

They got to the last cage, and Dee didn't go right to the lock. Instead she stared at the hybrid inside.

"I'll come back for her," she said, and Blayne caught her arm before she could move away.

"We're not leaving her." Blayne glanced at the silent female watching them. "She can walk." Hell, she looked like she could skip, jump, and dance, too.

Dee pulled her arm loose only to catch Blayne's arm instead and drag her away from the hybrid's cage.

"Let her out and that female is gonna rip us apart. You can see it in her eyes."

"How do you know that?"

"Ever seen a pit bull that's been in one too many dog fights? They got eyes just like hers. We leave her."

"Hell, you say. We're not leaving her."

"Don't argue with me on this, teacup."

"I'm not leaving her. And I thought you never left a man behind."

"I don't leave Marines. She ain't no Marine."

"No. But she's one of us. I'm not leaving her."

"You'll do as I tell ya."

"Like hell I—" Blayne's ear twitched, hearing footsteps behind her, coming in the way she'd let the hybrids out. She tackled Dee, the pair slamming into the last hybrid's cage, bullets ripping up the air around them.

Growling, Dee shoved Blayne away and fired her weapon twice. The full-human went down, but Blayne saw more full-humans heading toward them.

"Dee?"

"Here." Dee pulled a bowie knife out of a holster she had attached to the back of her jeans, and a thin blade she had tucked inside her leather bomber jacket. "All this time I thought it was the hockey player." Dee pushed Blayne away. "Go on, teacup. Show me what you've got."

Knowing she couldn't get the hybrid out on her own, Blayne decided she'd show the She-wolf exactly what she could do.

Blayne leaped on one of the cages and climbed up and around until she had one leg on a cage and the other pressed against the small overhang that was over the door. She waited, watching the door ease open all the way and several full-human males walk in, their automatic weapons raised, their fingers on the trigger. She glanced at where Dee was and adjusted her weight slightly. The last thing she wanted was the gun to go off and kill Dee and that poor hybrid.

When the men had passed a little bit in front of her, Blayne moved.

Dee didn't know when she'd lost her mind, but she clearly had. Giving Blayne Thorpe the bowie knife her daddy gave her for her tenth birthday and letting the teacup poodle watch her back while Dee unleashed some dangerously unstable hybrid was the height of stupidity. But standing around and arguing about it all damn day didn't sound like much of a plan, either.

Besides . . . she wanted to see what the teacup poodle could do. It was one thing to see bodies on a slab, but you really don't know a gal's skill until you could see her in action.

Crouching in front of that cage, Dee picked up the padlock. The hybrid inside still hadn't moved. She only watched her with those cold, dead eyes. Dee would rather face twenty guys with guns rather than this female, but Blayne had a way about her and, Lord, was that woman stubborn.

Dee moved her fingers around the padlock, getting a quick feel for it before she unlocked it. A skill any self-respecting wolf had, but apparently not the wolfdogs. She'd found the right spot and was about to unlock it when she glanced behind her and saw Blayne above the barn door. She only had a split second to think, "What the fuck is she up to now?" when Blayne flipped forward and down, the blades in her hands slamming into the shoulders of the man on the far left. He screamed, his finger automatically tensing on the trigger as his body naturally turned. A swath of bullets exploded, tearing two of the men in half. The other three jumped out of the way in time. For humans, though, they were fast, getting back to their feet once the dying male was down and his weapon dry.

Blayne pulled the blades out of the man's shoulders and without hesitation ran forward. Dee watched, her mouth hanging open, as Blayne Thorpe—teacup poodle—slashed one male across his arm, the tendons splitting, his weapon dropping uselessly to the ground. She lashed at another male with her left hand, cutting his throat and then burying the blade in his chest with one hard hit. She yanked the blade out and turned, the blade slamming into the eye of the man whose arm she destroyed as he tried to pick up his weapon with his other hand.

The third got off two rounds, Blayne ducking them both, before she moved in on him and caught hold of his gun by the barrel. She pulled the weapon forward then shoved it back, breaking the man's nose. She tossed the gun, the man's nose bleeding as he reached for the handgun holstered at his side. She slashed with one of her blades and the male screamed, three of his fingers falling to the floor. Blayne slashed with the other hand, and parts of his face flew off. She spun, giving herself a little momentum, so her back kick could knock him to the floor. She landed on him, her arms raised high above her head before she slammed both blades into the man's chest.

"You done?" Blayne called over to her, her hands twisting the blade to make sure she killed him quick.

"Uh . . ." Stunned as she'd never been stunned before, Dee looked back at the lock. "Yeah, uh . . ." She quickly toyed with the lock until it opened. Letting out a breath, she started to tell Blayne she'd done it when a rather healthy sized and scarred hand gripped hers through the bars. She only had a second to look up and see the hybrid staring at her from the other side of the cage before the bitch grabbed Dee's head and slammed it into the bars, knocking her out cold.

Blayne pulled the blades out and stood. She only had a second to realize someone was standing behind her. She turned, but the hybrid slammed her hands into her, sending Blayne's much smaller body flipping across the room.

Holy shit. The female hybrid was part grizzly, part canine. And really, *really* pissed off.

Blayne hit the wall and then the floor, but after breaking all her bones during the abduction, they'd healed up stronger than before. So she scrambled back to her feet, unharmed, with the hybrid advancing on her.

"Wait," Blayne said, her hands up.

Christ, she was young. A sub-adult sow. *What did they do to you?* Even though she was still in human form, it was like she wasn't human anymore. Like that part had been beaten and fought out of her. There were so many scars and so much pain she'd endured. It was all over her. "We just want to help you. I just want to help you." The sow didn't answer Blayne, just sort of huffed and snuffled a little. Not a good sign, but Blayne didn't want to have to kill her. She didn't deserve that. Yet Blayne was also trying to avoid death here. "Let me. Let me help you." Blayne held her hand out. "Just take my hand."

The sow stared at Blayne's hand for several excruciatingly long seconds before she reached out and gripped it.

Blayne smiled. "It'll be okay. I promise."

The sow still watched her, as if she didn't quite understand Blayne's words. Behind the sow, Blayne could see Dee getting up. Blood poured from an open gash on her head and she had her .45 out. She had the weapon raised at the sow's back, Blayne about to tell her not to do it, when the sow's head came up. She sniffed the air once and before Blayne could do anything, the sow sent her flying right into Dee.

The two females hit the floor and rolled until they ran into the barn wall. At that point, Blayne was beginning to think she'd had more physical contact with Dee in the past hour than she'd had with Bo in the last week.

Dee scrambled up, her .45 raised again but Blayne bounced up and between the two females.

"Move, Blayne!"

"No. I won't let you hurt her."

"Blayne . . ."

"She's young, Dee. A kid. We can help her. Really help her."

"Help her? How?"

"By giving her a chance. Please?" Blayne placed her hand on Dee's arm, pushing the weapon down. "Please, Dee?"

"This is stupid."

"It's the least you can do after what you did to me! Microchipping," she hissed.

"Oh. That." Dee's eyes rolled to the ceiling. "You're not going to let that go anytime soon, are ya?"

"If you protect her, take her back to the city and keep her alive—all's forgiven. I swear."

"Huh."

"No, really. I . . . I'll tell everybody how great you are and"—she snapped her fingers—"I'll even come up with a cheer just for you! Goooooooooo—"

"Stop!"

Both Blayne and Dee jumped, slowly facing the sow behind them.

"No cheering," the sow said. "Just . . . no cheering."

Blayne smiled at Dee. "You two should get along like a house on fire. You're both surly."

The sows head snapped up, her fangs unleashing. Dee caught Blayne's arm and pulled her behind her. But the sow faced the open backdoors.

Knowing more full-humans were coming through that door, Blayne went around Dee. "Get her out of here, Dee."

"What are you going to do?"

"Get her out," Blayne said again then she took off running, right out the door and heading into the tree that was outside the building.

Bo was annoyed. Why? Because his uncle wouldn't give up Bo's toy. No matter how much Bo pulled one way, his uncle pulled the other, both of them snarling and growling at each other. So unfair! Ursus County bears didn't know how to share, something his mother used to warn him about. And when the toy tore in half, neither of them wanted it anymore because it was no longer screaming and begging for mercy. Tossing his half aside, Bo looked over at the chopper landing by the beach. Armed, MacRyrie came out first and, with one look, Bo knew the grizzly had done this before. Bo had been around enough Marines to know one when he saw one.

After MacRyrie came Van Holtz and Blayne's father. The older wolf carried a mechanic's tool bag in one hand and a .380 in the other.

Wanting to make sure Blayne's father remained safe, Bo headed toward the males but he saw the full-humans running out of the corner of his eye. He turned, lowering his head and ready to charge them. But Blayne came tearing out of the open barn, running right toward a nearby tree that stood tall and ancient in front of the men. When she was inches from it, she sprang up, one foot hitting the tree, and catapulting her into the center of the small group of full-human males. Once there, Blayne went to work, using blades to slice and dice every man there before they could get a shot off.

Bo glanced over at MacRyrie and Van Holtz. Their mouths open, they watched Blayne while Blayne's father wandered off.

Bo followed after him, figuring he could use some protection. By the time he tracked the wolf down, he found him crouched by a small well. As Bo eased up behind him, Mr. Thorpe glanced at him over his shoulder. He snorted, shook his head. "I bet she loves those fangs. Trust me, at some point, if she hasn't already, she's gonna ask to hang from them."

Blayne could hang from any part of Bo that she wanted to. He didn't care.

"Although I'm guessing you won't care, right?" The wolf stood, picked up his tool bag and had his gun tucked into the back of his jeans.

"Come on," he said, walking off. "Couple more spots."

With a shrug, Bo followed after the wolf, batting or ripping apart any full-humans who came near them.

It was a nice bonding moment between him and his future father-in-law.

* * *

Blayne cleaned blood off the blades before tucking them into the tops of her boots. By the time she stood, she had Lock and Ric standing in front of her . . . gaping.

"What?"

Ric pointed at the full-humans at her feet. "You . . . you killed them all."

"I had to."

"But you did it with some . . . uh . . . skill."

"Uh-huh."

Ric looked like he wanted to say more, but she saw her father waving at her. "We better move out. Daddy's going to blow the place."

"Wait . . . what?" Lock snapped out of his gawking. "He can't blow Ursus County."

She laughed. "Don't be silly." Blayne brought her fingers to her mouth and whistled, all the bears still entertaining themselves with the full-human remains focusing on her. "Get everyone out, Grigori!"

The polar nodded and went up on his hind legs, roaring a signal that had the bears scattering off the property. Blayne ran toward the chopper. Dee-Ann and the rest of her team, plus the hybrid sow long gone. She reached the chopper and a big hand reached out for her. She grabbed it and Bo pulled her inside. Ric and Lock came in after and her father signaled to the pilot to go.

The chopper lifted off, and Blayne leaned over Ric to see. Once they were clear, she saw a very small explosion, sand from the beach bursting up in a small ball. Then the ground shook and everything in that quarter-mile radius jerked hard once and crumbled in on itself, disappearing into the ocean.

She grinned at her father. "You still got it, Daddy."

He shrugged. "Some skills you don't lose."

Blayne sat back and let out a breath.

"What a day, huh?" she said to them all, and Bo laughed.

CHAPTER 29

Gwen paced impatiently in front of the check-in desk at the private airport. The She-leopard watched her close until Gwen finally said, "Keep staring at me, I'll tear your eyes out."

The females hissed at each other until Gwen heard the doors leading to the tarmac open. She charged over, trying to see through the large males blocking her view.

"Blayne!"

The two females ran at each other, bodies colliding, arms wrapping around each other as they squealed and hugged.

Seeing Blayne, knowing she was safe, meant more to Gwen than anything else. It was hard in this vicious, cruel world to find someone you not only could trust as you could your own blood but who you actually liked to be around—unlike your own blood.

"Are you okay?" Gwen asked, pulling back so she could see Blayne's face. She wiped Blayne's tears with her thumbs.

"I'm fine. I'm great!"

Of course she was. She was Blayne.

"Don't cry, Gwenie." She didn't realize she had been. "I'm really okay."

"You better be. Or I'm going to hurt people."

Blayne threw her arm over Gwen's shoulder. "It won't be necessary. Everything is okay."

"If you say so. I'm just glad you're . . . you're . . ." Gwen studied her friend for a moment.

"What?"

Instead of answering, Gwen buried her nose against Blayne's neck and sniffed. The scent of bear and cat hit strong and her back snapped straight, her gaze on a suddenly silent wolfdog.

Gwen looked over at the three males standing behind them. Lock looked resigned, Ric concerned, and Novikov amused.

"You want to tell me what's going on?" she asked her friend.

"Not really."

"Blayne."

Both women jumped, her father's booming military voice always managing to make them feel guilty when they had no reason to feel guilty. Usually.

"I'm heading home," he said, marching around them. "I'll expect you on Sunday. As planned."

"Is that all you have to say to me?" Blayne demanded.

"Well, I could remind you to stay out of trouble—*but that always seems to fall on deaf ears!*" Ezra Thorpe raised a brow, immediately calm after his bellow. "Anything else?"

"No," Blayne said with a very resigned sigh. "That was it."

"Good." He leaned in and kissed his daughter on the forehead. "Sunday," he reminded her, walking toward the parking lot. "Bring the freak with you."

"Daddy!"

Funny thing was, Gwen knew old man Thorpe liked Novikov. He'd invited him to his and Blayne's monthly Sunday dinners. If Ezra Thorpe didn't like a man, he wasn't inviting him anywhere. Especially if he didn't like the man for his daughter.

But just because Blayne's father seemed to have accepted Novikov—or at the very least was willing to give him a shot—didn't mean Blayne's collective brother system was about to accept him.

"Why don't I give you a lift home?" Ric asked Blayne.

"Well—"

"I've got it," Novikov cut in, standing behind Blayne.

"I'd like to hear Blayne say it." Ric stepped closer. Now Blayne was trapped between two predators, and she didn't look happy about it. But Gwen knew Blayne well enough to know it wasn't fear or anger that had Blayne like this. It was something else. Something she was desperately trying to hide. "Unless you're trying to keep her quiet," Ric went on.

"We both know that's not even possible."

Lips pursed and eyes rolling, Blayne let out another sigh.

"You really wanna do this here, tiny little wolf boy?" Novikov asked. "Do I need to prove my point again with you?"

"You can try. If you've got the guts."

"Or," Lock said, grabbing Blayne's hand and pulling her out from between the two males. "We can go to the hospital."

"What?" Gwen knew what Lock had been heading into when he left, and knew it was dangerous. "Are you hurt?"

"It's a girl."

"Maybe he hit his head," Blayne whispered.

Lock held his cell phone between the friends. "Just got a text from Phil. It's a girl."

Blayne squealed, bouncing up and down on her toes. "Jess had the baby! Jess had the baby!" She grabbed Lock's arm and pulled before running off. "Come on! Jess had the baby!"

She cartwheeled toward the exit. "It's a girl!" she cheered, ran out the door, and ran back in. "Let's go!"

Laughing, probably as relieved as she was that Blayne was a-okay, Lock followed after her.

Gwen turned to Novikov, raising her head to try to see his face. Poor guy. He had no idea Blayne had just run out on him—again.

"Thank you," Gwen said to him, and she meant it. Without even talking to Blayne yet, she knew that Novikov had protected her best friend—and that he loved her.

"Not a problem."

She winked at him and followed after her friend, stopping long enough to say, "Come on, Ric. You can keep Lock and Blayne calm while I explain why I'm *not* going into that death trap." When the wolf kept staring at Novikov, she whistled, catching his immediate attention and making Novikov laugh.

"Don't make me get the choke chain, Ulrich."

Bo stood in the middle of the private airport, alone. Blayne had left to check on her friend. Did she forget he was in the room? Very possible. This was Blayne after all. Or was she panicking and running on him again? No. No way. She'd call him soon. In the hour, he bet. Gushing over the baby and whatever. He'd hear from her. He was sure of it.

CHAPTER 30

Bo now understood that he couldn't assume anything when it came to Blayne Thorpe. He couldn't take for granted that she'd do what he expected her to do.

He *expected* her to go see her friend in the hospital and come back to his apartment later that night. When she didn't, he figured she'd gone back to her apartment, but she hadn't picked up any calls or answered her door when he knocked. A good sniff told him the apartment was empty—and that she hadn't taken out her trash. Blayne didn't have her cell because the Brooklyn bears had brought by all the personal stuff they'd left behind in his truck. The bears had also taken care of his truck, bringing it to a bear-run service station to be repaired, and had returned that as well. Bo would get a bill for all that great bear service, but who cared?

Besides, his biggest concern at the moment was Blayne.

Finally, he'd headed to the hospital, tracking down which shifter-run medical center the pregnant wild dog would have gone to. And the female wild dogs there with their Alpha were really nice but Blayne had already split . . . leaving him alone with really nice female wild dogs who thought he was just "adorable"!

And three hours later, when he was still at the hospital and holding the tiniest newborn in the world, a bunch of She-dogs grinning at him, and a bunch of She-wolves watching him like he was Satan—he knew he'd blame Blayne for this. He was blaming Blayne! But first he had to find her so he could blame her to her face!

The problem was, no one seemed to know where his wolfdog was.

"She was here for hours," Jess Ward-Smith told him. She'd been the one to put the newborn in his arms, the kin of her mate looking downright horrified when she had. But one look at the newest hybrid to make it into the world and Bo knew he'd never let anything happen to her. "Then she said she had to go and that she'd talk to me later today."

"Is Blayne going to do this a lot?" he asked, unable to take his eyes off the baby in his arms.

"She doesn't stay in one place too long, but she doesn't usually go far, either." He hated to admit it, but he could kind of see why Dee Smith had microchipped Blayne. He still knew it was wrong—but he understood why. "You're good with kids."

"I am?" Maybe they were only saying that because he hadn't accidentally crushed the baby in his big paws.

"Yeah. You are. Which is good because Blayne's got breeder written all over her. While Gwen and Lock will probably stop at two, a certain amount of years apart, the whole event perfectly and logically planned and executed—Blayne will just be dropping kids around your house."

Bo shuddered, even while he laughed. "Don't say that."

"Don't worry. Blayne's officially part of the Kuznetsov Pack now. You'll always have babysitters available."

"Thanks."

Grudgingly, but feeling like he should before he became too attached, Bo handed the newborn back to her mother. "Do you have a name for her yet?"

"Nope. We're still working on that. Personally, I like Galadriel."

Bo asked, "From *Lord of the Rings*?"

The wild dog's brown eyes lit up. "You know *Lord of the Rings*?"

"Doesn't everybody?"

"Book or movie?"

"Well, I loved the movies, but the books were my favorites in grade—"

The wild dog gasped, her hand briefly covering her mouth. "She's chosen so well!"

"Sorry?"

"No. Nothing. I'm just proud of my Blayne." She snapped her fingers. "I forgot. When Blayne left, she left with Dee-Ann. Smitty's cousin."

Bo tried hard not to panic. "Why did she leave with her?" he asked, keeping his voice low and even. But Jess immediately seemed to understand his concern.

With her baby tucked into one arm, she placed her free hand over his and said, "Oh, don't worry, sweetie. I don't think Dee was planning to, you know, kill her or anything." Jess gazed off. "I don't think."

Dee watched Blayne behind one-way mirror glass. "Sorry," she said to the bear next to her. "About everything."

"Thanks," Lock said. He adjusted his stance, his arms folded over his chest. "It's not me you really need to apologize to, though, is it?"

"Heifer broke my nose and nearly got me killed by a crazed sow. I think me and Blayne are beyond apologies, don't you?"

"You've got a point." He motioned toward the room. "Is she going to help you?"

"No. She's going to help them. Got a whole speech about it, too." Dee had asked Blayne to help with the hybrids because although they took the Group's free food and clean beds, most of them weren't much for doing anything else. But instead of giving up on them, Dee forced herself to remember that these pups, kits, and cubs hadn't had an easy time of it. Chances were strong Dee was their last chance. They'd either end up dead, in prison, or on the wrong end of a pit fight. So Dee adjusted her perspective, something she was learning to do more and more these days. And that meant asking for some help when she could, even if she was asking for help from Blayne Thorpe.

Besides, Dee had always prided herself on being able to overlook someone being an annoying little twit for the fact that they had a genuine skill or two that Dee could use.

And, after less than an hour, Blayne had the troublemaking, "always looking for a scam to perpetrate" hybrids sitting on the floor, in a circle, and staring at her like she was a goddess.

Yeah. The girl had a way. She'd won over bears, antisocial hybrid teens, and even the most hated male in shifter sports. Dee had no idea how Blayne did it but she knew true skills when she saw them.

"So you going to pay her for this gig or just use her humanity against her?"

Dee snorted. "She sure does have y'all fooled."

"What does that mean?"

"She told me she wasn't doin' shit without pay. Apparently good quality hair products—honey-infused was the term she used—don't come cheap."

Lock laughed and Dee felt better hearing it. She normally didn't give a shit when people hated her. But Lock MacRyrie wasn't just anybody, was he? Good friends you could trust, not easy to come by.

"We're not going to have this issue again, are we, Dee?" Lock finally asked her, and Dee knew that question had been coming.

"Nah."

"Good. You don't want me cranky."

There was truth to that.

"So what are you planning to do with these kids anyway? Start your own little hybrid army?" he joked. But when Dee only stared at him, Lock shook his head. "Forget I asked. Just . . . forget."

"Will do, hoss."

Lock's phone chimed and he pulled it out of his pocket. He

glanced at the screen, smirked. "Novikov is still looking for Blayne." He shut his phone off and put it back in his pocket.

"You gonna do the man like that?"

He folded his arms over his chest again. "Damn right I am. Bet it wouldn't take much to convince Blayne to spend the night at our apartment, either. You know, so the girls can rebond."

"And everybody says I'm a bitch."

"Yeah, but with you they mean literally."

Blayne slipped past the two former Marines chatting amiably by the room she'd just been in.

Following her nose, Blayne headed down the hallway and out a back door. It led to a gorgeous hot house, filled with beautiful flowers and plants. She walked down one of the rows until she found what she was looking for.

The sow sat on the floor, her back against the wall, her scarred forearms resting on her raised knees. She had a pretty face that she was trying to hide under brown and gold hair with black tips, and a powerfully built body. Almost six-three, she wore a white T-shirt and loose blue jeans along with All-Star canvas high tops on large feet. Yet even with her size, she looked like any freshman kid in college—except for the scars. So many scars.

Blayne dropped into the empty space beside the sow. "How are you holding up?" she asked.

"Fine."

"I'm Blayne."

"Hannah."

"Nice to meet you, Hannah. They're treating you okay, right?"

"They haven't threatened to put me down yet, if that's what you're asking."

"Actually, yeah. That's what I was asking."

Blayne's candid answer had the sow finally looking at her.

"They were planning to put us down?"

"Pretty much."

"But you stopped them. Why?"

"They have an excuse to put you down today, they have an excuse to put me down tomorrow. Besides, all hybrids are in this together. We have to watch out for each other. God knows, no one else will."

The sow relaxed her head back against the wall, her gaze moving around the room. "How long do I have to stay here?"

"As long as you want. Or as little. I won't let them force you into anything."

"And you have that much power?"

"I do right now." Blayne grinned. "Let's enjoy it while it lasts."

Hannah didn't smile, but she scowled a little less. It reminded Blayne of Bo. Maybe it was a bear thing.

"Dee says you're nineteen, making you the oldest within the group she's training."

"Yeah. So?"

"So if you don't want to stay here full-time, you can crash at my place. It's not big but it's cute and, right now, extremely clean."

"You're not worried about having me in your apartment? The fighting dog?"

Blayne raised a finger. "The fighting dog-*bear*." Blayne grinned again. "Which sounds much cooler than bear-dog, don'tcha think?"

"Sure. Right. Whatever."

"Anyway, a place to stay and a job if you need it."

"A job? Doing what?"

"Plumbing."

"Plumbing? You want me to be a plumber?"

"My, my, how snobby we sound. There's nothing wrong with being a plumber. It's good and usually steady work, good money, and I can make sure you have time to come here every day to train."

"Train to do what exactly? When I ask they don't really answer me."

"Train you to take care of yourself without forcing you to wear a muzzle twenty-four hours a day or worrying you're going to dismember people with your teeth."

"Thank you," she said with a heavy dose of sarcasm. "That was very nice."

"I'm known for being nice, but in this instance, I went for honest. I want you to start having some choices, Hannah. You can't do that if I'm lying to you."

"You don't even know me. Don't know anything about me."

"Yet. I don't know anything about you *yet*. But I plan to learn all about you. And, when you're happy and calm, and all is right in your world, we'll talk about you becoming a blocker for my derby team."

"Because it's logical to put me back into violent situations I have no control over."

Again with that sarcasm. "Well, when you put it like that, it just sounds all sorts of wrong."

"Explain to me why I kind of like you."

"Because I'm charming and sweet and endearing. Plus I have this award-winning smile." Blayne hit the sow with a grin, and even though Hannah immediately turned away, Blayne knew what she saw from the hybrid in that brief second—a smile. Or a snarl.

To be honest, Blayne sometimes had a hard time telling the difference.

It was almost seven in the morning when Bo snatched open his front door before Sami could get the key in the lock. She blinked up at him. "You're back!"

"Where have you been?" he demanded.

"Nowhere," she immediately answered, but Sander who came in behind her carried new, expensive suitcases that had the initials GCA etched into brass nameplates. Something told Bo nothing in those cases actually belonged to the foxes. "I heard you had some trouble and ended up back in Ursus County."

"It's a long story. But I need you two to track down somebody."

"Who?" She took the slip of paper Bo handed her. "Lachlan MacRyrie? Isn't he one of your teammates?"

"Yeah. But his number traces back to a PO box in Jersey. I can't track the fucker's address down."

"How hard can that be?"

"He's ex-Unit."

"Ohhh. Gotcha."

She walked into his living room, dropping into one of the club chairs, her feet up on the ottoman. "I'll see what I can find out." When Bo scowled at her, she dug her phone out of the top of her boot. "Now. I'll find out now."

Sander dived onto the couch, immediately going to sleep; and Sami began to dial numbers. "So does this guy owe you money or something?"

"He has my wolfdog. I want my wolfdog!"

"Okay. Okay. Control the mane. It's sprawling across your shoulders. Just give me a couple of minutes." She grinned. "I know some people." Bo already knew that.

Sami waited patiently while, he assumed, the phone rang on the other end. She looked him over a few times, finally asking, "Any messages from home?"

"Your mother sends her love and details on an incoming shipment of emeralds, which I wasn't going to tell you about"—he glared at the emerald choker she had on—"but I see we're a little past that now."

She shrugged, the fingers of her free hand running over the priceless jewels she wore with jeans and a T-shirt. "Foxes love the sparkle."

And for the first time in twelve hours, Bo laughed.

Unable to continue sleeping with two females giggling hysterically in his bathroom, Lock headed to his kitchen. Coffee. He needed coffee.

He was walking through his hallway, heading toward his kitchen, when he caught a scent, stopping him in his tracks. He focused on the door at the end of the hallway, blinking when the industrial strength door he'd had installed was torn off at the hinges.

The slightly larger bear-cat hybrid walked into his house like he'd been invited. "Where is she?" Novikov demanded.

"And a happy morning to you, too."

The hybrid stormed up to Lock, scowling the entire way. When he stood in front of him, the bastard slammed his forehead into Lock's, knocking the grizzly back a foot or two. Lock shook his head, trying to get the ringing out of his ears. Once he'd done that, he butted the idiot back.

They had each other in mutual headlocks by the time a hearty laugh floated from the bedroom. Novikov threw Lock off and followed the sound.

Wiping the blood from his jaw and nose, Lock grinned.

Okay, yeah. Sometimes . . . I am a dick.

He found her in a bedroom with Gwen. And the sight wasn't nearly as interesting as it probably sounded since Blayne was stretched out, stomach down on the bed, reading a magazine and Gwen was sitting on the floor painting her toenails.

Scenting that this was the room Blayne spent the night in, he stormed over to the bed and began picking up the magazines she had laying all over the bed, the floor. *Everywhere!*

"How can you live like this?" he demanded. "This isn't even your house!"

Without even looking up from the copy of *Mademoiselle,* "This is how you say hello to me?"

"You're lucky I don't wring your scrawny chicken neck. You couldn't call? Check in? *Something?*"

"I thought about doing that . . . then I forgot . . . then I remembered . . . then I forgot again." She shrugged, still focused on her magazine. "I figured I'd see you today or something."

Unsure of what the hell was going on, Bo looked over at Gwen. She shrugged, looking as confused as Bo felt.

Not sure how to handle this situation, he handled it as his uncle would. He dropped the pile of magazines he'd picked up back on the floor, grabbed the base of the frame of the bed, and flipped Blayne's cute ass right off it.

"Hey!" she squealed.

Bo dropped the bed. "See ya," he said, and walked out the door.

"You're leaving?" she yelled after him.

"Yes!" he yelled back. "I'm leaving, Lady Spoiled Brat of Spoiled-Bradington. Have a good life!"

Bo was near the front . . . hole—the door was still in the hallway, the grizzly trying to figure out how to get it back on—when he heard feet run up behind him and felt something small, cruel, and heartless land on his back.

"You," she accused, "are so rude!"

Bo stopped walking. "I'm rude? *I* am rude?"

"You heard me."

Reaching behind him, he caught Blayne by the ass and swung her off his back. She squealed again until he placed her safely on her feet.

"You left me!" he accused. "You left me and didn't even bother calling me!"

"You knew I was with Gwen." She sounded so reasonable, like he was the out-of-control one.

"Nope. I can't do this." He took a step to walk around her, but she stepped in front of him, blocking his exit. He tried to ignore the fact she only had on a big Philly Eagles jersey and thick socks, her hair in two ponytails. She looked adorable and it wasn't fair. It was *not* fair at all!

"You can't do what?"

"Put up with you."

"Put *up* with me? I didn't know I was such a chore."

"What time is it?" he asked.

"Well, since I still can't get this goddamn watch off . . ." she muttered before looking at it. "Nine thirty."

"Right. And the first game of the Cup finals less than a week away. And what am I doing, Blayne? What am I doing at nine thirty in the morning before Cup finals?"

"Uh . . ."

"Well?"

"Looking for me?"

"Do you think I'd be looking for you if I weren't worried about you? Because I hadn't heard from you? Because I hadn't heard from anyone?"

"I needed some time to think, okay? And I didn't know if I was supposed to go back to your place or my place or if I was being kind of presumptuous thinking either way. I figured a night apart would do us both some good."

"You're thinking too much again."

With her eyes downcast, the toes of her right foot pushed into the floor, she countered, "Maybe I am, but you could have called *me*."

"Well, since I have your cell phone"—he threw that on the floor—"and you weren't home to pick up your landline, the wild dogs didn't know where you were, and Van Holtz and MacRyrie ignored my calls, I'm not exactly sure how I was supposed to call you."

She cringed a little. "Okay. You have a point."

"Thanks. I'm glad you think I have a point. I've gotta go." He grabbed Blayne around the waist and lifted her out of his way, then he walked out. He was at the elevator when she cut in front of him, blocking the exit with her arms outstretched.

"I'm sorry," she yelped. "Okay? I'm sorry, I'm sorry, I'm sorry!"

"You're making me crazy!"

"I know!" She took a breath. "I know. I'm not trying to drive you crazy."

"Not trying but succeeding nicely. Now move."

"You're going to end it because I'm unreliable, flaky, and often thoughtless?" She stopped, blinking hard. Her shoulders slumped. "Wait. I'd actually end it for those reasons."

The last thing he wanted to do was end it with this impossible woman, but he wasn't one of those guys who enjoyed constant drama in his life. It was distracting, and he couldn't afford ridiculous distractions. Instead of saying that, though, he said, "Let's talk about it later."

Ice time. He needed ice time and twenty miles on the treadmill at fifty miles an hour to make him feel better. It would clear his head.

He pressed the elevator button and stepped inside when the doors opened. Blayne stood there, watching him. Seeing that wounded look on her face was killing him, but he didn't know what else to do at this moment. They were really different, but he knew that wouldn't matter if they both worked together to make their relationship perfect. But he would not subject himself to one of those relationships where only one person was doing all the work. Life was simply too short for that kind of misery.

"I promise I'll call you later," he said, punching the button for the first floor.

She nodded, stepped back. "Oh." She leaned over and pulled out a piece of paper from the top of her sock. "If you're looking for me later," she said, handing him the slip, the old elevator slowly closing. "Here's my schedule." She gave a little chuckle. "I promised to do a bunch of stuff for Jess over the next couple of days before she brings the baby home, so I took your advice and wrote it all down."

She gave one more wave and the doors closed, shutting her out.

Bo unfolded the sheet and stared at the lined notebook paper. She had a list of twenty things with lots of scratch-outs, that was in no particular or discernable order, written in bright purple ink, except for the important stuff that was in red, and random notes written in the margins.

And, at the bottom of the page she'd doodled two hearts. One had the initials G.O. and L.MR., and between the initials she'd drawn one of those honey containers shaped like a bear. The other heart had B.T. and B.N. and between them she'd drawn a seal, which she'd scratched out and replaced with a plus symbol instead.

The elevator doors opened on the first floor and Van Holtz was waiting there with several bags of groceries in his hands.

"Oh. You," he said. He started to walk in and, without thinking, simply reacting, Bo shoved him back out of the elevator by his head and hit the elevator button again.

"You asshole!" Bo heard as the doors closed.

Blayne sat at Lock's kitchen table, her chin in her hands.

"I'm sorry, Blayne," Lock said, putting a bottle of water in front of her. "I should have told you he'd been trying to track you down."

"It's okay." Blayne could be the bigger person here because she had Gwenie.

"It is *not* okay!" Gwen slugged her fiancé's arm. "Not okay at all. You need to talk to Novikov and straighten this out."

"Isn't there something else I can do? *Anything* else?" Lock begged.

"No!"

Usually Blayne would try and stop the argument and soothe the hurt feelings, but she wasn't in the mood. She was miserable. And had no one to blame for it but herself. But what could she say? She'd panicked. Panicked because for once she had a reliable, smart, non-sociopath as a boyfriend. Not a gentleman caller, but a boyfriend. And he loved her—despite her many fuck-ups.

To be honest, once she realized all that—panicking was her only option.

"Giving me your list"—a voice said from the kitchen doorway—"makes it impossible for you to actually *use* your list, unless you made a copy. Which I'm doubting."

Blayne swallowed and looked over at the doorway.

"And maybe," Bo Novikov went on, holding Blayne's list up, "with some patience on my part and another forty or fifty years of hard work, we can get a list that makes a modicum of sense."

"It makes sense to me."

"That kind of says it all, doesn't it?"

Smiling, Blayne scrambled out of the chair, over the kitchen table, and into Bo's arms. He lifted her off the floor, and she put her arms around his neck, her legs around his chest, her ankles locking behind his back. He kissed her, and she felt all his love in that kiss.

When he pulled away, he said, "I missed you last night."

She hugged his neck tight, burying her face against his throat. "I missed you, too."

"We're going to get some breakfast," Gwen said, easing by them.

"Ric's coming over to make us breakfast," Lock argued.

"Ric can buy us breakfast instead."

"I'm not leaving so this idiot can have makeup sex in our apartment."

"Come on, man," Bo pleaded. "Can't you help an Asian brother out?"

"No!"

Blayne pressed her mouth against Bo's shoulder to stop the laughter from spilling out.

"This is your fault," Gwen reminded Lock, storming past the couple again and grabbing his arm. "And this is your punishment."

"But we haven't showered or anything yet."

"We'll go to Bren's hotel, book a room, and shower there. Hotel sex! And waffles. That sounds promising, doesn't it?"

"But I need to fix the door—"

"Suck it up, MacRyrie."

Bo pressed his forehead against Blayne's, holding her tight. Blayne was counting the seconds before Gwen and Lock grabbed their shit and left—and she loved Gwenie because the feline was making that slow bear "Move, move, move!"—when Ric came down the hall.

"Lock? What happened to your door? Was it that Neanderthal?" He stopped when he saw Blayne and Bo still in the kitchen doorway. "Oh," he said flatly. "The Neanderthal. And the Neanderthal's woman."

"Good, Ric," Gwen said. "You're here." She grabbed the bags of food Ric had with him and dropped them to the floor.

"There are eggs in there!"

"That's not your problem. Come on. We're going out for breakfast."

"I have enough food to even feed this cretin."

"This may come as some surprise to you," Bo said to Ric, his scowl terrifying if Blayne didn't already know how safe she was with him. "But I do know what those words mean, you magniloquent prat." And when Blayne's head came up, Bo added, "And no, Blayne, I didn't make that word up either."

"You mean like that boda-chica word?"

"It's Boadicea and I—why am I arguing this with you?" He glared at Ric. "You need to leave."

"Like hell I—"

"We're out!" Gwen said, shoving the wolf toward the door. "Blayne, call me when you're done, there's condoms in the top drawer of our dresser—"

"Jesus, Gwenie!" Lock barked, and Blayne didn't know if he was disgusted or merely embarrassed.

"—don't forget to change the sheets. Love you, sweetie!"

The trio argued all the way to the door, down the hallway, and into the elevator, but once they were gone, Blayne knew they were gone.

"Okay, fine." Bo grinned. "I find Gwen an acceptable human being."

"That's so big of you."

"I know." He pulled Blayne off him, launched her up in the air—Blayne squealing the entire time—and when he easily caught her on her way down, tossed her over his shoulder. "Now we find those condoms."

"Are you awake?"

Bo's eyes opened wide and he stared up at the energetic and naked wolfdog straddling his chest.

"I am now," he told her.

"Good." She wiggled on his chest and Bo caught her hips to stop her from moving.

"What's up, Blayne?"

"I'm bored."

"Okay." He pointed at the floor where he'd tossed the box of condoms after taking out a handful. "Get the rest of the condoms."

"Orrrrrr . . ." she said, drawing out the word.

"Or what?" She grinned and he tried to turn away from her. "Forget it."

"Please? Please!"

She wiggled again on his chest.

"Stop doing that." She was making him hard and if she wasn't in the mood that was simply irritating.

She leaned in, nuzzling his neck. "Please?" she begged.

"Fine. But we have to clean up first and I'll need to fix that door." He was pretty sure the grizzly didn't consider shoving the door back into place technically fixing it since anyone could simply take it off again without tools.

"Okay! I'll change the sheets!" She jumped off his chest and cartwheeled naked out of the room. When he heard panting, Bo raised himself up on his elbows and watched Blayne chase her tail.

"I've never seen anyone this excited about going to the gym."

She shifted back to human, stumbling into the door from the dizziness. "You've got the Cup finals coming up and the Babes have the championship. And we will win. Because we rock!" She raised her arms into the air. "Woo-hoo!"

Bo threw his legs over the side of the bed and sat up, wincing from the scratches and bite marks he'd gotten from his mouthy little mate. "Just remember, you're going to have to bury that nice shit if you want to win against the Texans."

"Derby is not hockey. Derby girls are loyal and nice."

"Loser talk," he muttered, scratching his head, once again wishing he could cut his hair and have it stay short for longer than twenty-four hours.

When he raised his gaze, he jerked back a little. "What?" he asked Blayne. When she didn't answer, he shook his head. "You said you wanted to go to the gym."

"We've got time."

"That's not the point," he said, climbing across the bed to get away from her. "We had a plan."

"Plans change," she laughed, coming after him. "And you look so cute covered in me!"

He made it off the bed, but the vicious wolfdog grabbed his leg and lifted, flipping him forward.

"How do you do that?" he demanded once he hit the floor.

She landed on his chest, small hands pressing into his flesh, wet pussy rocking against his cock, although he wasn't in that pussy—yet.

"Skill." She leaned in and kissed his chest, moving up until she reached his throat. "Now come on. Let's fuck so we can get to the gym before we lose a shot at all the best treadmills."

Like there was ever a time he didn't get the best treadmill. But Bo wasn't in the mood to hear how mean he was.

"Okay," he sighed, grabbing her shoulders and dropping her to her back, Blayne giggling the entire time. "But only because you're *making* me do this."

"I know. I'm such a bad influence."

"My God. You so are."

EPILOGUE

The end-game buzzer went off and Blayne took a quick look at the scoreboard. A blow-out. A fucking blow-out! She'd done it! Just like Bo had told her she could in a really sweet pep talk before the bout started. She'd battered, abused, and maimed the entire time, following each assault with a "Sorry!" said in her sweetest voice. And because of that, because she'd played like Bo Novikov, the Babes had won the championship!

Of course, it was also the reason her entire team was surrounding her. Not to pat her on the back and carry her around on their shoulders but to protect her from the Longfangs who were coming to kick her ass. It was a nasty fight, too, but the refs and security guards finally calmed everyone down.

With both teams under control, the Babes all gawked at Blayne.

"What?" she demanded. "You wanted to win."

No one argued with her, and, instead, Gwen, their captain Cherry, and Blayne all headed up to the makeshift dais to get their trophy. But because it was the Championship, there was a rather long, bullshit ceremony to sit through with a former derby star giving a long-winded speech before handing over the damn trophy. Unfortunately that wasn't working for Blayne. Leaning in, she whispered to Gwen, "Dude, we've gotta go. The Carnivores have gone into overtime." The only tragedy of this night was that what should be the final game of the hockey Cup finals was taking place at the same time. But overtime at least gave Blayne and Gwen a chance to see their men play.

"How do you know that?" Gwen asked.

Blayne motioned to the wild dogs in the audience, Phil holding up a sign that said, "They've gone into overtime."

"Cherry?" Blayne asked, making sure to use her puppy dog eyes. She'd found feline hybrids couldn't resist that.

"Let's do it," Cherry said. "'Cause I'm bored anyway."

The presenter turned, her hands around the trophy. "And it is my great pleasure to give this year's championship trophy to—"

"Thanks!" Blayne and Gwen said together, each grabbing hold of one end of the trophy and jumping off the dais.

"Let's go, Babes!" Cherry called out, the rest of the Babes falling in behind Blayne and Gwen as they tore out of the stadium and into the hall. They skated down to the elevator, people diving out of their way or plastering themselves against the wall to avoid getting hit. They dived into the elevator, the entire team forcing its way inside. The doors closed, and they waited for it to get to the main stadium floor.

The doors opened, and the Babes skated out, pushing drunk shifters lingering in the hallway out of their way.

"Left!" Cherry called out. "Left!" As one, they turned left and skated down a flight of stairs to the VIP seats that had been held for them just in case. They moved in, Blayne and Gwen tossing the oversized trophy to the male lions sitting behind them and several seats over.

"Oh, come on!" Mitch said. "I can't see around this thing!"

"Too bad!" Gwen snapped. "I can't believe you came to this instead of our bout."

"Hockey," Mitch said.

Ignoring the bickering siblings, Blayne focused on the ice and Bo. They were up against the Alaskan Bears, and the blood on the ice and protective glass was pretty dramatic.

Bo's right eye was swollen shut and the left side of his jaw had been torn open. But he had the puck . . . and every one of the Alaskan Bears was on his ass.

The rest of his team was working to get him free so he could take a shot at the opposition's goal but the Alaskan Bears weren't having it.

Bo skated behind the other team's goal. Although they were all similar in size, no one had Bo Novikov on speed, so they went at him from both sides, blocking him in.

A hand fell on her shoulder and Blayne looked behind her. "Grigori!" She jumped up and went over the seats, throwing herself into the big polar's arms.

"Watch the skates, woman!" Mitch complained next to them.

Ignoring Mitch, Blayne hugged Bo's uncle. "I'm so sorry I couldn't pick you up at the airport."

"No problem. The boy sent a car and driver." Then he made his eyebrows dance a little, but she knew he probably felt like king of the world about it.

"And how's Mr. Peabody?" Blayne asked, making sure the name sounded particularly persnickety.

"He still won't get out from under my couch when I'm home," Grigori complained. "And I'm not calling that damn dog Mr. Peabody."

"Then you better come up with something," she shot back. "Or I'm sticking with Mr. Peabody!"

"Hank," Marci Luntz cut in. "He calls him Hank."

Aaaah. Blayne smiled in relief. If Grigori named the pittie, then the newly christened Hank would be safe and now had his "forever home." Woo-hoo!

"Hi, Marci." Still holding on to Grigori, Blayne leaned over and kissed the doctor on the cheek. "How are you?"

"I'm fine, dear. Fine. And you look . . . like you've been through hell."

"Only a little." Blayne shrugged. "We won."

"Of course you did," Marci said as if talking to the stupidest woman she'd ever met. "We're so sorry we couldn't go to both games, though."

"No. You've gotta be here for Bo. Besides," she grinned, "I had my—"

"Could you embarrass me more?" her father snarled, moving into the aisle and dropping into the seat Bo had reserved for him, just in case. "Couldn't you have at least waited until that woman finished her speech?"

"She was taking too long. And don't snarl at me, old man!"

Marci shook her head and chuckled. "I swear. You two."

"He started it."

The crowd roared, and Blayne turned to see that Bo had dropped the gloves and gone at it with one of the bears. She winced when Bo got the bear on the ground and then smashed in his face—repeatedly—with the bear's own helmet.

"And I heard," Marci sniffed, "that *some* people were worried my Bold had gone soft now that he was in love."

"Who said that?'

In answer to Blayne's question, Marci glanced over at Dad and then Grigori. *Who knew these two jokers would become friends?*

"Well," Blayne began, "I hope you both realize now that"— Blayne jumped when Bo roared and threw the bear he'd been assaulting down the length of the ice, the grizzly slamming right into and *through* the protective glass—"the chances of him becoming a less aggressive player will probably not happen."

"I think we see that." Grigori placed Blayne back into her seat beside Gwen.

Once she was settled, she grinned over at Gwen. "Don't be jealous I have more bears who love me than you do."

Gwen laughed. "Shut up."

They were down to the last twelve seconds, and Bo had the puck again. He was forced toward his own team's goal, Ric crouching and ready. "What a position to be in for two to three hours," Blayne thought as she watched Bo trying to find a way out of the pack of bears swarming him. He was keeping the puck away from the other team but he wasn't scoring either. She glanced at the scoreboard. No one had gotten a goal? Holy shit. The game would go on all night at this rate.

Bo lifted his head and she saw his eyes narrow.

"MacRyrie!" he suddenly called out and, the entire crowd gasping in shock, Bo Novikov slammed that shot at the only one of his teammates not trapped in by a bunch of Alaskan bears. The only one near Lock was one of the opposition's foxes and, after snapping out of his initial shock, Lock sent the little guy flying before he caught the puck with his stick and sped off down the ice toward the other team's goal.

The two teams scrambled to follow, but Bo shot out from the rest and was in the goal crease by the time Lock arrived. The grizzly passed the puck to Bo but the goalie was already on him, waiting for that move. A move everyone had made because Bo almost always made the goal. But, with both teams bearing down on him, and two seconds left on the clock, Bo passed the puck right back to Lock.

Startled, the grizzly slapped it away and into the back of the Alaskan goalie's head. It ricocheted off and into the net. There was a weird moment of shocked silence throughout the entire stadium even as the buzzer went off. Because someone other than The Marauder had made the winning goal in a final playoff game. It had been unheard of for years.

But, for once, Bo had done what was right for the team. And that's why she was the first one up and screaming, *"Yes!"* Both her arms raised high in the air. And once Blayne said it, the rest of the crowd joined in. The cheers, roars, howling, and stomping, shaking the walls of the entire sports center and probably freaking out any full-humans on the top floors.

The grizzly stared at Bo, brown eyes wide, mouth open. It probably wasn't MacRyrie's first goal, but most likely his first winning goal in a season-final game. Bo grinned and winked at him seconds before the entire New York Carnivores team slammed into the grizzly, swarming over him.

Bo wiped blood off his face and started to skate away, but Van Holtz cut him off.

The wolf removed his goalie mask and said, "Nice."

Bo nodded. He started to move again, and again Van Holtz moved in front of him. "Should I contact your agent about re-upping your contract?"

Tricky canine. But it was a good time to ask wasn't it? Not because of the win, though.

Bo looked across the ice to the VIP seating. Blayne was hugging Gwen, the two females still in their derby gear. For once, Bo didn't feel the need to move on. And the goddamn wolf knew it, too.

"Yeah," Bo said. "You can call him."

"Excellent."

"But I want a seal farm."

Van Holtz gaped up at him. "You want a what?"

"A seal farm. With fresh seals."

"How . . . revolting."

"I don't judge you killing Bambi."

"Not every deer we take down is Bambi."

"And I want more control of the team." Before the wolf could freak out at that particular request, Bo said, "I may want to coach one day." He thought about it another second and added, "Or own my own team. One or the other."

Van Holtz skated off. "We'll talk more later."

Bo headed back to the team's bench, but before he reached it, he had to stop and watch a woman try and roller skate across ice. It was . . . interesting.

"What are you doing?" he asked when she was close enough.

"Trying to reach you."

"Leap for it, or we'll be here all night."

She did, Blayne landing right in his arms.

"How did you do?" he asked, enjoying how she immediately put her arms around his shoulders and her legs around his waist. She let him hold her like this a lot, and he loved it.

"We won! But apparently I'm as hated as you now." She pouted. "I said I was sorry every time. I even meant it!"

"Then they're just being unreasonable."

"That's how I feel." She grinned. "But you . . . passing the puck." She hugged him. "I'm so proud of you!"

"I wanted to win. If that meant passing my puck to that idiot—"

"Sha-sha-sha." She put her hand over his mouth. "Don't ruin the moment for me." He caught her fingers in his mouth and tickled them with his tongue.

Giggling, Blayne said, "Maybe we've changed places. I'm the heartless cruel one now and you're the nice one."

"I've learned anything is possible—"

"Excuse me, Mr. Novikov, can I have your—"

"—*Do you not see I'm busy?*" he bellowed into some wild dog's face. He focused back on Blayne so he didn't have to witness the wild dog–male sobbing that followed. "Where were we?"

Blayne's smile was soft, her palm pressing against his cheek. "It doesn't matter."

"I guess we have to go out with the old men brigade tonight?"

They both looked over at the VIP seats where two males were talking, Dr. Luntz—he'd never call her Marci—sitting on his uncle's lap.

"I never thought they'd become so friendly. He invited Dad to visit next month."

"Maybe we can all go." Blayne perked up—if it was possible for her to perk up more—her smile huge.

"You mean like a vacation?"

"A vacation with skating."

"Yay! Ice pond skating! And running in snow! I can't wait!"

He had the perkiest girlfriend in the world. It should annoy him. It didn't.

"It'll be a family trip. I like your father," he added honestly. How could he not? The man had told him exactly how to handle Blayne's clutter problem: "Since you have the space, give Blayne her own room and let her mess it up as much as she wants. Never go into it, and never ask about it. As far as you're concerned, it doesn't exist. Just make sure she keeps all her shit in there with the door closed, and you can keep the rest of the place just as you want it. In the end, you'll both be happier." His idea had worked like a charm too.

But the time management thing? "Forget it, kid," Ezra Thorpe had said. "You're on your own."

"Hey," Van Holtz called out, motioning to them with his hand. "We're taking team pictures with the Babes. You two get over here!"

"In a second," Bo told him. He hitched Blayne up a little higher. "I have a question first."

"Of course I'll marry you!" Blayne cheered, throwing her arms around his neck.

"I wasn't going to ask that."

"Oh." She un-hugged him. "Sorry."

"I was going to ask you that on Sunday. At three forty-five p.m. Before the surprise romantic dinner but after my Sunday laps in the pool. *It was on my schedule!*" he finished on a bellow.

"*I know!*" she bellowed back. "I saw it. You left it right out on the kitchen table! Was I supposed to ignore it?"

"Since you never look at the schedules you've been writing for yourself, much less mine—yes!" He scowled at her. "You know I hate when you mess with my schedule Blayne!"

"You're rude," she accused. "*Rude!*"

"Yeah. But you're going to marry me anyway, aren't you?"

That thousand-watt smile made Bo feel warm from the inside out. "Of course I am! Then again, I can't officially tell you that until three forty-six, p.m., Sunday. Mostly because you're a freaky hybrid with a schedule fetish."

Skating over to the rest of the group to take the picture, Blayne in his arms, Bo laughed and said, "Yeah, and I love you, too, Blaynie."

Donna Kauffman knows SOME LIKE IT SCOT, so go out and get her newest book today!

Just then he heard the loud reverberation of the chapel's pipe organ ring out the beginning of Mendelssohn's wedding march.

He sprinted back around to the front of the church and slipped inside behind her, just as she began her walk down the aisle. His heart sank, but he shook off the disconcerting feeling and edged as quietly as possible into the end of the last pew once she'd made her way down the aisle. All eyes were on the bride. No one noticed the man in the kilt. He pulled the now crumpled photo of Katie McAuley out of his sporran, and forced his gaze away from the bride and down to the picture in his hands. He needed to find her and start focusing on what he planned to do next.

He unfolded the photo . . . and frowned at the face smiling back at him, blond tendrils were blowing wildly about her face, as were those of the brunette and redhead mates she was clutched between. All three women were laughing, smiling, as if enjoying a great lark. Or simply the company they were in, regardless of location or event. He couldn't fathom feeling so utterly carefree. Or so happy, for that matter. It was both an unsettling discovery, and a rather depressing one. He enjoyed the challenge of his work, but . . . was he happy? The carefree smiling kind of happy? He knew the answer to that. What he wanted to know was when, exactly, had he stopped having fun? He could hear Roan's voice ring through his consciousness, as if he were an angel—or more aptly, a devil—perched upon his tartaned shoulder. *"When did you ever start?"*

And then the pastor began intoning the marriage rites, and Graham's gaze was pulled intractably back to the woman standing in front of the altar. She turned to her betrothed and he lifted the veil. Graham felt himself drawn physically forward, the crumpled photo in his hands forgotten, as he shifted on his feet and tried his best to—finally—see her face. It was only natural, he told himself, to want to see what she looked like, after talking with her in the garden.

But why he was holding his breath, he had no earthly idea.

Then she turned her head, just slightly, and he could have sworn she looked directly at him. His heart squeezed. Hard. Then stuttered to a stop. Only this time he knew exactly why. He looked down at the picture in his hand, and forced himself to draw in air past the tightness in his chest. He distantly heard the pastor urge everyone to be seated. And one by one, everyone did.

Everyone, that was, except him.

He turned over the wedding program that had been handed to him as he'd entered the church. He looked at the lengthy name engraved on the front, then lifted his gaze to her. "It's you," he declared, his deep voice echoing loudly, reverberating around the soaring chapel ceiling. "Katherine Elizabeth Georgina Rosemary McAuley." Katie. The nickname that had stuck. He held up the photo, as if that would explain everything, while he stood there, acutely dumbfounded. His mind raced as fast as his heart, as everything suddenly made perfect sense. And no sense at all.

He lifted the photo higher, stabbing it forward, as if making a claim. And perhaps he was. He felt driven by something unknown, a force he could neither put name nor logic to. If he were honest, it had begun outside, in the garden. It was something both primal and primeval, driven by what could only be utter lunacy. Because clearly, he'd lost whatever he'd had left of his mind. Yet that didn't stop him from continuing. In fact, he barely paused to draw breath.

"You're meant to be mine," he declared, loudly, defiantly, to the collective gasp of every man, woman, and child lining each and every pew. He didn't care. Because he'd never meant anything more in his entire life. And he hadn't the remotest idea why. Yet it was truth; one he'd never been more certain of. It was as if all four hundred years of MacLeods willfully and intently binding themselves to McAuleys pumping viscerally through his veins.

Clan curse, indeed.

Don't miss Cynthia Eden's I'LL BE SLAYING YOU, out next month from Brava!

"Let me buy you a drink."

She'd ignored the men beside her. Greeted the few come-ons she'd gotten with silence. But that voice—

Dee glanced to the left. Tall, Dark, and Sexy was back.

And he was smiling down at her. A big, wide grin that showed off a weird little dent in his right cheek. Not a dimple, too hard for that. She hadn't noticed that last night, now with the hunt and kill—

Shit but he was hot.

Thanks to the spotlights over the bar, she could see him so much better tonight. No shadows to hide behind now.

Hard angles, strong jaw, sexy mouth.

She licked her lips. "Already got one." Dee held up her glass.

"Babe, that's water." He motioned to the bartender. "Let me get you something with bite."

She'd spent the night looking for a bite. Hadn't found it yet. Her fingers snagged his. "I'm working." Booze couldn't slow her down. Not with the one she hunted.

Black brows shot up. Then he leaned in close. So close that she caught the scent of his aftershave. "You gonna kill another woman tonight?" A whisper that blew against her.

Her lips tightened. "Vampire," she said quietly.

He blinked. Those eyes of his were kinda eerie. Like a smoky fog staring back at her.

"I hunted a vampire last night," Dee told him, keeping her voice hushed because in a place like this, you never knew who was listening. "And, technically, she'd already been killed once before I got to her."

His fingers locked around her upper arm. She'd yanked on a black T-shirt before heading out, and his fingertips skimmed her flesh. "Guess you're right," he murmured and leaned in even closer.

His lips were about two inches—maybe just one—away from hers.

What would he taste like?

It'd been too long since she'd had a lover, and this guy fit all of her criteria. Big, strong, sexy, and aware of the score in the city.

"Wanna dance with me?" Such dark words. No accent at all underlined the whisper. Just a rich purr of sex.

Oh but she bet the guy was fantastic in the sack.

Find out. A not-so-weak challenge in her mind.

Why not? She wasn't seeing anyone. He seemed up for it and—

Dee brought her left hand up between them and pushed against his chest. "I don't dance." Especially not to that too fast, pounding music that made her head ache.

He didn't retreat. His eyes bored into hers. "Pity." His fingers skated down her arm and caught her wrist. He took her glass away, sat it on the bar top with a clink.

She cocked her head and studied him. "Are you following me?" Two nights. First, sure, that could have been coincidence. A coincidence she was grudgingly grateful for, but tonight—

The faintest curl hinted on his lips. "What if I am?"

His thighs brushed against her. Big, strong thighs. Thick with muscle.

Dee swallowed. So not the time.

But the man was tempting.

She couldn't afford a distraction. Not then. "Then you'd better be very, very careful." Dee shoved against him. Hard.

He stumbled back a step and his smile widened. "You keep playing hard to get, and I'm gonna start thinking you're not interested in me, Sandra Dee."

Who was this guy? Dee jumped off the bar stool. "You'd be thinking right, buddy."

He took her wrist again with strong, roughened fingers. The guy towered over her. Always the way of it. When you couldn't even skim five foot six with big-ass heels, most men towered over you. And since Dee had never worn heels in her life . . .

The guy bent toward her when he said, "I see the way you look at me."

What did that mean?

"Curious . . . but more. Like maybe you got a wild side lurking in you. A side that wants out."

Maybe she did. The guy sure looked like he could play. *After the case.*

"I don't know you, Chase," she finally told him, too aware of his touch on her skin. Too aware that her nipples were tightening and she was leaning toward him as her nostrils flared and she tried to suck up more of his scent. "I don't know—"

"I saved your life." A fallen angel's smile. "Doesn't that count for something?"

Catch THE DEVIL SHE KNOWS, the latest from
Diane Whiteside, out now from Brava!

"This is no place for a lady," he observed, ancient eyes studying Gareth without fear.

"She has a suite booked at the best European hotel—and I will continue to keep her safe."

"Most excellent." He bowed. "Peace be upon you."

"And upon you be peace," Gareth returned in equally excellent Arabic.

Portia could read nothing in Gareth's face after they'd left, unlike her wedding day, the last time they'd met. She sighed, wishing for so many things.

"Hmm?" Gareth asked noncommittally, just as he would have when she was twelve. Back then, he'd been surprised at her presence on his expeditions out of Uncle William's house. But he'd never refused to take her along and he'd always answered her questions, even if he didn't start any conversations. At least in the beginning, he hadn't.

"He looks so helpless, unlike the charming—"

"Charming?" Gareth's tone sharpened fractionally. He turned toward the large, comfortable barouche that Sidonie had just climbed aboard.

"Parrot? Or maybe a mynah bird?" Portia spread her hands a little helplessly, before following his lead. A seagull soared overhead, effortlessly free unlike herself. "Abdul Hamid always reminded me of a tropical creature, with his vivid waistcoats and eternal, colorful chatter. Seeing him crumpled up like this makes him look like a broken bird."

"I doubt there's any serious damage." Warmth softened Gareth's eyes for the first time until they gleamed blue as the water behind him. He offered her his hand and she took the first step up into the carriage.

"Are you sure?" Standing on the metal step, she was almost at eye level with him.

"They didn't have enough time to tie him up and truly start working him over. The police here have a pattern they like to follow." His expression hardened for a moment then he kissed the tips of her fingers. "But that didn't happen. Once he sees a good doctor, is bandaged up, and has a long rest, he should be fine."

"Are you truly certain?" She searched his face. They had never, ever lied to each other.

"As much as I can be."

"Very well then." She tightened her fingers around his, feeling his strength flood into hers once again. "Thank you for rescuing us."

"It was my pleasure, Portia." He kissed her hand again, brushing his lips across her knuckles. It was still no contact at all, nothing like all the men who'd tried to seduce her into an affair while she was married, saying she needed to distract herself from St. Arles. She'd always refused them, telling herself and them it was because St. Arles would never tolerate a cuckoo in the nest. He'd have known in a minute if another man had sired his heir and heaven knows, the son of a bitch kept hauling himself back to her bed to breed one.

She hadn't realized until now it was because no other man made her bones shiver, even when her skin hadn't been touched.